AS

DON'T YOU REMEMBER ME, ICELIN? OF COURSE YOU WOULDN'T. I SHOULDN'T HAVE EXPECTED . . .

Cerest watched her go. He was too shocked to follow. What had caused the reaction in her? A breath ago she'd been grinding his teeth in the dirt and giving him a dressing-down for carelessness, and now she was a frightened waif running away from him as fast as she could.

Come back to me, Icelin. I'll explain everything.

He laughed out loud. Icelin was a strange woman and fascinating. Gods, he was almost glad she'd run. It made everything more exciting. Now he had to know her better.

I'll make you remember.

D1484063

FORGOTTEN REALMS®

ED GREENWOOD
PRESENTS
WATERDEEP

BLACKSTAFF TOWER
Steven E. Schend

MISTSHORE
Jaleigh Johnson

DOWNSHADOW
Erik Scott de Bie
April 2009

CITY OF THE DEAD
Rosemary Jones
June 2009

Also by Jaleigh Johnson

THE DUNGEONS
THE HOWLING DELVE

FORGOTTEN REALMS

ED GREENWOOD
PRESENTS
WATERDEEP

MISTSHORE

JALEIGH JOHNSON

Wizards of the Coast

Ed Greenwood Presents Waterdeep

MISTSHORE

©2008 Wizards of the Coast, Inc.

All characters in this book are fictitious. Any resemblance to actual persons, living or dead, is purely coincidental.

This book is protected under the copyright laws of the United States of America. Any reproduction or unauthorized use of the material or artwork contained herein is prohibited without the express written permission of Wizards of the Coast, Inc.

Published by Wizards of the Coast, Inc. Forgotten Realms, Wizards of the Coast, and their respective logos are trademarks of Wizards of the Coast, Inc., in the U.S.A. and other countries.

All Wizards of the Coast characters, character names, and the distinctive likenesses thereof are property of Wizards of the Coast, Inc.

Printed in the U.S.A.

The sale of this book without its cover has not been authorized by the publisher. If you purchased this book without a cover, you should be aware that neither the author nor the publisher has received payment for this "stripped book."

Cover art by Android Jones
First Printing: September 2008

9 8 7 6 5 4 3 2 1

ISBN: 978-0-7869-4966-3
620- 21771740-001-EN

U.S., CANADA,
ASIA, PACIFIC, & LATIN AMERICA
Wizards of the Coast, Inc.
P.O. Box 707
Renton, WA 98057-0707
+1-800-324-6496

EUROPEAN HEADQUARTERS
Hasbro UK Ltd
Caswell Way
Newport, Gwent NP9 0YH
GREAT BRITAIN
Save this address for your records.

Visit our web site at www.wizards.com

DEDICATION

Dedicated to the members of WAG, past and present, for bringing me to the party. Most of all to Tim, my husband and friend. You've been there since the beginning, and now, I could never do without you. All my love.

ACKNOWLEDGMENTS

Grateful acknowledgement to my editor, Susan Morris, for abundant patience and sharp eyes. My clothes are on straight only because of her. Much affection goes to Ed Greenwood, and not just for his guidance with this book. He doesn't know it, but fourteen years ago he inspired a shy, awkward girl to keep scribbling in a notebook until she became a writer. Old Mage, how can I ever thank you for opening the Realms to me?

INTRODUCTION

At its heart, the Forgotten Realms isn't geography, it's people. Those "people" may be dragons or elves or scaly shape-changing monsters rather than humans, but good writers bring characters to life in front of our eyes, making us see and care about what unfolds in their lives.

Waterdeep is a whole bunch of people dwelling together, all striving to carve out lives and riches for themselves (sometimes out of each other). A relative few of them are wealthy, and live in splendid mansions in Sea Ward and North Ward. Most of them are hard-working, "caught in the middle" types, who dwell all over the city.

And then there are "Those Below." The poor, the outcasts, the misfits, the shunned. In Waterdeep, they may literally be "Below," under the surface wards of the city, in the Warrens or Downshadow. Or they may dwell in the mean streets of Dock Ward, or a fog-shrouded, eerie neighborhood that has been slowly growing in the "home" Realms campaign (the Forgotten Realms game I run, at home) for some years: an unmapped, rotting, waterlogged backwater of lashed-together, sinking, mildew-shrouded boats at the northern end of the Waterdeep's inner harbor.

A corner of Waterdeep much whispered about by the fearful, who believe all manner of sinister half sea-monsters, half-humans lurk in its sagging riggings and rotten cabins. Creatures with webbed fingers, gills hidden under high-collared robes, and sly, stealthy tentacles waiting to throttle or snatch.

Welcome to Mistshore.

The book you hold in your hands opens in the Year of the Ageless One. A hundred years on from its beginnings, Mistshore has become part of Waterdeep. Not a part many Waterdhavians would care to visit, mind you.

A place you can safely venture into, in these pages, to see and smell it without actually risking a dagger between your ribs, or the suspicious glare of the Watch if you should happen to prudently flee wildly back out again.

It's a journey you'll make in good hands. Jaleigh Johnson knows Waterdeep, and can make us all feel and taste Mistshore. From my few paragraphs of description, she has made this damp, fish-stinking, mist-shrouded, sinister neighborhood come alive.

"Alive" because she brings us not just a rotting chaos of ships, but people. Real people: Icelin, and Ruen, and Cerest, characters who have problems and personal mysteries, too. Not to mention officers of the Watch whose lives and careers we can understand, whose heavy boots thud with the ring of believability. There's the beauty of it: without ever risking humdrum, this book makes the fantastic believable. No marching armies, lost princesses, or glittering throngs of nobles this time (oh, we'll see those in other novels, no fear, and they have their powers and places, too).

Jaleigh brings us some of the folk who dwell behind the tattered curtains and shuttered windows of the mean streets of Waterdeep, a city of a thousand tales.

Here's one of them. A darned good one. Enjoy.

Ed Greenwood
March 2008

PROLOGUE

Dear Granddaughter,

I leave today on a new adventure. Faerûn calls to me, and I find I must answer her gentle whisper. You are too young, as I write this, to understand such a call, or even to speak the name of your homeland. All I can tell you about Faerûn is that it is a vast, lively, and aching world. The adventures found on her soil incite equal measures of bravery, recklessness, glory, and tragedy. I have learned much of adventure, and much of Faerûn, in my life.

I hope to be able to return to you one day, to spin you tales of the places I've been and the people I've met. But the decision is not mine. It is in the hands of the gods. I can only write you this letter, before you are old enough to read it, to tell you not to be afraid for me, or for yourself. Leaving you behind was the hardest battle I have ever fought, but I believe you will have a far better life growing up in my brother's house than traveling the dusty roads with me. Brant can give you the home I never made for myself. Your parents would understand. Someday, you will understand as well. I expect Brant will keep these correspondences from you until you are of an age to comprehend them, but I will write diligently, my dearest one, so you will know you are never alone in this large world.

Night rises around my quill, and so I will close. There are many dreams I wish for you to realize. I beg that you remember two things: The past is part of us; it shapes us irrevocably, but never allow grief and regret to rule your heart. The second is that I love you, more than my own life. I act as I do out of love, and if I have acted wrongly, or hurt you by my absence, please believe the wound was unintentional. Adventure attracts the foolish as well as the mighty.

Someday, you will go forth into the world and find your own adventure waiting. I want this for you, above all things, granddaughter. The world is spread out before you, and life is meant to be lived. Be well, and be happy, Icelin.

Your grandfather,
Elgreth

CHAPTER 1

22 Eleint, The Year of the Ageless One (1479 DR)

Icelin pressed her back against the warm chimney and watched an island of rock drift across the sky. Like a roughly hewn barge, it cut through cloud wisps and shrugged aside winging seagulls on its way to some unknown destination, far across Faerûn.

If any living beings walked upon its surface, Icelin couldn't see them. Tiny lightning bolts chased each other across the rock's surface, flashing bruise purple and deepest black. They might have belonged to some otherworldly creatures at play. Icelin ignored them. She was far more interested in the events unfolding below her tucked-up perch on the rooftop.

Dawn had come, and with the first rays of sunlight, the city of Waterdeep came alive.

She heard the wagons first. The commerce of South Ward turned on the spokes of caravan wheels. Merchants carting goods in from the trade routes formed a jagged line that funneled through the south gate from Caravan City. The scent of animal sweat, spices, and earth saturated the air, like threads in a familiar tapestry.

From her vantage, Icelin couldn't see the lines of traffic moving up and down The High Road and The Way of the Dragon. But the huge dust clouds they caused drifted up from the streets to mingle with the dawn fog. The dry air stung her eyes.

Voices shouted from the alley below her. A rear door opened. Icelin caught the sharp tang of yeast in new bread. A tired-eyed woman of middle years stepped into the alley, lugging a bucket of soapy water. She emptied its contents into the alley and glanced up to where Icelin sat. She threw a careless wave and turned to go back inside the bakery. Icelin smiled and waved back.

Most of the buildings, including the bakery and her great-uncle's sundries store, fronted The Way of the Dragon; behind they hitched up together against the darker shades of Blacklock Alley. Icelin preferred the quiet of her high perch, especially at dawn, when the rougher alley folk had gone abed or collapsed with a bottle.

Across the alley another door opened. Light spilled from the House of Dust, an affectionately named tavern where much of the caravan traffic ended up at the close of their long journeys. The tavern keeper, a man named Sintus Farlhor, shuffled through the door, sweeping out the leavings from the previous night's business. Muttering and cursing under his breath, he beat the broom against the wall to loosen the dust.

Icelin watched the man impassively. She lifted a bulky sack from a nook behind the chimney and placed it on the ledge next to her. The small lump of burlap had been tied tightly with a leather cord.

"Not sleeping again, lass?"

The voice made Icelin jump. She hadn't heard her great-uncle's approach.

"I thought Waterdhavians considered it virtuous to rise before the dawn," she replied, and she pressed an ivory finger to her lips. "Hush, now. I'm on a mission of deepest revenge this morn."

"Oh, is that all, then?" Brant came to sit next to her on the ledge. He was dressed for work in breeches and a double-pocketed vest of moss green, exactly the shade of the sign over his door. Brant's General Goods and Gear catered to the wagon folk, just like everything else in South Ward.

Brant pressed a mug of something steamy into her hands. Icelin inhaled the sugar and cinnamon in the tea and nodded her thanks, but she refused to be distracted.

"I heard Farlhor was at it again last night," she said, nodding to the tavern keeper, who had not yet noticed them.

"Shouldn't believe everything you hear." Brant loosened the ties on Icelin's sack and wedged a finger in to touch its contents. He brought the brown substance to his nose and gagged. "Gods, Icelin! You aren't ten years old anymore."

"My poor great-uncle," Icelin said, "you have never appreciated the subtle art of revenge." She put an arm across his thin shoulders. "Watch now. I promise you'll enjoy the spectacle."

"Whatever you say, lass." Brant swiped her tea and took a sip for himself. He wiped his other hand on the shingles.

Three stories below them, Farlhor finished his mad beating of the broom and seemed about to storm back inside the tavern when the door opened in his face. A bouquet of blonde hair and lively chatter spilled out.

"Her name is Eliza," Icelin said for her great-uncle's benefit. "She is sixteen this winter."

The girl was small but compact. Her brown arms showed a slight definition of muscle, but not so much as to make her unattractive. She was built well for barmaid's work, with animate features and friendly brown eyes.

A shutter closed over Eliza's face when she saw Farlhor. She started to back away, but the tavern keeper put himself in the path of escape.

"You're late," he said. He slammed the door, sealing them both in the alley. "I told you to be here before daylight."

Roughly, he grabbed her wrists, hauling her away from the building. The angry glaze in his eyes softened, became something more personal and far more sinister.

"Gods' teeth!" Brant hissed, slamming the tea cup down on the ground. He leaned so far over the ledge Icelin had to grab his belt. "I know that girl's father. Son of a whore! He better not touch her."

"I don't think he shares your sensibilities, Great-Uncle," Icelin said. She lifted the sack and let the cord fall away. In one motion, she upended the vessel of sweet revenge and emptied fresh dung into the alley.

The cow pies showered down on Farlhor, turning the tavern keeper into a mosaic of straw and animal filth.

Farlhor let out a lusty, inarticulate cry of rage and instantly released the barmaid's wrists. Eliza, who had missed the worst of the dung, bolted down the alley and disappeared around the corner of the tavern. Icelin hoped the girl would be smart enough to find a new place of employment.

"Oh, that was glorious," her great-uncle said. He rocked back on the ledge. "I wouldn't have appreciated the story nearly enough if I hadn't seen it!"

Icelin smiled. But she wasn't done with Eliza's tormentor.

"Sintus Farlhor," she said. Her voice echoed off the surrounding buildings, carrying to the tavern keeper's ears. "Heed me."

Farlhor tried to look up at her, but there was dung in his eyes. Icelin wondered what he could see of her. Her voice was strong, almost masculine—her great-uncle claimed that was because she used it so frequently—but her body was small. She had a thin, pale face curtained by long strands of unruly black hair.

"There are no fouler men than you in this city. But darker still are the eyes that watch this alley," Icelin said. "If you want to tryst here, let it be with yourself and not the girls under your care. If you forget, I will rain more than animal filth on you."

"Who are you?" Farlhor yelled, trying to sound fearsome. He squinted at her. "I know you! You're Brant's little she-witch! Come down here, then. I'll crack your bones." He reached for his broom.

"Will you, now?" Icelin said. Her voice was very soft.

She could feel Brant's eyes on her as she started the spell. No words came to her lips, not at first. Instead she hummed, finding the tune of an old song. She could recall it without breaking her concentration on the magic. The rhythm of the song steadied her until she was ready to cast.

The words and gestures felt foreign to her at first. She used them so seldom that recalling each aspect of the spell was a chore. Patiently, she worked her way through the complex patterns.

When she was done, the air crackled. Farlhor's broom snapped in half.

The tavern keeper shrieked and dropped the broken pieces. Cursing, he grabbed for a pouch that hung around his neck. The trinkets inside were meant to ward off harmful magic, but Icelin knew for a fact that they were owl pellets and painted stones, sold at the markets as arcane charms.

Rubbing his precious forgeries, Farlhor opened the door and darted through it into the safety of the tavern.

Icelin leaned back against the chimney, breathing hard.

"Icelin—lass!" Brant grabbed Icelin's shoulder as she swooned, but the faintness passed quickly enough. Then came the nausea, but she mastered it as well, swallowing and gulping air like a drowning swimmer.

It had been too long since she'd used such magic. She hadn't been properly prepared. The spell was not difficult, but she had worked herself up into a fury before the casting.

"I'm all right," she said. She squeezed his hand. "I'm just weak."

"You shouldn't have spent yourself like that," Brant scolded her, his good humor forgotten. "It's not like you to be so careless."

"You're right." Icelin grinned and pulled back her sweat-soaked hair. "But revenge is such a demanding creature. You have to be patient, day after day, until your chance comes in a wondrous spark of inspiration. The stableman down the south end of the Way; his son has a devious heart the equal of my own."

"I find that hard to imagine," her great-uncle said dryly.

"He selected the dung personally: aged one day inside a fat, cud-fed cow. I'm told she has loathsome intestines."

"Oh, I hope that's so," Brant said. "But you didn't need to use magic, Icelin. The dung was enough."

"I know." Her gaze flicked briefly to his. "Eliza and I used to play together as children."

"I remember," Brant said. "I don't fault your feelings. But you could have given Farlhor over to the Watch if you feared for her safety."

"Yes, and you know precisely why I didn't." Icelin leaned her head back against the chimney and closed her eyes. "Hush, now, while I bask in the sweet glory of my victory."

"Perhaps you should take to sleeping on the roof always," Brant observed. "Up here, you seem to have command of the whole world."

"If by world you mean Blacklock Alley, then I'll warrant you're right." Icelin didn't open her eyes. "I will reign over it as queen—or witch—and never have to sleep again. The Watchful Lady, I shall be, with her raven-black tresses and bloodshot eyes."

"We all need to sleep sometime, lass," her great-uncle said seriously. "Tell me truly: are the nightmares getting worse?"

"No. They are what they are."

"It's been five years, Icelin. Maybe, if we found you another teacher, he could help. You clearly still have the ability. It's only the control you lack."

"No," Icelin said. "I don't want to get into all that again. Today was a lapse. I lost my temper. It won't happen again."

She stared down at the alley, refusing to meet Brant's eyes. After a breath, she felt her great-uncle take her hand. She leaned sideways and allowed him to gather her up. They sat together, silently, against the backdrop of the awakening city.

"You never knew my Gisetta. But when you were humming that song, you sounded just like her," Brant said quietly.

"The music calms me," Icelin said. "The rhythm it makes in my chest. . . . Spells are just like music, only more. And more frightening," she added. "But the song braces me." She looked up at him. "You used to sing it to me. 'Give me eyes for the darkness, take me home, take me home.' " She knew Brant liked her singing voice. It was the only untainted gift she could give him, so she sang in his company as often as she could.

Brant patted her shoulder. "We should go below," he said. "The day has started without us, and you've an appointment with Kredaron after highsunfest."

"I haven't forgotten." Icelin said, wrinkling her nose.

"He's a respectable merchant, Great-Niece," Brant said. He always called her "great-niece" when duty and responsibility were involved. "You made a contract, and you have to honor it."

"It's not the honor part that I'm dreading," Icelin said. "But you're right. The price is more than fair, for one afternoon's work."

"What's he having you guard?"

"He wants to sell jewelry—family heirlooms, mostly—to boost his coin while he establishes his spice business. He's offered me first selection of the pieces before he sells them. All I have to do is ensure their security before and during the transaction."

Brant whistled. "That is generous. You remember what I taught you about appraising?"

Icelin shot him a wry look.

"Right, of course you do." Brant offered a hand to help her up. "You'll do well by him. This will be a good day."

"Assuming everything goes smoothly." Icelin plucked up the discarded cup, got to her feet, and drained the rest of her tea in one swallow. Brant sighed at the gulping noise.

Icelin wiped her mouth. "Yes, Great-Uncle, I slurp my tea and will therefore never be a proper lady." She widened her eyes. "Didn't I horrify you with that revelation a long time ago?"

"Can't an old man hope for a miracle?" Brant smiled. "In

with you. The least you can do is meet Kredaron in something more than a dressing gown."

"Anything to make you happy, Great-Uncle."

The sun was warm and high in the sky by the time Icelin got out of the house. She and Brant shared a small, neat set of rooms above the sundries store. Her great-uncle had few possessions, and Icelin had no great desire for baubles. The space was more than adequate for them both.

As promised, she'd shed her dressing gown, and even washed her face. But then Brant had cornered her in the kitchen and forced her to eat some bread and a bowl of the simmer stew he'd prepared the night before. He claimed she never ate enough. Her usual chores were after that—washing the windows and sorting coin from the previous day's business—before she had to prepare for her afternoon meeting with Kredaron.

She'd braided her hair and put on an ankle-length dress of light linen—brown, of course, so it wouldn't show the dust. One had to measure beauty against practicality in South Ward. Clouds of dust were everywhere on the dry days, and the mud slowed traffic when the rains came. But she had tall boots for those wetter occasions.

Crossing the High Road, Icelin wove among carts and shouting drivers until she reached Tulmaster's Street. She slowed her pace and walked in the shade of the crowded old stone shops and warehouses. The cries of cattle and horses mingled with the constant chatter of people coming and going on the busy streets.

Icelin knew the way without marking it. She knew that two streets north sat Shureene's Clothiers, and after that The Lone Rose, a flower shop that had been vacant since the winter but still smelled of fresh blooms. New violets grew in boxes outside the empty shop's windows. Someone had been watering them, though Icelin knew the shopkeeper had left the city months ago, with no expectation of returning.

This perpetual motion of travelers and traders, old and new settlers making their marks, left a strange mixture of restlessness and comfort in the city's inhabitants. Change could come in a day, yet commerce carried on. There was always more coin to be made and more to be lost. Icelin had been born to this function; it was the one thing you could always count on, according to her great-uncle.

Between the flower shop and the Inn of Spirits were two condemned warehouses. Icelin turned off Tulmaster's before she reached them, opting instead for Caravan Street to take her to the designated meeting spot.

The Watch claimed the warehouses were not dangerous, but Icelin had heard rumors, whispers that Spellplague workings had made the buildings unstable. Icelin avoided such places, as did all sensible folk in Waterdeep.

The city had been lucky—or gods-blessed enough—to escape much of the destruction that came in the wake of the Spellplague, an event that Icelin only comprehended through her great-uncle's stories. The explosion of wild magic had swept through Faerûn decades before her birth. Icelin and the rest of the younger folk had been spared the phenomenon and many of its aftereffects.

Icelin glanced at the sky. In the distance, she could still see the floating rock mote and its lightning play. One could get lost watching the strange islands drift over the city.

She blinked and saw the impression of a tower: white stone buried in sand. The spire appeared grown from the rock itself. Icelin shivered and looked away. When she looked back, the tower was gone. She must have imagined it.

That was another reason folk were quick to come and go from the city. All over Faerûn, the Spellplague had made life an uncertain notion at best. At times you couldn't trust your own eyes. And the strange, deadly spell ravages always seemed to spur people in one of two directions: to the cities, for relative comfort and security; or to the wilds, so that the travelers might comprehend some small piece of this changed landscape. Whatever strangeness had been wrought in Waterdeep by the Spellplague, Icelin wanted nothing of that outside world and all its upheaval.

Quickening her pace, Icelin tucked up closer to the familiar buildings, structures that didn't change shape or sprout new heads.

She reached the end of Caravan Street and a small, open square between buildings. Portals had been cut in the side of the nearer building, and folk leaned out to serve handpies and cold drinks to laborers and passersby. Wooden benches lined the square, and a handful of people sat at tables and sipped while they conducted private business.

Kredaron sat at the far end of the square. He was an aging man, with white hair that curled at the ends and papery skin that had seen the sun too often. He carried a rolled bundle of silk close to his chest. He rose and waved when Icelin caught his eye.

"Greetings, Kredaron," Icelin said, taking the seat across from him. "I hope you haven't been waiting long."

"Not at all, lass," the merchant said. His voice sounded soft and reedy. "I appreciate you coming. I trust Brant is well?"

"Yes, and he sends his greetings," Icelin said. She spread her hands. "So, where is this trove you would have me safeguard?"

Kredaron smiled. "Brant said you didn't enjoy wasting time—how rare in a young person. To business then, but if I may: would it be rude of me to ask for a small demonstration of your qualifications?"

"Not at all." Icelin's polite smile held. She listened to the sounds of the square. After a breath, she put her hand on the warped tabletop and made a gesture against the wood grain.

Light glazed her fingertips, and a warm glow spread across the table. No one sitting nearby could see the light except Icelin and the merchant. When the light faded, Icelin took a moment to gather her wits. There was no nausea, just the edge of weakness that came with every spell. Fortunately, she'd eaten heartily before leaving home—her great-uncle had seen to that—and barely noticed the pull.

She focused on Kredaron. "There are three occupied tables behind me. One is a lad and lass, roughly six summers my junior. They are lovers planning how best to tell the lass's father that she is with child, and they not yet hand-fasted. The second is a gnome sitting alone. He talks to himself, lives in the Warrens, and thinks it's too warm this Eleint day for being out of doors. The third table bears two women, pocket-thieves, who until a breath ago were very interested in your roll of silk. I've since disguised it to appear as if you're holding an ugly and very sulky dog, wrapped in a silk blanket. We should be undisturbed."

Kredaron shook his head in admiration. "Brant didn't exaggerate. You are remarkable, lass. Did you determine all that with your magic?"

"No," Icelin said, chuckling. "Mostly I listened to their conversations. Folk reveal more about themselves when they feel they are unobserved than most magic could tell you about their entire lifetimes."

"True words," Kredaron said. His forehead wrinkled. "You have an extraordinary memory, to note so much detail."

Icelin's smile twisted ruefully. "My means of living is spellcraft, but it is not my only gift. If you would know my full qualifications, you should be aware that my memory is flawless. I can recall any piece of information I am confronted with, no matter how trivial."

Kredaron smiled uncertainly. "That's quite a statement. I would dismiss such a claim entirely, especially coming from so young a person, but you don't seem to take any joy in the admission."

Icelin lifted a shoulder. "I only speak of it when it's necessary to the task at hand. Whether you believe me or not, you should know what you're getting when you hire me. Would you care to test me?"

"I would, for curiosity's sake," Kredaron said. "How?"

"Spread out your pieces," Icelin said. "I've shielded the table from prying eyes."

"As you say." Kredaron unrolled the span of silk on the table in front of her.

Icelin looked at the spread for two breaths and then back at Kredaron. "Cover them," she instructed.

He did as she asked. When the pieces were safely hidden, so that not even their shapes could be discerned in the wrappings, Icelin folded her hands on the tabletop.

"I am by no means an expert," she said, "but by my estimation your heirlooms would easily bring in enough coin for you to establish a presence in the spice market, perhaps even secure property for a small shop. You have three opals: one in a silver ring, thumb-sized; one in a clawed brooch; and one alone, ripped from its setting by some force. There is a ruby with a well-concealed flaw, and a silver braided neckpiece, like a spiderweb but with links missing. You shouldn't have any trouble repairing them; the damage is minimal. The gold chains are problematic—one is a clever forgery, but nested with the others it appears just as fine. I would of course remove that one before trying to sell the lot.

"You won't have trouble with fakery when it comes to the matching circlets. Those chains are genuine, and the diamonds they hold are the star items of your collection. But I didn't have to appraise them to know that. Your displaying of them in the exact center of the collection shows your pride. The sunlight catches the stones and sets them aflame with color.

"There is magic swirling in all the pieces," Icelin said, "of varying degrees. It would take further study to determine how much and of what type."

"What about the bracelet?" Kredaron asked her. "The charms on the chain, what were they?"

"The charms were a lock and key, both tarnished, a tiny slipper, and a rose," Icelin said. "The rose was pink topaz. There was no bracelet. Shall I keep going?"

"How long could you recite them?" Kredaron asked, fascinated. "Will you remember the pieces tomorrow, or is this just a mind trick you've mastered?"

"I will remember them tomorrow and every day for the rest of my life, if it serves me," Icelin said. Kredaron was right. She felt no joy in the admission. "Since it likely won't serve me beyond this day," she added, "I will put the knowledge away, find some dusty corner where my memory has space—there's always space, of course—and there it will stay. Once I've put a recollection like that aside, it's difficult to find again, since I don't have a ready use for it. It's much like locating a single crate in all the warehouses of Dock Ward. It may take hours, days, but I can remember them all."

Kredaron shook his head. "Well, lass, you are a wonder, which is rare in a city full of them. You have shown me your skills. I am assured of success in this transaction."

Icelin inclined her head. "Then let us proceed." When he'd spread out his items again, she laid a finger on a cameo brooch. The figure was of a thin woman sheathed in lace. The piece was smooth with age, but the detail was still astonishing, from the creamy relief to the oval background. She'd briefly touched the magic in the piece, but that was not her reason for choosing it. Her interest lay in its value to a jeweler.

"May that be my payment, Kredaron?" she inquired.

"You have excellent taste," said the merchant. He lifted the brooch for her inspection. "It's not the most valuable, nor the most ostentatious of the lot. But there is history here, I think."

"You *think?* You don't know the origins of the pieces?"

"Not all of them," Kredaron admitted. "They came from my father's family, and he's been gone a long time. I don't even know who the woman is, so I haven't formed any particular attachment to the piece. You may have it with my gratitude."

Icelin slid the brooch into the coin-purse fastened around her neck and tucked the pouch away in her dress. Kredaron ordered them light wine from the vendors. The glasses were just being poured, the wine's buttery color glowing warm in the sunlight, when Kredaron's buyer arrived.

CHAPTER 2

Icelin was surprised to see the gold elf approach their table. She didn't know what sort of man she'd expected to be interested in Kredaron's pieces, but this one was an anomaly, even among the varied folk of South Ward.

The elf was unusually tall. Not gangly, but thinner than he should have been. He was dressed in a tailored, deep blue doublet with a subtle river of silver thread ornamenting the shoulders. The cloth was only marginally above workman's material, however. She recognized the style from what Brant sold in his shop.

He buys for resale, Icelin thought, not for his own collection. Yet his style and carriage suggested he had at least some means of his own.

When her eyes reached his face, Icelin took care to keep her expression politely blank. His own features were impossible to read. The right side of his face appeared robust and healthy, the color enhanced by his dark clothing. But the left side was a patchwork of burn scars.

Puckerings of deep red skin quilted his forehead and all the way down to his jaw. From what she could tell, his left eye appeared to see normally, but it moved slightly out of concert with his right. The strikingly blue orb in the left socket looked like it was being chewed up by the field of angry red. Part of the elf's ear on the scarred side was missing, skewing the pointed end. The disfigurement caused a jarring, asymmetrical appearance to his face.

An elf, but not an elf, Icelin couldn't help thinking.

"Well met, Kredaron." The gold elf bowed to the merchant and took a seat at the table. Icelin watched in silence while the pair conversed. The merchant did not introduce her, but she hadn't expected him to. Kredaron's buyer was well aware that her purpose in the transaction was security. Icelin watched him closely, but she could detect no deception in him when he bargained for the jewelry.

It was well into late afternoon by the time a price had been decided for each piece. Kredaron chose the type and denomination of coin, and the elf agreed to his terms. Through it all, Kredaron was calm and eloquent. Icelin had no doubt his new business venture would do well, and she was glad of her small part in bringing that about.

When they were alone again, Kredaron beamed at her. "I thank you, Icelin, for all your help."

"It was my pleasure."

"Cerest is a good businessman," Kredaron said. "He has always dealt fairly with me, but it never hurts to ensure the success of a transaction."

"You've had dealings with the elf before?" Icelin asked, surprised.

"Oh, yes." Kredaron wiped perspiration from his brow. The sun baked the dusty streets during the day, though it would be cold once night fell. "Cerest came young—a relative phrase for the elf folk—to his trade in Waterdeep. A handsome eladrin and shrewd bargainer—he was born to be a merchant."

"Handsome?" Icelin said. "Then how did he come to be . . . as we saw him today?" She knew she was rude to ask. It was none of her affair, but she couldn't fight her curiosity.

Kredaron must have sensed her discomfort. He chuckled. "Don't worry, you're not the first to gossip about him. There's been wild speculation about Cerest's scars and his business dealings," the merchant said. "I first heard of him when he was buying antiques from the poorer upstarts, like me. I had little to sell back then, but he treated me politely, never made me feel as if I were less a man for having little wealth. For that I was grateful. I didn't realize then what he was truly seeking."

"But you know now," said Icelin. She considered, remembering how the elf had examined each of the pieces. In most cases he'd passed over the fashionable items in favor of the older pieces—the ones that sparkled with magic. "He is not a jeweler or an antiquities dealer, is he? He's hunting for treasure."

"Exactly right," Kredaron said. "Magic in all forms draws Cerest's attention. Of course magic is unstable at the best of times, but Cerest knows his market well. Folk seek magic trinkets now more than ever. They trust them. And I think solid objects sit better in their hands than spells cast by strangers."

"I can see how they would be justified in their fear," Icelin said. She stared at the tabletop, her eyes following the swirling patterns in the wood. "So Cerest buys and resells the magic items?"

"And anything else of value he can get his hands on, these days," Kredaron said. "He had a good eye and a bright future in the city, or so I thought."

"What happened?" Icelin asked. "Was it anything to do with his scars?"

"I don't know how he received them," Kredaron said sadly, "but I've heard he has spent most of his accumulated wealth trying to repair the worst of the damage. The whole affair is mystery and rumor. He disappeared for a time and left his business in the hands of his employees. When he returned, he was as you saw him today. He never spoke of what happened to him, and none of the clients who relied on him has dared to ask."

"What do you think it was?" Icelin asked.

"I think he dabbled too closely in dangerous magic and paid the price," Kredaron said. "We'll likely never know the full story."

"But if he deals honorably in business, why should he be judged for his appearance?" Icelin said. "Whatever mistakes he made, his scars have more than paid for them."

"You are right, of course," Kredaron said. "I shouldn't have doubted his character. But if I had not"—his eyes twinkled—"I would never have met and conversed with you. So you cannot fault me too harshly."

"True, I cannot," Icelin said, smiling.

The merchant glanced up as evenpeal sounded. The bells in Castle Waterdeep's turrets could be heard all across the city. "I've kept you too long. My apologies. May I escort you home? It will be dark soon, and I don't want your great-uncle to be distressed at your absence."

"Thank you, but I know the way well. I can be home before gateclose," Icelin assured him.

She parted ways with Kredaron at Caravan Street and headed in the opposite direction, back to The High Road. As she walked, she slipped the brooch from her coin-purse and examined its surface in the dying sunlight.

The woman in lace had a stunning profile, and the blue agate of the cameo gave her face an ethereal quality. Her delicate eyes held secrets Icelin could not begin to guess. Pressed silver bounded the piece in a teardrop design, forever capturing the woman's enigmatic beauty.

"You are an elegant lady," Icelin murmured dryly, "just as I am not. But I am practical, as many elegant ladies are not. You will keep Brant and I well fed, though I hate to part with you."

She slowed when she approached The Way of the Dragon. Normally, she would have cut between buildings and walked the alley, but dusk was imminent and the brooch too precious to lose to thieves. On impulse, she decided to stay on the Way and stop at the butcher shop at the end of the street. Brant would be glad for fresh meat, and they could afford the luxury, just this once.

She picked up her pace, excited at the prospect of surprising her great-uncle with a sumptuous meal. She was so absorbed with her thoughts and plans that she didn't hear the first scream.

She heard the second; the sound made every hair on her neck stand up.

It was not unusual for horses to neigh and cry on the Way. The caravan traffic brought animals that were in as many and varied conditions as their handlers: robust, sick, starving, even dying.

But everyone in South Ward knew the sound of a mad horse's scream. It was the scream that caused drivers to bring their carts to a dead halt in the middle of the road. Mothers yanked children up into their arms, and anyone who stood on foot near the dusty Way found cover with haste. The crowded road was unforgiving to those who walked it unawares.

Such was the man cutting across the Way twenty feet in front of Icelin. He walked with his head down, shoulders hunched. Impossibly, he didn't appear to have heard the horse's scream.

The animal, a brown velvet streak in the sunset gloom, reared and broke from its handlers. A coil of rope dangled from its neck. It bolted down the Way, heading straight for the man.

People were screaming, Icelin among them, but she was running too. She charged down the Way, her hair flying, and launched herself at the man's back.

She had a brief impression of orange sunlight and a horse's hooves flashing over her head. Four deadly clubs, poised to strike, Icelin thought. She closed her eyes, waiting for the weapons to come down and crush her skull.

Cerest Elenithil had never been in South Ward on foot before. He'd never liked the notion of walking here, having no strong desire to plod among draft animals and caravan lords. But he'd had two exchanges in the Ward today, and one of them had required his wagon to haul the goods. It was a simple transaction of silver for two antique tables.

The seller had insisted the markings on the edges were

arcane. Cerest had sent three of his men to confirm the claim and transport the tables, leaving him alone to conduct the affair with Kredaron. If he'd had more men—or more wagons—he might not have had to breathe the dust and detritus of Caravan City at all. Perhaps, if one of those tables did have arcane powers, he would never have to breathe here again. But after years of merely scraping by in the City of Splendors, Cerest doubted his luck would be running that high.

So when the elf found himself crossing The Way of the Dragon after evenpeal, he paid no particular attention to the traffic around him and the shouts and conversations of the predominantly human throng. He wanted only to get back to his men and his wagon.

A few folk ceased their chatter when he came near. They met his good eye and then quickly looked away, not wishing to offend him. He was dressed near enough to nobility that they paid him deference, but they could not keep their reactions to his scars in check.

Cerest wanted to be home, back in his stone house with its quiet garden. None who served within those walls would ever remark on his disfigurement. He'd seen to that a long time ago, at the point of a sword.

"I'm tellin' ye, that horse won't take a whip crack more than a fly's arc from its rump," he heard someone saying. "'It's not right in the head. Too jittery."

Cerest turned, and so didn't hear the horse master's reply. The damage to his left side was immutable. There were too many scars to salvage his hearing in that ear. Sound simply died when it came to him from the left.

"Clear the way! Move!"

The scream came at him from the right, and a shower of black suddenly exploded in Cerest's face.

Blinded, Cerest lost his balance as a dead weight slammed him from behind. The force knocked him completely off his feet, and he went down on his stomach in the dirt. Numbness shot up both arms. Cerest thought he heard bones crunch. The weight landed on top of him and stayed there.

For a long time Cerest tried simply to breathe. The air had been completely knocked from his chest, and a black curtain blocked his vision. He could hear more shouts and screams now, all filtered to the right. The effect unbalanced him. He felt sick to his stomach.

Breathing through his mouth, Cerest forced his arms to move. He levered himself up and slid the offending weight off his back. He turned and sat down in the road, ignoring the pangs from his protesting bones.

When he looked up and saw the black curtain again, he realized it was a woman's hair, dangling loosely from a ruined braid. She pushed the strands out of her face and massaged her neck gingerly.

Gods, a human lass had brought him low in South Ward. There was no pride left in the world.

"Are you all right?" the girl asked. She appeared to be about twenty, with milk blue eyes and pale skin. He recognized her. Where from?

Kredaron—that was it. She'd been his security. He'd tried not to be insulted by her presence and ignored her during their transactions—a gesture that had been rendered pointless now she'd planted her rump on top of him and ground his bones into the dirt.

Cerest coughed. "I think you broke my back."

"Oh no. You wouldn't be hacking like that if I'd done any such thing; you'd be screaming," the woman said, and she offered him her arm.

Cerest reluctantly let her pull him up. She was a petite thing, half a head shorter than he. Something about her seemed oddly familiar, but he didn't think he'd ever seen her before.

"Why?" he asked.

"Why what?" She cocked her head.

"Why did you almost break my back?"

Her expression slid from tight concern to full-blown incredulity. She pointed over his shoulder. "I hoped to do you a favor, and that's why."

Cerest turned and saw the carnage for the first time.

A broken wagon was twisted around a crushed archway that had once been a storefront. Blood splattered the otherwise pristine windows. A dead horse lay among the wreckage. The tall stud had been brought down near the wagon. An arrow jutted from the beast's neck. Foam still dripped from its lips. Its eyes were open, frozen in half-crazed fear.

"It went wild and broke its reins," the girl explained. "Everyone could see it going, but the fool with the whip didn't. He won't last long in South Ward with a whip hand like that, and neither will you, the way you wear your head so low on your neck. You have to look *up* when you walk, or else you'll be trampled." Her words crowded together. She shuddered, clearly unsettled by what had happened.

"I didn't hear it," Cerest said. "I don't hear well, from the left side." He turned back to the girl. "My deepest gratitude," he said. "You saved my back, and the rest of me, such as I am." He smiled wryly. "My name is Cerest Elenithil. We met earlier, though not formally. May I know you?"

The girl hesitated. "My name is Icelin Tearn."

"Icelin Tearn," he repeated. The shadow of familiarity snapped abruptly into a picture—a memory—and the elf lost his breath.

He was not often caught so completely off guard, but at that moment, Cerest simply stared at the woman before him.

Framed by swirling dust clouds and the curious onlookers who'd come to see the accident, she was a vision, a ghost given life.

Memories surged through him, phantoms he could draw

from the air: Elgreth, the fire, an opportunity lost forever, or so he'd thought. Yet here she was, standing before him like a small, dark angel.

Icelin Tearn, he thought. You are all grown up. I would never have known you.

An awkward silence had settled between them. Cerest recovered himself and hurried to fill it. "You must allow me to repay my debt. Please, I would like to escort you home. The Way of the Dragon is no place for a girl to be at night."

Cerest was careful to maintain a cordial manner. He didn't want her to realize how off balance he was. Did he imagine that she looked at him strangely, or was it just his scars that unsettled her? Before he'd been maimed, it had been effortless to charm people, in business or in his bed. Now it was more difficult to get folk to trust him.

"That's not necessary," said the girl. "I know the way well, and I like to walk."

An error. He'd been too forward. Cerest cursed himself. She was being cautious now, businesslike, just as she had been with Kredaron. He would have to snare the rabbit carefully, or she would run.

"I'm afraid my home is a far walk from here, but I have a wagon somewhat closer." He offered a mock wince. "I've learned my lesson. I shall never leave it to go on foot in South Ward again. I will retrieve the wagon and come for you here. Please, I could have you home to your family very shortly, and it would ease my mind to know you hadn't suffered any injuries preserving my poor neck."

"You're very kind, but I'm afraid I can't."

She was starting to edge away. Cerest could see she didn't trust him. He sighed inwardly. This was going to be more difficult than he'd thought. Ah, well. Perhaps his scars would serve him in this case.

He slipped his hand over her nearer wrist, as if it were the most natural gesture in the world, and not an intrusion in her space.

"Does my appearance unsettle you so much?" he asked, pitching his voice low.

That gave her pause. She flushed attractively. "I'm not troubled by your face, but by your sudden interest in me. You showed no such attentiveness before."

"Perhaps I am enchanted by the woman who just saved my life."

Her eyes narrowed. "Your hands are cold and dry, when any other man's should be shaking and clammy. You don't seem the least bothered that there is a dead animal reeking in the street behind us, an animal that almost killed you in a grisly fashion. You look as serene and collected as if you were hosting a dinner party and I had suddenly become the honored guest. Please let go of my hand."

She jerked away and immediately began walking in the opposite direction. Cerest had to admire her quick wit. She would be difficult, just like Elgreth had been.

"Wait, please." The elf matched her stride easily. "Icelin. Icelin, listen to me. Please don't run away. I don't want our acquaintance to start like this."

"We have no acquaintance," Icelin said curtly.

Oh, but you're wrong, Cerest thought. You don't know how very wrong you are.

He allowed her to pull slightly ahead of him before he fired his next shot, "Don't you remember me, Icelin?"

That stopped her cold. She spun to face him. "What did you say?"

"Of course you wouldn't. I shouldn't have expected . . ."

"Stop it." But she was looking at him now, her eyes raking his features, searching for something recognizable. No one had ever looked at him so intimately after he'd been maimed. His heart sped up. Gods, she was beautiful, more beautiful than Lisra. . . .

She raised her hand to her mouth. Her chest heaved up and down. "Gods, no, it can't be. No. I'm sorry, I have to. . ."

She turned and fled, cutting down a back alley. Two carts jammed the way. She slid underneath the closest, ignoring the shouts of the drivers who had to steady their horses.

Cerest watched her go. He was too shocked to follow. What had caused the reaction in her? A breath ago she'd been grinding his teeth in the dirt and giving him a dressing-down for carelessness, and now she was a frightened waif running away from him as fast as she could.

He laughed out loud, startling the men who'd come to clean up the horse gore. Icelin was a strange woman and fascinating. Gods, he was almost glad she'd run. It made everything more exciting. Now he had to know her better.

He wanted to keep her forever.

The elf turned and broke into a run down the Way. He had to find Riatvin and Melias. They were better trackers.

His men would get her back. Now that he'd seen her, he didn't want to lose her again. His hands trembled from an excitement that was almost sexual. Come back to me, Icelin. I'll explain everything. I'll *make* you remember.

Cerest's men were waiting for him at the wagon. Riatvin and Melias were gold elves, like himself; Greyas was the only human who served him. Cerest sometimes thought that, despite the inferiority of Greyas's race, the human understood him better than most eladrin. On a more practical level, Greyas was the only human who possessed tact enough to avert his gaze from Cerest's scars. A burly man with black hair sprouting from his head, chest, and nose, Greyas looked anything but tactful. He was sorely out of place between the two smooth-skinned elves.

"I need you to retrieve someone for me," Cerest told them.

"Deal go sour?" Greyas asked.

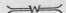

"The deal is in progress," Cerest corrected. He turned his attention to the elves and described Icelin in detail. He would never forget her face now. "You two go and find her. Bring her to the house. Hurry!" he snapped. "She moves fast, but someone will have seen her on the streets. Question them if need be, but discreetly."

The elves nodded and took off, moving like glowing streaks through the crowd.

She won't outrun them, Cerest thought. "Greyas, I want you to find out where she lives."

"How?"

"Go to Kredaron. He'll still be in the ward." Cerest's mind raced. An idea started to unfold. "Ask him politely where Icelin Tearn dwells. Apologize, but tell him you bear unhappy intelligence. Tell him that Icelin has stolen the jewels he sold to me. Ask him to please give an inventory to the Watch of the items in the transaction, as I had no time to make a record of them before I was robbed. That will remove Kredaron from the situation and assure him that I have no ill intentions."

"Do *we?*" Greyas asked.

Cerest looked at him, but his mind was still occupied with other things. "Find out if she has any family left. If she does, that will be problematic for what I intend."

"You want me to remove the problem?"

That was why Cerest employed Greyas. He was unlike most humans, just as Cerest was different from other elves. His tone was businesslike; he passed no judgments, nor offered any reassurances on the consequences of Cerest's actions. For all his human frailties, Greyas was an instrument that cut quickly and without emotion. Cerest needed more men like that, but for now he could not afford them.

"Yes," he said. "Remove the problem, but do it tastefully. I don't want Icelin to suffer more than necessary."

Icelin ran all the way back to Blacklock Alley, pausing only once for breath and to see if she was being followed.

Rustling movements disturbed one of the trash piles in the alley. Icelin nearly swooned. But it was only a small gray dog, snuffling through the garbage. It raised its head, sniffed the air around Icelin, and went back to foraging.

Shaking, Icelin pressed a hand to her stomach. She was nearly home now, but she couldn't go to her great-uncle like this. She glanced in one of the glazed shop windows. Her hair stuck out crazily from her braid; her dress was caked in dirt from her tumble with the elf. She couldn't let him see how wild she was, how terrified. And what if the elf still trailed her?

Leaning against a building, Icelin hid herself in the shadows. She would wait, for a while at least, to make sure the elf wasn't coming for her. In the meantime, she tamed her hair as best she could and tried to relax.

Cerest and his scars floated in her memory. Gods, did the elf truly know her? Had he been there five years ago? She hadn't known the names of any of the folk involved, except Therondol. She hadn't wanted to know their names or faces. How could she carry them in her memory and survive? Nelzun had been bad enough. Her teacher.

Don't blame yourself.

She heard his words again. They haunted her. If the elf came after her for what she'd done, she could hardly blame him, could she?

Icelin pressed her forehead against the cool stone building. She would ask her great-uncle. Brant would know. He'd raised her, protected her, even after what had happened. He would know what she should do.

Icelin stepped around the side of the building and glanced at the sign above the door. She saw with some surprise that it was the butcher's. "Sull's Butchery," it stated, in blocky brown letters over a painted haunch of meat.

I didn't even notice where I ended up, Icelin thought. A dangerous lapse, in Blacklock Alley. Well, she'd wanted meat. . . . Maybe the everyday chore would calm her. Anything was better than being in the street alone.

A bell jangled loudly when she entered. Icelin gritted her teeth at the sound. She wanted to be home where it was quiet and safe.

"Be right out!" The bellow sounded from somewhere in the back of the shop, a cross between a lion's roar and a ram's gravelly tenor.

A breath later, a giant human figure crowded the doorway. He carried a half-carcass of deer, dangling by a metal hook. Grunting, he heaved it down on a covered portion of counter at the far end of the room.

"Sull?" she inquired. She half hoped the imposing man wasn't the name above the door.

"That'd be me." He turned to give her a friendly smile, exposing a wide gap between his two front teeth. Red, frizzy hair covered his head, ending in two massive sideburns at his jowls. A shiny bald circle exposed the top of his head. "What can I do for you?"

"I need some. . . ." she trailed off, watching him wipe the animal blood on his apron. The streaky red stains reminded her of the dead horse.

"Aye?" He looked at her expectantly. "Are you all right, lass?"

"I'm fine." Icelin swallowed. "I'd like two cuts of boar and one of mutton, if you have them."

"I do, and you're welcome to 'em. Just let me take care of this beauty." He took a long cleaver from a padded pocket in his apron and cut into the carcass on the counter. "Lass a little older than you is comin' in for this one." He took a fistful of salt from a jar on the counter and sprinkled it like snow on the cut meat.

"Aw, you can make a hearty stew with deer or boar, and that's the truth. I got my own seasonin's—best recipe you'll find at any fine inn. Most folk have me prepare 'em in advance, tenderize 'em, let the juices mingle a while. Delicious."

The big man reached into another apron pocket and pulled out three small jars. "Peppers, some ground-up parsley, and more salt. Nothin' fancy. The key's in the quantity. I'll show you what I mean. It's best on the raw meat, when it's drippin' just a bit."

The bell at the door jangled again as the butcher headed for the back room. "Be right back," he hollered.

Icelin turned. A pair of gold elves stood in the doorway. They were dressed in servants' liveries. Neither paid her any attention, but Icelin felt sick in her gut.

They were Cerest's men. She knew they were.

CHAPTER 3

The shorter of the two elves took up a position by the door. The other came forward to lean an elbow against the long counter.

They all move like dancers, Icelin thought, as if the ground beneath them could be measured and controlled through their feet. Would they fight the same way?

Pinned between them, Icelin weighed her options. She could run, but they would be on her before she reached the street. If she screamed, would the butcher come to aid her?

The last thing she wanted was for harm to come to him or his shop. She couldn't use her magic for the same reason.

"Your master is persistent," she said, stalling for time. If she could just get them to move, take the inevitable fight to the alley. . . .

The elf at the counter regarded her coolly. He said something to his companion in Elvish. Sharp, elegant words to match their looks. The other elf nodded.

"You know, that's terribly rude behavior," Icelin said. She crossed her arms. "Talking as if I'm not in the room. If you're going to execute a successful kidnapping, the least you could do is be straightforward with your intentions."

The pair exchanged a glance. Icelin couldn't tell if they were amused or annoyed.

The elf at the door looked her over. "You've a blunt tongue," he said in Common. "I don't suppose if we were 'straightforward' and asked you to come with us, you'd cooperate without resistance?"

"Ah, if only a woman's intentions bore any degree of

predictability," Icelin said, smiling. "Let me think. If I kick and scream and conjure fire to boil the flesh off your lovely cheekbones, does that count as resistance?"

"I believe it does," the elf said, genuinely amused now. "But I think you're bluffing."

"You think I don't have magic? I suppose I don't give much of an appearance of sorcery." Icelin reached up to grasp the coin-purse at her neck.

"Hands at your sides!"

Her head cocked, Icelin obeyed. "But I thought I was bluffing," she said. "The pouch is too small to hold any useful weapon."

"Mefilarn stowil!" the elf at the door said sharply to his companion. "Make her hold her tongue, Melias."

"Your friend's right, Melias, I do talk too much. And that's a fault to reckon with," Icelin said. "But don't interrupt me now, I've only just got going. The pouch can't contain any weapon deadly to you. So what am I keeping in here, if not some dark magic that you both fear?"

"Empty it," Melias commanded.

"Not here," Icelin said, "in the alley. We can have a nice, quiet conversation—"

"Sorry to be so long!" Sull's booming voice cut through the tension in the air like a saw grating on wire.

"Watch your hands." The butcher tossed a pair of bundles wrapped in brown paper onto the counter next to Melias. "Seasonin's, I was talkin' of." He uncapped the jar of salt again and poured a fistful into his large hand. He gestured at Icelin and sprayed salt across the counter.

"Large crystals, that's what you want," Sull said. "Not ground as fine as for a noble's table in North Ward—that bleeds the flavor out—but try talkin' sensible cookin' to a noble, eh? The salt's what teases the tongue. You put some pinches of this on the fire while your boar meat's simmerin' in my spices, the whole thing'll be so tender it falls juicy onto your spoon. Make a man weep unashamed pleasure, that's the truth." He looked at the elves as if he'd only just remembered they were there. "Sorry 'bout that, gentlemen, I like to blather. What can I get the pair of you?"

"Nothing," said the one by the door. "We didn't see anything worthy of our master's tastes. The lass and we are leaving."

"Aw, shame, that," the butcher said, looking crestfallen. "This is prime meat, you know. Here now, maybe you'd like this cut instead."

The red-haired giant turned, yanked the meat hook from the deer carcass, and swung it in a downward arc. The hook sank into the countertop, the curved metal trapping Melias's delicate wrist against the wood.

Screams of elf fury filled the shop.

"Told you to watch your hand," Sull admonished. He threw his handful of salt at the elf by the door, grabbed Melias's head in his other hand, and slammed the elf's skull against the countertop.

Blood poured down Melias's face. He fell back over the counter, his hand still pinned awkwardly under the hook.

The elf by the door took the salt in the eyes. Crying out, he drew his sword and scraped a hand across his face.

Stunned by the violence, Icelin almost didn't react in time. Reaching into her neck purse, she chanted the first simple spell that came to mind. The elf at the door brought his blade up, but Icelin got to her focus first and hurled a handful of colored sand into the air.

A flare of light consumed the sand and shot at the elf's face. Luminous colors filled the small shop; Icelin covered her eyes against the brilliance.

She heard the elf fumble his sword, but he didn't drop it. Instinctively, she ducked. Wood splintered from the wall.

"Run, lass!" The butcher yelled at her.

Icelin broke for the door, stumbling over her dress. The noise betrayed her. The elf dived at her from the side and caught an arm around her waist. They went down together, arms and legs tangling.

Pain lanced along Icelin's flank. The elf's weight pinned her to the floor. She kicked out viciously, trying to find a vulnerable spot. He forced her arms against her sides and put his boot on the back of her head. When she tried to move, he pressed down, hard. Icelin thought her skull would crack from the pressure.

She heard him groping for his sword. He dragged the blade over to them and brandished the pommel. He was going to knock her out, Icelin realized. The fight had come down to kicking and screaming after all, but she was still going to lose.

The elf's head snapped to the side. Steel clattered on wood, and he pitched forward, sprawling heavily on top of her.

Her arms free, Icelin heaved the elf off and kicked his sword across the room. She raked the hair out of her eyes and felt moisture on her back. She could smell the blood.

"It's not yours." The butcher stood over her, clutching a mallet in his hand. "For tenderizin'," he explained.

"I think you killed him," Icelin said. She rolled the elf onto his back and put her hands over his heart. "There's no beat. What about the other?"

"He's breathin,' " Sull assured her.

Icelin had to see for herself. The butcher had strewn Melias across the counter next to the dead deer. Blood and bruises darkened his temple. His chest rose and fell intermittently. He would need healing soon, or he would join his friend.

"Why did you kill him?" Icelin demanded. Fear shook her voice. How had everything gotten so out of control? This could no longer be a private matter. The Watch would have to be called, if someone hadn't already heard the commotion and summoned them. She would be questioned; Gods, she would have to go through all that again. . . .

"Lass." The butcher was speaking to her. She'd almost forgotten he was in the room. "I had to, lass. Beggin' your pardon, but I was eavesdroppin' just now. These two, or whomever they serve, meant you harm. No man sends his own men—men he knows might be traced—after a person unless he plans for that body never to come home. After they'd trussed you up and made you gentle, they would have killed me for witnessin'. I'd be just another abandoned shop."

Icelin felt light-headed. "I have to go home," she mumbled.

"Best to wait for the Watch."

"The Watch be damned!" She lowered her voice. "Forgive me, but my great-uncle—he must know about this. I'll bring him back here—"

"Wait! What if there are more of them out there?"

More? She couldn't comprehend it. She was one small woman squirreled away in a shop, in a city full of folk much larger and darker. Why would someone want her so badly?

Cerest's scarred face appeared in her mind—the puckered red skin, the ruined ear.

"He wants revenge," Icelin said. "There's no other explanation." She glanced at Sull. The butcher looked extremely uncomfortable. "You know who I am," she said. It wasn't a question.

Sull cleared his throat. "Aye, I know. I recognized your face when you came in the shop. Someone's after you because of that business?" He shook his head. "It was years ago."

"He has burn scars all over his face," Icelin said flatly. "He recognized me too."

Sull sighed and nodded. "Go then, to your great-uncle. I'll speak to the Watch. But you'd best be runnin'."

Full dark pressed down on the city by the time Icelin reached her great-uncle's shop. The place was closed up, and there were no lamps burning in the second-level rooms. Brant always left a lantern in her bedroom when she was gone after dark.

Icelin fumbled her key in the lock at the back door. Sometimes her great-uncle lingered downstairs after closing to review his accounts. Meticulous in his records and his housekeeping, Brant never let anything stray out of order. That patience and painstaking attention to everything—including his great-niece—made her love him all the more.

Icelin stepped into the dark shop, leaving the door ajar for Selune to light the entryway. The shadow of a tall wooden plant stand caught her eye as she groped for a lamp. The piece of furniture had been moved slightly away from the wall, and the vase of lilies that had been displayed on it lay overturned on the floor. Water funneled through cracks in the floorboards.

Water, not blood. And no other earthly thing was out of place in the room.

But Icelin screamed anyway, screamed and dropped to the floor, clutching her hair and sobbing. In the dark, she crawled across the floor of the shop, feeling her way, fighting the dread bubbling up inside her.

Someone had already been here, seeking her. But how had they known? *How?*

"Great-Uncle," she whispered. Her fingers found a rack of boots, then a stand of belts. Long, leathery softness caressed her fingers. She crawled on, her skirts collecting dirt and dust that her great-uncle should have swept outside at the end of the business day. She found the broom in the next corner; the worn bristles reminded her of insect legs.

She reached the front of the shop. Clear glass jars lined the counter, each filled with a different herb or spice.

"Salt, mint, comfrey, basil." She named each one out of habit, stopping before she reached the wall. Selune's glow poured in a window and over her shoulder. She put her hand tentatively into the beam of light and followed it down to the floor. At the edge of the light, her hand found her great-uncle's chest.

Brant lay on his side, tucked against the back of the counter. There was very little blood; he'd clutched most of it in and made gouge marks in the wood with his other hand where he had held on. The sword thrust had been quick and precise, slipping right between his ribs.

When she touched him, his eyes fluttered open. Icelin could see he was already going. She had no time, no breath to explain that he'd been killed because of her, no time to say anything of meaning.

"Great-Uncle," she choked.

His eyes widened when he recognized her. He let go of the wood and grabbed for her, catching hair and dress and skin all together. He pulled her close.

"Get out of here," he said, his voice a terrible rasp.

"I'm not going anywhere," Icelin said. "I'm not leaving you."

"Get . . . the . . . box." The words came out broken by gasps and blood dribbling from his lips. "The floorboards, by the bookcase. Take it with you. Should have . . . been yours . . . before."

"You've given me everything I've ever needed," Icelin began.

"No!" He said it so viciously Icelin flinched. He held her tighter. "I lied, Icelin. I loved you, but now he's going to. . . ." Brant started to sob. She had never seen him cry before, not even when he spoke of his dead wife, Gisetta.

"I won't let him," Icelin said. She put her forehead against his. His lips moved, but she could barely hear what he said next.

"Run. Leave the city. Make something . . . new . . . better. Don't blame yourself. . . ."

"Shh, Great-Uncle, please." Icelin held his hands, but they'd gone boneless in her grip. He had no more strength.

"Rest now. I . . . I'll s-sing to you," she promised him. He could still hear her voice. Haltingly, the words came.

The last falling twilight
shines gold on the mountain.
Give me eyes for the darkness,
take me home, take me home.

"Do you remember, Great-Uncle?" she asked. She cupped his wrinkled cheek in her hand. His eyes stared glassily up at her. He nodded once. She felt the moisture at the corner of his eye.

"You always remember," he said. "I'm sorry . . . for that too." He closed his eyes, and his head slid away from her. She lost him in that last little breath.

Icelin curled protectively around the still-warm body, cradling her great-uncle's head in her hands. She stayed there, hunched, until she couldn't feel anything except a burning ache in her legs. The pain was the only force that kept her sane. As long as it was there, she wouldn't have to feel anything else. She would never leave that floor. She would stay there until the world withered away.

Moonlight still bathed them when Icelin heard the shop door close. She raised her head and saw the butcher's bulky shape crammed in the doorway. He seemed brought to her from another time, another century, one in which her great-uncle wasn't dead.

"Sull?" She didn't recognize her own voice.

"It's me, lass." The big man knelt beside her and lifted Brant's head from her lap. "Are you all right?"

"My throat hurts," she said.

"You were singin'."

"Was I?" She hadn't been aware, but now she thought of it, she could recall every song. Of course she could. She would remember them and the look on Brant's face when she sang. She would carry those memories with her until she died.

"You always remember. . . ."

"Icelin, you need to come with me," Sull said. He took her

hands. She was dead weight, limp as one of his carcasses, but he pulled her to her feet easily.

"He told me to leave the city," Icelin said. She might have laughed at the jest, but she didn't want to alarm Sull.

"I think he was right," the butcher said. He took her chin in his hand, forcing her to focus on him. "I've been to the Watch, but that elf bastard got away while I was gone. Guessin' he wasn't hurt as much as we thought. Ransacked every damn tool and stick of furniture in the place before he left, as if you were a mouse he was trying to scrounge up. Maybe to him that's what you are, but the Watch thinks differently."

"They've never liked me," Icelin said, and this time she did laugh. She could feel the hysteria bubbling up inside her. "Small wonder, I suppose. I'm the she-witch of Blacklock Alley, didn't you know?"

"Lass, that's not it," Sull said. "They've instructions to bring you in."

"For what?" she asked incredulously. "I didn't kill anyone!"

Not this time. . . .

"It's not like that," Sull said. "You're wanted on suspect of jewel thievery. The one who placed the request was named Kredaron, actin' on behalf of Cerest Elenithil."

"Kredaron?" Icelin closed her eyes. "Of course. That's how Cerest found out where I lived. So it's suspicion of thievery, unless they can prove I'm a murderess as well."

"I didn't tell 'em you were comin' back here. I told 'em I left you unconscious in my shop. But they'll check this place soon," Sull said. "I can get you out before that."

"Why should you care what happens to me?" Icelin said. Her voice held a bitter edge. "How can you be sure I'm innocent?"

Sull's brows knitted in a dark red line. "You and your mouth might be famous in this ward, but now's not the time to let loose on me," he said. "If he was alive, your great-uncle would give you a smart slap for takin' that tone with your elders. Brant Tearn was a fine man, he raised a good girl, and that's plenty of reasons for me to bother with you."

He left her at the counter and roved about the room, lighting a small lamp and placing it on the floor away from the windows. He selected a pair of swash-topped boots from the rack and tossed them to her.

"Put those on," he said. "You'll need new boots for the road, and a pack." He pulled one down off the wall. It was a nondescript brown mass of buckles and straps. "Blankets and ration bundles. Where did your great-uncle store 'em?" he asked.

"On the shelf behind you," Icelin said. She watched him collect some flint and steel, a compass, a weathercloak, and one of the belts. He put them all in a pile next to her.

"Don't wait for me; start puttin' it on," he told her. "I have a friend at the gate. He doesn't respond well to moral causes, but he can be bribed, so it suits me well enough. Stop lookin' at him, lass. We have to move!"

"Where do you think I can go, Sull?" He paused long enough to look back at her. "I have never trod on soil that wasn't Waterdeep's. My only family lies on this floor. Where would someone like me find a kind place in the world?"

Sull opened his mouth to answer, but the silence stretched.

Icelin nodded. "Exactly. I can't leave. I have to hide, at least for now."

But where to disappear to? Cerest's men had tracked her easily, and the Watch now joined them.

"You'll have to leave Blacklock, that's a certainty," Sull said. "If I knew your face, others will too, and they'll be watchin' for you."

"So, I leave the Alley," Icelin said. She picked up the pack and the belt and put them on. The rations she took as well. No telling where her next meal would be coming from.

Reaching over the counter, she took out the knife Brant had kept for emergencies. He hadn't been able to get to it when they came for him. She used it to cut a slit up her skirt. She needed to be able to run full stride if it came to that.

"There is a man I know in the Watch," she said. "Kersh. Fortunately, he *does* respond to moral causes. I think he'll help me, or at least be able to give me some information about Cerest."

"Help *us,* lass," Sull said. "I'm goin' with you."

Icelin shook her head. "You've already gotten yourself in enough trouble on my behalf. What about your store?"

"Stone and timber," Sull said, shrugging. "It'll be there after I've seen to you. This man," he said, and he knelt to touch Brant's shoulder, "he was known in South Ward. Like I said, he's a good man, and so is his kin. I'll be goin' with you lass, so it'd be best if we don't waste time arguin'."

Icelin looked at the butcher in the flickering lamplight. He still wore his bloody apron. He'd tucked the mallet and several wicked-looking cleavers into a leather harness that he draped sash-style across his broad stomach. Even had she not known what he could do with those tools, he was a fearsome sight to behold. Yet he handled her great-uncle's body with infinite gentleness. He tucked Brant's arms against his body and laid a blanket over him. Icelin swallowed the emotion rising up within her.

"All right, then, we'll go together," she said. "But you'll leave me at the first safe place I find. I'll sort the rest out on my own." She paused with the pack in her hands. "Wait. I need one more thing." She remembered her great-uncle's cryptic words. "Something he wanted me to take. He said it was near the bookcase."

"Could have been gibberish he was talkin'. A dyin' man might say things that don't make much sense," Sull said.

"No, he was very specific. He said it was in a box."

"If you say so. But we don't have time to be solvin' riddles, lass. What do you need?"

Icelin thought about it. "A sledgehammer," she decided.

Sull blinked. "Wasn't expectin' that."

"Over here." Icelin went behind the counter, where a narrow stretch of floor fronted a bookcase containing her great-uncle's favorite volumes. They were bound in leather, with red ribbons draped over the spines. He loved to read them on slow days. Tipped back on his wooden stool, he'd lay the pages open on his lap. When she was a child, Icelin had perched on the counter to listen to him read to her.

"I need to break through these boards," Icelin said. She wanted to smash them with her bare hands, to howl out the rage boiling inside her. But she would need her hands, her whole body's strength, in case she had to cast spells. "Do you think you could break them?" she asked Sull.

The butcher hiked up a leg and brought it down against the floorboards. The old wood splintered and gave way.

"There's dirt here," Sull said. "I don't feel anythin' else."

"Let me in there." He made way for her to crouch over the small hole. She felt with both hands in the musty darkness.

"Hurry, lass," Sull urged her. "Someone will have heard that noise."

"Found it." The box was small and narrow. She could feel the ridges of some kind of scrollwork running along the outer edges. When she brought it up, Sull's gasp drowned out her own.

"Bring the light," Icelin said.

Sull held up the lantern. The box shone, eclipsing the moonlight in the glow of flame.

"Is that—"

"Gold," Sull confirmed. "Or I'm no judge of beef. A small fortune's worth of it, at least. You have a dragon's hoard of mysteries about you, lass, and that's a certainty."

"Let's hope this is the last one," Icelin said. Escape was her greatest concern. She had no time to ponder what the box contained or why her great-uncle had concealed it from her. She buried it at the bottom of her pack and blew out the lamp.

Cerest didn't bother to light the lamps in front of his Sammarin Street home. He bypassed the front entrance of the blocky stone structure, with its single tower braced against the main building. He headed instead for his private garden.

He'd spent the largest share of his hoarded coin here, where he could be among the wild things and the quiet. It was his place to think, and where he often met the two women whose company he sought now.

Moonlight cast milky shadows over the cobblestone path leading to the small gladehouse. It was not as grand as those found at a high noble's mansion. The long sheets of glass that formed the circular cage were expensive and fragile, but they ornamented his most exotic blossoms: panteflower, with its bell shape and dark red stems; yellow orchids, the most fragrant; and all the rose varieties he could afford.

He lifted the latch on the door and stepped inside. The elf women were waiting, perched on stone benches on either side of a long rectangular pond. A fine layer of green scum covered the water. He would have to tend it when he was alone. Cerest looked forward to such tasks, but the Locks would have to come first.

Ristlara and Shenan, the Locks of North Ward, were sisters, or so they claimed. Privately, Cerest wondered if they were lovers. Not that it mattered, as long as they came to his bed.

Both had fiery gold hair, bronze skin, and moss green eyes. They were too beautiful and knew it, but they were also the richest pair of professional thieves living openly in the City of Splendors. That position demanded respect.

The Locks had defined the market for rare antiquities in the city, and Cerest knew what pleased them best: magic, the older the better. Their private mansion resembled more of a museum, stocked with artifacts either stolen or recovered from tombs across Faerûn, all of it carefully tagged and catalogued. It was a concise history of thievery that covered almost two centuries.

The sisters were mostly retired, preferring to commission their raids among the eager treasure-seekers who passed through the city. They were still rabid collectors, and to date, Cerest was their most successful contact. But for all his dealings with the sisters—both in the bedchamber and out of it—he'd never been invited to see inside their residence.

With this venture, Cerest vowed, things would change.

"Clearly, *you* don't see the need to maintain your business contacts, Cerest, since we haven't heard from you this tenday, but my sister and I were hosting a dinner party when you dragged us away to your swamp." Ristlara leaned back on the bench, crossing her shapely legs and scowling at him. She looked like a bronze sculpture against the stark gray stone. Her hair was upswept and bobbed at the back of her head, giving her face and neck a long, elegant line.

"Let him speak," Shenan told her sister. The older elf wore her hair loose, almost wild, and was as sedate as her sister was furious.

"Ladies, I appreciate you coming on such short notice," Cerest began. "You know I wouldn't have contacted you after such an inexcusable absence—rousted you from tea with boorish human muck-rakers—if it wasn't important."

"How did you know who we were meeting?" Ristlara demanded.

Her sister smothered a chuckle with the back of her hand. "Those are foul words to use, Cerest," Shenan chided him. "The humans led a legitimate expedition—a feat you have not achieved in some years."

"Digging in farm fields and wastelands where no real magic has dwelled for a century, you mean." With a melodramatic flourish, Cerest slid onto the bench next to Ristlara. He pulled the bronze she-cat onto his lap. "No thank you. I don't take up after the spellplague's leavings. Your lovely human pets are wasting your coin, sucking you dry like parasites. I have something better for you," he said against the squirming female's ear.

He felt her face grow warm against his cheek. Cerest nuzzled her neck until she stopped thrashing. "Are you interested, Ristlara? Or should I be coddling your sister?"

"Will it make us a lot of coin?" Shenan asked.

"Darlings, you won't believe me when I tell you," Cerest said. "I've found Elgreth's granddaughter."

Ristlara turned in his arms. Their faces were inches apart, but she'd stopped flinching at his scars a long time ago. "Are you jesting?"

"Not a bit."

"Have you spoken to her?" Shenan asked. She eyed Cerest shrewdly. "Will she work with us?"

"Not yet," Cerest said. "She needs time. I made a terrible first impression, I'm afraid."

"Poor Cerest," Ristlara cooed. She tipped her head back against his shoulder, so he could not help but catch the scented oil in her hair, or notice the full effect of her cleavage in her green lace gown. "Did you frighten her away? Did she think she was seeing a mask and not a face at all?" She reached up to touch his melted skin.

Cerest caught her wrist before she could touch him. He laid his other hand casually around her throat. For a moment, the elf's eyes widened fearfully. The irony of where she sat only then dawned on her.

The Locks were well aware of the change in Cerest's demeanor since his disfigurement. One of his former servants, a retired fence named Tolomon Shinz, had been unable to keep from staring at Cerest's scars. Cerest had been too ill at first to respond with any censure, but later, when the immediate pain and horror had abated, a general wildness of temper took its place.

He was known to react with violent outbursts to any insult, real or perceived, and so when Tolomon Shinz had looked too long at his crooked ear one Kythorn morning, Cerest had reacted decisively . . . most would say harshly.

Cerest had since mastered his emotions to such an extent that he could ignore most people, no matter their reaction to his deformity. But that didn't change the fact that Tolomon Shinz was entombed beneath Cerest's fish pond, and Ristlara's shapely toes dangled above the water scant inches from where his skull was decomposing.

The pretty elf, staring up at him while his hand noosed her neck, was most likely wondering, if only for a breath, if a similar fate awaited her. Ristlara's uncertainty was Cerest's power, and the elf reveled in it.

Shenan cleared her throat, and the tense breath passed.

Cerest relaxed and pushed the golden bitch off his lap.

"I was insensitive to Icelin," Cerest admitted, continuing their conversation as if nothing had happened. "Too greedy for my own good."

"You made the same mistake with Elgreth," Shenan reminded him.

"That was different. We had history between us. I expected more from Elgreth. But Icelin—"

"How lovely. It has a name," Ristlara purred.

"I think he's smitten, Sister," Shenan said. "I wonder if the lady will feel the same."

"She will," Cerest assured them. "I'm eliminating all her safe places. The life she knows is ending. When she has nothing left, she'll come to me gladly. I will be the only one who can protect her."

"And we will turn a tidy profit besides," Shenan said before he could. "It is a tempting offer." She swept a hand down beside the bench to caress one of the rose blossoms. She took hold of a thorny stem and severed it from the bush with her nail.

"Shall we agree to be partners again?" She offered the rose to Cerest.

Cerest took the flower and clenched it in a fist. Blood welled where its thorns pierced his flesh. Shenan watched in fascination as the droplets ran down his golden skin.

It was just the sort of poetic, gruesome gesture she preferred. In bed, she was no different, her nails digging blood trails into his skin until he cried out.

Dangerous, sadistic cats, these two. Cerest couldn't help adoring them both.

"We are in agreement," he said. He held out the bloody rose and watched Shenan kiss the stem.

Glass shattered behind them. Cerest turned, his hand on his sword hilt.

Melias lay sprawled in the doorway of the gladehouse. He'd collapsed against the structure and shattered the fragile door panel with his weight. Blood trailed from a blunt strike to the elf's head.

Cerest crouched next to the dazed elf. Melias's pupils were huge. His mouth moved, but the words that came out made no sense. He'd suffered too much damage to his head to live.

"Melias." Cerest shook the elf, trying to get him to focus. Melias whimpered, and his head lolled to one side.

"I think you might be in for more of a game than you thought, Cerest," Shenan commented.

The small elf crouched next to Melias and cradled his head in her lap. "Dearest," she cooed in his ear. "Who did this to you?"

"She . . . ran," the elf murmured. He was looking past Shenan, up at the gladehouse ceiling and through it to the stars. "We're dead . . . butchered . . . us." A slack, vacant smile passed over the elf's face.

"Yes, my sweet. Unfortunately, she did." Shenan took the elf's chin and forehead in her hands and jerked his head to the side. The sharp crack echoed off the gladehouse walls.

"You take too many liberties, Shenan," Cerest told her. "He was my man. I wanted him questioned."

"It was a kindness to end it," Shenan said, rising to her feet. "Pain is only alluring when there is the possibility of surviving it."

"I have to leave," Cerest said. He headed for the main building, leaving Melias's body concealed in the gladehouse.

The death of his men complicated matters with the Watch. They would not easily believe a waif of a girl could overpower two armed elves. How in the names of the gods *had* she done it?

She must be more powerful than I imagined, Cerest thought. The idea gave him a thrill of excitement and trepidation all in the same moment.

So much the better he declaim her a murderess, Cerest thought. He would tell the Watch that his men had been killed trying to retrieve his stolen property. They would have no proof to the contrary, as long as Icelin kept running.

The she-elves trailed behind him. "Do you intend to track her down by yourself?" Ristlara said.

Cerest stopped at the door to his house. Another idea occurred to him. On the surface it seemed perfect: efficient, clean, and with no way it could be traced back to him. But could he trust the Locks?

When he turned, he addressed Shenan. "Those human muck-rakers you're employing—how many are there?"

"Seven," Shenan said. "But they can muster the strength of twelve or more for longer expeditions. Why?"

"What say you put them to a different use, something that might actually end in profit?"

He could sense Ristlara gearing up for a fight, but Shenan's look was speculative. "How much of the profit would be for us?" she asked.

"If I get Icelin—unharmed—the percentage will twice exceed what you take now," Cerest promised.

Shenan smiled. "You truly are smitten," she said. "We'll bring the men. I want to watch this spectacle."

CHAPTER 4

Watchman Kersh Tegerin turned off Copper Street, crossing a footbridge linking Dailantha's Herbs and Exotic Plants to Breerdil's Fine Wines. A small, man-made stream ran under the bridge. Breerdril and Dailantha spent a small fortune to keep the water enchanted to appear midnight blue.

Kersh counted the paces from one end of the footbridge to the other. It was a habit from childhood that he'd never quite broken. Meren, his old friend, used to tease him for it.

The bell for gateclose had rung long ago, but he still had a little time before he needed to join up with his patrol. Kersh wasn't looking forward to the night's work. The word had gone out when he'd left the barracks: the Watch had orders to bring in Icelin Tearn for questioning.

How in the names of the gods did the girl get herself into these situations?

Kersh nodded to the lamplighters as they passed him on the street. The trio of men waved back, their iron reaching-hooks resting against their shoulders. They were sooty standard-bearers. The soft glow of flickering lights followed in their wake.

This time of night always made Kersh think of Meren, and tonight the feeling was heightened. They'd been on patrol together ten winters ago and had become fast friends. Meren had been young and, with all the wisdom of youth, had believed the quiet streets of North Ward held no threat for someone as spry and as skilled as he.

Meren learned differently, and Kersh lost his first real friend in Waterdeep. Kersh remembered the day vividly. The boy had

had no kin, but his former employer had come with his great-niece to claim the boy's body.

Icelin had been only a child at the time, but Kersh had never met a person who acted as she did. Bristling with opinions and outlandish teasing, she had seemed a fully formed adult merely lost in a child's wrappings.

Kersh remembered how, in the midst of his grieving, this strange child had walked right up to him and greeted him by name, as if they'd been friends for all their lives. Later, Kersh learned that she'd memorized the names and faces of almost all the Watch officers, simply by passing through the barracks when she'd escaped her great-uncle's sight.

After their first meeting at the funeral, she visited him regularly. She told him stories about Meren—silly, adorable boy, she'd called him—and his time working for her great-uncle in his sundries store. No detail or behavior escaped her memory.

Their friendship had continued, and Kersh had watched the odd child blossom into a lovely, confident woman. But he never forgot the affection with which she'd reached out to him all those years ago. It had been a balm to the terrible grief. The only being she paid more attention to was her great-uncle. She trailed his heels as if he were the center of her vast playing field.

So when the order came down that Icelin was to be taken for thievery and questioning for Brant's death, Kersh knew something was terribly amiss. Icelin was in trouble. And if Kersh knew her at all, he knew she wouldn't prefer the idea of surrendering to the Watch.

After the lamplighters had passed by, Kersh slid to a crouch on the bridge. Directly below his feet, between two of the bridge's supports, stood Icelin herself.

She was knee-deep in the perfect, midnight blue water, her thin frame concealed by the shadows. Behind her, a huge man emerged from a metal grate at water level. He crouched beside her, hissing at the cold water. Kersh had never seen the man before, but the small bridge barely concealed his massive frame. If the lamplighters came back this way to chase an errant flame, they would spot the pair in a heartbeat.

"Icelin, what web have you gotten yourself caught in?" Kersh said through his teeth. "And why meet here, bare-bottomed to the world?"

"Hello, old friend," Icelin said, "lovely to see you too. I'm afraid the risk was necessary, as I'm a bit pressed for time."

She shivered with cold and had deep circles under her eyes. Her hands gripped the bridge pilings as if for support. There were dark stains under her fingernails. Kersh suppressed a gasp.

"Icelin, what happened?" he demanded. "The patrols are getting your description as we speak. We're supposed to bring you in—subdued, if necessary."

"Then it's fortunate I'm a master of subtlety," Icelin jested. "Stand up and pretend to enjoy the night, you dolt, so no one looks under the bridge."

"This is serious," Kersh said, but he did as she asked. "How can you be so reckless?"

"I am taking this situation *very* seriously, my friend," Icelin said coldly. "Brant is dead. I assume you heard that too. He died in my arms."

"I'm sorry, Icelin. Who did it?"

"You'll recognize the name. Cerest Elenithil."

Kersh started. "The one who wants you brought in?"

"The same," Icelin said. "Obviously, he has a grudge against me that demands attention. Setting the Watch on my trail was an expedient way to corner me. I need a place to hide from him, somewhere the Watch won't readily find me."

"Unless you're sitting with the gods, there's no such place," Kersh said. "All the patrols have been alerted, and if that wasn't enough. . . ." He didn't know how to say it.

She did it for him. "They all remember Icelin Tearn. I have no illusions about my reputation among your fellows."

"Told you we should have made a run for it." The big man spoke up for the first time.

"Who's that?" Kersh wanted to know.

"Sull's my butcher," Icelin said, elbowing the big man into silence. "There must be somewhere we can go, Kersh."

Kersh hesitated. "You could come in with me."

"Hah."

"I'd speak for you," Kersh insisted. "My word doesn't carry as much weight as a swordcaptain's, but I know your character."

"The Watch has no desire to help me," Icelin said. "And I will not sit idly in a dungeon cell, waiting for them to deliberate my fate, while Brant's murderer plots my demise."

She stopped speaking. Kersh heard a soft sob, then silence. He waited for her to gather herself. He had never seen her fall apart before, not in all the years he'd known her.

"Kersh?" Her voice sounded strained.

"I'm here."

"What if—I know this will sound like lunacy—I could find a guide, someone who knows the city well and could hide me for the time being? Just until I figure out what to do about Cerest." Her voice grew stronger. "There is one person I can think of who would be perfect for the job."

It took Kersh a moment to realize where she was leading him. "Absolutely not!" he hissed. "You're right. You're talking lunacy."

"Who are we talking about?" the butcher wanted to know.

"Kersh used to work a night watch in the dungeons," Icelin said. "He told me a story once after several goblets of wine of a famous rogue he made the acquaintance of. A man named Ruen Morleth."

"He's nothing special, except he stole a fortune in paintings from a noble in North Ward, a great collector of odd and obscure art," Kersh said. "Brought the largest bounty on his head I've ever seen offered in the city."

"So he was caught?" Sull said. "Doesn't sound like a very good thief to me."

"Exactly. And he'd been imprisoned for some years," Kersh said. It was a stupid story. He couldn't believe he was reciting it now. "He asked me to get his hat back from some guards who were dicing over the thing." Of course Icelin would remember the whole tale perfectly, damn her. "I don't know why he bothered. It was the ugliest hat I'd ever seen."

"Kersh said the rogue offered to tell him a secret if he got his hat back," Icelin added. "So Kersh, being the curious thickhead that he is, set out to win the hat back from the guards. Fortunately, our Kersh has a good hand at dice. Tell him how grateful the rogue was, Kersh."

"I gave him back his hat, and he informed me very solemnly that he believed the secret of my parentage involved a tavern wench and several barnyard animals, and did I want to hear more?"

"Sounds like a lovely fellow," Sull snorted. "But you can't blame him for being angry over losing his hat."

"Oh, but you see, Kersh didn't tell the rogue that to get his precious hat back, Kersh had to gamble away half his wage for all the month of Ches," Icelin said. "The rogue got wind of it though, and this is the important part. Go on, Kersh. Tell him what Morleth said."

Kersh sighed. "He apologized, told me that he appreciated my looking after his hat, and said that if I ever needed a favor in return, I should go to Mistshore."

"Mistshore?" the butcher echoed incredulously. "That's the worst section of the city. He wanted to send you to Waterdeep's bowels to reclaim a favor?"

"At the Dusk and Dawn Inn," Kersh said. "I was to inquire at the dicing rounds."

"Those were his exact words," Icelin said.

"You would know." Kersh rolled his eyes.

"Except it's bollocks and cream," said the butcher. "Even if you were to brave the journey to the harbor, how's this thief goin' to be any help to anyone when he's locked in a cage?"

"He's not in a cage," Icelin said. Kersh glanced down and saw her leaning against the slime-clad piling, looking like a smug queen surveying her holdings. "He escaped not six nights after he got his hat back. He's the only man who has ever escaped from Waterdeep's dungeons."

"You think because he offered me a favor he'll help you hide from the Watch?" Kersh shook his head.

"And the elf," Icelin reminded him. "All I need is permission to call in your marker."

"Icelin, he's dangerous—dangerous and strange. You don't want to get tangled up with someone you can't trust, not when I'm here to—" he stopped, cursing under his breath.

"I would trust you with my life," Icelin said softly. "But folk have been turning up dead around me today, and I don't want you joining them."

"Then what's the butcher doing here?" Kersh asked, a little sullenly.

"Noisome baggage, but I can't shake him," Icelin said. "Please, Kersh. Give me your marker and let me be gone."

Reluctantly, Kersh reached into his coin-purse and pulled out a pair of cracked dice. They fit comfortably in his hand, clicking softly together. It had been years since he'd examined them, but for some reason he always carried them close. He handed them down to Icelin's cold fingers.

"Thank you," she said.

The butcher leaned in to look. "Are those bosoms where the sixes should be?"

"They are," Kersh said. "He handed them to me, clasped my left hand between both of his for a breath, then he nodded, like he was satisfied with a shift in the weather. He said, 'enjoy a long life, friend,' and smiled like he was having some jest. But

I could have sworn, by any god you'd care to name, that he was serious—relieved, almost. That part of the story I never told to anyone, not even you, Icelin."

Kersh went about his patrol as usual that night. When he was finished, he headed back to the barracks to report to the rordan on duty.

Icelin was his friend. He would lay down his life for her, and he would not sit idle while she wandered the most dangerous paths of Waterdeep.

Mistshore was a product of neglect more than anything else, but it had grown into a rotting infection on the back of an already struggling city. Waterdeep's harbor had become a steadily growing source of pollution and despair over the last century. The water had turned murky brown, and the breeze that blew off the harbor was rank with filth.

Ships had been scuttled haphazardly on the north shore of the old Naval Harbor; their owners were dead, gone, or content to leave them to the poisonous waters. One atop another, they'd gradually stretched wooden talons out into the brown harbor, forming their own private continent. The landscape on this strange plain could shift dramatically from day to day, with old wreckages dropping off into the depths and fresh tangles being added to the pile.

No one knew who it was that first discovered you could live on the floating, twisted wreckage—if living was what it could be called—but since then the newly christened Mistshore had become a beaching ground for wreckage of a different sort: the poorest, most desperate folk of Waterdeep.

Mistshore had earned such a dark reputation that the Watch patrols rarely visited the place. Their efforts to restore order on the battered harbor had earned them several slain officers and grief from the rest of the city, who preferred that Mistshore be left to its own devices. Kersh thought it comforted them in some way to have all the worst elements in the city confined to one area. As long as the violence didn't bleed over into the other wards, the people were content.

But Icelin was striding right into the center of the chaos. Worse, Kersh had sent her there.

Kersh entered a low-ceilinged building that housed the Watch garrison. Passing through with a wave to comrades he recognized, Kersh kept going, ascending a short flight of steps to a separate complex. Torches clung to the walls on either side of his path. The soot piles they left on the stone gave the air a dense, pressed-in feeling.

Or maybe that's your conscience prickling you, Kersh thought. He knew Icelin was innocent; it was the elf that worried him. Icelin would need the protection of the Watch, whether she wanted to admit it or not.

Turning down a south hall, Kersh stopped in front of an iron-bound wooden door. He rapped twice on the solid planks.

"Come."

The gruff voice sounded much deeper than Taythe's—the rordan who worked the night watch. Kersh felt a sinking in his gut.

He entered the small office. A broad table dominated the center of the room, lit by flickering candles that dribbled pools of white wax down the table legs.

A gray-haired man stood hunched behind the table, surveying a crinkled map spread out before him. A bronze, boxed compass sat at his right elbow. He looked up when Kersh entered the room.

Kersh swallowed and immediately saluted, tapping his forefinger against his temple. Gods, he'd come looking for a superior officer and found the commander of the Watch himself.

The Watch Warden of Waterdeep, Daerovus Tallmantle, surveyed Kersh through steely, narrowed eyes. A gray moustache draped the lower half of his face. In Waterdeep he was known as the Wolfhound, and Kersh could well see why. He moved around the table with a graceful, predatory air, despite the years on his body.

"Well?" the Warden asked, knocking Kersh from his stupefied staring. "What have you, lad? Don't lurk in the door. Close it behind you."

Kersh shut the door and came to stand in front of the table. Now that he was here, before the Watch Warden, he felt even more the betrayer. Icelin would never forgive him.

"I have news," Kersh said, "on the whereabouts of Icelin Tearn."

The Warden nodded. "Your patrol spotted her?"

"Not my patrol," Kersh said, "myself alone."

"Did you apprehend her?"

Kersh felt his throat dry up, but he was an honest man. "I did not. I spoke to her, and I let her go."

The Wolfhound sank slowly into his chair. He leaned back, crossing his arms. "So you've a tale to tell me about why you acted thus. Out with it, lad."

Kersh had expected fury from the Watch commander. He hadn't counted on the man's cool-eyed assessment, which, by its sheer weight, was harder to bear than any shouted censure.

"I believe Icelin Tearn has been wrongfully accused of theft," Kersh said. He relayed to the commander the whole tale, as Icelin had told him from under the bridge. He didn't have her gift of memory, but he thought he recalled the details as near perfect as he could manage.

"Do you believe her?" the commander said when he'd finished. "Do you think this elf, Cerest Elenithil, is responsible for Brant Tearn's murder?"

"I do," said Kersh. "I believe he has a personal vendetta against Icelin, and that she needs our protection."

"You have no proof that your friend isn't spinning her own

tales," the commander pointed out. "Her name is known in this barracks, and among many in the Watch."

Kersh felt a flare of indignation. "That does not exempt her from our protection, should her claims prove true."

"You don't believe the murder of a Watchman should warrant our enmity?"

Kersh felt his face flush with shame and something else. Righteous indignation, he might have called it, though he'd never thought himself capable of such emotions. However you termed it, the wrongness sat bitterly in his mouth. "There was no murder," he said. "It was an accident, as all involved are aware. Blame the gods if you will, but no man or woman should be punished for the fell magic that has gripped this city since the Spellplague."

The Warden gazed at him steadily. Kersh felt his heart hammering against his ribs, whether from anger or fear of a reprimand, he couldn't say. He'd never been so bold before.

"As it happens," the commander said softly, "I agree with you, lad."

Kersh offered a quiet prayer of thanks. "I want to take a patrol into Mistshore." He spoke faster, planning it out in his head. "I should never have let her go. She could be killed—"

The Warden held up a hand. "Before you break ranks, lad, and start leading your own patrols, hear me out. You say she intends to seek out this thief, Ruen Morleth?"

"That was her intention when she left me," Kersh said.

"Then our solution resides with him."

Kersh kept his mouth from falling open with an effort, but he couldn't keep his tongue from moving, not now that it had got going. "He's an escaped criminal; he's not to be trusted with her safety. How can you consider such a thing?"

The Watch Warden almost smiled. Kersh could see the quiver in his moustache. "Ruen Morleth has never escaped from anything in his whole life."

This time Kersh did gape. "You know where he is?"

"Indeed. He is a fine thief and as crooked as they come, but he's also smart. Ruen Morleth is a survivor. He has contacts in Mistshore and the Warrens, and probably other places we aren't aware of. We made him a generous bargain: his freedom in exchange for access to those contacts in Mistshore. With Morleth as our agent, we can work within Mistshore, and none of our own men need die. It's a bargain both sides were more than willing to make."

"Why are you telling me this?" Kersh asked. He felt hollow, betrayed by his own ignorance.

"Morleth is many things, but he won't harm your friend," the Warden said, as if sensing his distress. "We'll contact him immediately. When he finds Icelin, he'll bring her in, and I'll see to her protection personally until this matter can be resolved to your satisfaction and mine," he said.

"How will you find him?" Kersh wanted to know.

"We'll attempt magical means. But as you know, such methods don't always function well within the city," the commander said. "Fortunately, we have other ways to get information into Mistshore. Go outside the door, lad, and call down to the commons. Then come back. I've work for you yet."

Kersh hastened to obey. He had no idea where the night would lead him. But when the Wolfhound spoke, he found himself eager to follow the man.

When he was alone, Daerovus Tallmantle spoke to the empty air. "You heard, I expect."

A figure stepped into view from nowhere and crossed the room. The train of her fine crimson cloak was last to appear from the empty air.

She had gray hair to match the Watch Warden, but hers was a frizzy mass gathered into a hasty tail at the back of her neck.

Her spectacles rode low on her narrow nose, held in place by a sharp upturn at its end.

"Will you want me to contact Morleth?" his assistant asked.

No one in the Watch or the Guard knew that the Warden employed the small woman as his spell guard. Tesleena had been with him for years. She never seemed to mind staying in the shadows while he conducted the affairs of his post.

"Yes. See if the girl has made contact," Daerovus instructed. "If she has, we'll have to move carefully. We don't want to lose her. If all goes well—and I expect nothing less—she'll be brought in safely. I want this Cerest Elenithil summoned as well. Then we can determine guilt and innocence."

"And if Ruen Morleth is forced to aid us in this, you'll have the opportunity for a clear test of his loyalty," Tesleena pointed out.

"He will honor his end of the agreement," the Warden said, "or he knows we will hunt him down. But," he conceded, "I would just as soon know for certain that our contact in Mistshore is secure."

"Then I will leave you." The gray haired woman bowed briefly and vanished into the invisible world all wizards seemed to gravitate to.

Daerovus sighed and rubbed his eyes. "Where are you tonight, Morleth?" he said aloud, and chuckled. "You have no idea what interesting encounters you have in your future."

CHAPTER 5

Icelin had seen jaw-dropping wonders throughout her youth in the City of Splendors, and just as many sights that had convinced her of the worthlessness of some folk. She had never seen anything that inspired such measures of both emotions as when she first set eyes on Mistshore.

Adjusting the hood of her long cloak so that she could see a farther distance, Icelin took in the sprawling mass of wood, rigging, and moving bodies that swelled the harbor.

The place reminded her a little of Blacklock Alley: twisting, narrow corridors, broken here and there by the half-exposed bellies of ships that had been turned into living quarters or hawking grounds for vendors selling food and ale, or drugs and flesh. Torches lined the walkways. Small boys pushed past her with buckets of water, which they emptied onto the path. The saturated wood kept the torches' sparks from erupting into fire.

The wind blowing in from the sea was cold, and plucked uncomfortable holes in Icelin's cloak. The air reeked of fish, stale sweat, and a prevailing, sunk-in pollution that arose from the harbor itself. Tainted forever, the brown, salty sludge clung out of stubbornness and spite to the wreckages of Mistshore, determined in time to drag the structures down into the depths.

Icelin stopped to make way for a grizzled man in a tattered cloak hauling a hissing, spitting cat under one of his arms. He paused long enough to offer her an open bag of half-rotted fruit that had obviously come from a refuse pile. Flies buzzed around the brown apples and pears.

"Copper a dozen," he hissed, sounding just like the cat.

He smiled at her, exposing an empty mouth and a scar across his gums.

Icelin started to shake her head, but the man was already moving off, a look of fear crossing his face. Icelin turned around to see Sull towering over her. His own cloak did little to hide his bulk, but the hood kept his bright red hair under wraps.

"You're going to draw more attention to us with that scowl than you would if we were both running around here stark naked," she said.

"I don't like this place," Sull said. He kept a hand on her shoulder, his eyes constantly moving among the crowd. "Shifts under my feet."

Icelin looked down. The rough walkway, reinforced to hold large numbers of plodding feet, was still a slanted, groaning mess. The wood had rotted or broken in places, allowing brown water to seep through when the wake kicked up. Anyone not minding his feet ran the risk of tripping and falling into the polluted harbor. Sull's weight made the rotting planks creak and bow.

"We'll find better footing closer to shore," Icelin said. "We only have to be out here long enough to find the Dusk and Dawn."

The structure they stood on now was at least a hundred yards across and roughly the shape of an octopus. The central head was marked by smoke plumes rising in massive clouds to the sky. The largest concentration of people gathered around an immense, controlled bonfire. Wooden paths branched off at odd angles from this single head, ending at other wrecks and sail-covered remains of ships that would no longer be recognizable to their former owners.

"Should never have come here," Sull muttered. He eyed the controlled devastation like a fish that had suddenly flopped onto the dock. Icelin knew she wore a similar, gaping expression.

They moved through the crowd slowly. Sull's presence soon warned away any eyes that lingered on Icelin, so they stayed unhindered except for the occasional vendor.

A woman carrying a tray of brown glass bottles stepped into Icelin's path. Each small vial had a cork stopper and a crudely inked label. She brandished them like a barmaid passing out ale mugs. Icelin could see down the cleavage of her low-cut dress. Water stains blotted the peaks and valleys of its hem.

"Need a pleasure draught, young one?" the woman said, "or something a little more fatal?"

Sheer curiosity drove Icelin to pick up one of the bottles. She ignored Sull's disapproving grunt.

"That's a good choice, that is." The woman took the vial from Icelin and popped the cork. "My own special brew. Call it Grim Tidings." Her laughter boomed over the crowd. "Completely odorless," she said, holding it under Icelin's nose, "unaffected by alcohol or sugar, so you can put it in your lord's tea or strong drink, whatever his pleasure. Course, it won't be pleasurable for very long!"

"So it's poison," Icelin said.

"Should bottle the harbor water," Sull said. "It'll get you the same effect."

The woman laughed again. "Oh, you've got a nasty one here, don't you? He your bodyguard?"

"You could say that," Icelin said. A gust of wind kicked up. Icelin buried her freezing hands inside her cloak. "Why aren't there more fires?" she asked. "You'll freeze to death out here in the winter."

"Some do," the woman said, and shrugged. "You won't find much heat on the fringes, 'cept from the torches on the paths. Didn't used to be that way, and whole ships'd go up when some poor drudge was careless with the cooking embers. Only fire allowed now comes from the path torches and the Hearth," she said, pointing to the thick smoke plumes. "Largest fire pit offshore anywhere in Faerûn."

Icelin heard the unmistakable note of pride in the woman's voice and marveled at it. "Who built the Hearth?" she asked.

"Same person who pays the boys to empty water buckets on the walkways, I expect," Sull said.

The woman nodded. "The gangs do it. The children are their children. The ones that enforce the rules are their enforcers."

"The gangs rule here?" Icelin said.

The woman chuckled. "You're round as a newborn babe, aren't you? No one 'rules' Mistshore. We're lucky to keep it floating. Everyone takes a little chunk of power, but no one wants it all. Who wants to be king of a rat heap? The ship's already sunk; we just haven't got the sense to get off. So we keep it floating, make coin, and everyone's happy." She smiled sardonically. "My power is bottles. So buy one or don't. But every breath I spend flapping with you, I lose coin. So what'll it be?"

Icelin took out a handful of coins. "Is this enough for the vial?"

"Not by my measure, nor any self-respecting poisoner." The woman sniffed and raised her nose a notch in the air. "More silver, young one."

"Perhaps we'll shop elsewhere." Sull took Icelin's arm and started to lead her away.

"Hold on, now, fleet-foots!" The woman scuttled around until she was in their path again. "Let me look a little closer at that handful of coins, I didn't get a good glance the first time."

"Count quickly," Sull said. "We're in a rush."

"Ah, there's the extra silver. You got it right." The woman scooped up the coins, buried them in the bosom of her dress, and handed Icelin the vial in exchange. "Enjoy," she said, and moved off.

"What was that about?" Sull said when she was out of hearing.

Icelin shrugged. "The way I see our situation, we have two weapons: your butchering tools and my magic, which is unstable under the most ideal circumstances. What can it hurt to have a vial of poison?"

"Just stay away from my tea," Sull murmured. "Why is your magic unstable anyway? From all I've heard, Waterdeep's the best place for wizards. They come in droves, sayin' somethin' about the city is better at keepin' the wild magic under control."

"That may be true in most cases," Icelin said. "Not in mine."

Icelin saw a break in the crowd at the end of the walkway. She started in that direction, as much to end the conversation as to get out of the throng. She felt Sull jerk the back of her cloak.

"I don't want to speak of this—"

"Hush, now. Look at the water." Sull pointed to a spot thirty feet out in the harbor.

Icelin looked, and through the wavering torchlight saw a faint, glowing shape pass close to the surface. Against the dark harbor, it shone as white as dust off a moth's wings. For a breath, she thought the shape looked human, writhing and clawing through the water. But that couldn't be. . . .

"What was that?" she said when it disappeared.

"A reason to get back to shore," Sull said. "And there's another." He pointed ahead of them, where two men faced each other on the narrow dock. Both held rust-covered knives. Cursing and grappling, they fought while a crowd watched. Some of the nearby vendors pulled out coins, calling for bets as to whose throat would be slit first.

The bigger of the two men shoved forward, driving his blade into the smaller man's thigh. Blood poured down the man's bare leg, and he stumbled backward into the water. Crimson flowed to join the torchlight dappling the harbor.

Icelin pulled against Sull. "We have to help him!"

"Too late," Sull said. "Look."

The flash of glowing white came again, just as the man went under in a swell of wake. His head broke the surface once, and he screamed, screamed until he was choking on the terrible water. He disappeared again beneath the waves. This time he did not resurface.

Icelin stood frozen. Her legs felt weak under her. She looked around for a reaction from the crowd, but the bettors and the gawkers had broken up. The crowd kept moving, the vendors kept hawking, and those that did stand by to watch wore vacant expressions. Icelin wondered how much of the vendors' drugs they had coursing through their blood, to be immune to such a strange, violent spectacle.

"What is this place?" she said. But she wasn't really talking to Sull.

"These are parts of the city you're never meant to see, lass," Sull said, patting her shoulder.

"And what of you?" Icelin demanded. "What have you seen of this kind of death? How can you just stand there and do nothing?"

Immediately she regretted her words. She had no cause to attack Sull. None of this was his fault.

"I'm sorry, Sull," she said. "That wasn't right."

But the butcher merely shook his head. "I been in my share of troubles, doin' things I'm not proud to tell you about," he said. "But this"—he spat in the water—"this is unnatural, even for Waterdeep. I didn't mean to patronize you, lass. My aim is to get you out of here safe. ""Keepin' our heads low and out of other folks' path is the only way to do that."

She knew Sull was right, but nothing about this place made sense to Icelin. The people—scarred by disease and wounds suffered from fights like the one they'd just witnessed—wandered around like refugees from a non-existent war. Where had they come from? And what horrors had they seen out in the world that made them want to stay in a place like Mistshore?

They passed a crude signpost driven into the side of the walkway. Dock beetles scurried over its painted surface.

"Whalebone Court—Dusk and Dawn, appearing nightly," Icelin read. She followed a painted arrow to an open space near a pile of rocks. Here the wood had been reinforced several times over with new planks and a fresh coat of paint. The footing still shifted, but Icelin no longer felt the queasy up and down motion that had accompanied all her other movements.

Twelve wooden poles jutted out of the platform like exposed ribs, six on either side. From a distance, they vaguely resembled the carcass of a whale. Men moved among them, tying off ropes and securing the flaps of a bright red canvas.

"Puttin' up a tent," Sull said. "Think they intend on having a show?"

"Make way!" A stumpy man with a blond, pointed beard shouldered past Icelin. He wore a red velvet coat to match the canvas. He hauled an armful of knotted rope whose ends kept sticking in the gaping planks. Cursing, he jerked them free and moved on.

"Is this the Dusk and Dawn?" Icelin called after him.

"Working on it," the man shouted back. "Should have been open an age ago." He threw down an armful of rope. "Aye, I'm looking at you, Grazlen. Now get moving with that! Every breath you waste costs me coin."

Icelin and Sull moved out of the way. While they watched, the men hauled two more long poles out of the water where they'd been floating against rocks. Five of the men moved together to stand the poles vertically in the center of the platform. The bearded man stomped over and put his hand around the base of each.

Icelin saw his lips moving, the rhythmic song of magic she knew so well. Light flared at his fingertips, and the poles snapped to attention like wary soldiers, rigid upon the platform.

"Bring down the red!" the man in the red coat yelled. He spat on both his hands, rubbed them together, and shimmied up the poles.

The men below unfurled the canvas to its full length, securing all sides with the rope. The man in the red coat took an end and climbed to the top of the long poles, draping the canvas over them. That done, he slid to the platform, and watched as the men dragged the canvas over the rest of the exposed poles.

While the men tied the ropes to the platform, the man in the red coat removed a crumpled parchment sheet and a slender nail from his breast pocket. He spread the parchment out flat and pinned it to the canvas.

The sheet fluttered madly in the breeze, and Icelin could just barely make out the writing. "Dusk and Dawn," she read. And below that: "Time of Operation—Dusk until Dawn. Proprietor: Relvenar Red Coat."

"Open for business," the man in the red coat shouted.

Icelin looked around and saw that a small crowd had gathered with them to watch the proceedings. They filtered past in clusters, pushing and shoving to get into the tent.

Sull shook his head, chuckling. "I thought I'd seen everythin'. But a moveable feastin' hall I'd not expected!"

"It makes a certain sense," Icelin said. "You were right about the planks. They're too unstable to support a permanent structure this far offshore, not without stronger magic or more coin, or both. With a tent, he can move his operation whenever he likes and still be in the most crowded area of Mistshore."

"So it goes in fair Waterdeep," Sull said. "Commerce moves ever forward."

"Let's go in," Icelin said.

Sull sighed loudly. "And so it goes with all young people. Stridin' in headstrong, not carin' a bit if they're walkin' into certain doom."

Icelin threw him a bland look over her shoulder. "What kind of bodyguard talks thus?"

"A smart one," Sull replied.

Relvenar "Red Coat" made a quick round of the card players in one corner of the tent before heading past the dicing area.

All the gambling areas were marked off with paint on the floor. There were no tables and no chairs, and the only bar to speak of was the mass of ale kegs and crates of foodstuffs hauled in every night. The setup suited him just fine. The only thing about him that bore any frills was his bright red coat.

Dancing lamplight cast large shadows on the tent canvas. He paid an aching amount of coin to the gangs to keep the private lamps, but it was worth it not to have his patrons stumbling or knifing each other in the dark.

Relvenar moved to the back of the bar, where the wind teased the loose canvas and the smell of the harbor mingled with food and drink. He counted the kegs to make sure they would have enough for the night's crowd. He knew he should keep a larger stock, but transportation was cumbersome in Mistshore. The Dusk and Dawn had all the problems of a normal tavern mingled with the worries of a ship's captain. Relvenar wore the dual roles as well as he could. Business was good, and his ship—such as it was—was intact.

The sound of fingernails scratching the outside of the tent brought Relvenar to a halt in his inspection of the kegs. The scratching moved along the canvas, and a shadow loomed suddenly in front of him. Relvenar recognized the slender, agile shape, with a bulky top where a hat might be perched.

A very ugly hat, Relvenar thought. But business was business, and this client didn't enjoy being kept waiting.

Casting a quick glance around to make sure he wasn't being watched, Relvenar huddled down and crawled under the loose canvas. Outside in the clear air, the smell of the rank harbor hit him square in the nose.

Relvenar brushed a hand in front of his face, as if he could banish the stench. He shivered in the cold night air. "Didn't think you were going to show," he said to the figure leaning casually against a wood piling. The man stood easily, his arms crossed over his stomach, unbothered by the cold and the stench. He did not look happy. But then, Relvenar had never seen Ruen Morleth wear any expression except for a kind of blank coldness.

It's the man's eyes, Relvenar thought. There's too much wrong with them.

"Is she here?" Morleth said.

"Came in right after opening," Relvenar said. "Her and a big fellow. Keeps pretty close watch."

"How unfortunate for your cut-purses." Morleth produced a folded bit of parchment from inside his vest. "Send them to this location."

Relvenar took the parchment but didn't look at it. "What if they don't want to go? I'm not forcing any trouble in my establishment. If folk don't feel safe, they won't come back. I'll have to close down."

"I have a difficult time imagining your clientele feeling 'safe' anywhere in Mistshore," Morleth said. "Don't worry. These two are lambs; they'll go wherever you tell them. They *want* to find me." For a moment, Relvenar thought he read amusement in the man's features. Morleth turned, his worn boots making no sound on the platform.

He's almost too frail to be a proper thief, Relvenar thought. Light on his feet, but it's like he's a wisp. All bone, hair that's as fine as dark spider's silk. . . . The lass was the same way. They both looked like brittle spiders, apt to break in a harsh wind.

"I wish the lass luck handling you," Relvenar said, and bit his lip when Morleth paused. He looked back at Relvenar, holding his gaze until Relvenar shifted uncomfortably and looked away. When he looked back, Morleth was gone.

"Just like a spider," Relvenar muttered, shivering in distaste.

Cerest paced the dark street behind his home. The night was slipping away. Where were they?

He had already entertained a visit from a Watch patrol, and

endured a polite but firm summons issued by the little bitch in charge. He was to give testimony against Icelin Tearn, before the Watch commander of Waterdeep himself!

Cerest knew they could have nothing with which to charge him. His men had been careful. The trails he'd left pointed to Icelin as a thief and now a murderer.

But what if he was wrong? Cerest leaned against the wall of the alley, his hands rubbing reflexively over his scars. The puckered texture of the burns helped to focus him, to remind him of how far he'd come.

All he had to do was find Icelin. Once he had her, he could leave the city if necessary. Baldur's Gate was thriving and swelling with more folk by the day. He and Icelin could start over there, disappear into the crowded cityscape, and make their fortune.

Everything would be exactly as it was before. When Elgreth had been alive, Cerest had had bright hopes for his future prominence in Waterdeep. Elgreth and his family were going to take him all the way to the circles of nobility. Even when he'd been scarred, Cerest hadn't been afraid of being shunned. He'd held onto the hope that Elgreth would save him . . . But then the man died, and all Cerest's dreams had died with him.

No. He wouldn't let it end tonight. He would find Icelin and make her understand the kind of man Elgreth was, and all that he owed Cerest. She would pay his debt, or he would kill her for raising his hopes all over again.

The crunch of booted feet broke the stillness. Cerest tilted his head to the right to hone in on the sound.

Ristlara strode out of the shadows, her golden hair caught up in a black scarf. Behind her stood four men of various heights, shapes, and degrees of armament.

"You're late," Cerest said.

"How would you know, standing there so oblivious to all the night?" Ristlara sniffed. "It's a wonder you're still alive, Cerest." She nodded at the men. "We had to move slowly, in smaller groups. We'll meet at a location I've designated, if you're prepared?"

"I am." Cerest pulled up the hood of his cloak. "You told them Mistshore?"

She glanced sidelong at him. "Yes. Shenan will be there to meet us. Are you certain your information is accurate?"

"It is." What coin Cerest hadn't spent on his garden, he'd used to garner information from one of the low ranks in the Watch. His pride wouldn't let him confess the amount to Ristlara. The Watch was notoriously hard to bribe. They acted swiftly and decisively to cull betrayers from their midst.

He hadn't been able to get Icelin's exact destination, but the thick-head he'd spoken to had been savvy enough to know that many eyes were turning closely to Mistshore this night. All that remained was for Ristlara and Shenan's muckrakers to find her out, wherever she was hiding.

"How many did you bring?" he asked Ristlara as they walked, slipping from shadow to shadow on the broad street.

"As many as you could afford," Ristlara said. At Cerest's scowl, she added, "With you, Greyas, Shenan, and I, we are twelve strong. I've divided everyone into groups of four. Our searches will be more effective that way, given the layout of Mistshore. All the 'muckrakers' are human, so Icelin will not see them coming this time."

"Good," Cerest said. He remembered poor Melias and felt a flare of regret. If they were to work together, Cerest would have to teach Icelin control and restraint. He'd done it before, when those that served him had first witnessed the extent of his scars. Icelin had already demonstrated she could look at him without seeing the marks. There would be plenty of time for her to learn what else pleased and displeased him.

CHAPTER 6

Icelin sat on the floor across from Sull, who nursed ale in a glass the length of his forearm.

Working Ruen's dice between her fingers, Icelin said, "I think we should join them." She nodded to a pair of men throwing dice near the rear of the tent. A third man stood beside a painted board with chalk markings. The dice clattered off the board, with one man hurling curses at the numbers, while the other threw back more ale and collected the pile of coins on the floor.

The other tent patrons were more subdued, playing cards or huddling in circles with their own drinks. Lamplight glowed all over the room. Icelin's eyes were already watering from the smoke and the stench of so many unwashed bodies packed into the close quarters.

Sull eyed the dicers. "How do you want to play this, lass?"

"Try the game, I suppose," Icelin said. "Might be we'll have to give them some coin before they'll help us."

"Do you even know their game?" Sull asked skeptically.

"I've been watching," Icelin said. She yielded to the smoke and closed her eyes. "They roll pairs. Highest roller gets to buy points on the board—one copper per point, up to two." She opened her eyes and pointed to the dice board, where the man running the game was putting up marks with a stubby piece of chalk. "He can use those points to add or subtract from his next roll. Lowest roller that round picks a target number. They both roll again. The closest person to that number wins the pot. But if the winner isn't the man with the points, the low roller gets the pot plus all the copper his opponent spent on points to the runner—the man at the board. Side bets could be—"

Sull thunked his glass on the floor. "You could tell all that from across the room?"

"I memorized the numbers being rolled," Icelin said. "The rest was just putting together the rules of the game."

"They've been rollin' since we came in. How many numbers did you memorize?"

"All of them."

Sull nodded slowly. "Is this somethin' you do often, breakin' down dice games for your own amusement?"

"Not if I can help it," Icelin said. The numbers were already crowding her head, putting a dull ache at her temples. She rubbed them absently. "The problem is that I memorize everything I see and hear. I can't not."

Sull raised an eyebrow. "How long have you had this gift?"

A gift. That's what everyone called it. Icelin was long past being amused by the notion. "Almost ten years now."

It had also been ten years since the headaches started. The blinding, heavy pain came whenever she was in a crowd, or had too many facts vying for space in her head. Schooling had been a chore. Brant had taken on the task of teaching her himself, but they'd had to move slowly. She was quick and eager to learn, but there was only so much information she could be exposed to in a day, before the load threatened to overwhelm her.

Not until she started studying the Art did she discover how to bind away the information in her mind. Nelzun, her teacher, had shown her how, and had saved her going mad from the constant headaches.

It turned out storing information was no different than storing a spell once you'd memorized it from a book. Icelin had simply set aside a specific place in her mind for the facts to rest until they were needed.

"Picture your mind as a vast library," Nelzun had described it at the time.

"No vault can hold all of what rattles around in my head," she'd complained. But her teacher had only smiled indulgently.

"Once you have walked the halls of Candlekeep, with permanent wide eyes and slackening of the jaw, you may feel quite different," he'd said. "But let us stay in more familiar territory. Picture a building like your great-uncle's shop, but with an infinite number of levels.

"Follow a winding stair, up and up until you reach the place where magic dwells. Can you see it? Be playful, be mysterious, whatever suits your nature."

Icelin remembered squirming. "But I don't see how—"

"A red, plush carpet, so soft you can sink your feet right in." Her teacher had carried on as if she hadn't spoken. "Gold brocade curtains that shine in the sunlight, a fireplace covering an entire wall. And on the others: row upon row of bookshelves—empty now—but soon to be filled with the wonders of the Art. Everything you will ever learn or discover will be housed on these shelves.

"Picture a large wingback chair with leather cushions. Draw it before the fire and find upon the seat a single book—a very old, worn tome. The leather is cracked, the pages heavily browned by fingerprints of students who long ago became masters. Open the book. See what secrets lie inside."

When Icelin had opened her eyes, her teacher had presented her with a book exactly like the one he'd just described. It was to become her first and only spellbook. Icelin had been fascinated, and had loved her teacher from that day on. She would have done anything, mastered any spell, to please him.

Better that she'd never opened that imaginary room in her mind. She hated the thought of it now.

"Come on," she said to Sull. Distraction was better than a locked door for keeping memories at bay. "We're wasting time."

She approached the group of dicers and cleared her throat. No one paid her any heed. She cast a pointed look at Sull.

"New player, lads!" the butcher boomed.

Three heads turned to regard Icelin with a mixture of curiosity and annoyance.

Hesitantly, Icelin let her hood fall back and held out Ruen's dice. Suddenly she didn't feel so confident. She felt exposed, naked under the gazes of the rough men.

She cleared her throat again so her voice would be steady. "I've been told these are lucky dice," she said. "Do you gentleman mind if I throw with them?"

"No outsiders," one of the men snarled. "You throw our bones or none, girl, 'less you'd like a private game." He leered at her.

Sull stepped forward, but the man who'd been chalking the board spoke up.

"You're not welcome at this game," he said, watching Icelin closely. His eyes fell on the dice she held. "You should try the shore. There's a woman there, prostitute named Fannie Beblee. Give your dice to her. She'll get you what you need."

"My thanks," Icelin said, and to Sull, "Let's go."

The men resumed their game while she and Sull headed for the tent flap. She glanced back once and saw the man in the red coat watching them from behind the makeshift bar. He looked away quickly.

When they were outside, Sull said, "Awfully accommodatin' fellows. Oh yes, I feel much more secure under their direction."

"You think it's a trap?" Icelin said dryly.

"I think I won't be puttin' my cleavers away any time soon," Sull said.

"Aren't you the least bit curious?" Icelin asked, picking her way along the unstable wooden path to the shore. "About this Fannie Beblee? Or Ruen Morleth?"

"Least it gets us to shore," Sull said, "and off this stinkin' water."

"And we'll be able to fight better on land, assuming it is a trap," Icelin said.

"Now you're thinkin'." Sull clapped her on the back.

The shore, for all its stability, was not in much better shape than the floating parts of Mistshore.

Crude tents and lean-tos had been erected all along the shoreline. There must have been hundreds of the structures. Fires crackled in crudely dug pits, for there was little to burn here. In most cases a pot or spit hung over the flames. The meat on them was meager, consisting of rodents or small fish.

The people moved around in a sort of forced communal camp, talking or sleeping, huddled together for warmth. Icelin heard snores, hushed whispers, and a baby wailing in the distance.

She bent to speak to the nearest woman, who was stirring a pot of fat white beans in a watery broth. The lumpy mixture and its smell turned Icelin's stomach.

"I beg pardon, but I'm looking for someone," she said.

The woman ignored her and kept stirring the pot. The slow, rhythmic task absorbed her entire attention. Icelin might as well have been a fly buzzing in the air.

Sull put in, "Her name's Fannie. She's a friend of mine—"

Tinkling coins interrupted him. Icelin had pulled two silver pieces—nearly all of her remaining coin—from her neck pouch, drawing the woman's gaze from the pot as if by a mind charm.

"She's a prostitute," Icelin said, handing the woman the silver. "Fannie Beblee."

The woman curled her fingers in a claw around the coins. She pointed with her spoon to a spot south along the shore where two fires burned, one next to the other, then went back to stirring. The tents behind them were tied shut.

"Thank you," Icelin said. She straightened, but Sull remained kneeling next to the woman. Her expression had not altered throughout the whole exchange. Her eyes were lifeless, rimy pools sucked down in wrinkled, parchmentlike skin.

"We have to go, Sull."

The butcher reached into his apron and pulled out a small wrapped packet. He tore one end off and emptied the contents into the woman's soup pot.

The woman's stirring hand froze. She gazed up at Sull with a mixture of fear and hope swimming in her eyes.

"Not poison," Sull said, "but salt. Keep stirrin', and add this to the mix when it's ready." He drew out another packet and handed it to her. "Pepper grounds, and a few other spices I added to make a seasonin'. Works for potato chowder, so why not beans?"

But the woman didn't seem to be listening to him. She opened the second packet and touched her tongue to the edge to taste the spices. Her eyes filled with tears. She seized Sull's hand and kissed it.

Sull's face turned bright red. "Oh, er, you're welcome." He stood up quickly, tripping over his own feet.

Icelin took the big man's arm to steady him, and they drew away from the fire. For a time, neither spoke.

"I would never have thought to do that," Icelin said. "I would never have guessed that she'd want spices. I just assumed coin would move her."

"Coin's more valuable, but easily stolen," Sull said. "Salt and pepper don't amount to much, but if I'd been eatin' that bean slop for as long as she has—and I'll wager my stock of good steaks that's all she gets—I'd be cryin' for somethin' to flavor it with."

"You really enjoy cooking, don't you?" Icelin said. They'd reached the closed tents, but she hesitated to approach. She felt like an intruder.

"Always have," Sull said. "My father taught me to hunt game. This was, oh, long before we came to Waterdeep, and my mother let me watch the right way of preparin' it. She was forever making up her own recipes. Lot of them amounted to a burnt tongue and watery eyes, but she could make some of those dishes sing. I learnt all the best fixins from her."

"Does she still cook?" Icelin asked.

Sull shook his head. "Ah, she died. Year or so after we came here. Birthed a second son for my father, but she was too old for it, and she didn't live to see 'im. The little one followed her."

Icelin nodded. "I'm sorry. What about your father?"

"He found another wife and lives, still," Sull said, "but doesn't know much of where he is or who he is, most days. He'll be gone by the winter, I think." He nodded to the tent flap. "You can't put this off forever, lass. Best get it over with."

"You're right." Reluctantly, Icelin approached the closest tent. She called out, "Fannie Beblee. Are you in there?"

For a breath or two, there was no movement or response from within the tent. Then the cloth flap shuddered and was torn aside by a small brown hand.

The woman who peeked out was so tanned Icelin could barely distinguish her from the darkness of the tent. She peered at Icelin through muddy brown eyes. Her hair hung in graying, lank halves from a part in the center of her scalp. Sand grains sparkled in the tangled locks.

An angry dust devil, Icelin thought.

"Did you call Fannie Beblee?" The woman spoke in a rush, shoving the two names into one.

"I did," Icelin said, stepping forward. "We were sent here from the Dusk and Dawn. I have something to give you."

The woman's jaw hung slack. She clicked her tongue against the roof of her mouth. "You come from Whalebone Court. A criminal's alley, that is. What you bring me from there that's any good?"

Icelin held Ruen's dice up to the firelight so the woman could see.

"The bosoms are on the bottom," Sull muttered.

Fannie took the dice, pressing them between her two hands. Her face lit with a wicked smile.

"You bring me cursed dice," she said. "The boy is cursed."

"Ruen Morleth?" Icelin said. "What do you know about him?"

"The world is cold to him," Fannie said, "even old Fannie Beblee. So why not be cold right back to the world, eh? That's his way."

"Is that why he's a thief?" Icelin asked.

"A damn good thief!" Fannie shook a finger at Icelin and Sull. "He gave me this." She worked the strings of her raggedy cotton dress.

"That's all right," Sull said hastily. "We don't need to see any of . . . ahem . . . whatever you got under there."

Fannie shot him a scandalized look. "You think I'm going to give you this show for nothing?" She propped a hand on her bony hip and stood on her knees, swaying back and forth. "You pay, then we talk, big fellow. But later. I'm busy now." She waved a dismissive hand.

Icelin didn't have to look at Sull to know his face was bright red again. She bit her lip hard to keep from laughing.

"*This* is what I mean." Fannie pulled a leather cord from around her neck. Attached to one end—which had been buried in the bodice of her dress—was a tiny quill. A black crow feather, the quill had been stripped of its barbs, and the shaft appeared to have been dipped in gold. There was no longer a hollow end for the ink to reach parchment. So far as Icelin could see, the quill was for decoration only, and served no functional purpose. Yet Fannie gripped the gold shaft like a writing instrument, her tiny brown fingers fitting perfectly around the tip.

"It's . . . lovely," Icelin said. "Ruen gave this to you?"

"From his collection," Fannie said proudly.

"Collection?"

"Darzmine Hawlace's collection. They say he is mad—Darzmine, not Ruen—but he is not. Smart was the word. Hoarded items of power, disguised as art. Ruen was smarter. He knows art and power too. Knew just what to take from old Darzmine."

"So this is one of the pieces Ruen stole, the theft that got him imprisoned." Icelin looked at the quill with new eyes. "What is its power?"

Fannie's smile broadened. "I show you, but only you." She waved Sull away. "He don't understand."

Icelin and Sull exchanged glances. Icelin nodded at the water. "Wait for me over there. If trouble comes, I'll scream until my lungs burst."

Sull hesitated, and nodded. Icelin watched him stride down the shore to where the brown water lapped at the sand.

"What wouldn't my friend understand?" Icelin asked. But the woman didn't seem to hear her. She squatted in the sand and bent close to the fire. By the light, Icelin could see her tanned skin hanging in tiny ripples off her neck. She must have been almost fifty winters old. How long had she lived out here, alone?

Fannie looked up to make sure Icelin was still watching, whistled like an angry bird, and went back to her work.

Icelin realized she was sketching a picture in the sand. The gold quill matched the fire in color and movement. Remnants of the crow feather quivered in time to Fannie's scrawling.

"Here it is," Fannie said. "Now look. Move, girl."

Icelin hiked up her skirt and crouched in the sand, bending her head close to the prostitute's. The figure she had drawn in the sand was a hawk. She could see the predator's talons and curved beak. For a sand drawing, the picture was remarkably vivid. The depression where Fannie had placed the raptor's eye almost seemed alive.

Icelin gasped. The bird's head and body were rising, drawing sand and separating from it at the same time, as if they'd been buried and not merely a sketch. The thing took on shape and mass before Icelin's eyes. She had seen castles forged from sand or mud, but she'd never imagined the childish images coming *alive.*

The bird shook out its wings. Sand flew, catching a shocked Icelin in the face.

"Is it real?" she whispered, afraid to disturb the air and cause the sand-bird to disappear.

Fannie laughed. "No, no. Magic tells it what shape to take, and magic holds it together. Won't last long, but it makes a pretty art. Turtles," she said, chewing her lip. "I like turtles better. They don't move so fast, and the shells make them last longer."

Icelin reached out to touch the slender bird's wing. When she pulled her fingers back, they were glazed with sand. The bird did not react to her touch. It spread its wings as if for flight, and collapsed into a pile of sand.

"See," Fannie said, disappointment heavy in her voice, "they try to fly and fall."

"That was amazing," Icelin said.

"Aha! I knew you would understand," Fannie said. "He will like you, poor man."

Abruptly recalling why she was there, Icelin sobered. "You mean Ruen. I need to find him. I was told that you could help me."

"Oh, I can," Fannie said. Her gaze turned shrewd. "But what can you give to Fannie for helping you?"

Icelin didn't know what to say. She was rapidly running out of coins, and she suspected a woman like Fannie had as little use for them as the woman and her bean pot.

Inspiration struck her. "My friend, the one you sent away"—she waved an arm to get Sull's attention down the beach and motioned for him to rejoin them—"is the finest cook in Waterdeep."

"Is he?" Fannie watched Sull with renewed interest.

In truth, Icelin had no proof that Sull was any good in the kitchen, but she hoped Fannie wouldn't know the difference.

"Sull," she said, when the butcher approached, "I wonder if you would be willing to cook a meal for Fannie, as payment for telling us where to find Ruen Morleth?"

Fannie nodded eagerly, but Sull was looking around at the barren camp.

"Be happy to," he said. "But I've got no tools here."

"I have them!" Fannie scurried back into her tent like a mouse going to ground. She came up with a small black frypan, which she handed to Sull. "You cook for me with this."

Sull scratched his sideburns. "I suppose I could do a little fishin'," he said slowly. "Don't know what I'll catch that's not contaminated."

"Just try. That's all I ask," Icelin said, and turned back to Fannie. "Sull will cook for you, but we haven't much time. I need you to set up a meeting for me with Ruen. Can you do that?"

"Ah, I do one better for you, since you cook for Fannie." The woman pointed out to the harbor. "You find him out there. He takes a little raft out every night, to catch his own fish. You take a boat, go beyond Whalebone Court, and you find him. You'll see his light on a sagging pole. Only he goes out far enough to waltz. You'll find him."

Sull shook his head. "I don't like the sound of this," he said. "You're not going out there alone while I'm here cookin'—"

"It's our bargain, Sull," Icelin said firmly. "Besides"—she lowered her voice—"if it is a trap, at least you'll be on the shore. If Fannie is involved, you'll want to keep her close by. If I'm attacked or kidnapped, she can help you find me."

"That's not a comfortin' thought," Sull said.

"We don't have our choice of comforts tonight," Icelin pointed out. "It's either this or we run on our own, and I don't like those odds."

Sull sighed. "If you're determined to go, be wary, and signal me with one of those bright color spells if somethin' is amiss. I'll come runnin' across the water if I have to."

"I know you will." Icelin touched his cheek. He blushed mightily.

She turned to Fannie. "Do you know where I can borrow a boat?"

Fannie sniffed. "I know where you can steal one."

I suppose I'm officially a thief, Icelin thought as she rowed out into the harbor.

On the shore, she could just make out Sull, dangling a driftwood pole he'd constructed in the water. He kept his head bent, shoulders hunched, trying to ignore the sounds coming from Fannie's tent.

Her latest customer had arrived in a tiny rowboat, which Fannie had offered to Icelin as soon as she'd gotten her man safely out of sight inside the tent.

Icelin prayed she'd be out and back without incident, and the man would never know she'd taken his boat.

The way was slow going. More than once Icelin had to turn the boat around and row in the opposite direction to avoid a shelf of rock or ship debris. Small wonder this section of the harbor had fallen into disuse. Any sound ship entering the area would soon have her hull scraped raw.

She rowed past Whalebone Court and the Dusk and Dawn's red tent. Behind them, she could see the distant glow of the Hearth fire. The sound of raucous laughter and clumsy lute music drifted along the water. At least here, there was some semblance of normal life, even celebration, in Mistshore.

Icelin left the noise behind and rowed out into the dark water. She didn't know how she would come upon Ruen Morleth, or what she would say when she did. Why he would dwell alone in the putrid harbor was a mystery to her, but she didn't have long to ponder it. In the distance, she saw a sagging light, just as Fannie had said she would.

It bobbed faintly—a lantern, she saw as she approached—on the end of a long, bending pole attached to a raft. There were no other boats so far out in the harbor.

When she got close, Icelin heard voices. Two shapes stood out in the weaving lantern light. She could not make out their features, but the profile of the nearer one was short and rotund, his head hairless. The other held a fishing pole as tall as his body. He was very nearly as slender as the pole. Icelin also noted that the man either had a very misshapen head, or was wearing a floppy hat.

Icelin stopped rowing. She lifted her oars carefully out of the water and listened to the voices.

"I'm a clever man, Ruen. You could do worse."

The tall man cast his line into the harbor and answered, dryly, "Oh, I'm aware of it. I could tread the catwalks of Mistshore with a viper around my neck. Come to think of it, the snake might not be so bad, if I walk lightly. No, I don't think I need a partner, Garlon, especially one who sells his own brother to the Watch."

"How did you know about that?" The other man's voice squeaked like a guilty child's. "That was family business, got nothing to do with you and me. Come on, Ruen, you know you can't go it alone forever. You already got caught once. Admit it, you need a man to front you. You're too well known in Waterdeep."

"This isn't Waterdeep. This is Mistshore. We're dancing on the city's bones out here. Leave, Garlon, before I decide you'd make a pretty skeleton."

"But, I rode out here with you. You have to take me back to shore!" The man whined so loudly Icelin's ears ached.

"Yes, but you see, the fish are biting now. And if I move, I'll lose my spot."

"There's no one out here but us!"

"Are you sure about that?"

Icelin stiffened. She waited, crouched low in the boat, but no one called her out. Ruen must have been jesting.

"I was trying to do you a favor," Garlon said. "Word is you've still got a pretty pot of that treasure you stole from Darzmine Hawlace sitting around. I could move it for you. I know people."

"Ah, now we come to the true reason you're soiling my raft with your boots," Ruen said. "What makes you think I didn't dump the lot?"

Garlon scoffed. "You enjoy giving presents to whores and dealing with piss pushers like Relvenar, but you're not stupid. You kept some treasure back for yourself. All I want is a little piece."

"No."

Garlon spat on Ruen's boots. "To the Hells with you then." He strode to the opposite end of the raft. He paused at the edge. Icelin could feel him weighing his dignity against jumping into the fetid water. She felt a pang of sympathy, but it disappeared when she saw Garlon reach for something at his belt. He slid a dagger noiselessly from its sheath. Her heart sped up.

"What say you, Ruen? Last chance. Row us back to shore, and I'll buy you a drink while we discuss our partnership."

"Turn around," Icelin said, but no sound came out of her dry mouth. Her eyes bored into Ruen's back, willing him to turn and look at Garlon.

"Do you mind keeping quiet, Garlon?" Ruen said. He twitched his pole in the water. "You're scaring the fish."

"Course, Ruen," Garlon said, his voice dropping. "Not a squeak." He snapped his arm back, and forward, so fast Icelin couldn't see exactly when the blade left his hand.

"Watch out!" she screamed.

Ruen pivoted, his slender shadow seeming not to move at all. He dropped his pole and tore the spinning dagger out of the air. Flipping the blade to his other hand, he hurled it back at its owner.

Distracted by her scream, the fat man spun toward Icelin as if he'd been jerked by a string. His eyes widened when the dagger stuck in his chest. For a breath he swayed in time with the lapping water. Then he reached up, clutching his own weapon hilt. Icelin turned her head away from his staring eyes.

Silence, and then Icelin heard an *umph* followed by a loud splash. She looked back. The spray of water caught the moonlight and fell back into the harbor, which had swallowed up the fat man.

When the noise died, the scene returned quickly to normal. The moonlight settled onto the gently rippling water. From a shocked distance, Icelin saw Ruen pick up his pole and sit at the edge of the raft, his back to her. He cast the line into the water.

Numbly, Icelin picked up her oars. She considered rowing back to shore. Maybe he hadn't heard her shout, or maybe he didn't care that she'd just seen him kill a man, albeit in self-defense. Icelin gripped the oars. She forced herself to move the boat forward.

He came into focus at the opposite end of the raft, sitting cross-legged and dangling the pole near the water. He looked something like Sull in that pose, his shoulders hunched, trying to remain oblivious to the world around him.

Icelin rowed her boat up to kiss the raft, but Ruen never stirred. She wasn't brave enough to step aboard, but she had to get his attention somehow.

Icelin took the dice out of her pouch and tossed them onto the raft. They skittered across the wood, bounced off Ruen's back and came up double bosoms.

"Yours, I believe," Icelin said.

CHAPTER 7

For a long time, Ruen didn't move. Icelin thought he must not have heard her. But eventually he turned, and his profile caught the lantern light.

He looked to be in his early thirties. His hat, which appeared much older, was as ugly a thing as Kersh had claimed: brown leather and so creased the edges of the brim were flaking off.

Beneath the hat his black clad body looked like a scarecrow, so slender Icelin thought he must be half-starved. His cheekbones were two carved, triangular hollows; intermittent beard stubble graced the contours of his jaw.

A scarecrow, Icelin thought, except for his eyes.

His eyes were red-brown, their deep centers forming pools of muddy crimson when they should have been black. Either his eyes were a defect of his birth, or else . . .

Icelin had heard stories of such oddities from the children in Blacklock Alley, back when she was only a child herself. The boys talked in menacing whispers about the plague-touched, the spellscarred—men and women who'd been brushed by the deadly fingers of spellplague. Most died from the exposure, but a few managed to survive its curse. They were never the same.

Some emerged deformed, their bodies twisted into hideous shapes by wild magic. Others bore their scars in less obvious places, but developed strange new abilities: powers of the mind, magic that even the wisest wizards on Faerûn had never seen. It was said that a strange blue radiance often accompanied such displays of power, but Icelin had always thought these were fanciful stories that bore little truth.

Somehow, looking at him, Icelin knew Ruen Morleth was spellscarred. She remembered Kersh's warning about the man being strange.

"You know, it's impolite to eavesdrop on strangers' conversations," Ruen said, speaking for the first time. He picked up the dice and looked at them. "Stealing is generally frowned upon, as well. These aren't yours," he said.

"I didn't steal them," Icelin replied. "They were given to me by a friend. He told me you could help me."

His eyes traveled up and down her body. Icelin worked hard not to flinch under the gaze. "You look capable enough. Why should you need my help?"

"I'm being followed by someone who wishes my death."

He raised an eyebrow. "You think that's a compelling argument to me?"

"It sounds a bit dramatic, I know, but it's been a fine motivator for me," Icelin said. "I'm in no rush to die."

"Death is a common occurrence in Mistshore."

"So I see."

Ruen removed his pole from the water and laid it on the raft. "On the other hand, if you knew a likely fishing spot, you'd catch my interest. What's your name?"

"Icelin," she said. She held out a hand, but he showed no interest in taking it.

"Where did you get these dice?" he asked.

"From Kersh. I believe you two knew each other while you were . . . er—"

"Imprisoned. You can say it, I'm proud of the distinction." Ruen stood up. At his full height, he was well over six feet, which only accentuated his odd slenderness. "I remember Kersh. He retrieved my hat for me. Quite a service, under the circumstances."

"You gave him your word you'd repay him," Icelin said.

"I did. But I don't see him hiding behind your skirt. My debt is to him. I owe nothing to you."

Ruen removed a dirt-speckled rag from his belt and began cleaning his pole. Leather gloves stretched taut over his long-fingered hands. He seemed content to ignore her.

Icelin was at a loss. Of all the things she'd expected from the man, blunt refusal had not been among them. But why shouldn't she have foreseen this? Kersh tried to warn her. Sull tried to warn her. The man was a thief. She'd had no reason to believe he'd be honorable in any dealings with her.

But Kersh's story . . . the man's gratitude at being treated kindly, the quill he'd given to Fannie—he could have sold it for a handsome profit, yet he'd made the powerful magic item a gift to a prostitute so she could draw pictures in the sand. None of what she'd heard equated to the aloof man before her.

"I'll pay you for your services," she said finally.

Ruen glanced up at her. "You don't look as if you have anything I need, or enough of the coin I'd demand."

"I have this." Icelin took the cameo from her neck pouch and tossed it to him.

Ruen caught it and held the piece up to the lantern. His muddy crimson eyes mingled with the gold light. "You steal this?"

"Does it matter?"

"No. What do you want for it?"

"I need a hiding place, for myself and a friend. We're being pursued by the Watch as well."

Ruen cocked his head. "Why all the interest?"

"Let's just pretend I'm a criminal," she said with a half-smile. "A notorious, irredeemable scoundrel. Would that be near enough to your understanding?"

"Are you?"

"Am I what?"

"Irredeemable?"

Icelin's humor evaporated. "Probably," she said. "Will you help me anyway, in exchange for the jewel?"

Ruen put the pole away and walked to the edge of the raft. He cocked a boot on the bow of her boat and looked down at her. There was no discernible expression on his face. It made his eyes so much more disturbing. They were distant and menacing at the same time. Icelin suppressed the urge to put an oar between them.

"I'll hide you for one day," Ruen said. "After that we renegotiate the price or go our separate ways."

"One day—that piece is worth at least ten!" Icelin said.

"Then find someone who'll keep you from the eyes of the Watch for a tenday," Ruen said. "I'm sure there are lads everywhere in Mistshore hopping eager to take on the job. I don't mind at all dispensing the honor to them."

Icelin ground the oars against their moorings. "I have your marker! You're honor bound to help me, with or without payment."

Ruen smiled. "You're very passionate, my lady. Hold to that. It'll take you far in the world."

Icelin contemplated bludgeoning the man with an oar, just to wipe the mocking grin off his face, but she decided against it. She had one night; it was best not to waste it. "Fine. We have an agreement." She snatched the cameo back and put it in her neck pouch. "You'll get the payment after my night's over."

He tipped his ugly hat. "Whatever you say, lady."

So it was done. Icelin was going to ask if he'd like to follow her back to shore, when below them, the light she and Sull had glimpsed earlier reappeared, gliding across the water like a fresh oil slick. Icelin lost her train of thought watching it. The humanlike apparition drifted past them and out into the harbor, moving fast. Several breaths later it illuminated a large, misshapen structure Icelin had not known was there.

It was difficult to make out many details in the dark, but by the apparition's light it was the strangest shipwreck Icelin had ever seen. The vessel had been boosted straight up on its bow, the length of it seeming to dance upon the air. Something, an even larger structure, was propping it up in that odd position, like two lovers embracing on the lip of the sea.

The apparition floated right up to the mass and joined with it, illuminating the whole before evaporating into darkness.

"What was that?" Icelin said, stunned.

Ruen looked out into the darkness. "The Ferryman's Waltz," he said. He looked at her askance. "You've never heard of it?"

Icelin searched her memory. Ferryman sounded vaguely familiar, an echo from her childhood. Her mind cycled back, peeling away the layers of invisible brick she'd used to close off the memories, until she could visualize ships: dozens of cogs, rakers, and greatships lined up in the harbor. Brant had taken her to see them; they'd gone for a ride on one. Icelin remembered the greatship was so large she could barely make out the fish leaping along the keel.

"Ferryman," she said. "It was a ship, a converted passenger carrier. A merchant of Waterdeep built it to hire out for pleasure-sailing, a way to say 'look at what a big toy I have.' She recited her great-uncle's words exactly. It brought a profound ache to her chest. She could picture his eyes sparkling as he told her the story. Quickly, she raised the mental wall again. "I never knew what became of the ship."

"Destroyed, in a tangle with a leviathan," Ruen said.

Icelin's eyes widened. "A sea monster, invading Waterdeep harbor?" It sounded too mythical to be real. "I thought we were supposed to be protected here, shielded from attacks of the Art and—"

"You mean spellplague," Ruen said. "Maybe that's so. But who's protecting Waterdeep from those scarred by the plague? No keeping them out. Even those that get dumped in places like Mistshore can cause their share of trouble." He nodded toward the Ferryman's Waltz. "Locked together in a lover's waltz. Poetic, don't you think?"

"You mean a wizard did this?" Icelin said. "To summon this creature . . . He'd have to be mad."

Ruen lifted a shoulder. "Perhaps it's just a story. Whether it's true or not, something draws the sea wraiths out to the wreckage. There's wild magic there. That's why they glow as they do. Ordinarily, you'd never be able to see them in the water. I'd bet any amount of coin the plague still thrives at Ferryman's Waltz, and the wraiths are drawn to it like moths."

"Sea wraiths," Icelin said. So the Waltz was the source of the strange apparitions. "None of this feels real." Her gaze swept the Waltz and Mistshore: Whalebone Court and the Dusk and Dawn's red tent, the Hearth fire and all of the other structures. They blurred together in the darkness just beyond her sight. She caught Ruen looking at her. "What?"

He shook his head, as if he couldn't believe what he was seeing. "You're just a child," he said. "You don't know Waterdeep at all. What are you doing out here?"

"Conversing with thieves"—Icelin spread her hands—"fearing for my life and virtue, all of that."

"Why should you fear for your virtue?"

"Oh, I'm not afraid of *you* taking it," she said. "I don't trust myself. I'm afraid I'll have to offer it up to every lad in Mistshore to get them to help me after your contract runs out. This night was expensive enough. I shudder to think what the price will be day after tomorrow."

"So you're not afraid of me?" Ruen said.

"You mean because of Garlon?" She squared her shoulders. "I think he had his fate coming to him."

"That's bold," Ruen said. He tilted his hat to see her better. "Considering how pale you were when you rowed up to my raft, I would have thought you were a terrified mouse."

Icelin swallowed. "I've had fresh perspectives on terror tonight. Nothing you can do will frighten me."

"Truly?" He moved so fast the next breaths were a blur.

His hands encased both of her wrists. He hauled her out of the boat, onto her back on the raft. The hard planks knocked the breath out of her. He forced her hands above her head and half-straddled her.

"What about now?" Ruen said. He'd moved like a demon, yet he wasn't even breathing hard. His crimson eyes were so close they filled her vision. He didn't wait for a reply. He put his head on her chest.

Icelin bit back a whimper, but he made no other move to touch her.

"I hear your heartbeat," he said, lifting his head. "It's a wild bird." He smiled. "Are you certain you aren't scared?"

He knew she was terrified, and Icelin hated him for that. She could do nothing about the wild hammering in her chest, so instead, Icelin forced her rigid body to relax, one muscle at a time. It was the hardest work she'd ever done. "You know," she said, pleased that her voice did not shake, "if it's my virtue you're after, I should confess I gave it away a long time ago."

"How unfortunate," Ruen said. "Who was the lucky lad? Another thief?"

"A stable boy, actually. We did it behind the chimneystacks on the roof of my great-uncle's shop. He was two years older than me."

"Was he handsome?"

"Not really, but more so than you. We were outside all night, and I took sick the next morning. These are much lovelier conditions." She met his gaze, forcing a look of bored expectation. "Well? Are you going to do this or not?"

"You've got hard nerves, lady," Ruen said, "but you don't know this world. If I was any other man you'd be raped and robbed and bobbing in the harbor by now."

Icelin felt annoyance flare above her fear. "You're right, I don't know much about the world. In the last five years, I've rarely been out of my great-uncle's shop. I would love nothing more than to be there right now, but my great-uncle is murdered, and that shop is a tomb. Everything I once trusted is gone. I tell you truly, I have no one left to put my faith in, except a criminal. The irony of this could fuel many comic ballads, I'm sure. I may be naïve to you, but I have a sharp tongue and more than half a wit and if you can keep me alive long enough, I will find a way to pay you for the services you render me, if it takes all the blood in my body to do it."

They gazed at each other, their faces inches apart. Something like admiration passed over Ruen's face. He started to speak, but suddenly his face was illuminated by a brilliant, arcane light.

Icelin looked down, and saw the source coming from the space of water between the boat and the raft. A second apparition glowed from the water, but this one shone clearer, and its form melded into a twisted mockery of a human face—

"Watch out!" Ruen shouted. He hauled her up, but it was too late.

The sea wraith burst from the water in a shower of wet and light. The force of its appearance blew the small boats into the air.

Pressure, then fire shot up her right arm, but Icelin didn't dwell on that calamity. She felt her body leave solid ground—she was flying, the world tilting—and then the fetid water closed over her head, blocking out all sensation except cold.

Frantically, Icelin kicked in her bulky skirt, propelling herself to what she hoped was the surface. She came up gulping air. Nothing but cold blackness surrounded her. Ruen's lantern had been extinguished.

Raising her hand above the water, Icelin chanted, praying all the while that the weakness she knew would come would not render her unable to swim.

Light burst from her hand, transforming her arm into a makeshift torch. Nausea hit her hard in the gut. The queasiness in her belly combined with the stench and motion of the harbor proved too much. Icelin turned her head and retched, spitting water and filth. Her throat burned, but she forced herself to ignore it.

By the light of the spell, she saw a crooked gash running from her elbow to the middle of her forearm. There were splinters in the wound.

Ruen was swimming for his raft, which had been flipped upside down. He reached it, hoisted himself up, and pulled a knife from his belt. The thin blade bore a coat of rust. It was a not a weapon at all, but a gutting blade for fish. Icelin watched, incredulous, as Ruen brandished the rusty blade confidently at the sea wraith. The apparition swooped down from the clouds to hover above the water.

He's completely mad, Icelin thought. The knife would not put a scratch on the undead horror.

A glint of silver on Ruen's left middle finger caught Icelin's attention. He'd removed his glove, and she could see a ring glowing with arcane power, illuminating his pale flesh.

The glow spread down his arm, then flowed across his body like a weird, sped-up river. The light died away, except for where it illuminated the gutting knife. A single strand of silver lit the blade, eclipsing the rust.

Icelin swam to the raft, searching her memory for some spell that might aid Ruen. She hadn't used magic to defend herself in years. The spell in Sull's shop had been a harmless light trick. Gods, could she bring herself to remember how to call fire and ice? If she could, would it affect the wraith at all? She'd never faced anything like it before. Nelzun had purposefully guided her training to suit a woman traveling alone on the streets of Waterdeep.

While her thoughts spun and her arm burned, Ruen moved with preternatural speed across the raft. His knife blade flashed, cutting into the creature where its shoulder might have been.

Icelin saw no wound, but she heard an unearthly screech issue from the wraith.

The apparition twisted away, blasting through Ruen's body in its incorporeal form. For a breath, Ruen appeared to be treading water as the ghostly mass enveloped him. Then it passed, and the thief fell back onto the raft. Icelin was close enough to see his muscles twitching from the brutal exposure to the wraith's body.

She grabbed the raft with both hands and hoisted herself up next to Ruen's prone form. The wraith circled above their heads, as if trying to decide which of the two posed the greatest threat. Icelin swung her glowing arm back and forth, trying to keep the creature's attention away from Ruen.

She could recall no spells, nothing to harm or to kill. She'd buried them all long ago, vowing no living being would be hurt by her hand again.

But the memories were there, if she wanted to find them. The arcane power, locked away in the topmost tower room of her mind, like a princess in a tale. She needed no spellbook to find them, only the will.

She could picture her teacher's words of admonishment. This thing before you isn't alive, he would say. It has no warmth, no compassion. It seeks only death. When confronted with such creatures as this in the world, you have no choice but to deal death first.

The wraith, finally distracted by the waving light, swooped low across the water, its face inches from the rippling current.

It was coming at her from the right. Icelin braced her feet, certain she'd be knocked from the raft if the thing hit her.

A sharp arc, and the wraith was up and over the side of the raft—

Suddenly, Ruen sprang up between them. He'd only been pretending to be injured. He planted the gutting knife in the wraith's chest and held on.

The wraith thrashed and screeched and lifted Ruen off his feet. For a scant breath, they hung suspended over the water. Ruen jerked, tearing ghostly flesh. He jerked again, and the wraith spun, flipping the thief over its body to shake loose his grip.

The move worked. Ruen's fingers slipped from the knife, and he plunged into the murky water. His hat floated to the surface, but Ruen did not reappear.

Alone on the raft, Icelin at last found a spell. Calmly, she waited for the wraith to circle again. She watched it come, a ghastly glowing arrow running parallel to the water. Ruen's fish knife protruded from its chest, but the light had faded from the blade. As the creature glided closer, Icelin saw the blade and handle crumble, sprinkling ashes over the water.

This time the wraith would not be distracted from its prey. Ruen was either drowned or too far down in the water to help her.

Trembling, Icelin extended both hands out from her body. Pressing her thumbs together, she chanted the dusty words and prayed that she would not be burned alive.

"Begone!" she screamed.

Nothing happened. The cone of flame that should have spread from her hands manifested as a feeble yellow sparking at her fingertips. The palms of her hands grew faintly warm, but the heat soon died.

"Get down!" Ruen shouted from somewhere to her left. Icelin was too shocked to react. She saw the wraith bearing down on her, but she couldn't think or move. There came a rush of air, and the creature enveloped her.

Light blinded Icelin. She closed her eyes, but it was all around her. Cold. A bitter, biting freeze crawled over her skin like wet snakes, immobilizing her limbs. She tried to take a step. Her boots scraped the raft. She opened her eyes, desperately seeking escape.

Hollow eye sockets stared back at her. Ghostly flesh clung to the wraith's lipless mouth. It was nothing more than a parody of a human face, but the body was smothering her, freezing her to death. In the faint gray light between consciousness and oblivion, her teacher's words came to her, propelled from her memories with a life all their own.

"If, gods forbid, you ever have to fight a monster in the wilds, remember that it does you no good to think like a human woman. Each being responds differently to magic, and some can resist even the most potent spells."

"How will I be able to survive," Icelin remembered asking, "if I'm too weak to fight?"

"By being smart before you are powerful," her teacher said. "Certain creatures owe their existence to magical perversions. They are drawn to the Art, and can be distracted by it. Remember that."

Sucking in a ragged, painful breath, Icelin choked out the simplest spell she knew, one that always worked and never caused her pain. Long ago, she'd used it to mend tears in her clothing.

An invisible pulse of energy engulfed her hands as she finished the casting. Every successful spell she'd ever cast brought the sensation. Her teacher explained it away as one of the physical effects of magic on the body. Since the Spellplague, arcane energy was in a constant state of flux, manifesting in different forms for different wizards. This was hers.

According to Ruen, the wraith was a slave to the spellplague. Her distorted spell energies, however slight, might be enough to get its attention. Icelin prayed her simple spell would be enough.

Arcane energy sparked inside the wraith's incorporeal form. Whether from surprise or some other effect, the creature recoiled, forcing her out of its body.

Icelin stumbled back, but she was too weak to steady herself. She managed one feeble breath before she fell into the water.

After her brush with the wraith, the harbor actually felt warm. Icelin tried to swim, but her arms were still clutched into tight claws at her sides. She couldn't get her limbs to function.

Black spots popped in front of Icelin's vision. A part of her mind urged that drowning would be a better option than returning to the surface to face the wraith. Her lungs disagreed. She expelled her breath in a rush of bubbles. Above her, she could see the wraith's darting light. It was back in the water again, disoriented, searching for the arcane energy it craved. But the creature and its light were growing smaller the farther she sank.

At first she didn't feel the arm that encircled her chest. The burning was too painful for her to notice anything. It jerked her upright, and Icelin felt herself smashed against a hard wall. The wall moved, drawing her to the surface. Whenever Icelin thought she would slip, the arm would pull her back from the abyss.

She broke the surface gasping, choking foul water when she tried to suck in air. Her muscles were on fire. But she was alive.

Ruen was treading water directly behind her, holding her afloat with his right arm. The wall she'd been crushed against was his chest. The light spell on her arm still functioned. She could see the wraith making mad, swooping circles all around Ruen's raft.

"What did you do to it?" he demanded. "Its senses are blinded."

"I'm not sure." Icelin coughed and spat water. "We have to get away from here."

She felt Ruen shake his head. "Won't get far without a boat," he said. "Drive it away. Use your magic."

The wraith burst into the air, spraying them with water. Its attention refocused on the swimming pair. A high-pitched scream rent the air, and the creature dived at them again.

Ruen dragged her underwater, and they barely dodged the attack. When they came back up, the wraith had circled around for another pass.

"Cast your spell," Ruen ordered her. "Make it a good one. You won't get another before it kills us."

"You don't understand. I have no magic." Icelin tried to swim away from him, but he pinned her against his chest.

"Your glowing arm suggests otherwise," he said.

"It's also bleeding. Let me go!"

"Listen to me." He raised his left hand in front of her face. Icelin remembered the silver band. It rested on his finger, its light dull. "Everything this ring touches grows in strength, including magic. As long as our bodies touch, your spell should work."

He didn't wait for her to respond. He put his glove back on and folded her left hand under his.

Icelin felt a tingle of electricity coming from the ring. She searched her memory again. The fire spell was gone, but there was another. . . .

"When I cast this, I will likely lose consciousness," Icelin said. She fought to keep her voice steady.

Ruen tightened his grip. "You won't drown—you haven't paid me my fee yet. I'll hold you up, only work your spell!"

Icelin blocked out his voice, the icy water, the wraith's screams. She waited for the creature to glide close to the water again. When it was in her line of sight, she muttered the spell.

Burning pain erupted behind her eyes, a side effect Icelin only vaguely remembered from her early lessons. She had not cast spells of this magnitude for years. Her body was not ready for the shock.

Fighting oblivion, Icelin thrust her free hand above her head. The arcane pulse came again, strong and sustained. This time, the spell was going to work.

A stream of white vapor unfurled on the air like a sheet. It snapped and coalesced into a savage-looking spear, which shot across the water, trailing ice shards in its wake.

The magic impaled the wraith through its eyeless head. Unholy screams shattered the air. Ice flew in all directions. The force of the magic drove the creature back a full ten feet, and the light in its body flickered and died. The wraith collapsed in on itself, disappearing into the water without creating a wake.

For a long time, there was no sound except Icelin and Ruen's breathing. Icelin saw her breath in the wake of the cold spell. A fine layer of ice rimed the water in a straight line to where the creature had been. She watched the shards flake off like so much paint.

"That's i-impossible," Icelin said. Her head swam. "Never should have been so much, so big."

"It was my ring," Ruen said. "I told you it would strengthen the spell."

"Oh, well." Icelin felt unconsciousness looming. She was more than ready for it. "That's nice, isn't it?"

CHAPTER 8

Ruen retrieved his hat and swam to his raft, dragging the senseless girl behind him.

"You live up to your name," he said, grunting as he lifted her onto the deck. The ice had melted, but he could still feel the brittle chill in the air, a chill that had nothing to do with the wraith's presence.

Ruen put a hand on Icelin's chest to make sure she lived. She breathed deeply—the sleep of exhaustion. Her light spell flickered and died, leaving him only moonlight for navigation.

He knew magic taxed a wizard's strength, but he'd never seen a spell affect anyone the way the ice spear had wracked Icelin's body. He'd felt her trembling in pain.

He held his ring up close to his face but found no answers from the plain silver band. It no longer glowed with power.

"Did I push too hard," he murmured, gazing down at Icelin. "Or are you more than what they told me?"

He reached into the pouch strapped beneath his right arm. Inside he kept only two items: the ring, when he wanted it hidden from prying eyes, and a black *sava* piece—a pawn. He drew out the piece and palmed it. It took several breaths for the pawn to warm to his flesh and attune to his identity.

"Tesleena," he spoke aloud, and the pawn's answering flicker told him the magic connection was functioning. "I have the girl."

"Is she unharmed?" The tiny voice issued from the pawn as if across a vast distance.

"She's well enough, but unconscious," Ruen said. "We fought a sea wraith in the harbor. You owe me a new boat."

"You *what?*" Tesleena's voice shot up an octave. "Your instructions were—"

"Not well received by the undead," Ruen said. "I wouldn't be worried. Your little girl killed the thing with one spell."

"She used magic to fight?"

There was something in Tesleena's voice Ruen didn't like. "We can talk about it when I hand the girl over," he said.

There was a long pause. "Very well. Where can we meet?"

Ruen glanced at the shore. "I'll contact you."

"Wait."

Ruen severed the connection by dropping the pawn back in his pouch. Let the Warden's pet curse him. He needed to get back to shore. Then he would find a safe location to drop the girl. The Watch would find her easily enough from his instructions. He had no intention of meeting them face to face.

He gazed down at the sleeping girl. She was a hardy thing. Already her color was coming back.

Better she remain unconscious. He didn't want her kicking up a fuss when he left her. Betrayal was much easier with the eyes closed.

"Did you see that?"

Shenan's fine eyes were just visible above her scarf. The watching elves stood in the shadow of Whalebone Court, near the water's edge.

Cerest followed the elf woman's gaze out to the harbor in time to see the spell erupt. It was nothing more than light from this distance, but Cerest felt a thrill of excitement.

"It's her," he said.

Shenan looked at him. Torchlight reflected off her burnished skin. "How can you be certain?"

"You heard the people whispering. No one goes out in that direction. It's Ferryman's Waltz."

Shenan looked around. People were hurrying across the planked pathways. They cast nervous glances out into the harbor, as if they expected the light to notice and follow them.

"It's possible," Shenan admitted. She turned and made a subtle gesture against her chest.

A pair of men standing twenty feet behind them on the pathway slowed. One of the men signaled back, and both turned around and headed for shore.

"We'll intercept them when they come back to land," Shenan said.

Cerest nodded, but he didn't move. He watched the light until it went out.

His big hands buried in his sleeves, Sull pulled the cooking pan off the fire and placed it with a regal flourish in front of Fannie.

"My lady," he drawled, "your mystery fish is prepared."

Fannie clapped her hands once and proceeded to scrape the hot meat off the pan. Juggling the steaming hunks of fish, she popped them in her mouth one at a time, pausing only long enough to spit the bones onto the sand.

Sull watched her gulp down the food and hastily put Icelin's fish, which he'd already cooked, on the other side of his body. He wanted to make sure Icelin ate some proper food before they moved on, and Fannie looked too ravenous to be trusted.

He'd cooked the blind, horned fish to a blackened crisp to boil away as many of the toxins as possible. Afterward he'd tasted the fish—crunchy, but edible enough. Not his best work, but Fannie didn't seem to mind.

They heard it at the same time, the sound of a raft scraping over sand. Sull jumped up, Fannie right behind him.

A man stumbled up the shore. He carried a bundle draped over his shoulder. Sull didn't recognize it for a person until the man strode into Fannie's camp.

"Lass!" he roared, and to the unknown man, "Put her down."

"Gladly." The man dumped Icelin unceremoniously into Sull's arms and kept on walking.

The butcher lowered Icelin gently to the sand and looked her over for wounds. When he saw her arm, his face turned an ugly crimson. "Who are you? What'd you do to her?" he demanded. He lowered a hand to the closest cleaver on his sash.

"Hello, boy," Fannie said when the man approached her fire. "You in trouble again, Ruen, eh?" She grinned, but Ruen didn't return her smile.

"Get her awake," he told Sull. "We need to move. Half of Mistshore probably saw the battle in the water, and the rest saw me coming in to shore. We'll have eyes on us, and worse, if we don't get moving."

Icelin stirred. Sull put a hand under her head to support her as she sat up. She looked groggy, as if she'd been asleep for days, but otherwise Sull couldn't see anything wrong.

"Lass?" he said, turning her chin toward him. "Are you all right?"

She blinked. "I think so. It was the spell." She looked around. "Where's Ruen?"

"Don't worry about him," Sull said darkly. "We're leavin' just as soon as I see to your arm."

"But—"

"Hsst!" Fannie scuttled around her tent, cocking an ear to listen. "Someone comes."

Ruen kicked sand onto the fire, dousing it instantly. "Friendly or not?" he hissed to Fannie.

"What's friendly here?" The woman snorted. "You go now."

With Sull's aid, Icelin got to her feet. "Where are we going?" Icelin asked.

"Just be quiet and follow me," Ruen said. With a nod to

Fannie, he moved away from the camp, crouching low to weave among the tents. He fumbled in a pouch as he went, but Sull couldn't see what he was after.

Icelin kept close enough to whisper to Sull. "We were attacked."

"By the elf?" Sull asked.

Icelin shuddered. "Worse, by the gods. A sea wraith. I'll tell you the tale later."

They moved slowly, Sull jogging along impatiently in the rear. Finally, he called out, trying to keep his voice low, "Faster, damn you. They'll be catchin' up."

But Ruen didn't seem to hear him. He passed the edge of the tent encampment and stopped, listening to something on the air.

"This way," he said, and began running.

Icelin hurried to follow. She could hear them now, the sounds of running feet pounding against the sand, gaining ground with each step.

They circled a caravel that had had its hull split in two. The jagged wood opened a dark maw into the ship's interior. Icelin thought Ruen meant them to hide inside, but suddenly, Ruen stopped short and cursed. He shoved her behind him and reached for a weapon at his belt. He'd forgotten the fish knife was long gone.

"They're herding us!" he shouted to Sull, just before the men jumped them.

Two figures leaped over the side of the ship, landing on either side of Ruen and Icelin. One had bright, corn silk hair, the other was dark and compactly built. Ruen skidded on the sand to avoid plowing into their sword points. He dropped into a crouch and swept out with his leg, catching the two men at the ankles. He hit so hard Icelin thought she would hear the bones in his leg crack. But they did not, and the two men stumbled and fell.

"Behind us!" Sull drew his mallet and cleaver. He charged a

second pair of men coming from the rear. Before they could reach for weapons, Sull cut a wicked gash across the first man's arm. He backed off a pace, clutching his arm and shredded shirt.

His companion came in low, dodging Sull's swinging mallet. He wore dirt-caked traveling clothes and a hooded, threadbare cloak. He brought a broadsword up to halt Sull's advance.

Sull was no trained fighter, Icelin knew. But what he lacked in skill, the butcher made up for in sheer ferocity. He twirled the cleaver once, letting the bloodied weapon dance in his hand. He smiled at the man with the sword, and the whites of his eyes were huge in the campfires' glow.

"Come on, dogs!" he shouted, stomping the ground, feinting left and right between his two opponents, letting his size intimidate the men and keep them on the defensive.

Caught between her companions, Icelin wrenched a loose board from the ship and swung it at the dark, burly man before he could rise to his feet. The plank hit him in the chest; a protruding nail tore into his skin. The man screeched in pain and fury.

"Run!" Ruen barked at her. The man with corn silk hair brought his sword down in an axe chop. Ruen dodged, and the blade buried itself in sand. He rolled away and came up practically between the man's legs. He snapped out a fist, connecting just below his attacker's ribcage. The blow would not trouble the man, Icelin thought. She had seen the glint of mail through his thin shirt.

To her shock, the man whooped out a breath and bent double. His sword dropped, allowing Ruen to come in around his guard. He locked an elbow around the man's neck, jerking sharply to the left.

The loud crack sent a sick coldness through Icelin's body.

"Beware, lass!"

Icelin turned in time to see Sull's mallet fly from his hand. The butcher fell back, clutching his arm against his chest. Blood dripped through the gaps between his fingers.

Horrified, Icelin dropped the board and started to run to him.

She felt a presence rise up behind her. She'd forgotten the dark-haired man. She tried to spin, but the sand slowed her. Large hands grabbed Icelin around the waist and slammed her sideways into the caravel's hull.

Icelin felt the breath leave her body in a rush. Her head hit an exposed board. Stars burst in her vision. She tried to call a spell, but her mind wouldn't function. She collapsed back against her attacker's chest. He manhandled her to the ground, pinning her arms in front of her while he fumbled for a piece of rope at his belt.

Icelin struggled wildly. Sand raked her wounded forearm. The pain was unlike anything she'd felt before, but she had to keep her hands free. She had to have magic. She wouldn't let them take her. . . .

Somewhere behind her, she could hear Sull snarling, his cleaver whistling in his hand. The dark-haired man wrenched her hands together, tying off the rope. Ruen leaped to his feet and started toward her, but was distracted by another figure coming out of the night. This one was tall, agile in motion. The moonlight revealed a face covered in puckered scars.

"Bind her mouth!" Cerest cried. "She is a wizard." He noticed Ruen and drew a sword. "Shenan!"

Icelin could see no one else, but a breath later, magic erupted behind Cerest. Icelin smelled the burning, and chemical heat seared her eyes as an arrow streaked through the night, aimed at Ruen.

"Acid!" Icelin cried.

The dark man grabbed her by the hair, jerking her head back. She couldn't see Ruen, could only make out the night sky and the distant flakes of starlight visible through the clouds. She heard the arrow impact wood, hissing as the spell fizzled out.

The dark-haired man used his teeth to pull off one of his dirty leather gloves. Stuffing it in her mouth, he looped more rope around her head, binding the glove tight to her face until she choked.

Icelin felt herself lifted, tossed over the man's shoulder. He moved off into the night, around the ship wreckage, away from the sounds of fighting. She could not see if Cerest was following.

Icelin squirmed and tried to scream, but she could force no sound through the gag. They moved out of the campfire light, and the night grew pitch black. She could see nothing of her surroundings except the dark-haired man's broad back.

She prayed Ruen would help Sull. Over and over she begged the gods that they would escape. But even if they did, Cerest and his men would be gone in the night. Sull and Ruen would have no idea how to track her.

Abruptly, the man carrying her stopped. Icelin felt his hands leave her. She heard him fumbling with something. Metal clicked against metal: a door lock.

Now was her opportunity. She might not get another. Bracing herself, Icelin threw all her weight to the right.

She toppled off her captor's shoulder, raising her bound arms in front of her. She hit the ground hard on her stomach amid the cries of the dark-haired man. He recovered from his surprise and immediately crouched, grabbing her ankle so she couldn't run.

Icelin grappled with the gag at her mouth, tearing away leather, rope, and hair that had gotten caught against her face.

Her captor was on top of her now, trying to wrestle her hands down, but it was too dark for him to get a proper grip on her. Wherever they were, there were no torches or lanterns nearby to provide illumination.

Icelin thrust her elbow into the man's ribs. The pressure on her back slackened. She ripped the gag aside and screamed at the top of her lungs. The shrill sound pierced the night, and even the dark-haired man shrank back in momentary fear.

Several things happened at once. Her captor recovered and pushed her onto her side, backhanding her across the face. Dazed, Icelin flopped onto her back. She tasted blood on her lips. Her face felt hot. At the same time, footsteps were approaching rapidly from somewhere in the distance. Icelin's heart lurched—had Ruen and Sull come for her?—until she heard Cerest's voice.

"Strike her again, Greyas, and I'll split your tongue down the center," the elf promised. "Shenan, would you mind?"

"Of course," said a new voice, feminine, and as peacefully melodic as Cerest's. How many had the elf set upon her? Icelin thought. Hopelessness seized her, and with it came a hysteric frenzy.

She struck out, and by chance caught the dark-haired man in the throat. Icelin screamed again.

"Sull! Ruen!"

"Quickly, Shenan," said Cerest calmly over the noise.

Icelin heard the honeyed voice speaking in an even, arcane rhythm. A cold mist stole over Icelin's mind. Her body felt heavy, and her eyes burned as if she had not slept in days.

"No," she cried. But the word came out slurred, feeble. Icelin trembled, fighting to stay awake, but it was no use. She went limp on the cold ground, and all the melodic voices receded.

Ruen's fist glanced off jawbone, and the latter of Sull's opponents turned his full attention to Ruen. His arm still dripped blood freely from the wound Sull had dealt him. Ruen tipped his hat to the side and smiled before launching a flurry of numbing blows to the man's torso. The ring on his hand burned silver; Ruen felt its magic coursing through his bones, propelled on by his natural speed.

In his peripheral vision, he noted the tracks Icelin's captors had left in the sand. They were not the tracks of the Watch. He'd known it as soon as the ambush hit them. If he hadn't thought it was Tesleena's party pursuing them, he could have outrun the men easily. He should have known when she didn't answer his summons through the pawn.

Sull dodged a thrust from his opponent's broadsword. The butcher was quick enough, but the sword still whistled close to his ear, too close for the man to last much longer in the fight.

Ruen aimed his next blow at the man's sword arm, putting all the force he could behind the punch. The man's arm spasmed; his sword fell from nerveless fingers. Ruen punched again. The man went down and did not rise.

Sull threw his weight backward to avoid another sword thrust. He landed on his backside in the sand. Scooting away, he kicked sand, spraying the air and creating a meager shield between himself and the flashing sword.

Ruen came at the man with the broadsword from behind. He grabbed the man's shoulder and turned him. Locking a hand on his wrist, Ruen twisted until the bones cracked. The man's sword fell to the sand to join his friend's. Ruen jammed his elbow into the man's throat, and he fell, unconscious next to his companion.

Ruen looked briefly to see if Sull was bleeding more than necessary and, satisfied he wasn't, began disarming the unconscious men. He took a dagger from one of them and slid it into his belt. He much preferred the fish knife—it was his favorite—but the wraith had stolen that from him.

He stood up and saw a red blur charging at him. He managed to dodge the bull rush, but Sull's fist still found his cheek. One side of Ruen's head erupted in pain.

Ruen danced back, retaining the presence of mind to raise the dagger before Sull could come at him again.

But the butcher seemed uninterested in continuing the attack. Instead, Ruen saw tears leaking from the man's wild eyes.

"You damn fool!" Sull bellowed. "You let 'em get away."

"I saved your life," Ruen said calmly. He tucked the dagger away and rubbed his jaw. "She wouldn't have wanted me to let you die."

Sull hiccupped and seemed to consider this. His eyes were still furious. "You led us right into their trap. Do you have any idea what they'll do to her? They'll—"

Ruen shook his head. "They want her alive. They took a lot of trouble to remove her from the battle unharmed. We can track them now."

"How?" Sull demanded.

Ruen crouched next to the smaller of the unconscious forms. He nudged the man, but he did not stir.

"We wait for one of these to wake up," Ruen said. Sull made a noise of displeasure, and Ruen finally looked up at the big man. "They won't get far—look." He nodded to the horizon, where gray, pre-dawn light was giving way to sunrise. "They're not stupid enough to move her out of Mistshore while it's light. With the Watch patrols out, they'll be seen. We'll question these, rest and move on."

"What if they won't tell us anythin'?" Sull asked, glancing pointedly at Ruen's fists.

Ruen shrugged. "We'll have to be convincing." He got to his feet. "Help me move them inside the ship's hull. We'll be sheltered there."

Together they hauled the bodies, the dead and the unconscious, through the torn gap in the ship. The interior smelled of must and mold. Driftwood and the tattered remains of hammocks were piled in one corner. Rats scurried out of the lumpy mounds.

Ruen sat down on a pile of rigging next to the bodies. Sull moved around the ship with an air of ripe impatience. Ruen watched the chests of the unconscious men rising and falling. He had beaten them severely. He did not know when they would regain sense, and if they would be in a fit state to answer any questions.

Sliding forward, he removed his glove and reached across the closest man's prone body. He pressed his hand against the man's open palm. He wasn't sure what drove him to do it—he always avoided touching people when he could help it—but he needed to know. He ignored Sull's curious expression.

Faint blue light outlined the cracks between his fingers. Ruen curled his hand under the man's, but he didn't think Sull could see the light. The man's hand stung with cold; it was like pressing his palm flush against a frozen lake. He'd expected some degree of chill, but not this. The feeling repulsed him. Ruen removed his hand from the unconscious man's and put his glove back on.

"What are you doin'?" Sull said.

"Checking for signs of life," Ruen explained. He turned his attention to the other man. "We'll need to question this one. The other won't survive. I hit him too hard."

"I didn't see you feelin' for a life beat—"

Sull stopped. The man's eyelids had twitched. A breath later they opened, and the man let out a rough moan. He focused on Ruen and the butcher with the bloody cleaver in his hand. His eyes widened.

"Welcome back," Sull said, smiling cheerfully. He seemed to have forgotten Ruen's odd behavior. "We've a few questions for you."

Icelin knew she was dreaming. The scene was familiar. Barefoot, she walked on green grass, up the side of a wide, rocky hill. Shafts of sunlight shone on her white dress. There were wildflowers blooming, gold and purple, all around her feet.

She stopped at the crest of the hill. A stone tower rose up before her. A single window had been cut into the curve facing her, a dark and unblinking eye. The western side had caved in, leaving a gaping hole into which birds flew and nested. Their cries were the only sounds on the hilltop. But Icelin felt she was not alone.

There were other figures moving up the hill toward the tower, indistinct shadows darting in and out of her field of vision. She tried to grasp them with her eyes, but they had no more substance than the wind brushing her cheeks.

I will follow them, Icelin thought. It seemed the most natural thing in the world to stride across the grass to the gap in the immense tower. She put her hands on the exposed stone. Warm from the sun, bleached with age, and ribboned with thousands of miniscule cracks, the stone held secrets. Someone had told her this.

"All the ancient places of the world hold secrets. Who knows what manner of men walked here, be they beggars or kings—men who now lie in dusty tombs, their memories husks. Will the stones remember who touched them, when you lie beside these somber lords of the earth?"

Icelin remembered the words vividly, but for the first time in her life she could not recall who said them. The thought was vaguely disturbing, but she pushed it to the back of her dreaming mind.

She had entered the tower now. The stones blotted out the sun at her back. The tower's wood floors had long rotted away, leaving the interior open from earth to sky. Crushed grass and the remains of a small human body were strewn on the ground.

Icelin tilted her head as far back as she could, taking in the circle of blue rimmed by blackened stones through a gap in the ceiling. The tower had been damaged by fire; she could see the soot stains streaking the walls. Had this small human been the only person to die here? How had it come to be?

She felt tired now. Icelin sat down in the middle of the tower, still staring up at the sky. The shadow shapes moved around her, but she wasn't afraid of them. She felt that if they would only be still, she would be able to name them. It was the same with the tower—a living presence that, if she knew its name, would open its secrets to her and welcome her inside. Unnamed, it cast an immutable shadow over her dreams, dominating everything.

"*Have you found anything?*"

The voice, so loud in the peaceful place, made Icelin jump. The shadows flitted closer to her, and Icelin felt their urgency. Something was happening. The stones around her changed color and became bright orange and blue like storm clouds. The sun pouring through the tower roof was too hot, too hot.

She looked down at her skin and found it melting off her bones. She was burning alive.

CHAPTER 9

Icelin awoke to darkness and more shadows moving around her. This time she felt real terror, for she knew where she was. The gag stank in her mouth, and voices floated around her.

Cerest was there, somewhere in the darkness. She heard him say, "We'll wait for gateclose. Bring her, if she's awake. Be careful of her arm."

Icelin looked down and saw the clean bandage tightly wrapped around her injured arm. There was a dull ache where the pain had been.

Two pairs of rough hands grabbed her shoulders and hauled her to her feet. The dark-haired man stood to her right. Her captors guided her over to the center of a large, rectangular room.

Icelin looked up, just as she'd done in her dream. Timber beams crisscrossed above her head. Tin sheets formed parts of the walls. Wooden crates lined the whole building, some stacked as high as the ceiling.

A warehouse, Icelin thought. She felt the floor slope down sharply; the ground the warehouse was built upon had shifted over the years. There was a good chance they were still in Mistshore, near the harbor.

In the center of the room, Cerest and the female elf stood talking. The two men guiding her sat her on a crate before them. The dark-haired man removed her gag.

Cerest faced her, a cloak hood tucked close around his face. He appeared to be keeping his distance from the human men. Did he fear their reaction to his scars? The thought came unbidden to Icelin, and she wondered why the murderous elf would be bothered to care how others saw him. He nodded to one of the men.

"Wait outside," he said. "Greyas, you remain here, but step back so we may talk."

With the men dismissed, Cerest focused his attention solely on Icelin. "Hello again," he said softly. The female elf—Shenan, he'd called her—brought a lantern close and handed it to Cerest. The elf held the flickering flame close to her face so he could see her clearly.

"What do you want?" Icelin asked.

To her surprise, the elf went down on one knee in front of her, so that he was looking up into her face. She supposed he meant to appear non-threatening, but Icelin found the effort he took more unsettling than comforting. He angled his body so that the unscarred portion of his face was most visible.

"I would like," Cerest said, "for you to tell me how much you remember of your childhood."

The question was so bizarrely out of context with the situation that Icelin didn't immediately answer. Cerest, intent on her expression, seemed to take her silence as defiance. He frowned.

"Icelin," he said, at the same time gesturing to the dark-haired man—Greyas, he'd called him. "I know you don't trust me. That's to be expected. You don't remember who I am." He smiled. "But I have known you for a very long time. Gods, I *named* you. I remember the night you were born—"

Icelin lunged at him. Shenan caught her by the throat and pushed her back, but Icelin's gesture had the desired effect. Cerest stopped speaking and stood back a safe distance. He regarded her with wounded curiosity.

"Why do you behave this way?" he asked. "I've not hurt you, and I don't intend to."

"You killed Brant," Icelin said. Her throat burned. "All your lies, no matter how prettily spoken, won't change that."

"I'm not lying," Cerest said. "Brant cared for you. He was a good man. I know that." When Icelin only stared at him, he went on, "But I think you'll discover Brant had his share of secrets, especially where you were concerned. I'm confident he acted to protect you, but in doing so, he shortened his own life."

"Master." Greyas stepped forward again, dragging a smaller figure. Icelin pulled her gaze away from Cerest's face to see who it was. Her heart dropped.

Fannie stood in front of Greyas, looking like a doll in the man's muscular arms. While Icelin watched, Greyas placed a hand on either side of Fannie's head. Fannie quailed, but he did not exert any pressure on her skull. He didn't have to. Fannie stood utterly still, held in place by the mere threat of what he could do to her with those large hands. She was gagged, as Icelin had been. Her eyes were huge above the scrap of dirty cloth. She looked beseechingly at Icelin.

"We took her at the same time we took you," Cerest said. He motioned for Greyas to bring Fannie into the light. He pushed her, stumbling and barefoot, into the small circle of illumination.

"Shenan," Cerest said, and the female elf stepped forward, taking Greyas's place at Fannie's back. She patted the woman on the shoulder, whispering comforting noises that made Icelin's skin crawl.

"What do you remember of your childhood, Icelin?" Cerest repeated the question slowly, glancing meaningfully between Fannie and Icelin.

"I am an orphan," Icelin said. She met Fannie's eyes, trying to silently reassure her. "My parents were killed when I was barely two summers old. Brant, my great-uncle, raised me."

"Your great-uncle," Cerest said. "What about your grandfather, Icelin?"

"My grandfather is dead. I have no other living family," Icelin said. "Why are you asking me these questions? If you want to revenge yourself on me, let this woman go and have your pleasure! What more can I possibly give you than my life?"

Cerest's brow furrowed in confusion. "Revenge?" he said, sounding almost amused. "My dear girl, far from it. I have no quarrel with you. What gave you that notion?"

"I—" Icelin turned away. Her mind raced. He wasn't after her. She'd been wrong this whole time. He hadn't been in the fire. . . .

Relief and fear vied for control of Icelin's emotions. She hadn't injured the elf. But if it wasn't revenge he sought, why had he killed Brant? Why had he hunted her so diligently?

"Shenan," Cerest said quietly.

Fannie's muffled scream snapped Icelin back to the present. She looked up in horror to see the female elf holding Fannie's head back by the hair. She placed a gleaming dagger blade against Fannie's arched neck. Blood welled where the blade pressed flesh. The dagger was so sharp, one slip and Shenan would slice open the prostitute's throat.

"Answer my question, please," Cerest said. He sounded like a father coaxing a child. "I think it important I hear this tale, so that we understand each other."

Icelin swallowed. She looked at Cerest, letting him see the undisguised hatred. "I studied magic under the tutelage of Nelzun Decampter, a skilled wizard," she said. "My great-uncle paid out most of his savings to apprentice me to the man because Decampter specialized in handling wielders of unstable magic. Such was mine. I studied under Nelzun for three years and acquired a reasonable level of skill in the Art."

"A reasonable level—did Nelzun believe you had the potential for greater power?" Cerest asked.

Icelin's jaw clenched at the eager light in his eyes. "Yes. He wanted me to travel with him, to test my skills out in the world. But I had no desire to leave my home. That mistake cost Nelzun his life."

"What happened?" Cerest said.

"First tell her to move the dagger," Icelin said, looking at Shenan but addressing Cerest.

Cerest nodded to the elf woman. Shenan appeared disappointed as she removed the blade from Fannie's throat.

"Nelzun took me into the city to test my powers. He wanted me to be able to defend myself in the rougher districts. None of the spells I was to cast that day were dangerous, and Waterdeep is more stable than many cities when it comes to magic going awry." Icelin knew she shouldn't care what the elf thought of her, but the need to explain, to justify what couldn't be justified, clawed at her.

"We were in Dock Ward. A fight broke out at a tavern as we were passing by, and the brawl spilled into the street." Icelin could see it clearly in her mind: the shattered door, the man being thrown into the street. Another pair of men followed, brandishing weapons. She'd thought . . .

It didn't matter what they'd intended. She never had the chance to find out.

"I ran toward the fight. I left Nelzun. When I saw the man about to be attacked, I cast the only spell I knew that would hurt. I'd never called the fire before, but Nelzun had showed me how it was done."

"To summon fire to your fingertips is one of the easiest attack spells to master, because you cannot burn yourself, as real flame would."

Her teacher's words, Icelin thought. But he'd never given a care to what might happen to him if things went wrong.

"The spell ran wild?" Cerest asked. He touched his face, rubbing the scars thoughtfully. "The fire spread?"

"I can still remember how high the flames soared," Icelin said. She was dimly aware of wetness on her face. She reached up with her bound hands and felt the tears. It didn't matter. They had already seen how weak she was. "There was a boardinghouse—old wood, and a dry season—next door to the tavern. The fire took the roof first, caving in the ceiling on the people inside.

Five people on the topmost floor were killed instantly, including a Watchman who'd been investigating a woman's disappearance. The people below escaped—miraculously, I thought." She took a shuddering breath. "Until the spell ended, and I realized Nelzun wasn't with me."

"What happened to him?" Cerest asked. But Icelin wasn't listening. She recited the tale automatically, numbing her mind to the most painful part of all.

"Nelzun had gone into the boardinghouse to save the rest of the people inside. He got them all out, and then he collapsed outside the building. I tried to get him to take healing, but he said he'd breathed too much of the smoke, that healing wouldn't save him. He spent his last breaths telling me not to blame myself."

Icelin looked up. The warehouse was utterly silent. Greyas stood somewhere in the shadows, unseen, but probably listening. Nothing seemed to exist outside the dim circle of lantern light: it was only herself, Cerest, Shenan, and Fannie. She glanced at the two women and was horrified to find them both looking at her with pity in their eyes.

Gods above, she'd never thought to be making a confession before two monsters and a terrified prostitute. She'd never imagined such beings pitying her.

"I understand now," Cerest said. "You believed I escaped the boardinghouse fire, horribly scarred and out for revenge against the lass who'd maimed me."

Icelin nodded.

Cerest smiled gently. "You have nothing to fear from me, Icelin. My scars are from a different fire. Like your teacher, I see great strength in you. I want to help you harness your gifts—"

"Never!" Icelin's shout shattered the stillness. "I swore I'd never pursue magic again."

Cerest and Shenan traded glances. Icelin couldn't tell what passed between them.

"She is untried, Cerest," Shenan said, voicing her thoughts aloud. "You have led us on a fool's chase." Her tone was mild, but she tightened her grip on the dagger.

Good, Icelin thought. Let them slay each other and have done with the whole business. For the first time in her life she felt grateful for being inadequate.

"She can learn," Cerest said. "She's already had a wizard's training, which is more than Elgreth had."

"Elgreth," Icelin said, surprised, "you knew my grandfather?"

"It's true," said Cerest. "Elgreth was my best friend."

"No. You're lying again," Icelin said. His words cut her. This couldn't be. Her family would never be connected to a murderer.

"You don't know your family as I do, Icelin. Your grandfather was afflicted with a powerful spellscar. Did Brant ever tell you that?"

Mute, Icelin shook her head.

"He should have. The scar gave Elgreth substantial abilities," Cerest said, "abilities that I believe you also possess."

"That's not possible. You have to be exposed to the spellplague to bear such a scar," Icelin said. "I have never been outside Waterdeep's walls."

"You were too young to remember—"

"I remember everything!" Her body shook with suppressed fury. "I possess all my memories, whether I want them or not. And you, sir, are not among them."

Out of the corner of her eye, Icelin glimpsed movement. A slender shape flowed down the sloping floor toward them. Icelin thought it was a snake moving in a crooked line, but as it drew closer, she recognized the metallic smell. The substance pooled in a thick circle at her feet.

Cerest recognized it at the same time. He drew his sword.

"Greyas!" he cried. But there was no answer from the shadows.

Cerest looked down at the blood pool and cursed. Shenan shoved Fannie away and brandished her own blade, moving into position at Cerest's back.

Icelin used the distraction to slide off the back of the crate, putting it between her and the elves. She heard Fannie stumbling for cover, but Cerest was no longer paying her any attention. He was watching the shadows intently.

"Show yourselves!" He shouted.

Tense, Icelin waited, but there came no answer from the shadows.

A breath passed, and a sound like beating wings came out of the darkness. A huge metal cleaver buried itself deep into the crate where Icelin had been sitting. The handle quivered from side to side.

Icelin reached up and snatched the weapon. As soon as her fingers touched the handle, the attack came.

Sull leaped from behind a crate, charging into the circle with a loud roar. The sight of the red-haired giant hurtling across the warehouse was enough to break apart Cerest and Shenan. They dived for cover, and Sull placed himself squarely in front of Icelin. He grabbed the cleaver from her and sliced her bonds.

"Get back!" Sull shouted as he parried a blow from Shenan's blade with his mallet. The dagger left a deep gouge in the wood.

Icelin backed away, seeking cover. Cerest broke to follow when another shadow moved—a large burst of darkness that came from above.

Ruen dropped from a column of stacked crates, landing behind Cerest. He grabbed the elf around the throat, dragging him away from Icelin.

"Greyas!" Cerest shouted, twisting to shove the man off. "Rondel!" He spun. Icelin saw the instant the elf locked eyes with Ruen.

For a breath, Cerest froze like a frightened deer. Icelin heard him mutter, "Spellscarred," before he went for his sword.

Ruen stood before him, unarmed and at ease. His knees slightly bent, he all but danced on the balls of his feet. Cerest thrust with his blade, and Ruen jumped back. The thrust never came close to his flesh. The elf swung again, and again Ruen dodged, this time finding an opening to punch Cerest in the gut.

The elf stumbled back. His sword wavered; he didn't know whether to attack or defend.

He has no notion of how to fight an unarmed man, Icelin realized. It would be more to his advantage if Ruen had a weapon.

The thief, on the other hand, appeared to be reading Cerest's attacks before he made them. He danced back, sweeping his foot out in a kick that connected solidly with Cerest's knee. The elf had his full weight propped there; he went down with a cry of fury.

This wasn't desperate street fighting. Icelin observed Ruen's measured stance, the balance between rest and motion. He stayed suspended between the two, almost floating, until Cerest's attack came. Only trained, disciplined warriors fought this way, facing whirling steel with an air of serenity and absolute comfort in the strength of their bodies.

Ruen Morleth was not a thief, or at least, not *only* a thief. He was a monk, a warrior trained in unarmed combat.

A loud pounding sounded outside the warehouse door. Icelin tore her attention away from the battle. Ruen and Sull must have sealed the door from the inside when they'd entered the warehouse. Cerest's men—gods knew how many had come running at the elf's shout—were trying to break down the door. The flimsy wood and rusted iron wouldn't hold for long.

Not this time. She wouldn't be caught again. Icelin took a deep breath and searched her mind, cycling through spell after spell in the vast tower library.

Wind. Force. Her teacher had shown her how the spell could be used if she was ever jumped in Blacklock Alley.

Good enough to seal a door. Spellbooks opened and flew before her mind. She discarded the safe spells, those that would do no harm. She threw them all into a dusty corner and pictured a black book, something fearful and dangerous. Yes. Those were the spells she feared most, but they were the only ones that would aid her friends.

Then it came to her: a black tome with a gold spine. The words were written in faded ink, as if her mind were instinctively trying to protect itself from the deadly power in the words. She forced herself to visualize them clearly. Her heart tripped rapidly in her chest. She thought of a song to calm herself, chanted in time to the music, but her voice quivered. She was no monk. There would be no serenity for her in this fight.

The spell manifested in a burst of energy. Icelin's hair blew straight back from her face. The hot wind made her eyes stream. She lifted her hands, and the wind rose, spiraling outward to the door in a contained funnel. The force of it grated against the wood, forcing the door tight into its frame. The pounding ceased.

"Ruen! Sull, let's go! I can't hold it for long!" Icelin screamed above the wind.

Sull turned, his mallet tangled with Shenan's dagger. He kept barreling into her, knocking her off balance so she couldn't cast a proper spell. "Hold on, lass. We're comin'!"

Icelin heard a loud thud. It sounded like someone had been thrown into a pile of crates. She was too focused on the spell to see whether it was a friend or a foe.

The breath burned in her chest. Too hot, she thought. The air thickened, and sweat poured down her face. The spell was too strong. It was happening just like before, but this would be much worse. She could feel the heat building. Paint bubbled on the warehouse walls.

Gods, don't do this to me. Not again.

Five years fell away like scales. She was losing control; the spell was slipping away, taking on a life of its own. Icelin was powerless to stop it. She could hear the screams coming from the boardinghouse. So many people, trying to get out. . . .

The wooden door buckled in its frame. Frightened shouts rang out from the other side. Icelin fought to contain the wind, to keep it caged in its deadly funnel.

Flames burst into being and flew along the funnel's rim. Icelin could do nothing but watch them, a dozen restless sprites spiraling through the air. Pain shot through her after each flame appeared, as if they were being torn from her body.

Icelin dropped to her knees, and the funnel burst. Freed, the fire shot in all directions. The deadly flame arrows buried in crates or ricocheted off the tin walls.

Everyone in the warehouse would be a target, Icelin thought wildly. She couldn't end the spell; the magic became unrecognizable once the spell went wild. She had no way to contain it now.

Through a haze of smoke and pain, Icelin felt a presence behind her. For all she knew, it could have been Cerest or one of his men, come to stick a dagger in her back. Somehow, she knew it was Ruen. The thief crouched behind her.

"Can you walk?" He had to shout to be heard above the roaring wind.

Icelin shook her head. The slight movement made her vision swim.

"I can't touch you," Ruen said. "My ring will enhance the spell. It could kill us all."

"Where's Sull?" Icelin said. "Fannie—she's here too." She couldn't see them through the smoke. The crates were on fire, the blaze spreading to every corner of the warehouse. Soon the ceiling would collapse, just as it had done five years ago.

"Sull and Fannie are fine," Ruen said. "The others fled in fear of your spell."

Relief flooded Icelin, bringing with it a sense of peace. This was justice, she thought. I will die here and never hurt anyone again.

"Go," Icelin said. "Get out of here. Make sure Sull gets to safety, and your marker is paid. That's all I care—"

A wave of energy shuddered through Icelin's body. She felt the last vestiges of the spell inside her explode outward. The door and part of the wall blew apart, but Icelin didn't hear the grinding, tearing metal. The force of the blast deafened her.

"How convenient," Ruen said. He was still shouting, but his voice seemed to come from very far away. He had his hands at her armpits, dragging her to her feet. "You made us a door."

"You shouldn't have . . . done that," Icelin said. She swayed on her feet. A beam broke away from the ceiling, trailing a sheet of flame all the way to the ground.

"We've got to run," Ruen said. He took her hand, yanking her behind him. "Put your arms around my neck."

"But the ring—"

"Do it!"

Icelin wrapped her arms around him. Ruen lifted her onto his back and sprinted to the gap in the wall. Icelin felt as if she were flying. More beams dropped around them, but Ruen found a path through as if by magic. The fire and smoke were everywhere, but he kept running.

Suddenly they were through. Cool air hit Icelin's face. It was daylight.

The twisted opening spat them out onto a small dock behind the warehouse. Parts of it burned with the building, but Ruen didn't stop to see if it would hold their weight. He charged down the narrow platform all the way to the edge and jumped into the water.

The impact shook Icelin loose from Ruen's back, but he stayed beside her. The cold water shocked her limbs into functioning. With Ruen's aid, she swam to the surface.

"We'll stay in the harbor," Ruen said when they'd caught their breath. "Swim underwater as much as you can," he told her. "They'll be watching to see if we survived. We've got to find cover."

He dived down. Icelin followed, keeping a hand on his flank so she wouldn't lose him in the murky water. As far as she could tell, they were headed roughly in the direction of the shore.

They surfaced in a thick stand of brush about thirty feet from the dock. Sull waited in the weeds.

"I saw you go off the dock," he said. "Fannie slipped away. No one's watching that I can see."

Icelin was shaking by the time she got out of the water. When she came within reach, Sull pulled her against his chest, hugging her so hard Icelin couldn't breathe.

"I'm all right," Icelin said weakly. She patted him on the back.

"Thought I'd lost you, little one," the butcher said roughly. He released her and mopped his eyes with his apron. Ruen stood a little apart, scanning the area. The warehouse continued its slow collapse, but they were clear of the devastation.

"Let's get out of here," Ruen said finally. He moved away, crouching low along the shoreline, not waiting for their reply.

"Where are we goin'?" Sull asked. He led Icelin by the hand, half-supporting her. "She needs rest."

"Back into the water," Ruen said. He waded in up to his waist. "Keep her head up. She'll be fine."

The water felt colder. Icelin's teeth chattered, but she swam with Sull's aid, following Ruen into the harbor.

They swam clear of the dock and out into open water. The sky was gray and overcast. In the distance, deep blue clouds threatened rain, but the day was still too bright. Icelin felt horribly exposed. At any moment, she expected shouts to go up from the shore.

"Don't worry," Ruen said, seeing her expression. "We're going under." He took in her chattering teeth and general state of disarray. "Sull, you'll have to tow her if she slows."

"I can make it," Icelin said, but she slurred the words.

"We'll stay under until we reach the wreckage," Ruen said, nodding to the floating mass of Mistshore's main body. "We should be able to swim under the docks and footpaths. Ready?"

Icelin nodded, and they dived. Sull kept one arm around her and used the other to swim close to Ruen.

They swam for what seemed like an eternity. After a time, Icelin simply floated in Sull's grip, concentrating on keeping her breath in her body. When she felt she could bear no more, Sull angled upward to the light.

They came up under one of the wooden pathways. There was barely room for their heads underneath the rotting planks, but the sound of the waves lapping against the pilings concealed their gasping breaths.

Icelin could hear footsteps echoing loudly just above their heads. "Where are you taking us?" she whispered.

Ruen put a finger to his lips. He disappeared beneath the surface, leaving her and Sull to tread water.

"We should swim back to shore," Icelin said. "I don't like this." She expected Sull to echo the sentiment, but the butcher shook his head. Water plastered his red hair over his ears.

"I wouldn't have found you without him," Sull said. "He tracked you. Persistent as a demon, he was. Ghosted into that warehouse and took out the meanest of the elf's men without a sound."

"But why?" Icelin said. "He never wanted to help me. He could have left you on the beach to die."

"Maybe he is everythin' you thought he was," Sull said.

Ruen broke the surface a few feet away and waved a hand. Icelin experienced a renewed shock of weakness as she slogged through the water. "We're here," Ruen said.

"Where?" Icelin asked.

"If you can hold on for a little longer, I'm taking us someplace safe," Ruen said. "Nine feet straight down there's a figurehead: the Blind Mermaid, they call her. She sticks up from the sand, so you can't see her fish half. She's buried along with the rest of the *The Darter*."

"The Darter?" Sull said. "You mean she was part of a ship?"

"She still is," Ruen said. "But she has a more important job now. She's the guardian of a door, a secret door we're going to need. So we'll be paying her a visit." He raised a hand to forestall more questions. "When I go down, you'll follow a few feet behind. Don't be afraid of what you see, or how deep we go. Just keep following me."

Icelin nodded, but her hesitance must have shown. Ruen scowled and shook his head impatiently.

"This is important," he said, speaking to both of them. "You can't turn around. Once we go down, it's all the way. Or you'll drown. That's how they keep out the ones who aren't supposed to be there."

Isn't that us? Icelin thought, but she didn't give it voice.

"We'll follow you," she said. She'd decided to trust Ruen Morleth once, and now Sull seemed convinced of the man. He'd saved her from the fire, risking his own life to do so.

They dived. The water seemed darker here, a creature stretching out inky black arms to envelop them. When they got to the bottom, Icelin and Sull stayed back. Icelin pushed her drifting hair out of her eyes and strained to see what Ruen was doing ahead of them. Craning around his body, she saw the figurehead.

The wooden mermaid was covered in a shawl of seaweed, the thin, green streamers trailing behind her like a living cloak. Buried to the waist in sand, the mermaid stared up to the surface through her sightless eyes.

Ruen put his thumbs to both her eye sockets and pushed. The wooden orbs disappeared inside her skull, and Ruen backstroked furiously, propelling himself away from the figurehead.

Light burst from the mermaid's eyes, beams of illumination that spilled over her wooden sockets and down her rigid face like tears. The rotting wood glowed golden, suffusing, impossibly, with life.

The mermaid's skin turned white, and her hair moved in the water, shifting colors from brown to blue-green. She uncrossed her arms from in front of her bare breasts, brandishing a trident in one hand, and a glowing green orb in the other. She turned her head at an odd angle to regard them. Though her body now throbbed with life, her eyes remained vacant.

She doesn't really live, Icelin thought. She's a construct of some sort. A guardian, Ruen had said.

"Welcome to the Cradle," the mermaid spoke. The words reached Icelin's ears clearly, magically propelled through the water. "Those who seek entrance, come forward. But do no harm in Arowall's house, or face a slow death in Umberlee's embrace."

With those cryptic words, the mermaid lifted her arms, crossing the trident in front of her. The orb flashed green, and the trident glowed in answer. She brought it down in one swift stroke, driving the weapon into the sand covering her lower half.

A deep rumbling echoed beneath them. Awestruck, Icelin watched the sand roil, parting on either side of the mermaid's body. Contained by magic, the tempest of sand and water swirled around the mermaid and revealed her glossy silver tail. Beneath the webbed fin, a dark space yawned.

Lit by spheres of magical radiance, the narrow passage led into the hull of what looked like an ancient sailing ship. The wood around the animated figurehead was rotting and caked with barnacles, but somehow it remained intact.

Ruen swam for the passage; Icelin and Sull followed quickly. Icelin's chest ached to draw breath, and as she swam down the dark tunnel, she realized what Ruen meant about not turning back.

The sand was already swirling behind them, sealing off the entrance. The mermaid resumed her frozen pose, her sightless eyes betraying nothing of what lay beneath her fin. There was no way out behind them. It was death or forward.

CHAPTER 10

Cerest paced in front of the burned-out shell of the dockside warehouse. He stopped long enough to kick a smoking timber against the tin wall. A rattling crash brought down a rain of ash and smoke.

Ristlara and Shenan stood a little way off, looking anxious and unamused by his outburst.

"Come away, fool," Ristlara said. "The Watch is sure to bring a patrol. We won't be seen here with you."

"Tell your men to regroup. I want to know how many we lost." Cerest already knew Greyas was gone. Greyas, Melias, and Riatvin. Now he was entirely dependent upon the Locks and their hunters. The idea galled him, but what choice did he have?

"She walks with two companions now," Ristlara said. "The big one is an oaf, but he's strong; and I'll lay odds the thin one is a monk, and quite powerful. Think, Cerest," she said, putting a hand on his arm. "How can you be certain she possesses the powers Elgreth did? Shenan says she is an untried child."

"Can Shenan deny the evidence of her eyes?" Cerest waved an arm to encompass the devastated warehouse. "My untried child did this. The men may have slain Greyas and the rest, but *she* brought the building down. You heard her, Shenan; it wasn't her first display of such power. She is more than Elgreth ever was. While she is alive, I will have her."

Ristlara and Shenan exchanged doubtful glances. It infuriated Cerest. How dare they show such disrespect?

"Where do we search now?" Shenan spoke up. "The trail is cold."

"They can't go far," Cerest said. "If she is as unstable as I believe, she'll turn up again. Until then, we wait."

Cerest rubbed his face. He needed to rest. If his own body sought reverie, Icelin would be near exhaustion.

We'll both rest, Cerest thought, and tonight—yes, it would be tonight—we'll talk again. He would help her work through the trauma of the past. She had been scarred too—not physically, but the pain was there, a raw wound that only another, equally scarred being would understand. Those scars would be the link that bound them together. They would make each other whole.

"Cough it out, there's a good girl."

Sull smacked her on the back, forcing up more of the loathsome harbor water than Icelin thought possible for anyone to swallow.

She crouched on the floor of the lowest deck of *The Darter;* Sull and Ruen stood on either side of her. Behind them, a wall of water stretched weirdly from floor to ceiling, kept from rushing into the cabin by an invisible magical field that faltered and sprayed jets of water at random intervals.

In front of them, a trio of large, armored guards stood with drawn swords, the unfriendly ends pointed at each of their throats. The one pointed at Icelin bobbed uncertainly as she threw up around it. Icelin tried to appear as contrite as she could, under the circumstances.

"Where are we?" she asked when she could speak again.

"I told you: this is the back door," Ruen explained. "They'll check our weapons here." As he said it, the guards stepped forward, divesting Sull of his sash of butcher's tools. They took nothing from Ruen but the ring on his finger. Icelin saw his jaw tighten, but he said nothing.

Icelin allowed them to take the pack off her back without

resistance. She saw one guard's eye linger on the gold box buried at the bottom.

"What's in it?" he asked.

"An heirloom," Icelin said, "bequeathed to me by the last of my family."

"Open it," the guard said.

Icelin looked at Sull uncertainly. He knew what she was thinking. She'd not yet opened the mysterious box, found buried beneath the floorboards of Brant's shop. Who knew what it might contain?

"Arowall's rules state that no one may lose their possessions while under the protection of his hospitality," Ruen said. Icelin wondered whether his words were for her benefit, or the guard's.

The man glared at Ruen and spat on the deck. "I know the rules better 'an you, Ruen Morleth." He looked at Icelin. "I said open it, girl."

Icelin took out the box and laid it in her lap. She ran her fingers along the edges until she found the clasp. Thank the gods it wasn't locked. Releasing the catch, she lifted the lid.

Red velvet lined the inside of the box, but it was frayed and soaking wet from their swim. Nestled in the small space was a stack of folded parchment sheets, tied together with a black ribbon. The parchment and the ribbon were dry and perfectly preserved, obviously via some magical means. "Icelin" was inked on the top sheet.

"They look like letters," she said. She traced her name and felt a stab of disappointment. She had hoped Brant's words would be on the pages, but she didn't recognize the thick, black script proclaiming her name so boldly.

"Some heirloom." The guard sniffed. His fellows chuckled.

Icelin clutched the letters and tried not to let her anger show. It would be foolish to provoke these men.

Ruen laid a hand on the closest guard's arm. Immediately, the other two raised their swords.

"Step back," the largest of them warned.

"My apologies," Ruen said. He smiled easily and removed his hand. "I couldn't help but notice how cold your friend's skin is."

The guard he'd touched paled. Reading the mocking light in Ruen's eyes, he gripped his sword as if he might strike out at the thief.

"Get on with you," he said, his teeth gritted. "Though if it were up to me, I'd stick your head through that wall and let you breathe seawater."

Icelin quickly sealed the box and stood up. She wished she could read whatever was in the letters, but this was not the place. Palpable tension thickened the air. She had no idea what Ruen had done to offend the guards, but they stared at him now with murder in their eyes.

"You know the way," the guard said, still eyeing Ruen hatefully. "He's expecting you."

"You know this Arowall fellow?" Sull asked when they were past the guards. "I hope he likes you better than that lot."

"Arowall was captain of *The Darter*," Ruen said, "a pirate vessel for twenty years. When his ship finally went down, he'd strung it with so many magics salvaged from old cargo that the ship stayed intact. It drifted into the harbor and stayed here, resistant to water and, mostly, to time."

"What is *The Darter's* purpose now?" Icelin said.

"Without a ship, Arowall had to turn his hand to another profession," Ruen said, running his hand along the wall.

"The Cradle?" Sull said, echoing the mermaid's words. "Sounds awfully harmless for a pirate."

"Not exactly," Ruen said. He pointed ahead, where another pair of guards flanked a door at the opposite end of the ship. "Fighting was Arowall's second favorite activity, so he created a shrine to the sport. He died years ago, but his descendents—one of them is the man we're going to see, he goes by Arowall too—have been keeping up the business, and they turned *The Darter* into a secret passage to their domain."

The guards opened the portal and Ruen ushered them through.

Icelin's mouth fell open in shocked amazement.

She'd expected to enter another cramped cabin, but instead she beheld a tunnel through the seawater. It extended eight feet above their heads, reinforced by another magical shield. Water beaded and dripped on their heads in a steady drizzle. The air reeked of salt.

"They drain the water periodically," Ruen said, "so it doesn't flood the passage."

"Don't look sturdy to me," Sull said.

"It isn't." Icelin pointed to the stutters in the shield. The sensation of walking on water unnerved her. She kept her eyes off her feet. "Was the shield here before the Spellplague?" she asked.

"Yes," Ruen said. "The enchantments held. Most people who come to the Cradle come from Mistshore, walking above water. Only the lucky souls who can't afford to be seen entering the Cradle use this entrance now."

"Who?" Icelin asked.

Ruen shrugged. "Maybe a young noble. He wants a night of fun but doesn't want his face known in Mistshore. Long as he doesn't mind a swim, this is the way he comes."

The tunnel began a gradual, upward slope. At the end loomed another water wall.

Ruen passed through the opening first. Icelin followed, with Sull bringing up the rear.

Behind the wall Icelin could tell they were in the belly of another ship. The hull had been reinforced several times over. No visible magic greeted them beyond the water wall. A ladder led up to the main deck, and Icelin could see a square of dull sunlight above. The breeze blowing down the ladder was cool and smelled strongly of rain. She couldn't see anything beyond the opening, but she heard muffled voices.

She turned around and noticed for the first time the pair of guards standing on their side of the wall. One of them, a young man not much older than Icelin, stepped forward to speak to Ruen.

"Arowall sends his greetings, Ruen Morleth, and I bear a message. If you wish his protection, the cost will be the same as when last you came here. Can I tell him you will fight in the Cradle?"

"Yes," Ruen said.

"No, he won't," Icelin interrupted. "Ruen, what is this? We're not here to fight. You told us you were taking us someplace safe."

"Safety comes with a price," Ruen said. "Haven't you learned that yet? Fighting is Arowall's business. So if we want to stay here, that's what we do. Tell your master that I'm in," he told the guard. "Expect his champion to fall tonight."

"Bold words," the guard said. His face split in an involuntary grin. "Bells has no equal this past tenday."

"Bells?" Sull said. He snorted. "The champion is called Bells?"

"Death knells, that's why," said the guard. "They nicknamed her after she sent that poor bastard Tarodall into the pool. She hates it, but everyone likes a good nickname, you know."

"We need time to rest," Ruen said.

"Arowall says if you're committed to fighting, you can stay here in safety for the day," said the guard. "Fight's tonight, after gateclose."

"Give him my gratitude," Ruen said. The guard nodded and climbed the ladder. His partner followed, leaving them alone in the cabin, which reeked of mildew and the general stink of the harbor. Icelin found she was growing used to the smell. She wrinkled her nose. Likely because she was soaked in it, she thought.

"You've been here before?" Icelin asked Ruen when they'd arranged themselves on the floor near the back of the cabin.

"I only come here when I need protection," Ruen said, "when I'm desperate enough. We're safe here for the day. You should both sleep." He looked at Icelin. "We'll need whatever spells you can muster if things don't go well tonight. I see no way Cerest could track us here, but I want to be prepared."

"You said one night, and then we'd renegotiate the price for your aid," Icelin said. "The cameo can't possibly cover all you're doing for us."

Ruen laughed. "That, my lady, is the most profound understatement I've yet heard you make."

Icelin bristled. "You don't need to throw it in my face. In fairness to me, I hardly expected to be menaced by the undead, ambushed by a dozen men, interrogated by an insane elf who knows more about my life than I do, which, considering my powers of recollection, is distressing in the extreme. Then you drag me underwater, half drown me, and where do we end up? Back in Mistshore, in the teeth of gods alone knows what type of men, with only a warm place to sleep as consolation." Her brow furrowed. "Come to think of it, that's not terribly awful under the circumstances."

"You talk a lot," Ruen said.

"Only when I'm under immediate threat," Icelin said. "Keeps me calm."

Ruen nodded politely—a ludicrous gesture, considering his previous attitude toward her. And he was letting the subject of his payment drop like it was nothing of concern.

"Why are you doing this?" she demanded. "In case you hadn't guessed, I have no idea where this little adventure is taking us. You'd be wise to get as far away from me as you can. I don't have any coin to pay you, now or later. The Watch will have secured all my great-uncle's possessions. We didn't have a great deal to start with. I have nothing to offer you at the end of this long tunnel."

There, she'd admitted it. He would abandon them now, Icelin was sure, but at least she'd offered him truth. She heard Sull, already snoring softly in the opposite corner. Gods, she hoped she could keep him safe. She would give anything if he would abandon her to her fate too.

Ruen looked at her for a long breath. Icelin couldn't guess what he was thinking. The man had no range of expressions she could measure. He wasn't cold, exactly. Removed, was more like it. His eyes curtained his emotions.

Ruen reached into her pack and pulled out the gold box. The feathery designs caught the dim light from above and sparkled.

"You can give me that," he said. "Keep the letters."

Icelin considered. "What about your friend's protection?" she asked.

Ruen's eyes hardened. "Arowall is not a friend. He won't give us aid unless I fight in the Cradle. You heard the guard. His champion's been on a streak for a tenday; his crowd will be getting restless for new blood. No matter how much they may like Bells, they love an upset even more."

"So if you beat his champion, you help his business," Icelin said. She was beginning to understand the stakes. "You have to win his aid, not buy it."

"Yes. If I can win, we can negotiate with Arowall to hide us all, maybe for days."

"Then . . . we are agreed?" Icelin could hardly believe it. "You'll stay with us?"

He kept his eyes on the box. "I'll stay with you."

"You have my deepest thanks," Icelin said.

Ruen slid the box away into her pack. "Keep it hidden for now. And don't thank me. We made a bargain, and I'll keep it."

And with that, he was removed again, aloof. For those few breaths, he'd seemed like a normal man. Now he was the scarecrow—a blank face and a floppy hat, which he seemed always to hold onto, no matter how many times they'd been dunked in the harbor.

Icelin leaned back against the hull. With her immediate concern assuaged, she could feel her body relax. The frightened energy that had kept her moving was beginning to ebb, and she could feel the effects of the wild magic on her body.

To say that she was more exhausted than she'd ever been in her life would be a vast understatement of what was happening inside her. She felt like a child coming around from a long illness—or descending into one.

Every time she cast a spell, her energy returned more slowly. She'd never felt that strain before, not during her most arduous lessons with her teacher. What would the implications be if she was forced to cast more spells?

Ruen was right. She needed sleep to recover as much strength as she could. Her eyes burned, but she couldn't drift off. Restless questions flitted through her mind: Cerest, Ruen, the letters, her family. She couldn't settle on which mystery baffled her most. To distract herself, she picked the easiest.

"Why did the guard recoil when you touched him?" she asked Ruen. She remembered vividly the shocked, frozen look on the man's face.

"Because I have cold hands," Ruen said. He shrugged dismissively.

"No, that was what you said about him."

"Did I?" Ruen leaned his head back and closed his eyes. "You have a good memory."

"I have a perfect memory," Icelin said.

"I know. Sull told me." He opened one eye. "Nothing to brag about there."

"Nothing to—"

No one has ever said that to me, Icelin thought. The observation was so simply, absurdly true, an echo of everything she'd ever tried to tell people, that she started to laugh. At first out loud, then under her breath, until tears streaked her cheeks.

The wave of grief shocked her with its intensity. She slid down the curving wall, curling into a tight ball. She covered her head with her hands, trying to be silent, unwilling to cry out her misery in front of her companions.

She heard Sull stir in his corner, but Ruen said, tersely, "Leave it. Go back to sleep."

He thinks if Sull comes over, that will be the end of me, Icelin thought. I'll be howling, and bring every damn guard above and below the water running to throw us off the ship. He was probably right.

Wiping her eyes, Icelin took out the box again and removed the stack of letters. She wanted to read them. Even if they weren't in Brant's hand, they were the closest link she had to her great-uncle.

She removed the ribbon and unfolded the topmost sheet, the one bearing her name.

> *Dear Granddaughter,*
>
> *I leave today on a new adventure. Faerûn calls to me, and I find I must answer her gentle whisper.*

Granddaughter. Icelin mouthed the word. The letters were from Elgreth. She read the rest of the letter, hastily scrawled in the same bold writing. There was no mention of spellscars or powerful abilities, just a farewell from an aging adventurer setting off on another journey.

Elgreth was my best friend.

Cerest's words haunted her. Did she really want to know the man who'd been friends with the monster that hunted her now?

She held the letter, staring at it but seeing Cerest's scarred face instead. She folded the parchment and laid it beside her with the other letters. They beckoned to her, silently, but her arms felt weighted to her sides. She couldn't focus her eyes. Sleep, so elusive, was claiming her at last.

You speak to me of adventure, Grandfather. Icelin sighed. I know the word. I've already had enough for one lifetime.

Ruen waited, alert in the dark hold. He watched the square of dull sunlight above him turn steel gray, and then the rain came with full force. The air in the hold grew chilled, and a puddle formed at the foot of the ladder. The rain did not abate until the sky began to darken and the gateclose bell was near to sounding. Through all the weather changes, his companions slept, the butcher snoring in intermittent gulps and wheezes.

Icelin lay on her side, twitching now and then in the throes of some dream. If not for those small movements, Ruen might have thought she was a resting corpse. Her face was pale, her cheeks etched with dark circles where exhaustion had worked on her.

Before the past night's ordeal, she might have been beautiful, in a fragile, glass-blown sort of way. Grief had certainly left its mark on her, but the unstable magic she wielded had drained her more than any emotional trauma. She was dangerous, to herself and those around her, anytime she used the Art.

Yet, what choice did she have, if she had any hope of survival?

With that thought in mind, Ruen took out the *sava* pawn and softly called Tesleena's name.

"Before you speak a word, I want you to relay your exact location and that of Icelin Tearn." Tesleena's voice was colder than the air in the hold. She sounded like she hadn't slept in days.

"Are we having a rough time, darling?" Ruen said, smiling to himself. He was going to enjoy this more than he'd thought.

"Is the girl safe?" Tesleena repeated, louder.

"She is," Ruen said. "I'm glad to see the Warden's ankle-nipper has her priorities intact, even if she is a liar."

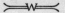

"You haven't been deceived, Ruen. You were only told what you needed to know—that Icelin is wanted by the Watch—"

"And a fair number of other interested parties," Ruen interrupted, "as I discovered last night. Had I possessed this information beforehand, we might not have strayed so dangerously close to death. What business is this, Tesleena? If you won't speak truth, I'll wait for Tallmantle's word. I give you nothing until then."

There was a long pause, during which Ruen imagined he could hear Tesleena planting her pretty fist into a wall, assuming wizards did such things. Perhaps she blasted it with fire instead.

"Icelin is being pursued by an elf, Cerest Elenithil," Tesleena said finally. "I assume you've gathered that much?"

"Yes."

"He claims she stole property from him, but he has yet to appear before the Watch to give personal testimony against her. And now he has disappeared to Mistshore, searching for her. We have information that Icelin confided to a Watchman friend of hers that the elf had a personal grudge against her. I have men questioning Cerest's contacts in the city, but there's little information to be had about him. We've determined he was not born in Waterdeep, but he came to the city at a young age. His conduct in business is without fault, but the details of his private life are sketchy. He was the second or third son of a noble house, but he was not raised in a state of wealth or privilege. Nevertheless, he would have been significantly above Icelin in station. The only event which might link them happened five years ago, at a boardinghouse in Dock Ward."

"It wasn't the fire," Ruen said, before she could relate the story he'd overheard in the warehouse. "The elf wasn't scarred by Icelin's hand; he admitted as much. He wants her for another purpose."

Stunned silence met this pronouncement. "Has Cerest

encountered the girl? You gave your word she was safe!"

"She is," Ruen said. "I can keep her away from Cerest, but I need to know how many men are after us."

"Ruen, by the gods, *bring her in* and the Watch will see to her safety. This is beyond your skill or caring. Why do you delay?"

"Perhaps you've turned me into a loyal Watch dog—officer—after all," Ruen said blithely. "She's safer with me, and she pays better. I'll be in touch when you have more information for me to work with."

He clenched the pawn in a fist until the magical connection died.

"What do you think?"

Daerovus Tallmantle pushed out of his chair and leaned over the desk. "I think you owe me new furniture."

Tesleena looked down at the desk. Her fingernails had left deep furrows in the wood. She waved a hand impatiently, and the marks smoothed out and disappeared.

"I'd wager Icelin Tearn wishes she had your control in magic, if not in temper," the Warden commented.

Tesleena nodded, but she didn't seem to be listening. "We'll track her from the warehouse. Her unstable Art will make her easy to find." The sorceress winced. "For Cerest, as well."

"All the more reason to step up our efforts." Daerovus took a sheet of parchment from his desk drawer and handed it to Tesleena. "Take this down, if you would. It's an order for a second, smaller patrol to join the first in Mistshore. These men will not be wearing Watch tabards."

"How will Ruen know them?" Tesleena asked.

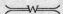

"You heard him. Ruen has no intention of cooperating willingly with our search," the Warden said. "Since his release from the dungeons, he's been sullen but resigned to his role as an agent. Something changed last night. He's regained some of his old arrogance. He hasn't shown such spirit since the night we captured him." The Warden looked thoughtful. "Icelin Tearn has lit a fire in him. Time will tell if that will work to our advantage."

Tesleena sniffed. "I don't see how it could possibly be to the good. He was going to be our eyes in Mistshore. We should have known his defiance would win out over sense."

"He still might be of use," Daerovus said.

The outcome of Icelin Tearn's ordeal would be revealing in more ways than one, if everyone involved survived.

Ruen slid the *sava* pawn away in his shirt and checked to be sure Icelin was still asleep. After sleeping through the butcher's heavy snores, he was certain it would take a cannon blast to wake her.

He looked up at the hatch. The square of sunlight had disappeared. A sliver of moonlight spilled down the ladder in its place. He could hear bodies stirring above decks. They would be coming to ready him for the Cradle in another bell.

Automatically, he felt for his ring. He'd known the guards would confiscate it, but he still felt naked. Whatever else came of the fight, his body was going to hurt like unholy fire after it was over. He just hoped the old man wouldn't let him die.

The dream took her again.

She stood in the center of the ruined tower, looking straight up at the sun burning through a gap in the ceiling. Her skin tingled. The hair stood up on her arms. She didn't like this place. The shadows moved when she wasn't looking. Frightened whispers—the footsteps of folk who'd walked and died here a century ago—made it impossible to hear her own thoughts. She turned in a circle, searching for the gap in the wall, but something impeded her.

I am a child, Icelin thought. Her limbs would not move properly. She stumbled and fell, scraping her knees on rock.

She started to cry. Her knees hurt. The sun burned her neck. It was so hot in the tower. Why didn't someone come to pick her up, to take her away from this place?

"Icelin," said a feminine voice. She didn't recognize it, but it spoke with enough urgency to make her turn. Icelin tried again to stand and was suddenly knocked from her feet.

"Get her out!"

The shadows were shouting at her. It was too hot. Icelin looked up, and her body burst into flames.

CHAPTER 11

Icelin awoke shivering, but her body poured sweat. Her bodice was saturated. She buried her head in her hands and waited for the dream fear to subside.

In the panic and grief of the night before, she'd almost forgotten the nightmare. After the boardinghouse fire, she'd been terrified of seeing the faces of the dead in her nightmares. But she only ever dreamt of the tower. It was a perversion of the tower Nelzun had created for her. She thought she'd left it behind when she'd left her great-uncle's shop, but the tower had followed her, to the warehouse and now here.

Drawing a slow breath, Icelin forced away the frightening images. Her heartbeat resumed its normal pace, and she drifted for a time, meditating, summoning the energy she would need to call her magic for another day. The words of the spells were there; she had no need to memorize them, but the power required concentration.

When she was finished, she opened her eyes and looked around, blinking in the darkness. Slowly, she recognized her surroundings. The ship's hold—their sanctuary for the day.

She longed to cover her head and sleep for days on end. The cold combined with the raw emptiness in her stomach forced her to a sitting position. Her hair, stiff from multiple dunkings in salt water, stood out in snarls all over her head. And the smell . . .

Icelin groaned. The smell was coming off her body.

Seeing she was awake, Sull ambled over to sit next to her. The butcher looked and smelled as unkempt as she.

"How do you feel?" he asked tentatively. His face was pale under his red hair.

"Food," Icelin said. She tried to run a hand through her hair and ended up getting her fingers stuck. Cursing a streak that would have made Brant blush, she yanked her hand free. "Food," she repeated, and smiled for Sull's benefit. "Succulent lamb's stew, to start, with fresh vegetables smothered in butter. Sharp cheese melted on bread slices. For the main course"—she scrunched up her face, pretending to give the matter grave consideration—"nothing whatsoever that includes fish." She waved a hand imperiously. "That's my order. Off with you."

Sull's deep chuckle filled the hold. "Ah, thank you, girl. I was worried you'd lost your good humor forever." He shot her a look of chagrin. "As to the food: the waterskins are fine, but the rations are soaked. I don't think they're fit to eat. But I found this next to me when I woke up."

He handed her a loaf of crusty bread. Icelin tore off a hunk and bit into it, expecting the worst. Surprisingly, the bread was flavorful and chewy inside. She took several more bites and a swig from her waterskin and immediately started to feel better.

"Where's Ruen?" she asked, noticing for the first time that the thief—monk, she reminded herself—was not in the hold.

"Don't know," Sull said, but I heard a lot of activity going on up there. Must be near fightin' time."

Icelin listened to the footsteps clattering above them. Sull was right. The voices were building into a dull roar. She wondered how many people would be present for the fight. Her earlier apprehension returned in full.

Ruen meant to win them protection by fighting in the Cradle. But for how long could they realistically hope to stay safe? Icelin had never met Ruen's contact, but already she didn't trust the man. If Cerest offered him coin enough, Icelin had a feeling he would betray them in a heartbeat.

"Sull," she said.

The butcher slanted her a look, his mouth puffed up with bread. The sight made Icelin smile and twisted her heart at the same time.

"If Ruen succeeds tonight, I want you to leave us. I trust Ruen to take care of me, and I don't want you in anymore danger on my behalf."

"Aw, don't go startin' that foolishness again." Sull wiped the crumbs from his mouth with an angry swipe. "Doesn't matter what that thief's done, you need me looking out for you, unless"—he hesitated, his face reddening—"unless you think I'm slowin' you down." He clenched his hands into fists. "I know I'm not much good in a fight."

"Sull, that's not what I—"

"I know it!" His face crumpled. He looked near tears. The sudden shift in mood caught Icelin completely off guard. "I know you're worried about me gettin' hurt on your account. It isn't fair—me strappin' myself to you, makin' you worry. Selfish is what it is."

"Selfish?" Icelin said incredulously. "You've risked your life over and over for me. I'm the one who's selfish and no good in a fight. Without you, Sull, I'd be lost." Icelin felt dangerously close to tears herself.

"But it isn't for you," Sull said, his voice barely audible. He dropped his head in his hands.

Feeling helpless, Icelin scooted closer to the big man and put her arm around his shoulders. "I don't understand," she said. "What do you mean, Sull? If not for me, why are you here?"

Sull sniffed loudly. He wiped his eyes but wouldn't look at her. "I love my shop," he said. "Always wanted one of my own, ever since I was a lad."

Guilt stabbed Icelin. "I'll get you back to your shop. I promise."

"No!" Sull roared. He jerked away from her as if he'd been

stung. "Serves me right if the place burns to the ground. Let me finish, lass, I beg you."

Icelin nodded, staying silent.

"I love my shop," he continued, each word a trial for him. "In the early days, all the folk knew me. Once I got established in the neighborhood, I helped others just startin' out. Wasn't anything to it, I just liked 'em and wanted 'em to have the same chance I got. So I gave meat to the baker and the blacksmith, kept 'em fed over two winters so they would have coin to spare for their wares. I spent the summer helpin' Orlan Detrent put a roof over his cow pen. Hot as the Nine Hells, it was, but we laughed over a pitcher of ale afterwards."

"That's wonderful," Icelin said. "They were lucky to know you."

Sull's eyes filled with fresh misery. "Not so lucky. You put me too high in your heart, lass, and I don't deserve it. I made friends with a lot of folk, so when Darthol and his boys came to the neighborhood, they knew to come straight to me."

"Darthol?" Icelin hadn't heard the name in years. Darthol Herendon had conducted a brief but lucrative extortion operation in Blacklock Alley and other parts of South Ward. Icelin remembered Brant had insisted on escorting her everywhere she went during Darthol's brief "reign." Her great-uncle hadn't wanted her to cross paths with any of Darthol's men, though Icelin suspected he'd paid a substantial amount to ensure her safety. Fortunately, they'd been spared any lasting strife. Darthol's body had been found in a garbage heap one night. Folk thought he'd been stabbed to death by one of his own men.

"I didn't know you ever encountered him," Icelin said. "I'm sorry for it. That was a dark time for many of us."

"Darker than you know," Sull said. He wasn't crying now. He looked old and sad. "I was cleanin' out the shop one night. I like to work late, when the streets are uncluttered, but I was being quiet so not to rouse folk. They didn't hear me at first."

The words hurt him. Icelin squeezed his shoulder. "You don't have to tell me," she said.

But he went on. "I had the big wooden washtub outside the back door, couple of candles lit so I could see. My cleavers were all in the tub, needin' a good scrub. I'd just picked up the rag"—he mimicked the gesture, lost in his tale—"when they came around the side of the shop, draggin' old Orlan by his bare feet."

"Oh, Sull," Icelin gasped.

"He wasn't dead," Sull said, "least not then. Face was covered in blood and sort of mashed in, but his eyes were open. He stared at me the whole time they were beatin' him, beggin' with his eyes for help. Somehow, I was stuck. I couldn't get my arms out of that washtub. I had my hand on a knife, gods forgive me, and I couldn't raise it up out of the water." He looked at his shaking hands, seeing a weapon that wasn't there. "I could have planted it in that son of a whore's back before his boys were ever the wiser. Worst of it was, Darthol knew I was there all the time. He beat poor Orlan to death in front of me. He *knew* I didn't have the guts to stop him."

"You were frightened, and rightly so," Icelin said. "Even if you'd killed Darthol, his men would have slain you."

"I wasn't afraid," Sull said. "Not for my life, anyway. All I could think was that they'd take my shop. Everythin' I'd worked for—I didn't want to lose it." Finally, he looked at her, but his eyes were bleak, unfocused. "The years haven't changed me any. You'd think they would have, but they haven't. I'm still selfish. When you came into my shop, and those elves were after you, I wasn't really aidin' *you*. I'm not so noble. All I could see was Orlan's bloody face, the whites of his eyes bulgin' out when he died. Whenever I look at you, I see him. You have to let me stay with you, Icelin. I know it's askin' too much. My burden's nothin' to do with you. But if I leave you, I'm never going to see anythin' but Orlan's face."

He started to cry then in earnest. Icelin laid her head on his shoulder so he would not have to see her. They sat that way for a long time while the big man sobbed quietly. Above them, the voices rose and fell, but that world seemed a thousand miles away from the cramped ship's hold.

Icelin reached for Sull's hand and found it waiting for her. "Sull?"

"Yes, lass?" He sounded remote, drained.

"Please stay with me." Her voice shook. "I'm selfish too, and frightened. Will you stay with me, until it's all over?"

He sighed deeply. "I'll stay. Thank you, Icelin."

Icelin felt his big body relax slowly, the knotted muscles loosening. The misery was still there, but she could feel him burying it.

When she lifted her head, Ruen was coming down the ladder. Their eyes met for a breath, and Icelin knew, though she could not read his crimson gaze, that he'd heard every word of Sull's confession. She nodded minutely. He mirrored the gesture.

"Thank you for the bread," Icelin said. "I assume you left it for us?"

Ruen nodded. "I couldn't arrange a bath for you. Perhaps if I win the tournament. Something to hope for, eh?" He wrinkled his nose.

Icelin glowered at him, but Sull said, "Tournament? You mean you have to fight more than once?"

"I'm a new entrant," Ruen said. "I'll have at least three matches before I get to fight Bellaril—Bells." He picked up Icelin's cloak and pack. "Keep these close," he said, handing them to her. "They're ready for us."

No matter how intense her apprehension about the Cradle, Icelin was grateful to climb the ladder out of the oppressive ship's hold.

On the main deck, night had fallen. Stars canopied the harbor, and the remnants of the day's rain glimmered on the wet wood. Torches lined the deck, lending smoky illumination to a sight Icelin could not have imagined in her wildest fancies.

The Cradle perched on the water, bounded by a loose circle of four half-sunk ships. The vessels listed at various angles, half supporting each other, their masts crisscrossing in a vast web work of rigging and wood. Rope bridges hung suspended from the main masts, allowing foot traffic to flow between the four ships. Figures swarmed the bridges or climbed, monkeylike, on the rigging to find a better vantage point for the activity.

On each of the four ships, wooden benches were bolted in rows to the deck, creating a sort of graduated seating on the listing surfaces. These rough seats were already packed with people, and the unlucky few who couldn't find a bench were perched on the rails, their feet dangling above the water. All told, there must have been hundreds of people crowded on the ships.

In the center of the Cradle, water was allowed to flow freely in a sealed off pool. Wooden platforms, not unlike Ruen's raft, had been arranged at various points, so it was possible to cross from ship to ship without touching the water. Four guards arranged themselves on the outer fringes and took charge of distributing weapons.

Icelin watched a pair of men walk out onto the platforms. Both carried the same weapon: a spiked ball and chain. To her shock, they bore no shields and wore no armor. The crowd screamed and pounded their feet when the fighters faced each other and swung the chains like deadly pendulums in front of their bodies.

"Gods above," Sull said, shaking his head. "I'd never have believed such a sight if I hadn't seen it with my own eyes."

"The platforms are stained red," Icelin said, half to herself. "What happens if they fall in the water?"

"Nothing, if they can get out fast enough," Ruen said. "They stock the pool with blindfin, shark, eel, and whatever else they can find that's vicious enough."

Icelin flinched as the combatants leaped at each other. The spiked balls whistled through the air, thudding sickly into flesh. The crowd cheered wildly. Both men fell back, clutching gaping wounds to the leg and flank.

"The winner will bleed to death before he claims his prize," Icelin said.

Ruen shook his head. "He only has to stay on his feet. Once the victor is confirmed, Arowall authorizes the winner to receive healing."

"Where is Arowall now?" Icelin asked, leaning close so Ruen would hear her over the crowd.

"You won't see him until after the tournament," Ruen said. "He watches the matches from there." He pointed to the largest ship in the circle.

In the Cradle, the combatants were already tiring. The heavy weapons were difficult to maneuver under the best of circumstances. On the water they were clumsy and shook both men's balance. The taller of the two swung with both hands. His opponent dodged back but tripped on an uneven board. He went down on his knees at the edge of the platform.

Sensing victory, the man still on his feet leaped across to his opponent's platform. Frantically, the man on his knees tried to scramble away, but there was nowhere left to go but into the water. Hurling the heavy weapon at his opponent, the man dived into the water.

The crowd went crazy, piling against the rails to see if the man would be devoured by sharks.

His head popped up a few feet away, next to another platform. He hoisted himself up, and for a breath it looked like he would make it. But the taller opponent had been watching, biding his time.

As soon as the man's shoulders came out of the water, the taller opponent swung the ball, releasing it to fly across the water.

The ball impacted between his opponent's shoulder blades. Blood spurted, and the man lost his grip on the platform. Jerking, he sank into the water.

Icelin thought the wound hadn't been very deep, but then she saw the water churning, the flash of a gray fin.

"Gods," she said, "how could he leave him for the sharks?"

"It was a clever move," Ruen said. He watched the man intently. "He'd already taken a wound to the thigh. He couldn't jump from platform to platform, which is what his opponent was counting on. Essentially, he had one shot, and it turned out to be a good one."

"Do they always fight to the death?" Icelin asked.

"No," Ruen said. "You have the opportunity to yield, but many don't. The winner's purse is too tempting, and the crowd doesn't like a coward."

A guard approached their group. "I'm to escort you down," he said to Ruen.

Ruen turned to follow the guard down a ladder. "Stay at the rail where I can see you," he told Icelin and Sull. "This will likely take all night."

"Good luck," Sull said doubtfully. He stood shoulder to shoulder with Icelin at the rail. Both were too tense for conversation.

There was no formal announcement when the fighters came into the Cradle—no names, no mention of how many victories each entrant had won. The crowd cheered their favorites and jeered others, according to no pattern Icelin could see.

She waited for the crowd's reaction when Ruen entered the Cradle. Would they favor him?

After what seemed like an eternity, she saw his old leather hat bob into view as he came up a short flight of stairs to the platform on the far side of the Cradle. Hushed murmurs ran through the spectators when they caught sight of him. He removed his hat and handed it to one of the guards standing at the bottom of the steps. When he returned to the platform, he raised both hands in the air, like a conductor readying his minstrels. He bowed low—Icelin could have sworn he winked at her as he straightened.

The crowd erupted in wild applause.

"Seems they like 'im," Sull said. "We should take that as a good sign."

Icelin nodded absently. She was waiting to see Ruen's opponent.

" 'E's a stick, this one," wheezed a man standing at Icelin's elbow. "Maltreth's gonna break him, you watch now."

"Oh, really," Icelin said, her temper prickling. "The crowd doesn't share your opinion."

"Ha!" The man slapped the rail. "Don't jingle your coins on this bunch. They're only cheering the poor bastard 'cause they know what's coming. Crowd loves to see the little ones get squished. Borbus!" he shouted across the deck. A pudgy man with skin the color of prunes looked up. "What're the odds on the skinny boy?"

"Ten to one, Sheems," the man shouted back. "There's a side bet says the sharks get to cut their teeth on 'im."

"You want in on that?" Sheems said, turning back to Icelin.

Icelin didn't bother to reply. She was watching Ruen stride confidently out to his starting platform. He waved to the roaring crowd, a lopsided grin stretched across his normally expressionless face. Icelin had never seen him look that pleased with himself.

"Gods give me strength," she murmured. "Tell me he's just playing the crowd, Sull. If he doesn't keep his wits, he'll get his head bit off out there."

"Among other parts of 'im," Sull said, pointing to the other side of the Cradle.

A man stepped away from the guards and climbed the stairs. He was not as big as Icelin had feared, but his musculature far outstripped Ruen's wiry frame. He carried a long, barb-tailed whip in his right hand. On his left, he wore a pair of polished brass knuckles.

The guard holding Ruen's hat stepped forward, raising his sword to silence the crowd. He then turned to Ruen and said something that Icelin and the watching crowd couldn't hear.

Icelin saw Ruen shake his head. The guard's face scrunched up in confusion, and he said something else, more emphatically this time. Ruen shook his head again. The same lopsided, complacent grin was still plastered to his face.

The crowd was starting to get restless, stamping their feet and whistling. This seemed to galvanize the guard, who waved a hand at Ruen as if to say, "good luck," and walked back down the stairs.

Maltreth, the man with the whip, assumed a crouched stance on his platform. Ruen stood, weaponless, with his arms loose at his sides.

"He was tryin' to get Ruen to take a weapon," Sull said, nodding to where the guard stood at the base of the stairs. A whip dangled from his right wrist. "Guess Ruen didn't need it," Sull said uncertainly.

The guard raised his sword again, and an ear-piercing whistle sounded from somewhere above their heads. It must have been the starting whistle, for Ruen's opponent immediately charged forward, leaping from his platform to the one floating adjacent. He swung his whip and snapped it above the water.

Shouts and wild applause erupted from the crowd.

"He's a peacock," Icelin said. "Strutting around like that's a waste of energy." She switched her attention to Ruen, but the man still hadn't moved. He stood, his arms at his sides, watching Maltreth with a bored expression. "Oh, that's perfect," she murmured.

"What?" Sull said. Icelin noticed he was gripping the rail as hard as she. "What's he doing?"

"Baiting him," Icelin said, "drawing him in. But he can't keep it up for long. The whip has reach. The barbs will tear him open."

Maltreth jumped again, and this time when the whip cracked, the edge of Ruen's platform splintered.

"That's done it. He'll have to move now," Sull said. "What's he waiting for?"

"I don't know. Oh, gods, he wouldn't go that far, would he?"

"What?"

"Move. *Move!"* Icelin shouted, but the crowd drowned out her voice.

Crack.

"Maltreth takes the first bite!" Sheems yelled gleefully from next to her.

Sull cursed. Icelin gripped his hand. A dark stain soaked through Ruen's sleeve. The barbs tangled in cloth and flesh.

Ruen staggered back, clutching his injured arm. He slid to his knees amid thunderous applause from the crowd. They might as well have been foaming at the mouth, Icelin thought.

Maltreth grinned at Ruen. He let the whip sway in his hands, swinging it back and forth like a skipping rope. The force was not enough to dislodge the barbs, but the whip pulled and tore new gashes in Ruen's skin.

He's waiting for Ruen to make a move so he can pull the whip out, Icelin thought. No matter what Ruen did, the wound would tear open when the barbs came out. Why had he let himself be hit? Icelin had seen Ruen fight. He could have dodged the blow easily.

She saw Maltreth take a step forward, then another, and suddenly Icelin wasn't paying attention to Ruen anymore. She was focused on Maltreth's shuffling steps, and remembering the way Ruen had dodged Cerest's attacks in the warehouse. Maltreth was far less graceful than the elf. His body was painfully readable.

"It can't be that easy," Icelin said.

"What?" Sull repeated, with a look of anxious annoyance. "If you're going to map out the battle, lass, at least let me in on the outcome."

"Watch," Icelin commanded.

Maltreth shuffled another step and jerked the whip. Ruen howled in pain. Icelin couldn't hear the sound, but she saw his face twist in agony. The whip hadn't come out of his wound. He pivoted toward her, and Icelin saw what she'd been hoping to see. She grabbed Sull and pointed.

Ruen wasn't holding his wound, which continued to bleed freely. He was clutching the slack end of the whip. Maltreth couldn't see it. He gave in to the cheering crowd and turned his face up, smiling in smug satisfaction. As soon as his attention left Ruen, the monk yanked the slack end of the whip with all his strength.

Maltreth's body teetered, his eyes bulging as the whip left his hands. He stumbled to the edge of the platform, but instead of pitching into the water, he jumped, using his forward motion to get him across the water.

He landed on Ruen's platform. The monk had already steadied himself in anticipation of the extra weight. Ruen tore the barbs out of his arm and threw the whip across the Cradle. Blood dripped copiously from his wound, but he ignored it and turned his attention completely to Maltreth.

Now he's within striking distance, Icelin thought. No more reach weapons to deal with. For Ruen, the match had not truly begun until now.

Maltreth, for his part, looked furious. Ruen had humiliated him in front of the mob, and now he was down to one weapon.

Raising his fists so Ruen could not help but see the brass

knuckles, Maltreth came in low, aiming for a quick jab to Ruen's ribs.

Ruen dodged, grabbed the man's wrist and twisted it away from his body. The crowd collectively winced and sat back in their seats. Their reaction might have been comical had Maltreth's arm not been dangling at an odd angle to his side. He staggered back but kept his other fist raised to defend himself.

The crowd waited, tense, for Ruen to finish him off. Maltreth was outclassed in a fistfight with the monk and everyone, including Maltreth, knew it.

Ruen kept his distance and spoke to Maltreth. They couldn't hear the words, but Icelin could see the guard at the base of the stairs preparing to draw his sword.

"He's offering him the chance to give it up," Sheems said. He'd been subdued ever since Ruen turned the fight around. "Crowd won't like that."

He was right. Jeers and booing came down from the crowd. People on the rope bridges stamped their feet, spitting at Ruen and sending dust and debris raining over the crowd.

Egged on by the violence of the outburst, Maltreth shook his head and spat at Ruen's feet. He charged, swinging his functioning fist for Ruen's head.

Twisting, Ruen caught Maltreth around the mid-section in a series of quick punches Icelin had trouble following with her eyes. When he ceased, Maltreth folded, collapsing to the platform. He was unconscious before his head hit the wood.

And just like that, it was over. The guard drew his blade and pointed at Ruen. The crowd cheered the newcomer's victory.

So it went throughout the night. Icelin and Sull stood at the rail, watching combatant after combatant enter the ring. Ruen fought three more times, and each time he took no weapon, but managed to disarm his opponent and end the fight with his fists. Sometimes it took longer, and he collected wounds over various parts of his body. He never showed it in his face, but Icelin could tell the injuries were taking their toll. Ruen wasn't moving as fast, and his punches were easier to track.

"He's going to be worn out for the final match," Icelin said. "How many damn fighters are left? It must be almost dawn."

"They're down to it now," Sull said. "Ruen's got where he needs to be. I heard Sheems say the winner's purse is a big one, on account of how long Bellaril's been champion." He leaned heavily against the rail, looking as anxious as she felt. "She won't give it up easy. Still, he's got this far. If he can hold out, he'll get healin' at the end of the match."

Icelin wondered what this Bellaril would look like. As reigning champion, she was only required to defend her title against the winner of the tournament, which meant she would be rested and, more importantly, she'd probably been watching the entire tournament to get a measure of her opponent.

Icelin saw Ruen climb back to the platform. He was still moving slowly, but his muscles were loose. He looked as relaxed as he had during the first match.

At the other end of the Cradle, the guards parted to admit a stout figure with a wild mane of strawberry blonde hair.

Bellaril was a heavyset dwarven woman with ruddy skin and large blue eyes. She wore plain brown breeches and a white vest cross-stitched with leather cord. Her face was as devoid of expression as Ruen's when she ventured out to her platform. She nodded to Ruen, and he returned the gesture.

Instead of cheering Bellaril, the spectators stamped their feet, and several of them produced small hand bells, waving them furiously above their heads. The din was shrill and loud enough to drown out Waterdeep's own great bells.

The guard raised his sword for quiet and approached the combatants. He spoke to each of them in turn. Bellaril answered his query regarding weapons with a shake of her head.

"Fist to fist, then," Sull said when the guard left the platform without distributing weapons.

This did not reassure Icelin. As soon as the guard was down the stairs, Bellaril darted forward, jumping nimbly from her platform to Ruen's, landing as far from him as she possibly could in the small space. The dwarf looked up, meeting Ruen's gaze and smiling.

CHAPTER 12

Watchman Tarvin surveyed the vibrant embers and ash clouds of the Hearth fire with one hand raised to shield his eyes against the wall of heat. It reminded him briefly of the burned warehouse he'd seen on the shore—or the smoking skeleton of a boardinghouse.

The metal basin from which the Hearth flames ascended had steep sides, but the bottom of the structure sat several feet below the walkway, allowing easy access.

The setup was ingeniously designed and protected the surrounding structures from damage quite well. The basin's inner shell had long ago turned an oily black color. The smells of cooking fish, meat, and the occasional spice were everywhere, but did nothing to mitigate the nauseating odor of the bodies gathered around the fire for warmth or sustenance.

There were no benches near the outside of the basin. People sat on the crude walkways built around the pit, cradling children in their laps or leading the elderly by the arm.

A pack of young girls, the youngest no more than five years old, was selling cooking spits for a copper a foot. Tarvin bought two from one of the older girls and shooed the rest away.

He leaned close to the child's ear when he paid her and asked in a confidential whisper if she'd seen a particular young woman walking by the Hearth.

"Black hair, white skin like a ghost's," he said, and he saw the girl's eyes widen. "Not a real ghost," he said quickly. "There's a man with her—tall, with red hair all over his head. Have you seen anyone like that passing this way?"

The girl shook her head. Tarvin gave her the copper coins and sent her off. He scanned the crowd a second time, his eyes coming to rest on a woman sitting alone near the edge of the fire. She was wrapped in a thin, dirty cloak, trying to blend in with the crowd.

In need of some amusement, Tarvin crouched next to the woman. He smiled when she averted her face. She had straight, drab brown hair and a tiny hooked scar on the bridge of her nose.

"Can I buy you dinner, pretty lass?" He held up his newly acquired spits, twirling them like batons.

The woman looked at him, but she didn't smile. "What are you doing here?" she demanded. "This is my territory."

"Lovely Deelia, I'd never infringe on your authority. I was just doing some independent scouting," Tarvin said. He made a vague gesture to the outer rim wreckages.

"You'd better hope she's not out there," Deelia said. "That's gang territory."

"Yes, it would be a shame if they dragged her off, had their fun, and didn't leave any pieces for us to find," Tarvin drawled.

Deelia shot him a look, but she didn't comment. Tarvin knew she didn't want to be out here anymore than he did. But the Warden had spoken, and the Watch had answered the Wolfhound's call. Icelin Tearn would be found and hauled in from Mistshore on the end of a leash if need be.

"Foolish to come down here," Deelia said. "This place'll eat her alive. What was she thinking?"

"She's afraid of the wolves," Tarvin said. "Us," he clarified when Deelia only stared at him.

The Watchwoman shook her head and turned her attention back to scanning the crowd for Icelin. Tarvin wanted to tell her not to waste her time.

The crowd huddled closest to the bright flames was mostly made up of women and children. Tarvin had thought this would be the first place she'd run to, with the late season darkness running cold and the wind colder still on the harbor. If the gangs hadn't already caught up to her, she'd need light, warmth, and especially food, if she hadn't had time to gather any. But so far, his search had come up empty.

"Did you know Therondol?" Tarvin asked abruptly.

"No," Deelia said. If she was surprised by the change in topic, she didn't show it. "I came to the Watch after his time."

"That's right. I'd forgotten how many years he's been gone. You'd have liked him, though. Steady, but he had eyes that could cut, you know? You could never lie to the man. I don't know why that made me like him, but it did. He was smarter than all the men in his patrol, but he never looked down on anyone."

"He sounds just like the Warden," Deelia said.

"Better than," Tarvin said. "But all that's gone, so no use dwelling on it, eh?"

Deelia shrugged. "Why are you out here, Tarvin? The Warden didn't send you. You should be on patrol in South Ward."

"What does it matter? We're all looking for the same woman, as if there wasn't a whole city of more worthy folk to mind."

"You'll be reprimanded," Deelia said.

"Be worth it, if I get to bring her in."

"Good luck to you, then," Deelia said. "Now either leave me, or stop talking."

Tarvin didn't get a chance to reply. A pair of women sat down directly in front of them, too close to their personal space to allow any private conversation.

Tarvin exchanged a glance with Deelia. After a breath, one of the women half turned to face them. Her left eye was swollen shut. Blood crusted the seam.

"Are you Serbith?" she whispered, addressing Deelia.

"Yes," Tarvin said, ignoring Deelia's sharp poke to his ribs. He loved to irritate her.

"Who are you, then?" The other woman turned. She had an open sore on her lip.

"I'm her bodyguard," Tarvin said without hesitation.

"Wasn't part of the deal, her bringin' another pair of eyes," the woman said. As she spoke, Tarvin found himself unable to look at anything except the ugly sore. "Never mind then, no hard feelings. I brought the goods. Let's see your coin."

"My bodyguard has it," Deelia said sweetly.

Tarvin smiled. "Of course. But I want to inspect the goods before I pay a copper."

"You hear that, Mabs? He wants to count fingers and toes," the woman with the swollen eye said.

"Oh, he's got 'em all, no mistake there." Mabs laughed and unwound a thin wrap from her shoulders.

Deelia hissed out a breath and a curse, but Tarvin kept his composure.

The baby was naked and new, probably only a handful of tendays old. His lips, fingers, and toes were blue from the cold. He should have been wailing his discomfort for all Faerûn to hear, but he was too underfed. He didn't have the strength to cry.

"How long has he been off his mother's milk?" Deelia said. Her mouth was set in a grim line.

"Never been on it," Mabs said. "It was the mother's fourth, so her teat's all dried up. But he's the best of the lot. Lord Theycairn's gettin' his coin's worth, don't you worry."

Tarvin stiffened. Lord Theycairn was a nobleman recently widowed. His wife had died in childbirth, but the family insisted the babe, a boy, had survived. No one had yet seen the child in public.

Deelia said abruptly, "I am satisfied." She removed her cloak and handed it to Mabs. "Wrap the child in this, please." She waited until it was done, then went on, "If Lord Theycairn should happen to have interest in . . . other children—"

"Lookin' to stock his larder with heirs, is he?" Mabs chortled. "We can do that. The other girls and us, we got just as many go in the harbor as not, on account of how we can't feed and clothe 'em all. But we could save back the best of 'em for you to inspect."

"That would be acceptable," Deelia said. "Could you remain here? Someone will be coming with your coin."

"Thought you said your bodyguard had it?" Mabs looked at them suspiciously.

"Lord Theycairn sent us to ensure you kept your end of the bargain," Deelia said quickly. "Serbith has your coin and will come to collect the babe. She knows nothing of us."

Mabs scowled, but she finally nodded. Her suspicion wouldn't keep her from taking the promised coin.

Deelia took Tarvin's arm and hauled him to his feet. When they were out of earshot, Tarvin said, "What was that about? I'll wager this Serbith is Lord Theycairn's washerwoman, or some such. If we'd waited, we could have caught her buying babies in Mistshore."

Deelia looked pale and angry. "And risk that baby being one of the discarded if the deal went badly? Better that one becomes Theycairn's heir. I'll report to the Warden when we see him next. We have to see about getting some food down to the prostitutes, at least those on the shore. You're right, there are more important things going on in Mistshore tonight than Icelin Tearn." She shivered. "I hate this place. Babies in the harbor—godsdamn bloody mutilated part of the city. That's all it is. A leech."

"Nice to see you again, Morleth," Bellaril said.

Ruen inclined his head. "It's been a long time, Bells."

The dwarf's expression darkened. "You know better than to use nicknames with me, Morleth. That's going to cost you."

They were circling each other now. "You don't like being called 'Bells'?" Ruen said. "I'd have thought you would have embraced the nickname. Your fans certainly have. Or are they plants by your master, to drum up support for his champion?"

He lunged, aiming a fist at the dwarf's face. The blow glanced lightly off her jaw, and Bellaril was already ducking under his guard for a jab to his midsection. Ruen fell forward into a roll. He tried to snag Bellaril's ankle as he passed, but she jumped out of the way.

Ruen sprang to his feet, his arms out in defense, but the dwarf kept her distance. He could feel the burn in his ribs where she'd jabbed him. Quick punches, just enough force to give pain. She knew exactly where and how hard to hit him. That was the damnable part of this fight.

"I did warn you," the dwarf said. "What is it you need from him this time, Morleth? Protection? Coin? Whatever it is, it won't be worth it." She moved in again, throwing a quick succession of punches, all aimed low where he had trouble defending. Ruen took another blow to the flank, but he caught the dwarf a heavy blow to the shoulder that had her backing off.

"I need a place to hide," Ruen said. He took the reprieve to catch his breath. The air burned against his cracked ribs. "There're two others with me. I assume he's seen them?"

"A bird and a butcher," Bellaril said. "Not the sort of company you generally keep. He'd love to hear the tale behind it."

"I'll happily throw the fight and tell it to him," Ruen said, "but I think he wants me to win."

The dwarf's swings faltered. Ruen got in another blow, a numbing shot to her arm. He pressed forward, but Bellaril kicked, catching his knee.

Ripples of pain shot up Ruen's leg. He wobbled, gritting his teeth to keep from collapsing to the platform. Breathing fast, he stepped back, unable to press his momentary advantage.

"Give this up, Morleth," the dwarf said. She massaged the feeling back into her arm while he seethed in pain. "It doesn't matter if Arowall wants me to lose. The title is mine. I'm not letting you or him take it from me."

"If you think so little of my chances, come ahead," Ruen said, opening his arms.

The dwarf shook her head. "I'm not to be baited like that, Morleth. I was giving you a chance." She dodged to the side when his fist came in, hooking an elbow around his arm. Securing her hold, she squeezed.

Ruen felt the bones snap. His mind momentarily blanked, but he kept his feet, largely by holding onto the solid dwarf. When he looked into her face, he could see she'd put very little effort into the attack.

"I'm the only person in the Cradle who knows how much pain you're in," she whispered. "I know how many of your bones are broken, and if I wanted to, I could drop you to the floor or the sharks. You can't win without your ring, and you know it." Her eyes softened. "One last chance, Morleth. Give this up."

"I have a better idea," Ruen said. He licked blood from his lips. The ribs must be broken, not cracked, he thought. "How about a side bet of our own?"

"You're mad," Bellaril said sadly. "What is it you want? Why are you fighting for those two?"

In response, Ruen jerked the dwarf close. He wrapped the palms of both his bare hands around hers. Bellaril's eyes widened in shock. She had not seen him remove his gloves. They lay discarded on the platform.

Ruen did not attempt to strike her. He waited a breath for her to see the blue light, to realize what he was doing, then he whispered against her ear. When she drew back, her expression was unreadable.

"Fine," she said, breaking his hold. "It's a bet. I'll try not to kill you, Ruen Morleth, but I make no promises."

"Fair enough." Ruen set his feet. He didn't trust his speed anymore. He would have to work on the defensive.

She struck at him again, hitting his jaw, his collarbone, his shoulder. Each time her fist glanced off a bone, Ruen felt himself come apart a little. She left him his legs. Aside from the blow to his knees, he could remain upright and maneuver enough to dodge the worst of her attacks. It wouldn't last. She would bring him down soon.

He took another blow to the shoulder, but this time he snagged her arm before she could dance back. Immediately, she began punching with the other, struggling to free herself. Ruen absorbed the blows, letting his weight shift against her. She stumbled, off balance by the sheer dead weight of him.

Ruen brought his good knee up, planting it in her stomach. She gasped and bent double, but he struck again before she could fold. Wildly, she clawed at him, but he kept pressing down with his weight, until they were both crouched on the platform.

He forced his knee across her throat, pinning her. Choking, she tried to sit up, but he kept her down. Her reach wasn't great enough to get around his long legs. She could keep punching him in the gut, but Ruen was beyond the pain.

The dwarf snaked an arm up, grabbing his leg. She twisted viciously, no longer concerned with his balance. Ruen bit his lip; blood filled his mouth. The Cradle wavered, the faces of the crowd blurring into indistinct smudges. He kept Bellaril down with his ruined leg. She hissed and sputtered and cursed him.

"You'll never . . . stand," she said. "Your legs are ruined." Her voice was nothing more than a whisper. He'd cut off her airway. If he could hold on long enough, she would lose consciousness.

"Maybe you are the better fighter," he said, as her body went limp. "The only thing that separates us is where we keep our pain."

He looked up. The crowd was on its feet, screaming and stamping at the turn the match had taken. Icelin and Sull were still watching from across the Cradle.

Directly behind him, the guards were clustered around a figure coming up the stairs. Long, meticulously trimmed gray hair fell across his shoulders. His face was pale, his skin wrinkled but not yet taken heavily by age. He might have been a handsome figure, but his eyes were yellowish, his jaw tight, as if some hidden strain were working on his mind.

The man stopped ten paces from Ruen. His gaze moved from the crowd to Bellaril's unconscious body and finally to Ruen's face. He raised his hand, and the Cradle noise died instantly.

"You know the rules, Morleth," he said, his rich voice pitched loud enough for the crowd to hear. "Stand and declare your victory. *Stand,* or forfeit."

He's playing the scene for all it's worth. A part of Ruen had to admire the man's gall. Whatever the outcome, there'd not be an empty seat in the Cradle after tonight.

Ruen slid his knee off Bellaril's prone body. He felt the grating of bone against bone, the pull of muscles and tissue twisting in ways nature had never intended. He shivered. Cold sweat stood out on his skin. The blood was still hot in his mouth.

Best to do it all at once, Ruen thought. It was the only way he would be able to gather the strength. One quick thrust to his feet, and the bastard would have to give him healing. The crowd demanded the rules be obeyed. Even the master of the Cradle couldn't deny the crowd.

Ruen closed his eyes and breathed. "Keep the pain locked away," he murmured. He pushed it all—the broken bones, the torn muscles—to a far corner of his mind, a box whose lid he could fasten tight and push away from conscious examination.

He waited until the pain was safely contained, then forced himself to stand.

Icelin covered her ears against Ruen's scream. She knew the cry was involuntary. He would probably never remember uttering such a sound, but she would forever remember the terrible, animal whimper that followed the scream. She'd known his wounds were severe, but now she was terrified he might have killed himself just by climbing to his feet.

He swayed. Icelin dug her nails into the rail, willing him to stay upright. His head lolled to one side; blood dripped in tiny rubies from his lips. But he stood, facing the tight-lipped man and his retinue of guards.

"I stand," she heard him say into the silence of the Cradle.

Arowall didn't react. He stood, watching Ruen with amused curiosity. A smile played at his lips.

"No," Icelin hissed. She grabbed Sull's arm. "No, *no!* He's going to wait until Ruen falls."

Sull cursed. He grabbed Sheems by the back of the neck and hauled him aside. "He can't do that! Tell me he can't."

Sheems cowered in the face of the butcher's livid expression. "Rules aren't clear on how long he has to stand. Depends on the master's mood. Makes for a good show—" He caught himself when Sull bared his teeth.

Icelin reached for her neck pouch, frantically searching its contents for a spell focus.

Sull grabbed her shoulder. "Lass, I appreciate the sentiment, but that's a good route to getting us killed."

"He's going to fall, Sull. Where in the Nine Hells is that wood!" She searched her memory to unearth the spell. "It's not an attack," she assured him. "He just needs to stay upright."

Magic for simple tasks. She could hear her teacher's words. "*The spells you'll use most often in the early days are spells to imitate simple tasks. Don't let the ease of their use make you complacent. A servant, unseen, should never replace your own two hands.*"

A servant unseen. An invisible hand to keep him standing that would escape the master's notice. Icelin's fingers closed on the focus in her pouch. She didn't bother to pull it out but chanted the spell, her will centered on Ruen.

"Go. Hold him," she chanted, mixing the plea with the arcane phrases.

A swirl of brilliant gray mist shot from her fingertips. The loop of magic descended from the deck of the ship to the platform, taking on shape, if not substance, as it went. The crowd shouted in warning and awe.

"Gods-cursed magic!" Icelin clutched her head, feeling the familiar pain behind her eyes. Sull tried to support her, but she shook him off. She had to see how the wild spell would manifest, and control the damage if she could.

The gray mist coalesced into a human shape. The unseen servant was now a woman in a flowing dress, her colorless hair drifting around her face. Arms swathed in ghostly lace encircled Ruen's body from behind. The spectral lady stepped forward, taking Ruen's weight against her chest.

"I know that woman," Icelin said, aware that the crowd and the master of the Cradle had turned to look at her in a great collective. She drew her hand out of her neck pouch. The focus she held was not a piece of wood, as she'd thought when she cast the spell. It was the cameo she'd been holding for Ruen. The woman's face gazed serenely back at her from the portrait—and from the platform behind Ruen.

Arowall regarded Icelin with interest. "You're building a fine and dangerous reputation in Mistshore, my lady," he called out to her. "I daresay some of the poor folk will be glad when you leave us."

Icelin heard the threat behind the words. "Believe me, sir, I will be equally relieved to escape this place, and I apologize sincerely for trespassing on your hospitality." She pointed to Ruen. "But I need that man alive, and I wonder if you will have it so."

There were titters from the crowd. Arowall looked up sharply, gauging the reactions. "I adhere to the rules of the Cradle," he said. "Ruen Morleth has not fallen." He flicked a glance to Ruen, who was watching the exchange with half-closed eyes. "But if your spell fails, will he keep his feet? That is the issue at hand. Your interference is grounds for his immediate disqualification."

"No," Ruen spoke up, his voice thick. "She interfered without my consent." He looked at Icelin, but his eyes were unfocused. Icelin wondered if he truly saw her at all. "Drop the spell," he said.

"You'll die," Icelin said flatly. "He'll feed you to the sharks."

Angry shouts arose from the crowd, surprising all three of them. The people stamped their feet. Refuse showered the Cradle, and the rope bridges swayed above their heads. Arowall's guards formed a protective wall behind him.

"The people have spoken," Arowall said when the noise finally died away. "If Ruen Morleth stands, he will be declared champion. Is this acceptable, my lady?"

"Yes," Ruen answered for her. Icelin shot him a withering look. "Drop the spell. Now."

Icelin raised a hand. She could feel the crowd cringing back in their seats, but the gray lady did not explode into fire like the spell in the warehouse. She melted away, leaving Ruen alone on his feet.

Icelin leaned forward, her hands on the rail in a death grip. Ruen faltered, steadied himself, and stood still. His posture was straight. All eyes in the Cradle watched him.

"Our new champion," Arowall said.

The crowd bellowed its approval. The wooden ships shook in their ancient moorings. Icelin thought the whole of Mistshore must be hearing the tumult.

The master turned and dropped a steel vial on the platform ten feet away from Ruen. "Accept your healing, champion." He ascended the gangplank to the largest ship and disappeared below deck.

Icelin vaulted the rail, landing at the edge of the Cradle. She ran out onto the nearest platform, crossing to Ruen's in three quick jumps, just as the monk started to fall.

She caught him at the waist and guided him to the ground. She heard Sull lumbering behind her, and a breath later he put the healing vial in her hand.

"Don't move him," Icelin said when Sull would have picked Ruen up. "We'll do it here." She pressed the vial to his bloody lips.

Ruen opened his eyes and drank. As the healing liquid poured down his throat, he sat up and moved away from her. "You made a spectacle of yourself again," he said, but he didn't sound angry. "Hundreds of people know your face now, to say nothing of your troublesome nature."

"Yes, but thank the gods for them. At least Arowall respects the crowd." Icelin put the vial aside when Ruen finished drinking. "He must be furious with me. He'll give us nothing now, I suppose."

Ruen laughed. His eyes looked clearer, more brown than red, as the healing potion took effect. "He's not angry, or he won't be for long. You gave the crowd a show they'll be talking about for a tenday. Even if he wanted to kill us, the man knows how to play his part. I'm the declared champion. The crowd expects to see us again. Come to think of it, your interference might have been the best part of the whole spectacle." He winced and fell silent.

"What is it?" Icelin asked. "Are you still in pain?"

"The bones are reknitting," Ruen said. "Stings."

Icelin ran her hands over his sleeve and across his torso. "You're right, they're mending," she said. "Gods above, she must have broken every rib. How could she hit so hard?"

"Don't let her height fool you." Ruen retrieved his gloves, took what was left of the healing draught, and poured it down Bellaril's throat. The dwarf was already stirring. When the liquid hit her tongue, she spluttered and opened her eyes. "She's much stronger than she looks."

Bellaril sat up and looked around at the crowd filtering off the ships. Icelin thought she must be looking for her master. She didn't realize he'd left her unconscious on the Cradle floor.

"Suppose I owe you congratulations," Bellaril said, offering a hand to Ruen.

"It was a good fight," Ruen said. "You're still too merciful, Bells. You should have taken my legs first."

"I won't make the same mistake twice," the dwarf assured him.

"Merciful?" Icelin said. "She broke practically every bone in your body."

"He knew the rules," Bellaril said. "No magic allowed in the Cradle."

Icelin decided not to tell the dwarf about her miscast spell. "Why would Ruen need magic to protect himself?"

"You didn't tell her." Bellaril snickered, her eyes alight with humor. "Well, that's interesting, isn't it?"

Ruen glared at her. "The ring I wear is magical, as you've already seen," he said to Icelin. "I told you it amplifies whatever it touches. I can shift that focus, a little, according to my will."

"He means his bones are sticks," Bellaril said. "Can't you tell by how thin he is? Without the ring to strengthen the bones, he's going to get pulped in any fight."

"Arowall knew that going in, didn't he?" Icelin said. "He knew how hard it would be for you to win."

Ruen shrugged. "He can't fix his own game. Like Bellaril said, there's no magic allowed in the Cradle. That's the rule."

"But he made you stand longer than was needed," Icelin said fiercely. "He wanted you to fall."

"Maybe, maybe not. He can't break 'em, but sometimes Arowall tries to bend the rules," Bellaril said. She stood. "He's a twisted creature, make no mistake."

"Why do you serve such a man?" Sull spoke up.

The dwarf looked at the butcher for the first time. "He pays me well. I don't want for anything, and I like the crowd's attention. Might be I'm a bit twisted myself." She shrugged.

"We should be going," Ruen said. "He'll be waiting for us. Coming, Bells?"

Bellaril's face hardened. "Don't have a choice, do I? You won the side bet."

"What did you win?" Sull wanted to know. They climbed the gangplank and joined an escort of guards.

Ruen smiled cryptically. "You'll see."

CHAPTER 13

Unlike the sparse ship's cabin they'd slept in, Arowall's quarters were carpeted with blue rugs that looked as if they'd been meticulously cleaned. The furniture was dark wood; a desk and matching chairs were arranged in one corner of the room. Arowall sat at the desk. A guard stood behind him.

In the middle space, a couch and another small table sat against the hull. Fist-sized globes of magical light floated along the ceiling. The portholes had been blacked over. There was no seeing in or out of the ship.

Icelin could sense the tingle of enchantments protecting the hull. This room must be where the master's more interesting audiences take place, she thought.

Their escort indicated the chairs for Icelin and Ruen, then returned above.

"You fought well, Bellaril," Arowall said, waving a dismissive hand at the dwarf. He looked at Ruen. "I'm pleased you survived, Morleth." He reached into his desk drawer and pulled out a familiar ring. He handed it to Ruen. "Yours, with my thanks."

Ruen took the ring. He slid it on his finger and covered it with the glove. "These are the people I wanted you to meet," he said. "Icelin you already know—"

"Of course," Arowall said. His gave Sull one disinterested glance before turning his full attention to Icelin. "My pleasure, Icelin." He held out a hand.

Reluctantly, Icelin took it, surprised at how warm his hand was. She'd expected a cold, clammy grip. He held her hand for a breath and released it.

"Well, Icelin, your champion has won in the Cradle," Arowall said. "You've earned the right to ask for what you need. If it is in my power, I will provide it."

Icelin exchanged a glance with Ruen. He nodded.

"I would request protection," she said, "for myself and my two companions. "We are hunted by the Watch and a party of elves and men. You've given us a place to rest, but we need concealment during the day. If you hide us, we will leave at nightfall and not trouble you again."

Arowall inclined his head. "Easily done. I have a place where you could be concealed quite well"—he leaned forward—"if you've the stomach for it."

Icelin met his calculating gaze. "What place do you speak of, sir?"

"He calls it the Isle," Ruen spoke up. "A half-sunk ship behind the Cradle."

"I appropriated it some years ago to take care of a minor inconvenience to my operation," Arowall explained.

"What sort of inconvenience?" Icelin asked, knowing instinctively she would not like the answer.

"Mistshore is a unique entity in Waterdeep," Arowall said. "We welcome all folk, no matter how desperate or murderous, so long as they've coin to spend. Unfortunately, being such a large enterprise, the Cradle attracts its share of . . . lesser beings."

"The diseased, the starving, the scarred," Ruen said. "The beggar folk, shunned even among the damned."

"We used to dispose of them—discreetly," Arowall said. "It was a mercy, I assure you. Their conditions were affronts to nature; whitewasting and darkrot, godscurse and worse. A few here or there were never missed."

"I wonder why you stopped," Icelin said sarcastically. The man's callousness knew no bounds.

"Some days I wonder that myself," Arowall said.

"Don't let him lie to you," Ruen said. "He knew that mass murders would not go unnoticed for long, no matter what sort of folk were dying. He devised a surprisingly merciful solution."

"I took them in," Arowall said. "They live on the Isle now, in relative comfort and, more importantly, out of sight of normal folk."

"No one goes there," Ruen said. "They're afraid of catching something."

"I know I would be," Sull muttered.

"Don't worry," Ruen said. "If he intends to send us there, he will provide us with disguises and spell protection against the sicknesses."

"Absolutely," Arowall said. "I would not send you off unprepared. You will have your disguises, which I daresay will continue to serve you after you've left us."

"Then we are agreed," Icelin said. She stood and extended a hand, but there was no warmth in her eyes. "We thank you for your hospitality."

He smiled and leaned forward to kiss her fingers. "You are not easily unsettled, my dear," he said. "I admire your nerve."

He looked past her shoulder, his brow furrowing in consternation. "Bellaril, you may go. I have no further need of you."

The dwarf shifted uncomfortably. "There is a matter I must discuss with you, Master. It concerns Ruen Morleth, and a wager we made during the fight."

Her master raised a brow. "I have the distinct impression I'm not going to like this, Bellaril."

"It was my doing," Ruen said. "I made a side bet with Bellaril. If I won the match, she promised to accompany us for three nights—to whatever destination Icelin names—as a bodyguard."

"And you agreed?" Icelin said, looking sharply at the dwarf.

"I did," Bellaril said. "No offense meant, lady, but at the time I believed I could win the fight."

"You discovered differently," Arowall said. He kept his voice even, but Icelin saw his cheeks flood with color. "Your arrogance will be the death of you yet."

The dwarf said nothing, only bowed her head.

"I will honor the wager," Arowall said, rising and coming around the desk. He towered over Bellaril. "Take her, but don't be gone long, little one," he said softly "And don't displease me again."

"Yes, Master," Bellaril said.

Icelin turned to leave, but Arowall held up a hand. "Morleth, a word with you in private, if you please?"

Icelin started to speak, but Ruen shot her a quelling glance. "I'll be along soon," he told her.

"If you say so." Icelin nodded to Arowall and climbed the ladder. She wondered if she would spend the rest of her life passing from the belly of one strange ship to another.

"Well," Ruen said to Arowall when they were alone. "What is she?"

"Your friend is a human girl and nothing more," Arowall said. "I detected no concealment magics, nor modifications to erase her memory. No wizard, in the Watch's employ or any other, has tampered with her."

"Why is she so powerful, then?" Ruen said. "Is it the spellplague?"

"You already know the answer to that," Arowall said, waving an impatient hand. "She is spellscarred, just like you; and like you, her powers are debilitating. But her condition is perhaps more serious."

"In what way?" Ruen demanded.

"I can sense the spellplague as clearly as you smell the rot coming off the harbor. I have met few individuals living with so strong a taint in them. To put the matter bluntly, you and that girl are rotting with spellscars; but while you can live with brittle bones, Icelin is dying."

"What?"

"Gods' breath, haven't you touched her yourself?" Arowall took in his expression. "If you did, you'd doubtless find her frigid."

Ruen lowered himself into a chair, in the way a cat sinks into a wary crouch. "Why is she dying? Explain."

"I am only speculating, of course, but I believe that whatever ability Icelin gained as a result of her brush with the spellplague is interfering with her magic. Her spells go wild more often than they succeed. Am I correct?"

"You are," Ruen said.

"Then, in effect, every time she casts a spell, her body wages war on itself—the spellscar fighting the ordered forces of magic. Her scar must be a powerful talent, to cause such a chaotic reaction. What is it, exactly, that Icelin can do?"

"That's for her to say." Ruen stood. Tension hummed in his blood. His body must be readjusting to the ring, he thought. He held up his hand. "Is there any magic like this ring that can calm the forces in her, make the spellscar sleep?"

Arowall smiled. "That's why I like you, Morleth. You think of it as a living thing, just as I do. It surrounds the city, weaving into the wood and stone. Folk think they're safe here, but they breathe the plague every day. They just don't realize it. You and I are the only ones who know how doomed the world is."

"You've spent too long in the harbor rot," Ruen said, "and you're wasting my time. If you can't help me—"

"There is no magic that can stave off the spellplague forever," Arowall snapped. "You know that as well as anyone."

"She's stronger than she looks," Ruen said. He turned away from Arowall. "Stronger than you."

Arowall laughed. "Yet I would not trade places with her for the world. My men will bring your disguises. Bring them and Bellaril with you when you return to the Cradle to fight for me. I'll give you a tenday before I hold another tournament. A tenday, Morleth. You've tried my patience more than any other man and lived. Don't displease me again."

Ruen nodded. A question burned on his tongue, but he did not ask it. He climbed the ladder and left the ship, but the thought haunted him.

How long does she have? He'd have to touch her—the bare skin of her hands—to know for sure. He could touch other parts of her and get impressions, but they wouldn't be as strong.

He'd never known why it had to be so specific a touch. The monks of his order believed the hands were the links that most strongly connected mortals to the world. A warrior's hands could take a life; a midwife's could bring a babe into the world. Ki manifested through the hands.

It didn't matter. He would never touch her. His hands—his whole body—were abhorrences, mistakes of nature. The gods alone were supposed to know how long a being had left to live, not mortals.

Especially not a cutpurse from Mistshore.

"Everywhere we go has a name," Sull said. "Mistshore, the Hearth, Whalebone Court; now it's the Isle." He gazed at the latest jumbled wreck of a ship. This one, a cog, had been hollowed out, the decking torn up to form one high-walled chamber at the bottom of the ship.

"There's a ladder here," Bellaril said, stepping onto a short gangplank off the raised dock. She pointed to a rickety ladder laid against the inside of the ship. It descended into the cog's belly, disappearing from sight. "That's our way down."

"We're at the nether end of Waterdeep, yet they still get around to namin' everythin' here," Sull babbled on. "Unsettlin', that's what it is." He shot a quick glance at the ladder. "Unnatural."

Ruen handed Sull a rolled bundle of cloth. "Put it on," he

said. "You'll feel better once you're protected. Arowall said even the stench is blunted by the magic."

"Why does he have these?" Icelin said, taking her own bundle and unrolling it. A simple cloak of layered rags, it hardly looked like it could stop a swift breeze, let alone be magical.

"He's never told me, but I suspect he uses them for spying," Bellaril said. "His own man poses as a beggar, then the master sends him wandering around the Cradle. Folk try to ignore him. They don't see him as a real person, with ears and a tongue that can tell what he's seen."

"So after he's done spyin', the guards grab him and throw him on the Isle, just like a staged play," Sull said, shaking his head. "Everyone serves a purpose. Tidy little business he keeps. Too bad someone hasn't killed him." He ignored Bellaril's narrowed eyes.

"He's offered us shelter," Icelin said, trying to head off the confrontation, "such as it is." She donned her cloak and felt a warm wave as the magic flowed over her. "How do I look—any worse than before?"

Sull turned green in the face. He looked like he might gag. "You could say that, lass. I wouldn't go searchin' for any mirrors if I were you."

"Some gallant gentleman you are," Icelin said. "Let's see yours, then."

Ruen and Sull and Bellaril donned their cloaks together. Icelin knew instantly when the magic had taken hold.

"That's . . . effective," was all she could think to say.

Open sores blossomed from Bellaril's and Sull's faces. Yellowish fluid seeped from the bulging skin. Sull's red hair turned gray and lifeless, and his skin had a distinctly wasted tinge. Ruen looked no better. His red eyes sank into his skull, and his already gaunt face looked skeletal. Icelin could see the crooked blue veins just below the surface of his skin.

"No one will recognize us," Icelin said. And indeed, she did feel better. Cerest's gaze would never linger on creatures like this. "We'll be safe, even in broad daylight."

"If we're so well disguised, why do we need to stay here at all?" Sull said. "We can walk about Mistshore as we wish."

"No," Ruen said. "They'll start searching magically for such disguises, if they haven't already. I don't want to test the limits of the cloaks in daylight. At night, perhaps. Besides, we need to sleep sometime, and I'd like to be as protected as possible."

And I'll be able to read grandfather's letters, Icelin thought. It was fast approaching dawn. She had until nightfall to find some clue as to the nature of Elgreth's relationship with Cerest. She had no idea if such knowledge would aid her in defeating the elf, but she had to know the truth. She had to know if Elgreth had been Cerest's friend.

"Dawn is coming," she said, putting her hands on the ladder rungs. "Let's get this over with."

She descended the ladder. Shapes moved below her—brown humps that stumbled and pushed each other out of the way in the small space. The farther down they went, the more she could distinguish the babble of voices.

"All at one end, you know better than to crowd the stage, Hatsolm, you old fool."

"I want to be able to hear the music this time. I'm a full ten feet back. You mind your own seat; it's wide enough to demand your full attention."

"I'm not fat, you imbecile!"

The voices died when they reached the bottom of the ladder. Icelin could see dozens of rag-cloaked figures angling for a space at the far end of the ship's belly. They all stopped what they were doing when Icelin's foot touched the ground.

A tense silence followed. Icelin stepped forward, raising a scarred hand in greeting. "W-well met," she said.

"Well met." A man with a crooked back ambled over to take her hand.

It was like greeting a skeleton. His fingers had no meat. Real sores peppered his arms and bare legs. Icelin swallowed hard and tried not to pull her hand away.

"You look like you could use a rest, friend," the man said eagerly. "I'm Hatsolm, and I won't bother you with the rest of the names for now, just you remember mine. Taken together, we're the Drawn Cloaks. Lovely and mysterious-sounding, isn't it? I came up with the name myself. Come and sit over here. We've some food and drink to spare."

Icelin let herself be led over to the others. Hands patted her on the back and guided her to a seat on the ground. Immediately, a cup of water was pressed into her hand, and a bowl of some unidentifiable substance appeared in front of her. Similar treatment greeted Ruen, Sull, and Bellaril.

Icelin sniffed the food and looked at Sull. Her mouth was already watering, but she wanted to be sure the meat wouldn't kill her. Sull sniffed his own bowl and nodded slightly. Icelin scooped up a handful of the stewlike substance and ate.

She tasted stringy meat and hard potatoes, liberally seasoned with grease that pooled at the bottom of her bowl. Not a king's feast, by any standard, but it was more substantial fare than her body had taken in days, and did much to clear her head and soothe the raw churning in her belly. She'd been so hungry, her hands shook when she brought the food to her mouth. She looked at Hatsolm, unable to speak, grateful tears standing in her eyes.

"Yes sir, that's what they all say." He chuckled. "Now then. Where do you come from?"

"We . . . don't hail from Waterdeep," Icelin said quickly. "We came in on a caravan. Our village was dying. Everyone was leaving, so we thought we'd come here, to start anew."

Hatsolm nodded gravely. "Aye, that's the story among many of us. And here we are"—he waved his rag-draped arms expansively—"in Waterdeep mighty, a city that looks precious little like a city and smells a bit like the rotting bowels of a once-fine ship. Alas, the bards, how cruelly they exaggerate!"

There was a smattering of applause and rude gestures from the beggar folk. Shouts of, "Save it for the real performers!" had Hatsolm throwing up his hands and laughing.

"Eat hearty, all of you," he said, and he waddled off to find his own bowl. "We're fed and clothed and grateful, and the troupe's comin' in. What more could kings ask for?"

"The troupe?" Icelin said. But Hatsolm was gone, and the others were immersed in their own conversations. The temporary distraction of their arrival had passed; the people seemed to be waiting for something. They kept shooting glances at the bow of the ship, but Icelin saw nothing except a stack of rotting crates. Rats weaved among the loose boards.

"Surely Arowall doesn't provide food *and* entertainment for 'em," Sull said. "Not when he'd just as soon be killin' 'em."

They looked to Ruen, but the monk shrugged. "They seem in high spirits, which is more than I expected. Perhaps one of them is a musician."

Hatsolm came around again to collect their bowls. Icelin tugged on his rag cloak. "Are they waiting to see a show?" she asked politely.

He grinned. "Aye, lass, the best in Waterdeep, though we're the only folk knows it. Sit you all right here and see what there is to see." He patted her arm and settled back on the ground.

A crow flew over their heads, descending into the ship to pluck a rat from one of the crates. The bird was large and sleek, with oily black eyes that watched the beggars even as it snapped the rat's neck. Icelin cringed.

The sun had risen outside the ship, but a shadow fell across Icelin and the rest of the crowd. She looked up; more crows were flying in an uneven formation, clustering close and snapping at each other as they dived down into the belly of the ship.

Instinctively, Icelin ducked. The birds flew over her head

and landed on the rotting crates. The air filled with restless caws, but a hushed silence had fallen over the beggar folk. Every face, including Hatsolm's, was tuned in rapturous attention to the crows.

"What's going on?" Icelin whispered to Ruen.

"Halt your lips, you ungrateful lot!" shouted a voice that made Icelin jump.

A crow's head stretched, its black feathers shrinking into pale flesh. The bird stood up on two spindly legs, which lengthened and shed more feathers. The creature shook itself, and was suddenly not a bird any longer, but a boy, a boy grown from the body of a crow. The ungainly creature hopped up on one of the crates and surveyed the crowd.

"Are we the show this night or not?" the boy demanded. He looked to be about eleven years old—human—with greasy black hair tucked under a brown cap. A crow's feather rested behind his ear like a quill. His eyes shifted around like restless insects, never settling on one object. "Answer me, dogs! Are we the entertainers?"

"Ho!" A chorus erupted from the beggar folk. For a breath, Icelin thought she was back in the Cradle.

"They're new arrivals, Kaelin, not true Drawn Cloaks," said Hatsolm. "Give them a chance."

The boy regarded Icelin's group with interest, his gaze fixing on each of them in turn. "They're false fronts," he said.

Ruen glanced up sharply. He'd avoided eye contact with the boy until that instant. "We're refugees, the same as any person here," he said. "What of you? What do you have to say for yourselves?"

The boy hopped from crate to crate, his arms spread. "Do you hear, friends? He wants to know who we are."

The crows flapped their wings in a grim chorus, and suddenly the air was full of feathers. When the black shades fell away, a dozen men and women stood where the crows had been.

Icelin gasped. The crates were gone, transformed into a wide, foot-high stage that stretched from the port bow to the starboard. The boy pranced from one end to the other, pulling lit torches from a bag at his hip. He placed them in sconces at the edges of the stage. Their fiery brilliance lit up the suddenly shadowed hold. It was as if all the sunlight had been sucked from the ship, replaced by torches that gave off light but no heat.

"They can't be real," Icelin whispered to Ruen. "It's wizardry. Illusion."

"Complex magic that can transfigure and interact by itself, all for a crowd of beggars?" Ruen said. "No one would take such trouble."

"Then what are they?" Sull asked.

It was Hatsolm who answered. "Ghosts," he said.

CHAPTER 14

A woman strode to the center of the stage and pulled a lute from her back. She began to play a lively tune for a pair of jugglers that somersaulted onto the stage. They tossed a dizzying handful of colored balls into the air and caught them before they gained their feet. Hatsolm laughed and clapped. The beggars were enraptured.

"They're such a motley troupe," Icelin said. "Shouldn't they be haunting a playhouse?"

"That's the charm of it," Hatsolm said. He leaned closer so his voice wouldn't carry to the stage. "They've never said, but I think the whole group was lost in a shipwreck. I'll wager they're chained to it still, so they seek out the audience that's closest. Before we came, they said they performed for the crows. After we arrived, they took the shape of the crows and performed for us. Isn't that lovely?"

"They sound friendlier than the sea wraiths, but are they dangerous?" Icelin asked.

"Not so long as you fix your attention on them and keep your tongue between your teeth," Hatsolm said pointedly. "They don't like to be interrupted."

"Of course." Icelin gave up and fell silent. She sat back against the hull and watched the boy, Kaelin, flitting through the crowd. He straightened a cloak here, shushed an errant tongue there, and teased an old woman who called him her boy. He seemed excessively fond of touching everyone. Icelin didn't know if they could feel him, but all the faces turned up eagerly at his approach.

The jugglers bowed and ran offstage, leaving behind a trail of balls that burst into sparkling fireworks. When the light spots faded from Icelin's eyes, the lute player was back, changing her tune to something mournful. It took Icelin a breath to recognize the tune.

The last falling twilight
shines gold on the mountain.
Give me eyes for the darkness,
take me home, take me home.

Icelin's heart stuttered in her chest. It was the same song she used to sing for Brant. The woman on stage looked directly at her while she strummed the lute.

"What's wrong?" Ruen asked. He reached out but stopped short of touching her with his gloved hand.

"Nothing," Icelin said, "I'm cold." She wrapped her arms around herself.

Ruen continued to watch her intently. Icelin kept her eyes forward, but she couldn't look at the woman's face. The song was painful enough. She stared at the bard's feet and tried to blank her mind.

She felt a weight across her shoulders. She looked up, off balance as Ruen pulled her against his side. His arm, hidden under the cloak, was draped across her shoulders. He was staring straight ahead.

"Ruen," she said, fighting a smile, "your arm seems to have fallen on me in a suspicious gesture of comfort."

"Is that so?" He still wouldn't look at her. "I suppose your virtue is distressed by this turn of events?"

"Terribly. I believe I will expire from shock."

"Better than expiring from the cold. Why is the song bothering you?"

"Brant, my great-uncle, loved this song," Icelin said. She let the words in. The lute player's voice enveloped her like a warm blanket covered in needles.

"It's a sad song," Ruen said. "He's lost in the wilderness. Does he ever find his way home?"

"The song doesn't tell," Icelin said. "What do you think?"

"I think a bard should say what she means. Otherwise what's the point of the show?"

"What's the *point?*" Kaelin shouted incredulously from right behind them. The lute player's song ground to a halt.

Icelin sucked in a breath. Kaelin's hand came down on her shoulder; it was ice cold and strangely invasive, as if he had put his hand inside her skin. She could tell by the lack of color in Ruen's face that he'd had no idea the boy had been behind them.

Kaelin patted Ruen on the back before the monk could flinch away. "The point, he wants to know. He wants the full story of the boy lost in the wilderness." Kaelin's eyes sparkled. "But will he want it told, after all's done?"

He looked at Ruen expectantly. Ruen shrugged. "Tell your tale. You're the bards, and it's no difference to me."

"Truly, then, I have your permission?" Kaelin bent in a half-bow, so that his face was close to Ruen's.

"Truly," the monk said through gritted teeth. "Be gone."

"How wonderful," Kaelin said. "It will be a fine tale. Clear the stage! Places!"

The lute player vanished. She reappeared a breath later, without her lute and wearing a black cloak. She flipped her hood over her face and joined the rest of the troupe assembling at the back of the stage. They were all dressed identically, their clothes and features covered by the cloaks.

Kaelin jumped onto the stage, taking his place at the front of the assembly. "Who will play the lead?" he asked. He put his hand theatrically to his ear to hear the response of the crowd.

"Kaelin!" they cried on cue.

"Yes, and don't you forget it," Kaelin said. "Tonight, I will be playing the part of the boy lost in the wilderness, the boy named Ruen Morleth." He swept an arm up, and suddenly he was swathed in black too.

Ruen sat forward, his jaw muscles rigid. "What are they doing?" he said.

Hatsolm answered. "They're going to tell your story," he said eagerly. "You're lucky to be chosen. Most newcomers never get picked until they've been here at least a season."

"How do they know what to say?" Icelin asked, as Ruen lost more color. "They know nothing about us."

"Silence before a performance! We know all we need, just by touch," Kaelin said from the stage. His voice sounded deeper, older. He swept off the cloak. It dissolved into a flurry of crows that flew out over the crowd. The stage transformed in the birds' wake.

The bow of the boat was now a forest glade, draped in dense green ferns. A small, stagnant pond dominated the scene, its watery arms wrapped around the exposed roots of an oak that crawled up the hull.

Icelin's eyes blurred at the sudden appearance of the illusion. She knew it wasn't real, yet she swore she could smell the moss clinging to the pond stones. Unseen, a sparrow chirped its shrill song. Wind rustled in the wild grasses.

"Not natural," Bellaril said. She swiped a hand across her nose, as if she could smell the green too. "Magic can't mimic life, not like that."

"Ah, but death can mimic life. The dead remember." Kaelin's voice echoed from the heart of the glade, though they could not see him. His voice still sounded strange.

Two cloaked figures, male and female by their shape, came from opposite ends of the glade to stand in front of the pond. They faced each other. Only visible were the skin of their hands and bare feet.

"Where is my son," the woman cried, "my foolish, fanciful boy, who runs through the forest like a wild animal?"

"He likes to run," hissed the man. "Loves to run away and worry his mother. What a terrible boy; he thinks the village is not good enough for him. Poor, foolish boy."

"That's not true," Ruen murmured, but only Icelin could hear him above the cloaked woman's wailing.

"Where are you, Ruen!" With her slender arm extended to the forest, the woman dropped to her knees as a blue light fountained from within the green pond. The light cast the ferns and the cloaked figures in glowing relief. The woman shouted, "He is doomed!"

She disappeared. The man crouched to address the audience in a stage whisper.

"But does the boy know why he is doomed? Did his mother never warn him of what lurks in the forest? Poor, poor mother. Poor, ignorant son."

The blue light faded, and the man vanished, his cloaked form revealing a small figure sitting by the pond, his back to the audience. Lazily, he reclined on his elbows and tossed a fishing line into the water. Somewhere, a bird called, and the boy turned his head to stare at the audience.

Icelin felt Ruen stiffen next to her. She made to put her hand on his arm, but he moved away, closer to the stage.

Icelin looked at the boy. It took her a moment to realize that it was not Kaelin sitting there, but an older boy. He lacked Kaelin's mischievous air and had an overly serious demeanor, his mouth twisted in an introspective frown.

His hair was dark, with brambles and grass clinging to its wild strands. But his eyes . . . they were common brown, yet so familiar.

Icelin looked from Ruen to the boy and back again. In her mind she filled in the progression of years—the widening jaw, the added height and musculature of manhood. Ruen was in his early thirties, the boy only thirteen or fourteen, but Icelin could see it. They were not so different, except for the eyes.

The boy was Ruen.

Icelin watched the young Ruen strip down to the waist and wade out into the pond. Up to his elbows in the green muck, he took swipes at the water, coming up with a bright green frog. He put it back in the water and watched it swim.

When the blue light came back, the boy didn't see it at first. He was too absorbed in watching a dragonfly glide in dizzying circles over the water. Its wings touched the edge of the blue light. There was a flash, and the dragonfly disappeared, vaporized by the magic surge.

Seeing the light, the boy waded to the spot, his hand outstretched.

"Don't do it," Icelin said. "Don't touch it, you'll be killed!" Hatsolm and the others were looking at her strangely, but she ignored them. She looked at the adult Ruen. His body was still tight, but he watched the scene with a kind of detached resignation.

The boy stepped into deeper water. The light wrapped around him, flowing up his legs and chest until he had to squeeze his eyes shut against the brightness. Panicked, he tried to back away, but he lost his balance and fell, his head going under the water.

The beggars gasped. Hatsolm murmured, "He's lost now. The plague'll rot his mind."

Icelin knew better. She waited, her hands clutching her skirt.

The boy's head burst from the water, and he was screaming, clutching his face, and thrashing while he tried desperately to find the shore. He crawled onto the bank and collapsed in a snarl of cattails. Their brown heads quivered above him.

The blue light continued to glow, but Icelin could see the pond's surface bubbling. The floating plants and moss shriveled up and turned black, their essences consumed by the spellplague.

Soon, the water itself began to recede, pulling away from the bank and leaving behind a jagged shelf of claylike soil.

The boy rolled onto his back, his eyes staring vacantly at the crater where the pond had been. Streaks of blood ran down his cheeks. He climbed unsteadily to his feet and ran blindly into the green glade, away from the empty crater.

He stumbled and fell against the oak tree. There was a loud, sickening crack. The boy screamed and clutched his arm. He stumbled and ran on.

The boy vanished, the glade melted from green to brown, and suddenly a small parody of a village square grew from the ship's hull. The tallest buildings stood to the port and starboard side. Each adjacent building was smaller than these, making the village appear to recede down a long tunnel.

An old woman hobbled across the dusty path down the center of the village, passing in front of a thatched house with no windows. In the open doorway, a sullen boy crouched, playing with the rocks at his feet. A dirty linen bandage covered his left eye. The other was red and swollen. He blinked rapidly when the wind kicked up.

That same wind yanked the old woman's shawl from across her shoulders. The scrap of green fabric tumbled through the dust and tangled with the boy's dirty feet.

Wearing an irritated expression, the boy tore the shawl away and started to hurl it across the square, but he stopped when he saw the old woman. They watched each other—the shawl dangling from the boy's hand—each unsure what to do.

Slowly, the old woman walked to the doorway and stood over the boy. When she stretched out her hand, he put the shawl in it and started to back away, but she caught his hand in both of hers.

"I am so sorry about your eyes, boy," she said. "My sight is failing me, just as yours is. Someday soon, we both of us will have to help each other."

"I'm not going blind," the boy cried. "I don't need any help! Let go—your hands hurt." The boy struggled to loose his hand, but the old woman clutched him tighter.

"It's all right to be scared," she said. "It won't be so bad."

"You're cold," the boy whimpered. His hand had turned blue in the woman's grip. "Your hands are too cold. Get away from me!"

He shoved her. She dropped his hand and fell in the hard dirt. Her cry of pain brought more figures running from the neighboring buildings. The boy ran inside his house, screaming, "Mother!"

The old woman's shawl drifted away on the wind. Icelin's eyes were still following the patch of green when the scene changed again.

This time it was the smoky interior of one of the thatched cottages. The old woman lay on a bed below a dark window. Candlelight illuminated her sunken features. She was clearly dead.

Kaelin's black-cloaked figures stood over the bed, talking in hushed whispers.

"They say he touched her, the day before she died. His hands were red and raw, like he'd been frostbitten. Frostbitten in the middle of Flamerule!"

"I say he made it happen," a female voice whispered. "The spellplague wormed through his fingers and killed poor Megwem. Any of us could be next. Don't let him touch you. He's got death in his hands!"

The black cloaks melted, and the scene changed again. Another cottage, a dirty kitchen, and the boy now sitting on the floor in front of a fire pit. A woman sat on a chair behind him. She had gray hair and bony arms. She cut herbs in quick little chopping motions on a board. Every few breaths, she would look up at the boy. Her eyes were shadowed.

"Where did you go to play today?" Her voice was strained. "I told you not to stray out of sight of the house."

"You mean out of your sight," the boy said without looking at her.

The board clattered to the floor. The woman yanked the boy to his feet by his belt. "You will not defy your mother, do you hear? If they find out you've touched anyone else—"

"I didn't kill Megwem!" He reached up to wrench her hand away, but she released him before he could touch her.

"You're just the same. You think I'm plague-touched!" he shouted.

"Darling, that's not true, I only—"

"She was already dying." Tears ran down the boy's face. "She was going to die anyway. I could feel it." He looked at his hands. They were still swollen. "She was so cold. How could she live like that?"

His shoulders shook. His mother turned him around and wrapped her arms around his waist. She stood behind him, rocking him slowly. The boy continued to sob, but eventually he quieted, soothed by his mother's arms.

Arms which were very careful not to touch his bare skin. Icelin could see the fear in her eyes, the fear she tried to hide from the boy.

The cottage vanished, whisking away the boy and his mother. In their place, Kaelin reappeared on top of a rotting crate. He held a rat comfortably in his lap. The rest of the troupe was gone.

"Well played!" The beggars were on their feet, applauding and whistling as enthusiastically as the crowd at the Cradle. Icelin could only sit and marvel at how quickly the illusion had come and gone. How fast a boy's life could change.

Kaelin slid off the crate, letting the rat run free. He walked over to stand in front of Icelin.

"Did you enjoy the show, false front?" he asked, his eyes alight.

Icelin shook her head. "You should have asked his permission. That wasn't right."

"Oh, but I did ask. He wanted to hear the tale of the boy lost in the wilderness. You should be grateful. He would never have told you himself."

"You still had no right."

"Ah well, then you have my deepest apologies," the boy said. He didn't sound the least bit abashed. "Perhaps I should tell him your tale, to even the ground between you."

"I have no secrets left from any of my friends," Icelin said. "You don't scare me."

Kaelin leaned down. "What about the secrets you're keeping from yourself?" he said, his words for her ears alone. "The tower where you've hidden them all?"

Icelin felt a chill. "I'm not the only one with secrets," she said unsteadily. "You are not truly a boy, are you? You are spirits imitating flesh."

"Of course we are," Kaelin said, sniffing as if he'd just been insulted. "But I remember what a child is, and so do they," he said, nodding at the beggars. "Everyone knows the best liars are children, and the best storytellers are liars. I am what I am, in service to my craft."

"So all that," Icelin said, waving to where the imaginary glade had been, "that was a lie?"

"To the senses, it was," Kaelin said. "As for the story itself—ask him."

Icelin blinked, and suddenly a sleek crow was sitting on her knee. The bird cawed once, loudly, and took flight. Icelin watched it until it disappeared beyond the wrecked ship.

The crowd of beggars broke up, each going to separate nooks of the ship to sleep or talk.

"We should all be resting," Bellaril said. She stood with Sull off to one side, where the beggars wouldn't hear.

"You two sleep," Icelin said. "Ruen and I will keep watch. I'll wake you in a couple of hours."

"Why should it be you?" Sull said. "You both look exhausted."

"We are," Icelin said. She looked at Ruen, who was staring at the crates and rats. He hadn't said a word. "Yet neither of us will sleep."

A quiet figure crouched in the shadows of two crates and gazed down on the beggar folk. He watched them settle in after their strange audience had concluded.

Imagine, watching a cluster of crows and rats for entertainment. Tarvin shook his head. His job had shown him some strange things, but this was a story for tavern talk if he'd ever heard one.

He stood up and faced the guard who'd come bearing a load of food: bread, dried meat, and a bushel basket of nearly rotting fruit.

"A hardy feast," he said, eyeing the fare. "I trust your master never neglects to bring the food?"

"None have died due to his neglect," the guard said. "Did you find what you sought? My master will require word of your departure."

"He doesn't like having me here," Tarvin said. "Well, there's some satisfaction in that. Tell him I'm leaving directly. I didn't find what I was looking for."

"A waif of a girl, wandering Mistshore; she's likely dead," the guard said.

"You think so?" Tarvin said. "I hope you're right."

The guard looked surprised. "I thought your orders were to bring her in alive?"

"Oh, I'm quite clear on my orders. My wishes are another matter." He crossed his arms. "I have little care whether Icelin Tearn lives or dies in Mistshore. She belongs here with the rest of the outcasts, as far as I'm concerned."

"Well then, I wish you good fortune in your diligent search," the guard said dryly. He pushed past Tarvin and began tying rope to the handles of the baskets.

"Are you judging me," Tarvin said, "when you're tossing food to the diseased with gloved hands and sweating because you don't want to get too close?" The guard didn't respond. Tarvin grabbed his arm and spun him around. "Answer me, wretch!"

The guard shrugged his arm off and put a hand to his sword hilt. "You won't be touching me, little watchman, not out here. You said it yourself: this is Mistshore, and we outcasts don't like to be looked at down the nose of Waterdeep's mighty, especially when he's all alone."

"Alone?" Tarvin said, laughing. "You have no idea how many of us walk in Mistshore this day. Best be holding those threats inside. You never know who might be listening."

"Be off with you," the guard said. He tipped the basket over the side of the ship and lowered the food. "Turn your wrath on the girl. I hope she keeps you running in Mistshore forever."

"You can be sure she won't," Tarvin said. He walked away from the guard, and walked back in the direction of Whalebone Court.

She couldn't hide for long, not with her wild nature. The burnt warehouse was just the beginning. It was only a matter of time before Icelin Tearn slipped up again and got somebody else killed.

Tarvin clenched a fist. Gods help her if she tried to turn her wild wrath on him or any of the Watch. Orders or no, he would bring her back to the Warden on a board before he let her magic kill any more of his friends.

He glanced toward the Court. He should meet up with the patrol to see if they'd gained any ground, but something held him back. His presence obviously irritated the master of the Cradle, so why not take advantage of the situation?

He settled back among the crates to watch the beggar folk a while longer. He found it strangely fascinating to see them from this distance, unobserved. Like watching the rats on a sinking ship. Except these rats were staying on board. Like the rest of Mistshore, they had nowhere else to go.

Icelin lay awake as darkness fell. She watched the stars come out, the tiny lights framed by a ship's hull. There were no floating crags tonight. She usually only saw them from her roof, on nights like this when she couldn't sleep. They were often illuminated in purple, their underbellies some kind of crystallized rock.

It had never occurred to her to wonder where the drifting motes came from. They'd been a part of that distant world for so long she'd never questioned what happened to them when they left Waterdeep's view.

Just as she'd never before questioned what her dreams meant, until Cerest, and Kaelin's whispered taunts. Now she wondered about the strange rock crags and the crumbling tower of her dreams. Why did she dream of a place she'd never been to? Why was an elf from distant lands seeking to possess her like an object of power?

"What are you thinking about?"

It was Ruen. He sat a few feet away from her in the dark. These were the first words he'd spoken since Kaelin's strange play had ended.

Icelin shifted so she could make out his profile. "How long did you stay in the village after you'd been scarred?"

"That's not what you were thinking about."

"I was thinking I should read Elgreth's letters. I have all this time to examine them, yet I haven't."

Ruen turned his head. She saw the slash of red in his eyes. "I didn't stay long. After Megwem, the whole village knew. They wouldn't touch me. When the monks came to take me into their training, I knew she—my mother—had arranged it somehow. That was fine. I didn't want to slip and accidentally learn or cause her death, anymore than she did. I'd rather they all died peacefully, without the knowledge of when it would happen."

"Is it such a certainty?" Icelin asked. "It doesn't seem possible to know when someone's going to die, just by touching them."

"Doesn't seem possible for someone to have a perfect memory either," Ruen said.

Icelin had nothing to say to that. "Were you happy with the monks?" she asked instead.

"For a time. The monks understood more than the others," Ruen said. "All things originate from the hands, they said. The ki. It's true. Otherwise Kaelin wouldn't have any stories for his stage."

"What do you mean?" Icelin asked.

"He touched all of the beggars. Not many barriers can keep the dead out, and the mortal mind is exceptionally fragile when it's weakened by illness or infirmity."

"If that's true, how did he know our stories?" Icelin said. "We're not sick."

Ruen looked at her a long time without saying anything, his gaze burning her with its intensity. It frightened her.

"What is it?" she whispered. "What's wrong?"

He blinked and shook his head. "Nothing. Maybe the boy could see through us because somewhere inside we wanted our stories told."

"Yet my letters sit unopened."

"So open them," Ruen said, his voice rough, tired. "Even I can't hide you indefinitely."

But I'm afraid. "Do you already know how all this is going to turn out?" Icelin asked. "Will I . . . die from this adventure?"

"I haven't touched you," Ruen said. "Not your hands, nor any part of your bare skin. I don't know how close to death you are." He looked down at her, and Icelin saw him chewing something over in his mind. When he spoke, it was hesitantly. "If you're afraid for your life, why not stop now? Turn yourself in to the

Watch, and you won't have to cast any more spells. I can see how they weaken you," he said when she started to speak. "Why do you hold onto magic, when it brings you so much grief?"

Icelin was silent for a long time. She knew exactly how to answer him, but she couldn't at first, because she'd never admitted it outright to herself. It felt strange to do so now.

"The first time I cast a spell, it was agony," Icelin said. "My head hurt; my stomach felt like it was being yanked inside out. When it was over, my teacher told me not to worry, that the pain would not always be so debilitating. I knew even then that he was wrong. I didn't care. I cast spell after spell; I learned every magic he taught me."

"Why?" Ruen said. "Why put yourself through the pain?"

"Because it made me *forget,*" Icelin said. "In that breath when I called the magic, the pain made me forget everything. Me, who can forget nothing. It was a miracle. All the memories I couldn't bury disappeared when the magic engulfed me. Their weight was gone. For that short time, I was free. Give up magic? I couldn't conceive of it, not until the fire. Even after I killed those people—"

"It was an accident," Ruen said.

"When I swore I would never use magic again, I broke my promise almost immediately. I locked all the dangerous spells away, yes, but even the little magics caused me pain. I kept those spells close, and cast them often. It was the only way I could forget."

"It's not so easy for the rest of us to forget," Ruen said. "The worst and the best memories stay with you. Some things you're supposed to experience, no matter how painful."

"Do words like that aid you, when you touch a man's bare flesh?" Icelin asked. "When you learn when he will die?"

"No," Ruen said. "But I still say the words. It's all I can do."

He turned his head away from her and tipped his hat down over his face. Icelin started to say something else but let it go.

She pulled the letters out of her pack and laid the bundle in her lap. The first she'd already read. She folded it carefully and laid it aside.

The second letter had dirt caked around the edges of the parchment. Icelin fingered the stains. This letter had come from outside Waterdeep. She wondered what it had gone through to make its way to her great-uncle's house.

Breaking the brittle seal, Icelin unfolded the pages.

> *Dear Granddaughter,*
>
> *I wish you could be with me as I pass through the Dalelands. You would love this country. The sun is rising, the air is crisp, but the dying hints of campfire keep me warm. If I listen closely, I can hear the most remarkable sounds. Brant would call me sentimental, but I imagine I can hear the voices of those who walked these roads long ago. What stories would they tell, these brave phantoms, if they could stop a while by my fire? Would their adventures be of storming perilous castles or tilling fertile fields? Would they slay dragons or raise daughters? All these things I wonder, as I sit by my fire and think of you.*

Icelin clutched the parchment in her hands. This letter and the handful following all came from a different land or city—some she had never heard of. Four years went by in a bell as she read. The only thing she could conclude of her grandfather, besides his affection for her, was that restless was too weak a word to ascribe to him. He never stopped moving.

> *Dear Granddaughter,*
>
> *Today I looked for the first time upon the city of Luskan. I pray you never have cause to enter this den of depravity and violence. There is no law but that of*

the thieves' guilds and street gangs. Ever at war with each other, they take no notice of a lone man seeking shelter.

I sat upon a rooftop and looked out over Cutlass Island, at the ruins of the Host Tower of the Arcane. The locals say it is a cursed place, and I cannot help but agree. The restless dead walk that isle, sentinels to its lost power. In my younger days, I would have longed for the challenge and promise of treasure to be found in such a forgotten stronghold. I can see the magic swirling under shattered stone. It drifts among the bones of the once mighty wizards who ruled here. The riches tempt me even now, but my strength would never hold out long enough to reach the isle, which seems as distant as gentle Waterdeep. No, tonight I long only for a warm blanket and unspoilt food. Strange how one's priorities shift with age.

Icelin stopped reading. Hatsolm rolled onto his side, bumping against her leg. He coughed once, deep in his chest, then again. A fit overtook him, and he curled upright into a ball, his body shaken by the hacks and wheezes. Icelin pulled his blanket up over his shoulders. He opened his eyes and looked at her.

"I'll get you some water," she said.

"No need." He wiped the blood from his mouth. "It's over." He pulled the blanket over his head and laid back down, his face turned away from her.

Icelin looked at the letter in her hand. Hatsolm had come to Waterdeep seeking refuge from the world, and he'd found it, in a way, through Kaelin and his ghostly troupe.

Elgreth spoke of being old. The tone of this letter was much different from his earlier messages to her. Perhaps he wasn't sick like Hatsolm, but he seemed in no fit condition to travel in Luskan. Her great-uncle had always said the city was not a city at all, but a damned place where only the desperate sought refuge.

She went back to the letters. They continued in Luskan for a year, all written from the same perch on the rooftop. Elgreth had constructed a rough shelter from abandoned slates of tin and wood, in the ruins of a condemned tavern. The more she read, the more Icelin suspected that her grandfather's adventure would not continue beyond the hellish city.

At the bottom of the pile, Icelin found an especially thick bundle. The seal was cracked; the wax had not been sufficient to hold the folded parchment. Was it a memoir? A deathbed request? It was the last letter. Icelin's fingers shook as she unfolded the sheets.

Dear Granddaughter,

The time has come. You are old enough now to be told the truth. But even if you were not, I have no time left to delay this tale. I pray it never happens, but if Cerest comes looking for you, you must be prepared.

CHAPTER 15

Ruen watched Icelin reading her letters. Her attention was completely absorbed by the writing on the page.

He sat up quietly, slid into the shadows, and climbed the ladder. When he got to the dock he glanced down to be sure he hadn't been followed. He slipped the illusion cloak from his shoulders and moved through the shadows in his own form.

When he was safely out of earshot of the beggars, he pulled the *sava* pawn from his pouch and warmed it between his fingers. He felt the connection at once.

"What is it, Morleth?"

Tallmantle's voice. "Where's Tesleena?" he asked. "Has she tired of me so soon?"

"She walks in Mistshore, seeking Icelin," the Warden said. "Know that if Tesleena comes to harm through your delays, none of the squalor in Waterdeep will be able to hide you from me." The Warden's voice was polite, even conversational.

"Your wizard will be fine," Ruen said. "Icelin is another matter."

"What's happened?"

Ruen hesitated before plunging into the tale. He left nothing out—his battle in the Cradle, Icelin's letters, her unique memory, and every instance of her spells going wild. He gave a detailed account of what Arowall had told him about Icelin's gifts. When he'd finished there was a long silence.

"Are you certain?" the Warden asked. "Certain she is dying?"

"I haven't touched her," Ruen said. "Nor will I, so do not

waste breath in asking. "But I see the evidence of my eyes. She needs help. Perhaps Tesleena—"

"Are you saying you're willing to bring her in?"

Ruen clenched the pawn in his fist. "Can you aid her, if I do?"

"Tesleena and I will do everything in our power. Tell me where you are, and I'll send a patrol to get you."

She won't forgive me, Ruen thought. But she'll be alive.

"Not yet," Ruen said. "It has to be her decision."

"Ruen—"

"Thank you, Warden. I'll be in touch. Give my regards to Tesleena." He severed the connection.

In the end, there was no choice. Perhaps, if he let the Watch capture them, the Warden would take pity on him and not reveal his identity to Icelin and the others.

"So it's the coward's way, as always." He shook his head. Soon he would be well and truly hidden in the Watch's skirts, a tamed dog they used for their own amusement. Or was he already there, and he just didn't realize it? If that was so, what more could the opinion of one dying woman matter to him?

Tarvin couldn't believe his luck. Ruen Morleth, expelled from the bowels of the beggar ship by the gods' own sweet blessing.

He considered subduing the man, but thought better of it when Ruen spoke into the *sava* pawn. Tarvin recognized the Watch Warden's voice, though he could make out little of the substance of the conversation.

If Ruen Morleth was here, then Icelin Tearn was somewhere nearby. Tarvin looked down into the ship, but he could see nothing except rag-cloaked bodies.

Odds were she was hiding among the sick. It was brilliant, in a twisted way. The wench must be truly desperate.

There was no chance in the Nine Hells he was going down

there to search for her. He could go back to the Court and warn the others. They would come in force and root the beggars out, but in the meantime Icelin might leave her hiding place for a safer one. If she did that, he would lose his chance to capture her.

Tarvin sank low in the shadows, hiding himself again behind the crates—abandoned food cartons, by the smell and the buzz of flies. For now, he would wait.

He watched Ruen Morleth clench his fist and slide the pawn away in his pouch. He looked angry, perhaps at something the Warden had said. Was he upset that he was about to lose his wild little plaything?

Go on and sulk, dog. The Warden will have you both. Tarvin smiled at the thought.

Cerest watched Ristlara and Shenan work their magic. Arcane radiance lit up the ship's cabin.

Ristlara had Arowall's hands pinned to his desk with two gold-hilted daggers. Magic pulsed down the blades into the man's skin. The pale blue light ran sickly up his arms, creating new veins while pushing others out of the way.

The man's face twisted in agony. A steady stream of blood and spittle ran down his chin. His eyes were fixed on some unknown distance. He would not look at either of the females while the magic sapped his life energies.

"I don't understand," Shenan said. She sounded like a parent disappointed in the performance of a beloved child. "We never have this trouble with the daggers."

"He's strong-willed," Cerest said, but Ristlara shook her gold tresses impatiently.

"He's human. He should have broken by now."

At her words, Arowall spat blood and a piece of what looked like his own tongue. He collapsed facedown on the desktop, his head between the glowing blades. Ristlara moved hastily out of the way.

"Pull the blades out," Shenan told her. When the magic faded from his skin, she rolled the man over and laid her head against his heart. "Dead," she said.

"Your daggers aren't as effective as you thought, Shenan." Cerest slammed his fist against the ship's hull. A waste of time, all of it. He was no closer to finding Icelin than he was a day ago.

"She's obviously here. Half the crowd saw her, but strangely, none of them know where she went," Ristlara said sardonically.

"They fear Arowall," Shenan said. She ran her fingers through the dead man's thin hair. "He's not so terrifying. Perhaps Mistshore has its own sense of loyalty. Incredible thought, isn't it?"

"Search the ships," Cerest said. "The ones circling the Cradle must belong to Arowall. If she's still here, we'll find her."

The Locks exchanged glances. Ristlara nodded at her sister and went above. Cerest could hear her gathering her men.

Arowall's domain had been shockingly easy to penetrate, despite the guards stationed on deck. Cerest supposed Arowall had put the majority of his resources behind maintaining the Cradle instead of seeing to his own protection. A fatal mistake.

Shenan stayed perched on Arowall's desk. She folded her arms across her chest and gazed at him with that parental expression he loathed.

"Well?" Cerest demanded. "Say whatever is on your tongue. I don't have time to waste."

"Cerest, why not give this up?" Shenan said. "We're all exhausted near to dropping, and we've come closer to the Watch patrols than any of us are comfortable."

"I never took the Locks for cowards," Cerest said.

The elf woman smiled faintly. "Oh, Cerest, sometimes I forget how young you are, how like a spoiled child who never gets his way. Do you believe those sorts of taunts will move either Ristlara or I to action?"

"You've been compliant so far."

"We have, because the chase amused us, in the beginning. Also, we recognized the profit to be made by aligning ourselves with you and the girl. But you're ruled by your impulses, Cerest. That's why you will never make a proper merchant, because your emotion gives you away. People can always tell when you want something so badly it threatens to break you. Isn't that why your father let you live but denied you your birthright, because he knew you valued it more than your own life?"

She knew it would provoke him. Cerest could see it in her eyes. He obliged her. He strode to the desk and backhanded her across the face. She fell over Arowall's body, her hair spreading wildly over the dead man's face.

Sitting up, Shenan put a finger to her split lip. Blood welled against her hand. Her face would swell and bruise, but she smiled as if he'd kissed her mouth instead of punching it.

"In the end, that's why we love you, Cerest," she said. "Allow me to be equally blunt: if you continue to pursue Icelin, you will likely be killed, by the Watch or by the allies Icelin has gathered. Perhaps Icelin herself will be your undoing." She raised a hand to stop his argument. "You may continue to hunt her as long as you like. I don't mind how many of the human dogs we lose—keep them and use them with my blessing—but I will protect my sister and our business interests."

"You would leave me?" Cerest said, and he realized he sounded very much like a bewildered child. But this was how it always ended. Everyone in his life had deserted him when he needed them most: his father, Elgreth, now the Locks.

"Where did I go wrong with all of them," he said aloud.

Shenan slid to the edge of the desk so her knees were touching Cerest's thighs. She put a bloody hand against his cheek. "You don't have any notion of what a conscience is, do you? Of how to trace your actions to consequences? Your mind doesn't work that way. It's fascinating. You don't realize what you did to them, to Elgreth and the others, do you?"

Cerest pulled away, wiping the blood from his face. He felt unsteady in the knees, but he didn't know why. Was Shenan right? Was there some part of his mind that functioned differently from other folk, beyond the differences that separated elf from human? He'd never considered it before. He'd always taken for granted that he was an oddity, an elf in a swell of humans. But to hear her say it gave him pause. "Icelin is different," he said. "We can start over."

Shenan shook her head. "You killed her great-uncle—"

"Brant is not her blood," Cerest said. Why couldn't they understand? "He lied to her about her family. She owes no loyalty to him."

"She loves him as she will never love you, Cerest. She will act precisely as Elgreth acted. She will resist you, or she will run. That is the truth."

"You're wrong," Cerest said. "I can convince her. I can make her see that it wasn't my fault."

She searched his face, read the conviction there, and nodded. Standing on her toes, she kissed him on the brow, on his scar, and finally on his mouth. When she was done, she put her lips against his good ear so he would hear her whisper.

"I wish you good fortune, my love, and I will mourn you when you are gone to the gods."

Cerest didn't reply. He stood, stiffly, and let her have her way. When she'd gone, he remained at Arowall's desk, staring at the dead man. Ristlara's men, he knew, would be waiting for him on deck. To leave him such resources was more than generous, but he wasn't feeling generous at the moment.

His head ached, and his mind screamed with the implications of Shenan's words. What if she was right? What if Icelin rejected him, as Elgreth had?

Cerest acknowledged that Shenan was probably justified in her concerns. Between Icelin's magic and the sheer number of hunters he'd had after her, they'd been attracting too much attention. Perhaps it was time for a different strategy.

When he climbed the ladder, Ristlara's men were waiting. "We're going separate ways," Cerest said. "The first man who sights the girl and returns to me at Whalebone Court will be paid in more gold than any of you have ever seen. Look, listen, but do not approach her. Follow her to whatever hiding place she's using during the day. Once we know where she goes to ground, we'll have her. Do you understand?"

They nodded. Cerest dismissed them. He looked around the empty Cradle, but he knew he would not see Shenan or Ristlara.

If Shenan was right, he wouldn't be able to keep Icelin from deserting him. But there were options, magics that controlled the mind and made a person's will pliable. Wasn't he the expert in objects of such Art?

Everything would work out this time. Shenan was wrong. He had it all under control.

Icelin stared at the words on the page.

> *I pray it never happens, but if Cerest comes looking for you, you must be prepared.*
>
> *I hope you will have no need of the tale I am about to impart. My absence from Waterdeep should dissuade Cerest from searching for you, and if it does not, he could hardly know where to begin in a city so vast. He did not know about Brant.*
>
> *To my sorrow, my brother and I were never as close as we should have been, but perhaps it's for the best. Now, to the tale.*

You must understand, and not be deceived by the good man Cerest once was. He grew up the third son of the Elenithils, a noble family of Myth Drannor. He was educated at the behest of his late mother's family, because Cerest's father would never acknowledge his son's existence or birthright.

There was much evidence that Cerest was the child of an affair between Lady Elenithil and a rival family's eldest son. He was several decades her junior. Cerest's mother died soon after his birth under mysterious circumstances. Lord Elenithil was a prominent suspect, but nothing could be proven; so his reputation survived, while Cerest was publicly shunned as evidence of the fall of a noble lady of Myth Drannor.

Cerest took his education, but he left Myth Drannor as soon as he came of age. I first met him in Baldur's Gate. He'd come to the city to establish himself as a merchant. He had a small portion of his mother's wealth to invest but no interest in the common trade in Baldur's Gate.

I was an adventurer at the time, wandering out from the city to the ruins of tombs and strongholds and floating motes fallen from the heavens. I made enough coin to survive by selling my findings, but I hadn't the resources or manpower to delve as deeply into Faerûn's changed landscape as I desired. Then I met Cerest.

He purchased some of the pieces I brought back from the ruins. During the third such of these transactions, he confided that he had been in contact with a newly wedded couple who were interested in cataloging the artifacts to document the changes to Faerûn and its magic, resulting from the spellplague.

Here at last was my chance. With Cerest and the young man and woman, I had an expert team to explore more of Faerûn than I ever could hope to on my own. They would have their research, Cerest would have his profit, and my obsession for the unknown would be satisfied. It seemed the perfect arrangement, and we became quite close.

The young couple, Lisra and Edlend, were of course your parents. We were exploring a tomb in distant Aglarond when Lisra was four months heavy with you. We found a name scrawled on the wall, the only marking in the lonely ruins: Icelin. When you were born, Cerest named you after her. Lisra and Edlend named me your grandfather.

I wish I could tell you all the things your parents longed to give you, Icelin. It was their wish that you would follow in their footsteps. I think Cerest wished this, as well—that we would all continue on together, one human generation replacing the last. We were the closest thing to family the elf had ever experienced in his life.

Considering all this, the happiness that we shared, I can't explain why Cerest brought it all crashing down. He lied to us, but you see, we had no reason not to trust him. He had always told us the truth, so we believed him when he swore it was safe. You must believe me, Icelin, you must! I would have given my life before I saw you or your parents hurt.

Icelin turned the page over, but there was no more writing. The letter simply ended.

"No," she said, her breath coming fast. "That can't be all." She went back over each page, thinking one had gotten out of order. When she didn't find another, she sorted through all the letters. Panic made her clumsy; the pages sailed out of her hands, blurring in a yellow haze as her vision swam. The world seemed to spin.

It was too much to take. Elgreth wasn't her grandfather. Brant wasn't her blood at all. She had always been alone in the world, she just hadn't known it. All because of Cerest.

"How," she said, her voice shrill. "How did it happen? Gods above, tell me!"

"Icelin."

She jumped, but it was only Sull. He looked like he hadn't slept at all. There were great red pouches under his eyes.

"What's wrong?" he asked.

Bellaril was sitting up too. She rubbed her eyes with a fist. "What's all the noise?" she demanded.

"Nothing," Icelin said. She slid the letters away in her pack. "It can wait. I'm sorry I disturbed you all." She looked around. "Where's Ruen?"

She heard footsteps on the ladder. Ruen climbed down to them.

"I've been scouting," he said. "It's almost full dark. We can move around soon." He looked to Icelin. "If you're ready to leave?"

"I've read the letters," Icelin said, aware of Sull and Bellaril listening. "My grandfather, Elgreth, tried to warn me about Cerest. He knew he might come after me." She looked at Sull. "Brant must have known. Even if he'd never read the letters himself, he must have known about Cerest. Elgreth wouldn't have left his own brother ignorant of the danger."

"Of course he wouldn't," Sull said soothingly. "Your great-uncle probably thought, after so much time, the elf had given up lookin'. And what was the sense in frightenin' you if that was the case?"

He had given up, until I saved his life in the street, Icelin thought. The bitter irony of it made her dizzy. She remembered thinking, in the moment she'd pushed the elf to the ground, that she was doing something good—a small act of penance for all the harm she'd done. The gods had a cruel streak in them.

"Why's he so interested in you?" Bellaril asked. "Begging your pardon, but you don't seem worth all the men and coin he must be losing."

"I couldn't agree more," Icelin said. "I thought Cerest wanted revenge, but he said he wanted me for my abilities. He said Elgreth had a powerful spellscar; he thought I shared it. Why he would pursue someone with such unstable magic is beyond me, though Elgreth did allow that Cerest's interest lay heavily with magic."

Kredaron had said the same, that Cerest was fascinated by the Art. He'd thought, just as she had, that the elf's scars were a result of a brush with wild magic. If that was the case, Cerest should want nothing to do with her.

"Is there more?" Ruen asked.

"Yes," Icelin said. "This is the part where things get muddled. Cerest used to work with my parents and Elgreth. They adventured together. But for some reason, Cerest betrayed them."

"Why?" Ruen asked.

"I don't know. The letters end. They were either lost or sent incomplete to Brant. I'm sure Cerest would tell you the tale, the next time he catches up to us."

"Maybe it's time that happened."

It was Sull who had spoken. Icelin looked at him. "You can't be serious?"

"I am," Sull said. "That elf's used to huntin' us, drivin' us to ground. Let's turn the tables on 'im, see how he likes being chased."

"We're outnumbered," Ruen reminded him, "even with Bells."

The dwarf snorted. "I'm not afraid of an elf with a mashed-in face."

"None of you are attacking Cerest on my behalf," Icelin said. "We're not discussing it."

"There's another option," Ruen said.

Icelin waited, but the monk didn't speak. She cocked an eyebrow at him. "This option involves throwing us headlong into more danger and strangeness, doesn't it?"

Sull threw up his hands. "I thought it didn't get any stranger than this!"

"I think it's time we go to the Watch," Ruen said.

CHAPTER 16

Silence fell over the group. Icelin thought at first he was jesting.

"You're mad," she told Ruen. "I'm not giving myself up to the Watch. I'd rather spend my life in Mistshore."

Bellaril regarded her as if she'd just asked what color the sky was on clear days. "You're just as daft as he is, if you mean that," she said.

"She's only a child," Ruen said, which made Icelin want to plant her fingernails in his eyes. "She doesn't know what Waterdeep is."

"Then what is it?" Icelin said, forgetting to keep her voice down. "Open my eyes, Ruen Morleth, to more horrors. I don't think I've had enough thus far."

"He doesn't mean to hurt you, girl," spoke a voice, and everyone except Ruen jumped.

Hatsolm rubbed the sleep from his eyes and regarded them blearily from his curled-up pallet. There was a crust of dried blood at the corner of his mouth.

"I'm sorry," Icelin said, ashamed. "I didn't mean to wake you."

"Doesn't matter, I wasn't sleeping anyway," Hatsolm said. He sat up slowly. Sull put his hand on the man's shoulders to steady him. "The problem is that when we're children we're only conscious of our own suffering."

"I don't understand," Icelin said. She felt like a child, and she didn't like it. Nelzun had never made her feel this way.

"You only know the safe space in which you were brought

up," Hatsolm said. "That's a wonderful thing, but it doesn't lend itself well to wisdom, or to understanding why folk do the things they do."

"So to understand why Cerest is after me, I have to go right back where I started?" Icelin said. "Into the hands of the people who think I murdered my own great-uncle, the same people who hate me for killing one of their own?"

"No." This time it was Ruen who spoke. "To understand yourself, you have to put your pride and fear aside. Believe me, I know what that costs a person. But the Watch can help you."

"How?"

"I think you know." He looked her in the eyes. "Your great-uncle would not have you live as a fugitive. More than that, the Watch have wizards, folk who can help the spellscarred."

Icelin felt like she'd been struck in the stomach. "No," she said automatically. "I have never been touched by the spellplague."

"Are you certain?" Ruen said, his eyes boring relentlessly into her. Those red eyes. Spellscarred eyes.

"Of course!" Icelin took a step back from them all. "I grew up in South Ward! Waterdeep is safe from the plague."

"Safe, is it?" Hatsolm said gently. "Waterdeep is a refuge to those scarred by the plague. They may be scorned, shoved into forgotten corners like Mistshore, but the plague is part of us."

"No!" Icelin wrapped her arms around herself. The weeping sores stood out on her arms. Repulsed, she ripped the cloak off, peeling away the layers of rags and rotting flesh. She needed to see her own skin, needed to see it normal.

"Put your cloak back on!" Ruen snatched the cloth and covered her. "You'll be contaminated."

"I'm not plagued or spellscarred. I'm not like—"

"Like me?" Ruen said.

She took a step back. "You know that's not what I meant. Stop twisting my words."

Sull touched her arm. Icelin tried to back away, but he held her fast. "You know I'm with you, girl. But just because you've got gifts others don't, doesn't mean you're not a Waterdhavian. You have the right to be protected. You shouldn't be afraid."

"Why not?" Icelin's chest heaved. "Look what my gifts have done." Her magic brought nothing but disaster, and her memory ensured that she never forgot any of it. Every experience, frozen in her mind, perfectly preserved.

Except one.

"I have the same dream every night." She spoke haltingly. Sull squeezed her arm. "I'm in a tower, surrounded by people whose faces I can't see. There's a bright light, a burning light, and I'm afraid." She looked at Ruen. "There's no such tower in Waterdeep. I've looked."

"If you've been outside the city, why don't you remember?" Ruen asked.

"I don't know," Icelin said. "You've no idea what it's like, to have everything lined up and catalogued in your mind, a vast library of things you can't ever be rid of; yet there's this huge crack in the wall, a terrifying maw, and *that's* the knowledge you'd give anything to have."

"What's the Watch going to do for her?" Bellaril spoke up. "If she's scarred, then that's that. Doesn't help her with the elf."

"There are too many missing pieces," Icelin said. "The rest of the dream, Elgreth and his spellscar. That's what Cerest wants. Bellaril's right. The Watch can't help me with any of that."

"But if you accept the spellplague is the source of your flawless memory, that's a place to start," Ruen said. "Waterdeep has done better than any city keeping the plague at bay. There's a reason for that. You won't find another realm in Faerûn where folk know more about the plague's effects."

Bellaril smiled grimly. "And you think she'll just stride up to them and start interviewing likely candidates to help her, do you?"

"The other choice is confrontin' Cerest," Sull said.

"He won't harm Icelin, but he'll have no compulsion to spare the rest of us," Ruen said. He looked at Icelin. "Do you want to risk Sull's life? Do you want to see the elf slide a blade into him the way he took your great-uncle?"

"Don't say that to her," Sull said sharply. "I can see to myself fine enough, and I don't need a magic ring to do it."

Ruen shook his head. "You're a fool. You claim you want to protect her? You're letting your guilt cloud your judgment. It makes you useless to her."

Sull went pale. His hand slid off Icelin's arm.

Icelin looked at Ruen. He was like a stranger, his eyes bright, almost feverish. "What's wrong with you?" she demanded. "The last place you would ever put yourself is in the path of the Watch. Your instinct for self-preservation is too strong." Her eyes narrowed. "Why is it so important to you to see me safely delivered to them?"

"Because he's finally smartened up to doing what he's told."

The voice rang out above them, and a crossbow bolt twanged into the hull a foot above Icelin's head.

The cluster of beggars, stirred to wakefulness by their argument, sprang into frightened motion at the shot. Filthy bodies crowded toward the ladder.

"Stay down!"

Another bolt stuck in the wood above the ladder. The beggars fell back, knocking each other aside in their haste to get away.

Icelin took an elbow to the ribs. Her feet and arms were jammed in the press of bodies. She tried to look up, but the sky spun wildly as she was pulled in one direction or another. She crouched down, trying not to be hit by the bolts she knew were meant for her.

Ruen slammed into Icelin from the side, knocking her to the ground. Her breath whooshed from her chest, and she lay, gasping, staring up at the sky. She tried to roll onto her back, but Ruen was suddenly on top of her. He threw his disguise cloak over both their bodies. Darkness closed in on her completely.

"Stop! Ruen, we have to get out—"

"Quiet!" he said in her ear. "He can't know which one you are, not after all that uproar."

Their attacker must have come to the same conclusion. The firing stopped, and the beggars gradually wore out their frenzy. Icelin could feel them pressing together and against her. They protected themselves by sheer numbers, blending into one form.

"Come out, lass." The voice, mocking and deep, rang out again. "I've already seen your pretty face. You look much better without the sores, Icelin Tearn."

"Gods, I'm a fool," Icelin whispered.

Ruen put a finger to his lips and listened. "He's pacing the dock," he said. "I can hear his bootsteps. I think he's alone."

"He's had plenty of time to reload," Icelin said. "If you try to reach the ladder, he'll put a bolt in your head."

"I'm not convinced he's that good of a shot," Ruen said. He pitched his voice louder. "Name yourself, friend, and we might invite you down to Eveningfeast. We're having stew and apples with the cores plucked out. Are you coming to us from the Watch?"

"I am. Tarvin is my name, and I won't be sharing your table, Ruen Morleth," the man said. "I'm here for the woman, but I'd just as happily bury a bolt in your eye, if you don't hand her over."

"I would *happily* oblige you," Ruen said, "but I'm afraid she doesn't want to go with you. She's a stubborn, difficult creature. I've almost drowned her a time or two."

"You're a smooth liar, Morleth, but in this I believe you. What of the rest of you, then?" he said, his voice rolling over the heads of the beggars. "You willing to give your lives to protect a fugitive? She's not one of you. I saw her. She wears a mask of disease. She mocks you and your suffering."

"She's fresh air to your foul breath," Hatsolm said, and the crowd laughed, tentatively. "If she wants to stay in Mistshore and deigns to walk among us, she's welcome. She's a lot braver than your Watch friends, who won't come to Mistshore at all."

There was a collective murmur of agreement from the crowd. Icelin closed her eyes. Gods, he wouldn't kill them, would he? Not for hatred of me.

The crowd tensed, waiting. Icelin couldn't breathe.

"Ruen—"

"Don't," Ruen said. He tightened his grip on her. "He's bluffing."

He was right. There must have been a spark of decency in Tarvin, for in the end he only laughed. "You're truly a wonder, lady. You've got the freaks lapping at your hand."

"Be silent!" The words burst from her before she could stop them.

"She speaks," Tarvin cried, and his voice moved past them. "Sing out again, lovely one, and show yourself."

"Tell your friends to leave Mistshore," Icelin said. "I'd rather die here than be taken and tried for what's in the past. Your bitterness makes my choice for me, Tarvin."

"How long do you think you can survive here?" Icelin could hear him toying with the crossbow string. "We'll drag you and your friends out of there one by one. Is that what you want for them?"

Ruen shifted, alert again. "Now that's an odd statement," he said. "You haven't yet mentioned your friends. Hard to believe they'd be waiting in the shadows while you have your tantrum. Hardly professional conduct for a Watchman. No, I think you're alone up there, and you can't quite figure out what to do about it. If you leave for help, we escape; and if you stay, you're outnumbered. I don't envy you, truly."

"Shut up," Tarvin snarled. "I can wait you out well enough. How would that be? A tenday with no food, no water, and no one to clean your filth—how friendly will you be to the pretty bitch then?"

"Maybe he's right," Icelin whispered. "If he keeps us here, people could get hurt. You said yourself I should turn myself in."

"Not to him," Ruen said. "Not to that one. He's no Watchman."

"I killed his friend," Icelin said. "He has reason to despise me."

"The beggars have done nothing to him," Ruen said. "No Watchman is so cowardly as to threaten the weak." He didn't realize his voice was rising.

"He thinks he knows so much about us," Tarvin said. "Don't you wonder why that is? You want to stake your chances with Morleth? Maybe you'd be grateful to hear some truth about him, eh?"

"Don't listen to him," Ruen said. There was a note of panic in his voice Icelin had never heard before. Dread stirred in her belly.

"Is she too shy to ask? Are you keeping her silent, Morleth, with the weight of your eyes? If you're innocent, what could you possibly have to fear?"

"What truth is he talking about, Ruen?" Icelin said. His body was rigid. He could have been carved of stone.

"Did you ever ask him how he escaped Waterdeep's dungeons?" Tarvin asked. "It must have been a marvelous feat. I'm shocked he hasn't bragged of it up and down Mistshore. Didn't you ever think it strange that a man like him, a thief, would risk his life to aid you?" Tarvin was pacing again. His voice came from directly above them. "Such men work only in exchange for wealth you've never possessed, my lady. Of course it was easy enough for Morleth to steal the treasure he wanted. He lived like a king, with Hawlace's collection to sell off piece by piece. You get used to that kind of lifestyle, well then you can't stand being put in a cage. Makes a man do things. Maybe make bargains he'll come to regret later."

Icelin twisted, trying to look into Ruen's face, but he pressed her down.

"Don't move," Ruen said tersely. "He wants you panicked. As soon as you throw the cloak off, you'll be staring down his crossbow. Don't be stupid!"

"Let me go," Icelin said. She pushed against Ruen's chest, but she couldn't move him. The cloak and his body were suffocating her. Smells of sweat and fear and sickness mingled together in her nostrils.

"Or maybe," Tarvin said, "the question you should be asking yourself is why a master thief turned Watch agent can't deliver one murdering wench to his betters?"

The strength left Icelin's body. She stopped struggling and lay still on the cold floor.

"Icelin," Ruen said. The guilt in his voice sealed everything. "Listen to me. He's baiting you. He knows your temper; he's using it to paw at you."

"Deny it," Icelin said. "Tell me he's not speaking the truth."

At last, he looked at her. Was it any harder for him now than it had ever been? His red eyes betrayed no expression, as always. Somehow that made it worse.

"What can I tell you that you will want to hear, Icelin?" Ruen said. "That I'm not a Watchman—with fervor I tell you I'm not."

"Are you working with them?" Icelin said.

"Yes."

Unexpectedly, Icelin had the urge to laugh. "It might have been easier if you'd tried a denial," she said. "At least then I would know you regretted it."

He clenched his jaw. "You'll never know how much. There were reasons."

"So many things make sense now," Icelin said. "It's very freeing, you know. You risking your life for so little payment, how easy it was to find you—I should have known my tracking prowess left too much to be desired. I suppose Fannie was in on everything? I probably had that one coming, though, since I almost got her killed. You should pay her extra for that."

"It was never about coin," Ruen said.

"Actually, that might have made things turn out differently," Icelin said. "On the raft, I should have offered up my virtue after all. It might have been inducement enough for you not to betray me."

"Spew venom at me later," Ruen said. "We don't have time for this."

"You're right," Icelin said. "Don't worry. You thought I should go to the Watch, and now the Watch has come to me. I'm going to give everyone what they want."

"I won't let you," Ruen said when she tried to push against him. "We've danced this dance before. You won't move me."

"Probably not," Icelin said, "but I have other weapons now."

She lifted her head and put her lips against his mouth. It wasn't a kiss, and not remotely romantic. But it was skin to skin contact, and that was all she needed.

For Ruen's part, she might have hit him with a lightning bolt and evoked a similar reaction. He recoiled so fast that, for just an instant, he lost his balance.

Icelin shoved him with all her strength. She couldn't roll him off her. He locked his legs around her knees, but she managed to get one hand free. She ripped the cloak from her body.

Fresh air and startled cries from the beggars swamped her. Icelin blinked in the darkness, trying to adjust her eyes. She heard a clattering on the ladder and looked up.

Tarvin stood halfway up on the rungs, the crossbow leveled at her chest.

"Well met, lady," he said. "I'm glad you could see reason."

Ruen released her and rolled to his feet. He was an easy target, but Tarvin kept the crossbow trained on Icelin.

"I'm not going to bother with you, Morleth," he said, his

gaze never leaving Icelin's. "Tales of your weapon-catching skills abound. But I don't think your lady is quite as talented. Step back, please. Give Icelin room to climb the ladder."

He climbed back up, slowly, keeping the weapon level on her. When he was back on the dock, he motioned to her.

"Climb up and keep both hands on the rungs," he said. "Bring your clever disguise."

Icelin picked up the cloak and spared one last glance at Ruen and the cluster of beggars. She made her eyes move unseeing over Bellaril and Sull, who were huddled near the back of the crowd.

They must have been herded there by the others, for protection, Icelin thought. Bellaril gripped Sull's arm to keep him from moving. Icelin inclined her head a fraction at the dwarf, as if to say, *keep him back*. Bellaril returned the nod.

"Thank you," Icelin said to Hatsolm, who stood at the front of the group.

"Be wary, lass," Hatsolm said. His eyes were sad. "Remember what I said. You aren't in a child's world now."

She nodded. She didn't look at Ruen.

The ladder climb was quick, much faster than the descent had been, though she tried to go as slowly as possible. When she was on the dock, she held out her disguise cloak to Tarvin.

"Put it on," Tarvin said. "I want to see what you look like."

The group below stirred angrily, but Icelin didn't react. She unfolded the cloak and draped it over herself. Immediately, the sores reappeared, and her flesh took on the ghostly pallor of disease.

"Is this to your liking?" Icelin said. "It's not a punishment equal to Therondol's death."

"You're right," Tarvin said. "I take my vengeance where I can."

"I understand, but if you march a plagued woman through Mistshore at the end of a crossbow, you're bound to attract unwanted attention. Is your vengeance worth that?"

"Worth my life and yours." He took her by the shoulder and spun her around so her back was to him. He put the crossbow at the base of her spine. "Walk, lady, and don't fret. We aren't going far."

Borion was cold, and he didn't like the harbor smell. Not that anyone asked his opinion.

He walked slightly behind Trik, his partner. The elf with the funny face had told them to split up, but Borion never went anywhere without Trik. When Trik wasn't around, things got fuzzy. If the elf was angry, well that was too bad.

"What we doing out here, Trik?" Borion asked. He must have asked this question before, because Trik turned around and made a dirty gesture at him. Borion grinned. He couldn't help it if his memory was short.

They fell into step together, but Trik was quiet for a while. That didn't bother Borion. He knew Trik would answer him before too long.

"You know, Boss, I'm walking here, asking myself that same question. Frightening that I'm starting to think at your level, isn't it?"

Trik always called him "Boss." Borion wasn't any higher rank than anyone else in the band, but he was bigger than all of them, and stronger.

"If you don't know why we're out here, Trik, how do you know where we're going?" Borion asked, not because he was overly curious, but because he didn't want to get lost in Mistshore. He didn't like the place.

He didn't like the city much, either. If they were traveling, he'd be happy. Outside the walls, the air was cleaner, and there weren't so many people. People scared him. They moved too fast, and he had a hard time keeping up with their speech.

It wasn't that way with Trik. Trik had lost part of his leg in a tomb raid, had it chopped off by a portcullis that hadn't stayed up like it was supposed to. So now he walked with a limp. Borion had no trouble keeping pace with Trik.

"We're going to stay close to those whale bones, or whatever they are," Trik said, "maybe go in for some ale. Let the elf rot for a while, I say."

"Boss won't like that," Borion said, referring this time to their actual boss, Rynin.

Trik stopped again, so suddenly Borion almost ran him over. "Have you got maggots for brains?" Trik said. "Rynin's dead. He got himself killed in that fight with Arowall's guards. We're thin in numbers, my dumb friend, and it's starting to make me anxious."

It took an effort, but finally Borion remembered. That's right. Rynin was dead. So were others of his friends. What if Trik was next?

Trik seemed to know what he was thinking. "Don't you worry, Boss, nothing's going to happen to me. I'm thinking the coin's not enough to find this little girl. I'm thinking we go off, round up the rest of the company what'll come with us, and leave the city tonight. What you think of that?"

Trik seemed confident, and that made Borion feel somewhat better. "Where will we find the others, Trik? We're all split up. Trik?"

But Trik wasn't listening to him. He was looking at something behind Borion. Without a word, he grabbed Borion's arm and pulled him behind a stack of barrels.

"What is it, Trik?" Borion asked, but Trik waved a hand for him to be quiet. He pointed across the harbor. On a walkway that ran paralell to their own, two figures stood. One of them, a woman, had a crossbow pointed at her face.

"That girl look familiar to you, Boss?" Trik asked. He sounded delighted.

Borion squinted at the woman. She was shaking out a bundle of rags. She looked tired and underfed. Pretty, though. He would have liked to have a wife as pretty as her. Then, the larger impact of Trik's question hit him.

"Is that her?" Borion said. "The girl the elf wants?"

"I'd lay any amount of coin it is," Trik said. "Looks like someone got to her first, though."

"He doesn't look nice," Borion said.

The man with the crossbow was talking to the girl; they couldn't hear what was said. The girl cast the rags over herself. Her body shriveled and transformed, assuming a horrifying shape.

Borion clutched Trik's arm. "What'd he do to her?" he said, frantic. "He's cursed her!"

Trik shook him off. "No, he didn't. He's no wizard, not a dark god's priest, either. It's just a disguise, so people won't know who she is. Doesn't matter, though, we've already seen her."

"We should tell the elf," Borion said. The elf would come and get the girl, and they could finally leave Mistshore.

"Still trying to think, are we?" Trik said. "Don't you remember, we're supposed to bring the *girl* to the *elf.* Then we get our reward."

"But it's only the two of us," Borion said. "I thought the elf wanted us to tell him so all of us could go after her together."

"The elf hasn't managed to do anything right since we started this chase," Trik said angrily. "We bring the girl to him, we get more coin than the others, and we get out of here sooner. That sounds right to me, Boss. What about you?"

The explanation sounded simple enough, but it still bothered Borion. He tried to put the doubts out of his mind. He could never remember anything properly. Maybe Trik was right, and it would be better to bring the girl directly to the elf. It would save time, and Borion wanted to get out of Mistshore more than anything.

"What's the plan?" Borion asked.

"Well, seeing as that fellow with the crossbow's not one of us, he must be a Watch spawn in disguise. First we take her from him, but we have to make sure he doesn't shoot her, or us. Think you can get the crossbow if I get him?"

"Yes," Borion said. The one thing he was good at was taking things. Lately they were objects from tombs and ruins, but he'd taken people before, for coin or food.

"Let's go, then," Trik said. "There's a lady in distress."

CHAPTER 17

Icelin walked slowly. It was difficult to see out from under the raggedy hood and difficult to think with the tip of a crossbow bolt shoved into her spine. Tarvin wasn't taking any chances. He kept her close, one hand on the crossbow trigger and the other on her arm to steer her in the right direction.

They were headed back to the Dusk and Dawn. It made sense as a meeting spot for the Watch patrols, especially if they were moving around without their official regalia. Would Kersh be among them? Icelin hadn't thought of her friend in days. Her former life seemed nothing more than a distant dream.

They reached an intersection. The pathway to the left ended in collapse, wooden planks floating on the water. The other three paths were intact. Tarvin pointed her to the right. Icelin paused to pick her footing and thought she heard the clicking of boots echoing off the planks behind them.

She tried to turn, but Tarvin twisted her arm painfully.

"No going back," he said. "Face front, keep marching."

"There's someone behind us," Icelin said. "Can't you hear?"

"To get behind us they'd have to swim," Tarvin said. "We're alone out here, and if you stall me again I'll put a limp in your step."

He forced her forward. Stumbling, Icelin went, but she could feel eyes on them. She couldn't hear the footsteps anymore, and that made the sensation worse.

Could it be Ruen? If it was, you'd never have heard him, she told herself. Not that she should expect a rescue from that corner, which meant the eyes behind them were probably unfriendly.

Icelin searched her mind for a spell. There were empty corridors all throughout her mind. She'd spent herself of all but the harshest spells. She couldn't risk her magic going wild now.

"Tarvin, please," she said, "think. What if—"

She angled her head in time to see the board. It was one of the planks from the collapsed walkway. She saw it pass out of her peripheral vision and instinctively dropped to the walkway.

She twisted; Tarvin still gripped her arm. He cried out, but the board silenced him. It smashed him in the side of the head.

Icelin heard a weird, hollow crunch. Tarvin slumped to a half-sitting position on the walkway. She could already see he was dead.

Icelin went for his hands, seeking the crossbow, but it was gone. Two pairs of boots filled her vision, one of the pairs at least two sizes bigger than the other. She looked up to see a man as tall as Sull and twice as round. He held Tarvin's crossbow like it was a toy. He had brown hair and a long shirt that he'd belted clumsily below his gut. His clothes were soaking wet.

His partner was slicker, his dark hair shaved to stubble. He had green eyes above a pointed nose. His clothes were saturated too.

"It's amazing how often, in Waterdeep, the goods change hands," the slick man said. In response, the giant pointed the crossbow at her. "You can take off the cloak, though. We're not so nasty as the Watch."

Icelin slid the cloak off her shoulders. She cast it into the harbor. "So you belong to Cerest?" she said.

The slick man took umbrage at that. "We're treasure hunters. You just happen to be the treasure tonight."

"I see," Icelin said. "How wonderful for me."

The giant looked uncomfortable. "Shouldn't we be going, Trik?"

"Soon, Boss," the slick man said. "Hands in front of you, lady. I haven't forgotten you're a spell hurler."

Icelin put her hands together while Trik tied them. They stood on the walkway, and a breath later they all heard the approaching footsteps. It was something akin to a herd of elephants charging in from the sea.

Icelin turned. Horror crashed over her. "Sull, no!"

The butcher barreled into the two men from behind. He got both arms around the giant, pinning the crossbow against his side. Icelin didn't think the man could be moved, but Sull hauled him off his feet and slammed him to the walkway.

He went for his cleaver, but the giant kicked sideways, sweeping Sull's legs out from under him. The butcher twisted and came down on top of the giant. Part of the walkway splintered and collapsed into the harbor, but the big men didn't notice. They were wrestling each other with a vengeance, punching and kicking and grabbing at hair. They might have been children, but the blows they landed were hard enough to break bone.

"Settle 'im!" Trik said. He started forward to aid the giant.

Icelin brought her bound arms up, smashing Trik in the face. He took the blow in complete surprise, his jaw cracking painfully into her knuckles. He staggered back. She drove him forward, trying to push him off into the water, but he caught himself against a piling.

He hooked an arm around her waist and swept her back. She tripped over his leg and fell on her side on the walkway. Her head smacked the wood, and her teeth clamped painfully together. She bit her tongue and tasted blood. Dazed, she tried to get up, but the world swam in and out of focus.

"Don't worry, lass," she heard Sull cry, "I've rolled bigger hunks of beef than this lout. I'm comin—" He took a punch to the jaw. Plucking the giant's fist out of his cheek, Sull gleefully bit the pudgy fingers.

Icelin saw Trik stand up, his shadow blocking out the torchlight across the walkway. He drew a knife from his belt and waded into the tangle of legs.

No, no, Icelin thought. She lunged for Trik's ankle, missed, and lost her breath again when she came down on her chest. Forcing herself to her knees, she bit into the knots binding her hands. She managed to loosen them enough to slip the rope off, but Trik had moved out of reach.

I'm not going to make it, she thought. "Sull, Sull!" she screamed. "Get back—Ruen!" Where was Ruen? And Bellaril?

"Hold him," Trik yelled.

The giant rolled onto his back, pulling Sull on top of him. He locked his arms in an arrowhead across Sull's chest. The butcher wheezed, his face turning bright red. He couldn't break the grip.

"You want to . . . get . . . 'fectionate . . . with me . . . do you?" Sull jammed his elbow into the giant's gut. The giant grunted, but he didn't let go. Sull drove the elbow in again, and again.

Each blow contorted the giant's face. He coughed, blood dripping down his chin. Both the men panted furiously, but the giant maintained his grip.

"Hurry . . . Trik," the giant moaned. His head lolled to one side. His eyes were black glass.

Icelin tried to call a spell. Ice. Fire. Wind. She couldn't find them. Pain and fear took her down twisting corridors in her mind, places that led to songs and stories and visions of her great-uncle, dead in her arms, and Sull's face, his wild red hair.

Concentrate!

But the magic wouldn't answer. The pain in her head blocked it all out. Her body was trying to protect itself, to preserve the few uncorrupted parts she had left.

Icelin gave up. She was searching blind. Instead she concentrated on Trik's dagger. He held the weapon crosswise in his hand. He wanted a quick slash to the throat. A quick cut, and Sull would be gone.

A quick cut. She repeated it, and suddenly everything crystallized in her mind. The alternate paths fell away, leaving her a clear line to the tower. She ran for the door, threw it off its hinges. The spell was waiting, had been waiting, for her to get past the fear. It appeared as a glowing tome of light in the middle of the room.

"Sull, roll him!" she cried. "Keep moving!" She whispered the spell, her voice cracking.

Over the arcane phrases, she heard more footsteps charging down the walkway. Shouts, Bellaril's voice. So far away. They might have been coming from the other side of the city.

She risked a glance at Sull, but kept her concentration fully on the spell.

He wasn't moving. He knew the knife was coming, but he wasn't struggling anymore. She saw a strange, peaceful expression settling over his face. He gazed over Trik's shoulder at her, and the look in his eyes held such a boundless affection and acceptance that Icelin felt her heart tearing open.

Go, his eyes told her. *I'm fine, now.*

Trik came forward. Icelin screamed the rest of the spell. The words were fire in her throat. She felt the spell hold, and the scene erupted in shadows of torch and spell light.

Icelin's world lost focus. The pain was unbearable. The spell burst from her like something newly born. She could only crouch on the walkway and hope that she lived through it.

Streams of metallic force shot from her outstretched hands. They quivered and solidified in the air. Passing each other, they encircled Trik at the chest and legs, tightening into two confining bands.

His balance gone, Trik pitched forward, collapsing half on Sull and half on the walkway. The magic held him immobile.

"Sull!" She came up to her knees, forcing her body to move. There was blood running down her forehead. She must have hit her head harder than she'd thought. Everything was tilting, the torchlight was too bright, but Sull . . .

The giant let go, freeing one of Sull's arms. The butcher

reared back, trying to get a hand on the giant's throat. He didn't see the giant pick up Trik's discarded knife, or turn it toward Sull's chest.

"Sull." The name framed her lips, but there was no sound. The dagger went into Sull's chest and pinned his leather sash to his body. He fell back, and the giant fell on top of him.

In the same breath, Icelin felt the backlash from her spell. There was a distant drumming, the blood forcing its way through her body. Her skull felt tight. Would the vessels burst and her mind go dark? Yes. She welcomed it.

Sull's lifeblood dripped between the planks, crimson on the brown water. The colors were just like Ruen's eyes.

Icelin felt herself fall, half-curled into a ball. She could see Sull's face. He was looking at her, the fear intense in his gaze.

Not for himself, Icelin thought. He didn't care at all that he was bleeding to death from a chest wound. He was trying to get up, to get to her. To see if she was safe.

She could hear Ruen's voice now. He came into view, running full out down the walkway. She saw his floppy hat bobbing. He grabbed the giant, peeling him off Sull like a fly. Before he could raise the dagger, Ruen grabbed him from behind, pushed his knee into the small of his back, and used both hands to pull the giant's head back.

There was a soft popping noise, and the giant went limp.

His spine, Icelin thought, snapped in one movement. Such a small sound on such a big man. But Ruen had known exactly what he was doing. He dropped the giant's body and went for Trik, a bland expression on his face. Same intentions, his course set.

He grabbed the spell bands that held the smaller man. When he was sure they were secure, he dragged Trik to the edge of the walkway.

"No, please!" Trik cried, when he realized what Ruen intended. He kicked and struggled, but Ruen kept dragging him. His expression didn't change. "Not the water, don't!"

"Ruen," Icelin said, but it was too soft for him to hear. He gazed at Trik's frantic expression reflected in the water. "Ruen," she said, louder.

The monk paused and turned to look at her. His face visibly softened. He started toward her but checked himself. He looked from the water to Icelin, as if he were suddenly waking from a dream.

"Leave him," Icelin gasped. The blood pounded a sick rhythm against her temples. "Check on . . . Sull."

Ruen nodded and left Trik at the edge of the walkway, face-down toward the water.

He crossed to Sull and examined the butcher's wound. When he saw all the blood, he turned to the giant's body. He fisted his hands in the giant's baggy shirt and ripped the fabric down the middle. The tearing was loud in the darkness. He stripped the giant to the waist and left the body where it was.

"Help me," he told Bellaril.

The dwarf came around to Sull's other side. Together they hoisted the butcher into a half sitting position. Bellaril put her back against Sull's to prop him up.

Ruen looped the ruined shirt around Sull's middle, tying off the end under his armpit to try to slow the flow of blood. Bellaril gently laid him back horizontal.

"He'll live for a while," Ruen said.

Icelin put her head down to quiet the spinning, the roaring blood. She heard Bellaril's footsteps, a short, heavy tread that stopped behind her.

"She's almost as far gone," the dwarf woman said. Icelin felt Bellaril gently roll her onto her back. She probed her chest for wounds, then started on her arms and legs. Icelin started to tell her not to bother, but she didn't have the strength.

"Well?" Ruen said when she was done. He hadn't come any closer. He used Sull's body as a buffer between them.

"Whatever's hurting her is going on inside," Bellaril said. "She needs healing, and even that might not be enough. Her eyes are strange—glassy, like yours."

"Ruen." Icelin sat up, gripping the dwarf's shoulder for support. "Tarvin's dead."

He followed her gaze to the Watchman's body. "He shouldn't have tried to take you alone."

"Ruen, can you call the Watch?"

He hesitated. The pain twisting his face was all the answer Icelin needed. "What do you want to tell them?" he said.

"Give them our exact location." The tide of pain was slowly leaving her. Icelin felt strangely calm, her body inert. She had no more reserves of strength to lose. This was where everything settled. She had to start the slow climb back up. "I assume they're still searching for me somewhere in Mistshore. Tell them we have wounded and need immediate aid. Go quickly, please."

Ruen stood and walked a little distance away. He removed something from his pouch and spoke a word Icelin didn't hear.

He's been connected to the Watch all this time, Icelin thought. Yet he never brought them roaring down on our heads. He and Sull had followed her, no matter where she went. They'd kept her safe.

The conversation was short. When Ruen returned, the familiar tightness was in his jaw, the only sign of concern he ever betrayed.

"They're not far away," he said.

"Good. Would you help me, Bellaril?" Icelin asked.

The dwarf helped Icelin to her feet. When she could walk steadily, she went to Sull.

He was unconscious, but he still breathed. His face had no color, and his skin was cold. Did it feel worse to Ruen?

"I never touched him," Ruen said, in answer to the unspoken question. "I couldn't know—"

"Of course you couldn't," Icelin said. "And I wouldn't have

listened, if you'd tried to tell me. I would have denied it until I was blind to everything else."

Ruen removed his gloves and slid his silver ring off his finger. Replacing his gloves, he picked up Sull's left hand. The ring would only fit on his smallest finger. Ruen slid it snugly into place.

"It'll keep his heartbeat strong until the Watch gets here," Ruen said. "He should live, if they hurry."

Icelin nodded. "How long do we have?"

"Not long."

"Then I need to get going."

She kissed the back of Sull's hand, folded it over his chest, and stood up. Her eyes fell on the bound man hanging over the walkway. The sense of detachment settled over her again as she approached him.

He watched her seat herself on the walkway so he could see her in his peripheral vision. She left him as he was, dangling over the water. The threat was there. She didn't need to tell him.

"He was your friend," Icelin said, pointing to the shirtless, dead giant. When Trik didn't answer, she said, "Sull is mine. You don't know how hard it was for me to tell that man"—she pointed at Ruen—"not to kill you. A tenday ago I could never have conceived such a thought in my mind, but time and hunger and desperation and fear work so many worms into the most pristine thoughts, and mine weren't clean to begin with.

"You can't imagine how much I want to kill you myself right now. It should matter that you're helpless, that you can't fight back. I know it should, but it doesn't. I just want to punish someone, for all of it. Perhaps it's the same for you, and that's why you could kill Sull without even knowing him. I don't care about that either."

She put a hand in the air. He flinched, and she took a gross stab of pleasure in his fear. "I talk too much. It's a curse Ruen warns me against, but I won't waste much more of your time.

I'm going to release you. You'll go back to Cerest—you've got no other employment, or you'd have taken it by now. Go back to Cerest, and tell him that I want to talk to him."

Out of the corner of her eye, she saw Ruen and Bellaril exchange glances. She didn't look at them or try to explain. They knew this conversation was as much for their benefit as Trik's.

"Do you know what the Ferryman's Waltz is?" she asked Trik.

For a breath the man didn't answer. Then he nodded, a quick jerk of the head.

"That's good. That will make things easier. Tell Cerest to meet me in the heart of Ferryman's Waltz."

"You're mad," Trik said, breaking his silence at last. "No one—"

"No one goes there," she said over him. "That's why it has to be there. No one to hurt, no more friends to kill. Only enemies. If you come there, Trik, I will kill you, with no words preceding the deed. If Cerest wants me, he'll have to come to the Waltz. Will you carry that message to him?"

Trik nodded again. Icelin flicked her hovering hand. The bands around his chest flickered and melted away. He exhaled sharply and slumped on the walkway. Until then, Icelin hadn't realized how tightly the bands had constricted his breath.

She sensed Ruen stepping toward her. His protective shadow fell across her, seen clearly by Trik as he got to his feet and took off running down the walkway.

When his footsteps receded, Icelin stood and faced the others. Sull was still unconscious, his head tossing fitfully from blood loss and fever. She knelt, dipped her arm in the harbor, and smoothed her cool, wet fingers across his forehead.

"Do you approve?" she asked Ruen without looking up.

"Of your plan?" Ruen said. "I don't know. It's very possible that if Cerest doesn't kill us, the wild magic at the Waltz will do the job."

"I know. I am tempted to wait for the Watch, as I should have done back at the ship. I'll be a long time regretting that." Her voice broke, but she plowed on. "There are some questions I need answered. Cerest has the knowledge, and I think he'll give me what I want."

"I'll go with you," Ruen said, "in case he proves reluctant."

"Thank you," Icelin said. "I know it's more than I deserve, after the way I've used you."

"Don't," Ruen said tersely. "You don't owe me anything."

"I never should have kissed you," Icelin said. "I made you feel my death, and you weren't ready for that. It was a very unromantic gesture." She put her head on Sull's chest. It took several breaths, but when she was strong enough, she looked up at Ruen. "How long have you known? You said you'd never touched me—"

"I haven't," Ruen said. "I only suspected. It was Arowall who confirmed it. He has a power to sense those touched by the spellplague, and how badly they've been afflicted."

Icelin nodded, accepting it. "I hope Cerest can tell me that too—why I'm dying."

"You don't have to rush to your demise so soon," Ruen said, his voice harsh. "You might have years yet, if you stop using magic now."

"But I have to use it, if I'm ever to be free of him," Icelin said. "One last time, that's all I need."

"No. We'll do it another way."

"You think you can change fate?" Icelin said.

He looked away. "Just yours."

"That's not true. You wouldn't have brought Bellaril with us if you didn't believe you could change things. I saw you touch her hands in the Cradle. You wanted her out of there, and not just to be my bodyguard. You knew her death waited in that place."

"She's stubborn enough I wonder if anything can kill her,"

Ruen muttered, but he didn't deny her words.

"You can't protect me by yourself," Icelin said. "Without your ring, we'll need my magic."

Ruen started and looked at his hand, as if he'd forgotten it was bare. He looked at Sull, at the ring keeping him alive. Defeated, he dropped his hand to his side and clenched a fist.

"Is your raft still intact?" Icelin asked.

"Enough to get us out to the Waltz," Ruen answered. He looked at Bellaril, and a spark of black humor lit his eyes. "What'll it be, Bells? Should I tell the Cradle you were too frightened to take on the fair folk, golden locks and all?"

"You won't be telling any tales when I have your head underwater for the sharks to nip at," the dwarf said, smiling sweetly. "But I'll go to the Waltz, and gladly."

"You don't have to do this, Bellaril," Icelin said.

The dwarf nodded curtly. "I do, but not for you, so don't let your conscience prickle you. After Tarvin led you off the Isle, we got word from the guards that Arowall's dead."

Icelin was shocked. "How?"

"How do you think? It was the elf. The survivors said he had a pair of pretty elf princesses with him." Bellaril looked at Ruen. "Might be you were onto something about my death waiting in the Cradle. I owe you thanks for letting me live long enough to get my revenge on the pretties. But in the meantime, do we leave the butcher here?"

Icelin didn't know what to do. The thought of leaving Sull alone on the walkway was a physical pain. He would be vulnerable to any attack until the Watch arrived.

"I have to protect him," she said to Ruen, half in defense, half in apology.

The spell had gone awry the first time she'd used it. For once, that would work to her advantage.

She put a hand in her pouch, grasping the cameo as she'd done in the Cradle. She pictured the woman's face in her mind, the blue curve of her cheek, carved forever in stone. Letting the image float in her consciousness, she wove the spell.

Mist slid off her hands and coiled in the air. It took on the shape and substance of the woman in lace. She stood before Icelin in her vaporous gown, her face impassive.

Icelin didn't know exactly what to do. The last time, the servant had automatically gone where her mind willed it. She remembered that she'd been mentally screaming for something to aid Ruen.

"Can you understand me?" she asked the strange apparition.

The woman didn't answer. Her expression didn't change.

"She has no consciousness," Ruen said. "There's nothing in her eyes."

"So she only has life when Icelin pulls her strings?" Bellaril asked. "Tell her to play guard dog, then."

"It wouldn't work," Icelin said. She raised her right arm slowly out from her body. She concentrated on nothing except moving the appendage. The lady in lace mirrored the gesture until their fingertips were practically touching. "She only does what I directly imagine her to do. Once I'm gone, she won't act independently."

Icelin slowly turned her body until she was facing Sull, who lay a few feet in front of the servant. The lady again mimicked the gesture.

"There," Icelin said. "As long as I picture her standing here, she'll remain. The folk of Mistshore should be wary enough of sea wraiths to stay away from this apparition until the Watch arrives."

Still, her gaze lingered on Sull. She took a step toward him, but Ruen laid a gloved hand on her arm.

"If we're going, we need to go now," he said.

"You're right. I just—"

"I know," Ruen said. "You'll see him again."

She looked at him. "Do you truly think that?"

He shrugged. "You were right. If I didn't think I could beat the odds, I'd never play the game."

They looked at each other for a breath. Then Icelin smiled. "So let's play."

CHAPTER 18

Ruen's raft was in good condition, considering it had gone through a sea wraith attack. Ruen and Bellaril worked the oars while Icelin sank into her thoughts. She kept a part of her mind fixed on the apparition watching over Sull, but she knew she would lose the spell soon. The battle ahead would require her complete concentration.

The Watch would be there by now. They would save Sull. Icelin could not consider any other outcome.

She took inventory of what magic she had left. She had never used so much in so short a time. Some of the spells left she hadn't meditated on in years. They were at the very edges of her consciousness. Her teacher had insisted that she be able to protect herself, but she'd put the harrowing magic as far from her active mind as she could.

Now, mentally, she entered the tower room. The sunlight spilling in the windows had become stygian night. When she entered the room, flames sprang from tallow candles, long unused in their brass candelabras. Black shadows stretched to caress the bookshelves. It was only her fear made manifest, but she was still unsettled at the changes.

Icelin walked to a place at the base of the shelves. A black tome floated down from a high shelf to meet her outstretched hand. Arcane writing was burned into the silver spine. The book opened in her hand, and she read.

The spells were powerful, but she was more concerned with the backlash. She'd been caught completely off guard and made helpless when she'd incapacitated Trik. All the offense she could muster wouldn't be worth anything if she were incapacitated herself.

Icelin blinked, and the tower disappeared. She stared out at an endless stretch of dark water. Ruen didn't have his ring. With his body unfortified, he'd be significantly weakened by any blow that managed to land on him. But she trusted his speed. If they couldn't catch him, they couldn't hurt him.

That left Bellaril. She would anchor all of them, and she would make Cerest's men answer for her master. It worried Icelin that she would be walking into a potential den of spellplague, but she knew the dwarf woman would not be dissuaded.

"What will you do when this is all over?" she asked.

Bellaril looked up from her rowing. "Go back to the Cradle," she said, as if it was a foregone conclusion. "No one to run it, the champion should step in. I don't think he's going to be doing it," she said, nodding at Ruen.

"The title's yours," Ruen said. "I have no interest in the Cradle."

"Don't know what you're missing," Bellaril said.

"What do you love so much about the fighting?" Icelin asked.

Bellaril shrugged. "I like the crowd, like it when they cheer for me. It's what everyone wants."

"She likes to be seen," Ruen said.

"Isn't that what I'm saying?" The dwarf woman looked irritated. "What of it?"

"Bells grew up in a family with eight brothers," Ruen said.

"Eight? Isn't that quite . . . prolific, for a dwarven family?" Icelin said.

"Not so much these days," Bellaril said. "I'm thinking our sire wanted a small army, not a family, so he got all of us on my mother. As far as he was concerned, I would grow my cheek fuzz and be indistinguishable from my brothers. Nine soldiers, nine sons. That's what he wanted. He cut my hair himself, when I refused to do it. My brothers held me down."

"Gods," Icelin said. "Your own family?"

"Blood doesn't mean much. The next time he came for me, I bruised him good before he could get the shears on me. After that, I almost took out his eye. Each time I hurt him a little more, until he stopped coming for me."

"That's when you came to Waterdeep?"

"Not at first. I wandered a little, busied my hands at different jobs before I ended up in Mistshore. But the Cradle." Bellaril shook her head. "They'd never seen a dwarf woman pretty as me who could fight as hard as the boys they bet their coin on."

Icelin smiled at Bellaril's pleased expression. "No one ever tried to make you grow a beard?"

"And they know better than to touch my hair," Bellaril said.

In the distance, Icelin could see the behemoth outline of Ferryman's Waltz. Wraiths circled in an endless dance in the water, occasionally swirling up to curl their bodies sinuously around the broken masts of the inverted ship.

The leviathan's bones twined seamlessly with the rotting greatship. There was no flesh left to suggest what the creature might have looked like in its original form, but the thought of it driving the massive ship straight into the air was boggling. The leviathan's remains kept the *Ferryman* from plunging into the deep by sheer force of an old will, a need beyond death to remain locked in battle.

Bellaril looked unimpressed by the sight. "How you thinking of getting past them?" she asked, nodding at the wraiths.

Icelin closed her eyes. She hummed the familiar ballad to brace herself against the magic. The lost boy, trying to find his way home. She didn't look at Ruen to see his reaction to the song. She couldn't let herself be distracted.

"Find a path into the wreckage," Icelin instructed them. She reached into her pouch for foci, careful this time to make sure they were the correct objects. "When the wraiths scatter, make for it with all possible speed."

Bellaril snorted. "They're not just going to let us glide in—"

"Quiet," Ruen said. "Let her work."

Help me, Nelzun, Icelin thought. The raft drifted closer. One by one, the wraiths slowed their restless circling. They sensed a change in the chaotic usualness of their domain and turned their attention to the small raft and its three distinctly human occupants.

Icelin finished the spell and threw her arms into the air. She released a handful of coin-sized stones, three in each hand. They soared high and burst into orange flame. She pictured them in her mind, the wild, soaring orbs, pulsing with arcane energy.

To the wraiths, arcane energy released from a body steeped in spellplague was like a bone cast in the path of starving dogs. Their bodies glowed in concert with the flames. They streaked after the orbs in clusters of three and four, leaving a clear path between the only three living souls on the water and a cavernous hole snugged between the wrecked *Ferryman* and the leviathan's bones.

The raft drifted up to a slash of sail draped across the upper half of the opening. Ruen pushed it aside with his oar. He maneuvered the raft between hull and rib and they floated on, into the Waltz.

Cerest listened to Trik's report in fascination. "You're certain it's only the three of them?" he said. Trik looked uncomfortable. Cerest narrowed his eyes. "I'm sorry for the loss of Borion, but if you're lying, it won't go badly for just me. We've lost Cearcor and Rondel."

Trik's eyes bugged out and he half-swayed on his feet. "How?"

"Arowall's guards," Cerest said. "They caught them just after we split up. I underestimated their loyalty. But don't worry, Feston is safe. He's gone to get three more of your fellows to aid us."

"Six of us," Trik murmured. "Six of us against three of them."

"More than passable odds, if Icelin is willing to cooperate."

Trik shook his head. He looked at Cerest in a way that made the elf's skin prickle with anger—disgust swimming in pity. But Trik wasn't looking at the elf's scars.

"You go find her on your own," he said. "Take the others if you want. Hells, they'll all fight 'til they're dead, if there's coin in it."

He turned away, the torchlight burning his profile orange.

"Don't you want revenge?" Cerest asked him. "They killed your friend."

"And I killed hers, or near enough," Trik said. "I'm out of it."

Cerest watched the man walk away. It didn't affect him the way it had when the Locks had left him. He felt nothing now, not in light of what Trik had told him about Icelin.

He'd finally worn her down. She was coming to him, and she was coming angry. He would have to fight to bring her to heel, but he wasn't worried about that. He would have the upper hand, because he had the truth Icelin wanted.

All he had to do was make her give up everything to get it.

Ruen's lantern flickered and went out. Icelin started to cast a light spell when she felt Ruen's hand on her arm.

She knew it was him by the cool touch of leather.

"Save your strength," he said. "I'll get the lantern going. Bells, keep rowing."

The dwarf grunted acknowledgment. Ruen moved away in the darkness. Icelin could only assume he was feeling his way.

She tried to get a sense of the interior of the Waltz by the moonlight filtering through the gaps in the rigging, but the sheer bulk of the vessel and bones prevented much detail from being discernible. The structures had massed together in one hive shape, eclipsing all the individual parts.

The raft bumped against something solid about the same time Ruen got the lantern lit. Icelin thought it was debris floating in the water. It took her a breath to realize that it was a boot, propped against the front of the raft. The boot's owner floated six inches above the water.

Icelin looked up into the most frightening collage of a human face she had ever beheld. Naked above the waist, the man's torso and shoulders were disproportionately wide. Veins and bone bulges stood out from his pale skin. Thin patches of hair grew like scrub grass all over his head. His bottom lip folded over on itself in one corner, giving him a perpetual sneer and allowing a stream of drool to escape from his mouth in a needle-thin waterfall. This type of deformity, the godscurse, Icelin had seen before. But the gods weren't done with their jest at this poor soul's expense.

From the man's neck sprouted a quartet of bulbous gray tentacles. He had them draped across his shoulders like a mane that ended at his belt. The tentacles were moving, seemingly independent of any conscious mental direction on their owner's part.

With his boot on the raft, the man brought forward a long polearm, its tip reaching well above his head. He swung the point down level with her chest. His arm muscles tensed. Icelin thought he was going to drive the weapon through her breast, but instead, he let out a keening whistle that threatened to shatter her eardrums.

Icelin folded into herself, clutching her head against the high-pitched whistle. When it was over, she noticed Bellaril and Ruen had adopted similar protective positions.

"We mean no harm here," Icelin said shakily. "We came here for refuge—"

A howling cry echoed from somewhere deep in the inverted *Ferryman*, cutting off Icelin's words. It rose in intensity, so that it mimicked the man's whistle perfectly. The sound rang out again, nearer, and with it came clicks and rapid pounding on wood.

"Get the oars up!" Ruen shouted. Bellaril was already hauling hers out of the water.

Ruen ran past Icelin and swung his oar. He batted the man's polearm away from her chest and reversed the swing for a swipe at the man's legs.

The deformed man backed off, blocking Ruen's swing with his polearm, but he made no further move to fight back. He smiled, and the expression was horrid, his lips curling like worms around uneven rows of teeth.

Ruen plunged the oar into the water, trying to push them away from the *Ferryman*.

"Beware!" Icelin cried, pointing to the ship. Pinpoints of light were visible from a gap in the hull. There came another howl, and a breath later, two enormous bodies leaped through the opening. In size and movement they resembled stags, but their faces were a cross between canine and badger. They launched into the air using massive haunches, one and then the other landing on the small raft.

The stink of rotting flesh and gamey fur swelled in Icelin's nostrils. Their craft was not big enough to contain the beasts. Icelin fell to her knees to avoid being slammed off the raft by the weight of the furry bodies.

The beast farthest from her whipped its head around, catching Bellaril by the leg. She fell on her backside. The beast shook her like a playtime doll, and for the first time Icelin heard the dwarf woman scream. Terror widened her eyes, but she fought back, and folded her body up to get at the beast's head.

It lifted her by her leg and swung her, tossing its head and snarling. On the second backswing Bellaril grabbed her belt dagger and planted it beneath the beast's eyes. She missed its burning orb by half an inch.

The beast keened and snapped its head down. The knife came

out of its flesh. It bit the blade in half, nearly severing Bellaril's fingers too. The dwarf woman dropped the ruined weapon. Her skull smacked the raft, and she went senseless.

"No!" Icelin cried. She tried to crawl between the second beast's legs. Ruen had his arms around its head. His muscles strained as he attempted to keep the beast's teeth from his neck.

"Get up," Ruen hollered when he saw her weaving between the beast's legs. "They're leucrotta. They'll trample you!"

Icelin lunged forward, but the second leucrotta had already seen her. It dropped Bellaril in favor of a moving target. Curling sideways, it lunged. Its massive weight hit Icelin from the side and bore her to the ground.

She hit the planks hard. The leucrotta's rancid breath was all over her. Bone-ridged jaws snapped inches from her face.

Icelin pushed against the leucrotta's throat. Her hands slipped off the oily fur and down its chest. She had the brief impression of a wild heartbeat and stone-hard muscles. She would never throw the beast off. Her only advantage was the size of the raft. The craft bobbed wildly between the leviathan's bones and the bow of the *Ferryman*. The leucrotta were positioned half on these shores and half on the raft.

Icelin couldn't see Ruen now, but she could hear his punches vibrating along the other leucrotta's body. It squealed in pain, and Icelin heard a splash when its back legs skittered off the raft.

She kicked up, into her own foe's belly. It hacked a foul breath and became meaner. Nine feet of muscle and bone settled on top of her. Icelin couldn't breathe. She flopped back and tried to pull her chest free, but the leucrotta latched onto her wrist and began to shake the appendage in its teeth.

Fire exploded up Icelin's arm. She cried out as the flesh was stripped from her wrist, exposing white bone. The pain was mythic. She felt the blood dribble down her arm and almost passed out. She tried to rip her arm out of the leucrotta's mouth, but that only made the pain worse.

Haltingly, she chanted a spell. Her concentration was in shreds, her attention too caught up in her trapped arm. She imagined how the magic would go wild, but she didn't care. Any pain was better than watching the leucrotta tear her hand off. It was playing with her, enjoying her pain before it ate her alive. She shrieked the arcane words and braced herself for the backlash.

Metal spikes burst bloodlessly from her skin. They were two inches long and curled at the tips. She felt them puncture the roof of the leucrotta's mouth. Willingly she gave the beast her hand, driving the spikes deep.

With a high-pitched wail, the leucrotta released her. The beast pulled its weight off her chest, but more of the spikes were growing from Icelin's skin. She felt each one as a tiny pinprick. They stuck and tore the leucrotta's skin until both woman and monster were drenched in blood. The beast ripped free and retreated, whimpering pathetically. It limped to the edge of the raft and licked its wounds.

Icelin could see the wicked intelligence in its eyes as it re-evaluated her. She stretched out her wrecked arm, daring the creature to come at her and taste more spikes.

It watched her with those frightening eyes like the burning edges of coins, but it came no closer. That's right, Icelin thought. I'm not as weak as I look.

She sat up and looked around, careful to keep one eye on the injured leucrotta. Ruen lay on his back; his beast had worked its way onto his chest, but it couldn't keep him still. He punched the leucrotta in the side of its wedge-shaped head over and over. His fists moved in a blur, delivering quick, alternating punches down either side of the beast's flank. Distracted by the constant stream of hurts, it couldn't bite his fists or sever fingers. He would wear it down eventually, but not before he exhausted himself.

Not far away, Bellaril lay in a wrecked heap. Icelin saw she'd taken a bite to the neck before the beast had grabbed her. Her leg flopped in a blood pool. The stench of copper and oily fur was dizzying.

Icelin crawled to the dwarf's side. Out of the corner of her eye, she saw the leucrotta's deformed master pacing the air among the leviathan's ribs. He was agitated, his tentacles writhing over his chest. He propped the polearm on his shoulder, but he didn't throw it.

He won't risk hitting the beasts, Icelin thought. She tore her sleeve, wrapping it three times around the deep gash in Bellaril's leg. The spikes made it take twice as long, but she didn't want to end the spell yet.

When she was done, she tore her other sleeve and wrapped her own wrist as tightly as she could. Blood immediately soaked through the makeshift bandage. She felt light-headed. She prayed she could kill the injured leucrotta before she passed out.

Standing on her knees, Icelin chanted again. The spikes sank back into her flesh and dissolved. On the heels of the dispel, she pushed her arms out from her body, the sweep encompassing both leucrotta.

Blue missiles of magical energy shot from her hands. They hit the injured leucrotta in the chest. The beast howled. The blue streamers sank into its flesh, briefly illuminating the beast's face.

Before the injured one could recover, the missiles rebounded, striking the leucrotta Ruen was fighting in the spine.

In the explosion of pain and surprise, the leucrotta lost its balance at last, its back legs collapsing underneath its body.

Ruen took the distraction and flipped himself onto the leucrotta's back, raking his body across the beast's singed fur. The leucrotta howled and bucked, trying to throw the monk off, but Ruen locked both arms around its head.

The leucrotta turned and charged toward the water. It would force Ruen off one way or another. When the beast turned its head, Ruen sprang up, contorting his body so that his full weight landed on the leucrotta's left flank. With his arms locked around the beast's head, Ruen had the leucrotta disoriented. It tried to twist free, but Ruen pulled straight up and to the right with all his strength.

The leucrotta's neck popped with a stomach-turning crunch. It sagged against Ruen, biting and snapping at random, its senses shattered by the trauma it had suffered.

Ruen grabbed the jagged remains of Bellaril's dagger and plunged it into the beast's throat. It coughed once and expired, collapsing half on top of Ruen. He shoved the body off into the harbor.

The injured leucrotta howled furiously, a cry echoed by the deformed man. He hefted his spear, aiming it at Ruen, while the leucrotta lunged for him.

"No!" Icelin cried. Ruen dodged, but the leucrotta grabbed him by the shoulder, tearing out a chunk of flesh.

He crab-crawled back, putting a little distance between them, but the leucrotta was already tensing to spring again.

Icelin gauged the distance and cast another spell. She twisted her arms together and waited, sweat from the pain pouring down her face, until the deformed man threw his spear. He aimed for Ruen's heart.

Icelin spoke a word, and Ruen and the leucrotta disappeared. She untwisted her hands and instantly they reappeared, but they had exchanged places on the raft.

The deformed man stared, his jaw slack with horror, as his own spear punched a hole in the leucrotta's flank. Its wicked point protruded out the other side, between two of the leucrotta's ribs.

The beast collapsed—dead before it hit the ground—and Ruen was up and moving, grabbing Icelin, hauling her to her feet.

She sagged against him, her strength gone. She'd done too much. Three spells practically at once, and she was losing blood, despite the bandage.

"He's still armed," Ruen said, and as he spoke, the deformed man drew a broadsword from a ratty leather scabbard. He let himself fall out of the air, landing on the raft with a crash that sent Icelin and Ruen to their knees and jarred the leucrotta's body.

Seeing the corpse up close seemed to incense the man more. He came forward, slashing wildly with his blade. Ruen let go of Icelin and rushed him. He ducked under the man's reach just before his slash would have come around and decapitated him. He brought his forearm up and blocked the slash at the man's wrist, leaving his other hand free for a counter attack.

One of the few things Icelin had learned to be true about Ruen Morleth—however much honor he showed as a thief, as a Mistshore fighter he would never fight fair.

So Icelin was not in the least shocked when Ruen brought his other hand up and snagged one of the tentacles writhing at the deformed man's waist. He wrapped it around his fist and yanked.

The man's sword arm flew out wide at the same time his face came down, until he was nose to nose with Ruen. The monk snapped his skull against the deformed man's and released the tentacle.

The deformed man staggered back. He tried to bring his sword up, but Ruen had him this time. The monk took his thick wrist in both hands, twisted and brought the sword point down, driving it harmlessly into the raft. The deformed man released the sword and it bobbed there, a scar in the wood.

Ruen brought his fist around and punched the deformed man in the stomach. He stumbled backward and off the raft. No spell held him as he plunged into the water.

Ruen went back to Icelin's side. "Are you well enough to walk? We have to get to a hiding place. We won't be able to fight Cerest like this."

"I know," Icelin said, "but Bellaril's wound is bad. I don't think we can move her."

A pitiful wail erupted from the water. Icelin and Ruen tensed. Ruen turned, his fists raised to defend against another attacker, but it was the deformed man. He thrashed in the water, his tentacles floating weirdly around his head. It gave the impression an octopus was latched onto his neck.

"Gods," Icelin said, "he can't swim." She took a step toward the edge of the raft.

Ruen latched onto her arm. "Or maybe he's a clever play actor who'll stick you with a hidden dagger when you get close enough to help him."

The cries intensified. Icelin flinched. "If that's so, you'll finish him when he makes his attack. If it's not—I can't listen to him die like that."

"He was willing enough to let us be eaten by his dogs," Ruen said, but Icelin had already shaken off his restraining hand.

She walked to the edge of the raft and got down on her knees. She buried one hand in the strapping that kept Ruen's raft together and extended the other out to the deformed man.

He thrashed for a handful of breaths, his eyes huge in the lamplit darkness. He watched her for sign of a trick, but she just let her hand linger in the air like a bird hovering before a cat.

The deformed man dipped down, catching water in his half-open mouth. He coughed and spat. Panting now, he reached out and grabbed her small hand.

Icelin tightened her grip on the strapping. She felt Ruen's legs on either side of her. He grabbed her shoulders to steady her, and hauled her up by the armpits with the deformed man in tow. Together, they dragged him up and onto the raft.

He lay on his side, in a pool of water and leucrotta blood, coughing up harbor filth from his slack mouth. Icelin stood over him, unsure how far the uneasy truce was going to stretch.

The hairs on the back of her neck prickled, like sudden heat in a cold room. She looked up and saw a man standing in the torn gap of the *Ferryman's* hull. She didn't know how long he'd been standing there, watching them, but the man looked to be about a hundred and ninety years old.

He had a narrow, jaundiced face, but his expression was not unkind. Green eyes peered out from eye sockets that were heavy on top and papery with age on the bottom. His thick, stark white eyebrows were raised in speculation. He was clean-shaven, head and face; and wore a long set of robes, white over gray. A black belt that looked like it had been chewed on by wild dogs circled his waist.

But the feature that demanded the greatest portion of Icelin's attention was the carved wooden staff he held in his right hand. The wood had been notched with arcane markings over every visible surface At its peak, a swirling red mist encircled thin shoots of wood, like foliage on a burning tree.

He had the staff slightly pointed forward. Icelin could imagine a ray of arcane power shooting from the tip and striking Ruen down before the two of them could flinch. This was not a warrior's polearm; this was a wizard's staff. It relied not on human strength, but on a connection with its master. The staff would respond to its wielder's slightest instinct, and it would do so in the space between heartbeats.

Icelin raised her hands, palms out. "We surrender," she said.

CHAPTER 19

When he heard the doglike howls, Cerest motioned for his remaining men to abandon the boats. At first they hesitated, their eyes drawn to the wraiths circling endlessly above the gap between the *Ferryman* and the leviathan.

The undead creatures did not appear to notice them. They chased and dove at three flaming orbs hanging in midair; but for all their frenzied efforts, they could never capture the arcane energy. Cerest thought the orbs must be Icelin's doing, and wondered for a breath if she had laid a trap for him here.

The dwarf woman's screams rang out in concert with the snarls of beasts. Cerest slapped the boat nearest him with an oar to get his mens' attention. Reluctantly, they slid into the dark water. Stealth was the wisest option for whatever lay ahead of them.

They were only five, but they were the deadliest of the Locks's muck-rakers, in Cerest's opinion. Up to their noses in the water, they swam silently through the gap between the *Ferryman's* corpse and the leviathan's. They carried no light source, trusting Cerest's vision to lead them through the complex tangle of ship and creature. Above their heads, the wraiths continued their oblivious circling.

One leucrotta was dead, and the second dying, by the time they came within sight of the raft and its torn occupants. Cerest watched the monk fighting a hideously deformed man, and then a breath later helping Icelin save the man's life.

So that was how it was between them, Cerest thought. He was her dog, awaiting the command to throw himself into death's path. He felt a strange surge in his chest, a heat that did not diminish, even with the harbor soaking his clothes to his skin.

He didn't like the way the monk touched Icelin, the rough way he hauled her back upon the raft, as if she were so much refuse he couldn't wait to cast off. Yet at the same time he stayed as close to her as polite proximity would allow. Like the dog Cerest had named him, he soaked up the energy of her presence; and his body practically vibrated, begging for more.

Cerest didn't want to see that type of connection between the monk and Icelin. Icelin was *his*.

"Kill the thin man," Cerest whispered to his men. But one of them lifted his hand to his throat, gesturing for silence.

Cerest followed the man's gaze and saw the old man standing on the *Ferryman's* ruins. His staff glowed brightly, illuminating too much of the ruins for Cerest's comfort. The old man looked shrewd, and comfortable in his power.

"Dive down," Cerest said. "We'll swim a safe distance away and watch. If we get the chance, kill the old man quickly and bring me his staff. Do whatever you wish with the thin man, as long as you kill him in the end. By that time, Icelin and I will be safely away."

He sank under the water, knowing the men would follow. The burning sensation remained in his chest.

"Who are you?" the old man asked.

Icelin felt a strange pull on her scalp, as if some invisible hand were tugging at her hair. The strange lifting sensation brought the truth to her lips, like drawing up water from a deep well.

"Icelin Tearn," she answered, and felt strangely calm, unafraid of this powerful stranger. "My companions are Ruen Morleth and Bellaril."

As soon as she'd finished speaking, the calm force shattered, and terror burst free in Icelin's chest.

"His magic compels truth," Icelin said, her words running together. "Don't answer his questions."

"My apologies," the man said. "I only wished to confirm your identities. I won't invade your private space again. I owe you thanks for saving my friend's life."

"It was her doing, not mine," Ruen said. "In thanks, why not tell us your name, friend, and how you know who we are?"

"The wraiths whisper things on the edges of my hearing," the man said. "Lies, mostly, and tantalizing hints about secrets that are better left unspoken. I can't help but listen. They have whispered your names in fear."

"Good," Ruen said. "And your name?" he prompted.

"Call me Aldren," the old man said, "faithful servant of Mystra's memory." He stepped down from the *Ferryman* onto the raft. He never lost his balance, and the raft did not stir in the water. Icelin suspected that like the deformed man, he was hovering inches above the water.

The deformed man was sitting up on the raft, his head dipped between his bent knees. He looked like he was going to be sick. Aldren touched the glowing nimbus of the staff to the deformed man's shoulder. Cast in red, his tentacles basked in the arcane heat. The deformed man looked up at his master.

"It is all right," Aldren said. "Take three deep breaths and you'll be feeling back to normal."

Icelin watched the deformed man do as he was told. The pain creases slowly left his face, and a peaceful resignation descended over his features, as if, for this man, "normal" was simply a chosen level of bearable suffering.

"Who is he?" Icelin asked. The unshakable trust in the deformed man's eyes when he looked at Aldren gave her courage. Surely, no one who could inspire that kind of love would hurt them without cause. "Why are you both here?"

"Darvont has been a friend to me for a long time," Aldren said. "He attacked you in defense of me. It is difficult for his mind to grasp the subtleties between intruder and refugee." He moved his staff back to its upright position beside his head. "Come inside my home, if you will. I can help your friend and give you the answer to your other question."

Icelin looked at Ruen, who shrugged. "He has the upper hand as either a friend or foe." He added, "Bellaril will not survive without aid."

Icelin nodded. Together they lifted Bellaril between them and followed the old man through the wound in the *Ferryman's* hull. Icelin cradled Bellaril's head gently and felt the lifebeat in her neck. She thought of Sull, and a fresh prayer surged within her, a plea for the lives of her friends.

They came through a dark passage and into a chamber of muted spell light. Aldren had cast a light spell on the preserved nests of insects clustered near the ceiling. A dank chill filled the air, creating the unsettling atmosphere of a tomb. Jagged planks and ripped sail gave way to what Icelin could only describe as a nest carved of rotting wood and arcane power.

Planks from the main deck had been stacked against the wall, their ends warped by magic so that they curled back on themselves like wood shavings. The rough chairs had been fastened to the hull for stability. Their curling ends seemed to have been done purely for style.

"Put her here," Aldren said.

Icelin and Ruen laid the dwarf woman in the corner, on a narrow straw pallet stacked with blankets. The crude bed had been stuffed into a wooden frame set six inches off the floor. Icelin saw a mouse burrow into the straw and disappear.

While Aldren moved his staff over Bellaril's body, Icelin surveyed the rest of the odd living quarters. Another chair and a table stood in the center of the chamber, reinforced by more wood to make a crude desk. Like the wizard's staff, the surface had been covered with inscribed symbols, some scratched and some burned into the wood. Icelin couldn't imagine how long it must have taken to carve the symbols so meticulously.

Aldren stood straight. The light in his staff dimmed. His eyes looked more sunken than ever, but he smiled wanly. "She will sleep heavily for a time, but she is healing. There will be no permanent damage."

Before Icelin could speak, he brought the staff up and passed it in front of her face. Briefly blinded, Icelin felt warmth and strength flow back into her body. The terrible pain in her wrist went away in an instant. She didn't realize how close the agony and weakness had been to consuming her until they were gone. When the light faded, she saw Aldren make the same gesture before Ruen.

"I'm in your debt," Icelin said. "I am truly sorry to have brought my burdens to your door."

The old man waved a hand dismissively. "I am not so easily intimidated at the prospect of other people's burdens. I welcome the distraction from my own." He followed her gaze to the desk and its writings. "Wood is the only reliable substance to hand," he explained. "The harbor and the wild magic together are so toxic the ink is eaten and the parchment crumbling before a decade is out."

"A decade?" Icelin said. "You've been here that long?"

"What is that?" Ruen asked. He pointed to the back of the chamber, which was cast in shadow outside the spell light.

Aldren spoke a word, and two candles jumped to burning life from the back of the hold. They sat in brass dishes on another wooden table, this one free of symbols but draped in a cloth runner of purple velvet. Faded gold braiding lined the edges of the runner, and in its center, true gold glinted in the candle light.

"Is that an altar to Mystra?" Icelin asked. As she approached, she thought the glintings were jewels, but when she got close she realized her mistake. They were not jewels, at least not in the sense that a high lady of Waterdeep would value.

They were holy symbols. She recognized Mystra's symbol, and Deneir, Helm, even Mask and Eilistraee. There were several others she didn't know.

"I don't understand," Icelin said, turning to Aldren. "I thought you served Mystra's memory?"

Aldren seated himself on a chair and propped his staff next to him. Darvont sat on the floor across from him. His eyes never left the old man's face.

"I first came here in the Year of Blue Fire," Aldren said. "I was a man of thirty, then. I awoke on a slope of sand with water lapping my face and found that I had been brought to the place by this man," he said, gesturing to Darvont. "I remembered only that I had been caught in an arcane storm of the magnitude you only imagine in nightmares."

"The Year of Blue Fire," Icelin said. "You were there at the beginning of the Spellplague? But that would make you—"

"Over one hundred and twenty years old," Aldren said.

"How is it you're still alive?" Icelin asked.

"Your spellscar keeps you alive," Ruen said. He stood next to Icelin at the altar, but he did not touch any of the pieces arranged there.

"In a way," Aldren said. "I have died several times over the course of these nine decades, but my scar, as you call it, restores me."

Icelin stared at the old man. She thought she'd ceased being surprised at the suffering endured by those the plague had touched, but she was wrong.

She looked at the holy symbols. "You were a priest of all these gods?"

"Over each of my 'lifetimes,' and sometimes more than one," Aldren said. "I served them all, faithfully, not realizing at first that they, like Lady Mystra, had passed on. How could they cease to be when I could not? It was one of the more horrifying truths I've had to face: to accept immortality when the gods were dying around me. When I realized that none of them would be able to grant the long sleep I desired, I dedicated myself to what the Art had lost—to Mystra's memory."

"How does your magic function?" Ruen asked. "From whom do you receive your divine power?"

"The gods are silent to me," Aldren said, "even those I know to be alive and thriving. I don't know why. Fortunately, the magic in this staff has remained strong. It is my only link to the power that once was Mystra's, and so I will watch over it, this small shard of the unbound weave that no longer has a weaver."

"But why stay here?" Icelin asked. "Why not live in the city?"

"Because I feared the day I would be struck down. I imagined awakening in a sealed crypt, enduring a slow death over and over until I descended into madness. And I couldn't leave him." Aldren touched the side of Darvont's head. "He saved me and shares my curse. I suspect part of his mind dwells forever in the heart of that arcane storm."

"So you'll live here forever, custodian of the same magic that scarred you," Icelin said, "venerating gods who won't answer your prayers?"

The old man shook his head. "You should not anger yourself on my behalf. Many others suffer greater trials. You yourselves are touched, are you not?"

Icelin and Ruen exchanged glances. "How do you know that?" Icelin asked.

"Because we are all the same, now," Aldren said. "Weavers—custodians of the Art that was lost."

"Only Mystra could control the weave," Ruen said. "We aren't gods, and we aren't immortal."

"Then what is magic, without its caretaker?" Aldren challenged. "Lost, ungovernable. Yet in some few individuals it finds a vessel. You're quite right: we are not gods, and most of us do not survive the blue flame that burns our flesh and bores our minds. But without the Lady, where can the Art go? It's been too long mastered. I say it cannot survive on its own, so it clings to the mortal realm and threatens to destroy what it loves most."

Ruen snorted. "You can think that, if you find it comforting. The truth is magic doesn't have a soul. There's no beauty left in the Art. The only thing it can do is burn."

"Is that why you gave Fannie the quill?" Icelin asked softly. "Why you stole a collection of magic at amazing cost to yourself? Did you risk your freedom because you believed there was no beauty left in the Art?"

Ruen stared at her. He pressed his lips into a hard line, but his expression wasn't exactly angry. "What has the Art ever done but bring you misery?" he said. "Why would you defend it?"

"I would defend *you,*" Icelin said. "I don't know if what you say is true," she said to Aldren, "but my friend and I must leave soon. We're being pursued by a group of men. I led them here, thinking only the wraiths would be disturbed by our presence. I would lead them away—"

"But there is no better place than here for confronting demons, real or imagined," Aldren said, "Please don't fear for my safety. Darvont and I will be protected within the *Ferryman's* hold. You are welcome to share its sanctuary, but I suspect that would defeat your purpose."

"It would," Icelin said. "Yet I would beg sanctuary for my friend Bellaril. I've no right to ask, and I have nothing to offer you in return. But if I live long enough I would find a way to repay you."

"She's true to her word," Ruen said. "Stubbornness has never known a more faithful lover than Icelin Tearn."

Icelin shot him a look, but Aldren said, "Of course your friend will stay. No one will harm her while I keep watch."

"My deepest thanks," Icelin said. She looked at Ruen. "Are you ready, clevermouth?"

Ruen nodded. They made their way to the gap in the hull.

Icelin paused by Bellaril's pallet. The dwarf was still unconscious, her skin the color of the moon, but she breathed evenly and deep.

"She truly would have been killed," Icelin said to Ruen, "if you hadn't made her come with us. Cerest killed the master of the Cradle—such a mad action even someone so well protected as Arowall couldn't have predicted it. And Bellaril wouldn't have abandoned her master to save her own life."

"Doesn't mean she'll live any longer than she was meant to," Ruen said.

"Maybe," Icelin said. She looked at Aldren. "Do you think your fate can be changed?" she said. "That one day the plague will allow you to die?"

"That is my fondest hope," Aldren said. "Until then, I will live as best I can."

"You and I are two halves of the same curse," Icelin said. "The plague lives in me. It causes my memory to be nigh perfect, for a price. Ruen says it will take my life before age does. The more I use my own magic, the quicker that fate will come for me."

Aldren's soft green eyes reflected the spell light. "I am sorry for your burden," he said.

Icelin shrugged. "I am sorrier for other burdens—loss and pain done to my friends because of my own fear. I think you're right. We, all of us, can only live as best we are able, and hope to change our fates—" She stopped as something took hold inside of her.

Memory came, this time uncalled. With trembling fingers, Icelin removed her pack from her back and dumped its contents on the floor. The deformed man skittered out of the way.

"What are you doing?" Ruen said. Seeing her face, he crouched beside her and helped her gather the scattered letters from Elgreth. "What's wrong?"

"He tried to live as best he could," Icelin said. "Just like us, like Aldren, retreating to this place."

She found the letter she was looking for and practically tore it in her haste to unfold the old parchment.

"Cerest isn't after a perfect memory," Icelin said. "Elgreth's scar was different from mine. Here!" She read part of the letter aloud. "I sat upon a rooftop and looked out over Cutlass Island, at the ruins of the Host Tower of the Arcane. The locals say it is a cursed place, and I cannot help but agree. The restless dead walk on that isle, sentinels to its lost power. In my younger days, I would have longed for the challenge and promise of treasure to be found in such a forgotten stronghold. I can see the magic swirling under shattered stone. It drifts among the bones of the once mighty wizards who ruled here."

Icelin stopped reading and looked at Ruen. "Do you see?"

Ruen shook his head. "What are you talking about?"

"I can see the magic swirling under the shattered stone," Icelin repeated. "He could detect powerful magic, through stone and earth, just with his eyes. What gift would tempt a treasure hunter more?"

"Cerest will be disappointed when he finds out you inherited a very different gift," Ruen said.

"Yes," Icelin said. "A perfect memory is of little use to him. His hunt was for nothing."

It was all a tragic jest. Icelin was grateful to have the one mystery solved, but there were still missing pieces. "I have to know why he betrayed my family," she said. "If Cerest won't confess it . . . *how* do you remember something you've managed to forget so thoroughly that even the spellplague can't penetrate the defense?"

She'd meant the question rhetorically, and was surprised when Aldren answered, "If your mind has seen fit to bury something so deeply that even the spellplague can't touch it, I would count the power a blessing."

"Blessing?" Icelin said. "I don't see how. If I had this memory, it would explain so much about my life. Why would I want to bury it?"

"You mistake me," Aldren said. "I didn't mean it was a blessing that you be denied a piece of yourself. I meant to say that if you could find within you the same power that pushes the plague back from this one, vital memory, you might find the power to change your fate."

As Icelin digested this, she noticed Ruen looking at the old man intently. "Can you help her?" he asked. "Is there any priestly magic in that staff that can help her remember what she needs to know?"

"There are ways of bringing memories to the surface, if you truly want to relive them," Aldren said. "When dealing with the spellplague, such methods are never certain to work and carry their own cost. I have stored the memories of each lifetime I've lived," Aldren said. "I don't know if I can impart such a thing to your friend, but if she is willing, I would try."

"At what risk to yourself?" Icelin said. "No. We've caused you enough grief."

"Are you afraid, Icelin?" Ruen said.

Icelin could hear the challenge in his voice. "No," she said, "I'm not afraid. But I'm tired of other people risking pieces of themselves for me. I think it's time Cerest was made to answer for what he's done. I will make him tell me."

She stepped to the gap in the hull. She could feel an invisible presence. The old man's magic formed a protective seal over the opening.

"Thank you," she said to Aldren. "Whatever happens, I'm glad to have met you."

"And I, you," said Aldren. "The gods go with you."

Icelin nodded and stepped through the opening. Ruen followed behind her.

She didn't know what she expected to happen once she crossed the seal. An ambush, another monster, or a spray of magic from the elf woman who'd taken her on the shore? She got none of those things, but she sensed the change in the air as soon as the harbor scent hit her nose.

"Look above you," Ruen said quietly.

Icelin looked up and lost her breath. She could see slivers of moonlight through the *Ferryman's* tangled rigging. The skeletal forest canopy swelled with movement. Sea wraiths circled each other and the wreckage. More were floating up from various parts of the ruins to join the mass. The unearthly choir keened softly, as if singing to the moon or some other, invisible celestial body.

"You said there was wild magic here," Icelin said, "that it draws the wraiths. Can they feel it—the three of us here together?"

"I don't know," Ruen said. "But it's possible we're stirring up whatever's been lying dormant here since the *Ferryman* was destroyed."

"Not just us," Icelin said, "him too."

Cerest sat cross-legged on Ruen's raft. He was alone, and looked completely at ease beneath the canopy of swirling wraiths. Icelin knew his men would be nearby, but wherever they were, Cerest had them well hidden. She wondered if Ruen, with his sharper eyes, could detect them. The only illumination came from the lantern on Ruen's raft and a torch Cerest had propped in front of him.

He looked up when they appeared, and smiled in genuine pleasure. "Well met, Icelin," he said. "I received your message. I'm happy to see you are well."

He didn't seem to notice or care that there was a puddle of drying blood—leucrotta and Bellaril's—behind and to his left. The copper scent combined with the leucrotta's naturally pungent stink must have been overwhelming. But like the dying horse that day on the Way of the Dragon, Cerest took the horror completely in his stride. His pleasant expression never faltered.

Somehow, though, the sight of him amid the blood was less intimidating instead of more. Here at last he wasn't trying to hide what he was, the deficiency of mind that had set him on her like a crazed hunting hound. She could see him in this true state and feel pity, though it was a fleeting emotion.

"Greetings, Cerest," she said. "I hope you haven't been waiting long."

"I'm accustomed to being patient. I was more than willing to wait for you," Cerest said. "In the end, I knew you'd come back to me."

Icelin felt Ruen tense behind her. She reached back to touch him, but of course he moved just out of her grasp. She dropped her hand.

"Are we alone?" she asked, deliberately affecting a teasing tone.

"There's at least one in the crow's nest," Ruen said. "Ten feet up." He pointed, and Icelin heard the scuff of boots on wood, a figure hastening to conceal himself in the shadows. Ruen smiled. "I don't think he enjoys heights."

Cerest was not so amused. Hatred came alive in his eyes when he looked at Ruen, an emotion so intense Icelin wondered at its root. "I would be more than willing to dismiss my men, Icelin, if you would send your friend away," he said. His voice was unsteady. He swallowed.

"But that's hardly fair," Icelin said. "I have so few friends left, thanks to you." She reached into her pack and pulled out the stack of letters. "Do you know what these are?"

Cerest stood and walked toward her outstretched hand. Icelin allowed him to approach but kept her body squarely between Ruen and Cerest, noting the irony of her protection of the elf.

Not for long, she thought, as the viper took the letters from her hand. I won't need you for long.

Cerest shuffled through the letters, and Icelin could tell he recognized the handwriting immediately. "These are Elgreth's," he said, handing them back to her. "I never would have credited him with the strength to write them. He was in poor shape when I left him in Luskan."

She thought she'd been prepared for anything, but at his words, Icelin felt a cold kiss on the back of her neck, as if one of the wraiths had drifted down to whisper hateful truths in her ear.

Anger bloomed in place of the cold, and the contrast made her tremble. She felt the letters flutter from her hands. They landed on the harbor's surface and became tiny, worn boats carried away by the rippling current.

She had felt many things upon learning of her grandfather's identity and subsequent fate: grief, confusion, loss, but always a place removed from her heart. It wasn't that she was callous. It was simply that nothing could surmount the pain and anger that lived there after Brant's death—until now.

"Why?" she said. "If you found Elgreth in Luskan, why didn't you bring him home to Waterdeep? You said he was your best friend. How could you leave him in that godscursed place?"

"He was too far gone to walk," Cerest said, "and I didn't have enough men. I never would have made it out of the city with him. We would have been set upon—fresh carrion for the vultures."

"Of course," Icelin said bitterly. "You wouldn't have risked yourself to make your old friend comfortable in his last days."

"Whatever you think of me, Icelin, I *was* Elgreth's friend," Cerest said. "I would have given anything to have brought him home. He should never have gone to Luskan."

"He went to protect me," Icelin said. "He must have been terrified you would find me. What was it, Cerest? What did you do to betray my family's trust in you so completely?"

"I never intended to betray them," Cerest said, "just as I didn't intend for Elgreth to run from me. You are too young to understand. My family was composed of artisans. They had centuries to hone their skills. My father could craft weapons that sang with arcane music. He only made a handful of blades in his lifetime, but they were *named*. If not alive, they were near enough to sentient that men in Myth Drannor craved the bond between sword and man more than they craved a mate. And it was all because my father could sense magic and make it bend to whatever shape he desired. It didn't matter that the Spellplague was ravishing magic all over Faerûn. My father might have been a god. He was master of the unbound weave."

"But his son did not inherit his ability," Icelin said.

"No," Cerest said. "I tried, but the gift never came. There were reasons, my father said. A question of birth."

The naked longing in his eyes was of a kind Icelin had never seen except on a grieving person. Cerest had long ago realized what he could never be, but he refused to come to terms with his inadequacy.

"It was easier after I left," Cerest said. "I comforted myself by thinking that this kind of gift was an aberration. I would never see it again, even in my long lifetime." His voice was ragged, emotion breaking through at last. "I met Elgreth, and your parents, and everything was perfect. We would have continued together, year after year, explorers all"—his face contorted—"if Elgreth hadn't wanted to explore the Rikraw Tower."

These were the words Icelin had waited to hear. Cerest had given the tower a name, and names were power. She felt the bonds around her memories snap.

CHAPTER 20

As Cerest spoke, Icelin felt a kind of stupor descend upon her mind. The fog thickened and deepened. This was not like the other times she'd gone into her mind, seeking a stray piece of lost information. This was not in her control. She was being led down the twisting corridors by a hand that belonged to a person that was her and yet not her. This person was a child and yet possessed of more wisdom than her waking self.

Icelin was only half-aware, in this state, of Cerest moving closer to her and Ruen farther away. This repositioning made no sense to Icelin, but she had no time to consider the implications. The hand pulling her was moving faster, sweeping her along with its urgency.

The corridors turned to aged stone; dust and cobwebs clung to the corners. Was she going backward in time? An appropriate metaphor, Icelin thought. Brant always said her mind worked with the same practicality of a history text. Past was old, present was new.

She came to the end of the passage and found a swathe of green cutting brilliantly across the stone. Stepping out of the passage, Icelin found herself in a vast field.

At first she was afraid. The space was too open. The smells of the city were gone. She could only detect grass and the distant smell of smoke in the air.

This was what outside the city smelled like. This was what *space* smelled like. Gone were the constant press of animals and South Ward wagon traffic and the refuse of so many folk living side by side. She felt—remembered—the grass tickling her ankles, the movement of insects in the living carpet.

She breathed deeply and caught the hint of smoke again. Mingled with the ash and fire was the scent of onions cooking, and fresh game nearby.

A dusty ribbon of road, stamped many times over with hoof prints, snaked out in front of her. It led up a steep hillside and out of sight. She followed it, and when she crested the rise saw the campfire, the stew pot cooling in the grass, and the circle of figures waiting for their meal.

The feeling of familiarity cascaded over Icelin with such intensity that it left her dizzy and unmoored in her own memories. It was like encountering beloved friends with whom she'd corresponded for years but never seen face to face.

Elgreth cradled a spit stuck with flaming venison. He looked young, his dark brown hair showing only a few threads of silver in the sunlight. He had a thick moustache and wide arms like ale barrels. His cloak fell around him in a pool of darker green against the grass. He pulled the venison off the spit, snatching his hand back from the steaming meat. He sucked on his fingers and pulled faces at the child seated across the fire from him.

Icelin recognized her young self only distantly. Her black hair was trimmed short. She looked like a boy, except she was delicately framed and wore a dress of thick cotton and indeterminate shape.

How strange to see herself this way. She was no longer walking through vague half-memories, as she had been in her dreams. Her mind was spinning the completed story, as vividly as Kaelin had staged his play.

A woman stepped into view and dropped a blanket over her younger self's head. The child squealed and crawled out from under the quilt, her eyes staring adoringly up at her mother.

Her mother and father. Icelin saw them more clearly than she saw her younger self. Her father sat behind her mother, pulling his wife back into his lap, trapping her between thin arms. He was not nearly as burly as Elgreth. His back was slightly hunched under the weight of the pack he wore. His spectacles had been bent and repaired so many times they gave his face a misshapen appearance. When he looked at her mother, his face was so full of love. And in that breath he became the most beautiful man Icelin had ever seen.

Her mother looked exactly like Icelin. She had the same dark hair, trimmed short, but there was no mistaking her curves for a boy. She had the full mouth and healthy weight Icelin lacked, but their eyes were the same, their cheekbones as finely chiseled.

How did I keep you away from my memory for so long? Icelin thought. Where have you been hiding? She sat down on the grass, determined to stay forever in the field, content to bask in the presence of the family she'd never met.

When she looked back at the scene, she noticed the tower for the first time. An ugly gray spike that was slightly off center from the rest of the landscape, the tower cast a shadow that reached nearly to the campsite.

She noticed other things. Her father kept shooting glances in the tower's direction, a look of barely contained excitement stretching his face.

Thirty paces from the fire, Icelin saw another figure, small with distance, agile when he moved. The figure had his back to her, but Icelin could see he was male. Two points of flesh stuck out from his golden hair. When the figure turned, Icelin was shocked to see the smooth, handsome features, the lively eyes unmarked by grief and trauma.

Cerest was an angelic blight on the idyllic scene, Icelin thought. She could see how anyone, man or woman, human or elf, would be taken with him. His face, in its symmetry, was more beautiful than any she'd ever seen. He motioned to her family, his face bright with exhilaration.

The camp broke up. Elgreth left the venison smoking in the grass. Her mother scooped her younger self up in her arms and tossed her over one shoulder. Her delighted squeals trailed away down the hill toward the tower.

Don't do it. Don't go. Stay, and be with me always. Icelin got to her feet and followed her family. She tried to run, but the tower seemed always at a safe distance from her footsteps, and no shout would reach the ears of the living memories before her.

She closed her eyes, and when she opened them, she was inside the tower, just as she had been in every nightmare that had haunted her from childhood.

This time, she was no spectator. She resided in the body of her younger self. She could feel the cool ground beneath her bare feet, and the shadows swirling around her had form and substance. They were her family. Her father was taking scrapings from the brittle stone walls and placing them in vials on his belt. Her mother was chanting in an undertone, her hands on the spine of what had once been a massive tome. The spine was all that remained. Her mother's eyes were closed. Yellow light encircled her fingers.

Her mother—a wizard! Icelin couldn't believe it. Her mother had carried the gift of the Art, and Icelin had inherited it. Gods, how much her mother could have taught her, guided her, if she had lived to see to her daughter's tutelage.

"Be cautious," said a voice.

The sudden interruption jarred Icelin from her thoughts. She looked to see who had spoken and saw Elgreth standing next to her mother.

"It's all right," her mother said. She touched Elgreth's arm. "I sense no pockets here. Cerest was right. The plague has abandoned this place. Have you found anything?" she asked, addressing her husband.

"Where's Cerest gone to?" Elgreth asked.

"I think he's putting out the campfire," her mother said. She touched Elgreth's cheek affectionately. "I expect we forgot to douse it in our excitement."

Icelin only half-listened to the rest of the conversation; her attention was caught by the ruined book. She got on her knees and turned her head to see the letters on the spine. They were outlined in blue fire, the edges of the script blurring and fluttering like wings on a dying butterfly.

As she watched, the flames punctured the leather binding, leaving blackened curls in their wake. The smell of charred leather rose in her nostrils. She looked up, and saw that her mother was watching the book too. Her eyes widened, and the color drained from her lovely face.

Icelin, hampered by her younger body, could not get to her mother. She tripped over a pile of wood and fell. Her face caught the sunlight coming from a gaping hole in the tower ceiling. The light beating down was too intense. The ground had been cold only a breath ago, yet everywhere around her she felt heat. It was like she'd stepped into the middle of the campfire.

"Icelin."

She heard her mother's voice. It had never sounded like that before. With a child's certainty and an adult's memory, Icelin knew this was the end.

The spellplague pocket, awakened by her mother's simple magic, swirled to life from the rafters of the ruined tower ceiling. A cerulean cloud that looked like a tiny, confined thunderstorm, it crawled along the walls, finding cracks in the stone and exploding them, spraying shards of rock on the helpless people below.

Someone was at her side, hauling her roughly under a cloak.

"Get her out!" she heard her mother scream. Then her voice faded. Icelin was running, running on legs that didn't belong to her. Elgreth had picked her up. The blue fire was everywhere—in her eyes, her mouth. She was blind. She couldn't see either of her parents.

They broke free into daylight, but the blue fire wasn't done with them. It stretched out hungry tendrils and snared her hair and her arms. Elgreth dropped her to the grass.

She started to cry. The heat was too intense. It was the worst sunburn she'd ever had. Her flesh should be melting from her bones. She heard Elgreth next to her, screaming. She reached for him, but she couldn't touch him. The blue light was everywhere. There were other screams, shouts her young mind couldn't comprehend but that the adult Icelin recognized as the Elvish language.

Cerest was nearby, crying out in agony. His beautiful face was melting and being reforged into something new, a visage that more closely matched his soul. Icelin curled up in a ball on the grass and waited for it to be over. She didn't care if she died, as long as the pain stopped.

Oblivion came, sweeping its cool hand across her body. She was resting in a dark place. She wanted to sleep there forever. To wake was to re-enter that world of horrid pain.

When she opened her eyes again, she was still on the ground. She could see the tip of the tower, weirdly, in her peripheral vision, as she stared up at the sky. Star and moonlight illuminated the scene now, and somewhere, far off, she smelled another campfire burning.

Elgreth leaned over her, adding another blanket to a growing pile on her small body. Her nose was cold. Elgreth's breath fogged in the night air.

"Is she awake?" It was Cerest's voice. He spoke in the human tongue. He sounded weak.

Elgreth didn't reply. He stroked her cheek, and threaded his fingers in her hair to push it away from her face.

He looked broken, the adult Icelin remembered. Gone were the light-hearted smile and the fringes of youth that she'd seen by the campfire. They had been replaced by a tremendous weight and sadness.

She reached up to touch him. His skin was warm, his moustache hair brittle. He smelled like smoke. It was no campfire that burned, only the remnants of the Rikraw Tower—the funeral pyre for her parents.

When Elgreth left her at last, she crawled out from under the blankets and walked to the tower. Elgreth called to her, screamed for her to stop. But she couldn't. Her parents were somewhere in the wreck of stones.

The tower's collapsed wall was a black blemish on the landscape. Scorch marks sprayed out from it in jagged, oily streaks. Viewed from above, the tower might have been a stygian sun.

Elgreth was still screaming. He's injured, Icelin thought, or he'd be running after me. I am wrong for leaving him. But she couldn't make her feet stop walking.

She caught her foot on a rock. When she looked down, she realized the rock was a hand, clutching her ankle. The fingernails were black, the palms blistered and oozing white pus.

Frightened, Icelin jerked away. She followed the arm attached to the hand and found Cerest, curled on the ground. He had one arm thrown across his face. The appendage was out of its socket. His other arm stretched toward her, trying to stop her.

Icelin looked at that blistered, trembling hand for a long time before she turned and resumed her long journey to the tower.

The stones vibrated with a power beyond sun-warmth. Everything was cold now, but she could feel where the energy had been. When her eyes adjusted to the dimness inside the tower, Icelin could see there was nothing left. Her mother's hair, her father's spectacles—the spellplague had burned them to ash.

She touched the blackened stones, caught the ash-falls drifting through the air. Illuminated in moonlight, they might have been dust or the remains of flesh. She caught as many as she could in her small hands and clutched them against her chest. She started to cry and found she was too dehydrated for the tears to form.

Carefully, she got down on her hands and knees and placed

her cheek against the ground. The ash stirred and warmed her skin. She stayed there, imagining her mother's arms around her, while Elgreth screamed for her outside the tower.

Daerovus Tallmantle was a patient man, and his office demanded discipline, but, as he surveyed the wraiths circling the distant Ferryman's Waltz, he concluded that he'd been patient long enough.

"That's the place," he said.

"Can we trust him?" Tesleena asked.

The Warden thought of Tarvin, his head crushed by a plank. His body had been borne away to the Watch barracks and then to his family.

He surveyed the group of men and women that stood before him in homespun disguises. Their eyes flitted between the Ferryman's Waltz and his face.

"You know what's expected of you," he said. "If any man or woman among you feels he cannot perform his duty, you may accompany Tarvin's body back to the barracks. I look you in the eyes and ask this plainly: will you see justice done?"

A chorus of "ayes" answered him. As promised, he stared each of them in the eyes, hunting deceit. He found none, and was satisfied.

"On the boats," he said. " 'Ware the wraiths, but Icelin is the one you want. Bring her in."

"You have to untangle yourself from this," said a voice Icelin did not, at first, recognize.

She looked up, and for some reason was unsurprised to find Aldren standing in the shadows of the tower.

"I didn't think you could weave yourself into memories," Icelin said.

"Only yours, it would seem," Aldren replied. "But I would rather not be here. This is a foul place, and you're needed elsewhere."

"I don't know how to leave," she said. "What if the plague won't let me?"

Aldren made a motion with his gnarled hand, and his staff appeared in the clawed grip, as if it had always been there, invisible.

"To weave magic requires discipline," he said. "At the best of times, anything can go wrong, because the Art runs unchecked. We are its only shepherds now." He held out his staff to her. "To be a weaver requires a focus," he said, "a tool to channel your energy. You should never rely on such a thing completely, but in the worst of times it can help you endure the wildness of the raw Art."

Icelin touched the staff and felt a pulsing energy. The Art ran through the staff like blood in wooden veins. She could feel the contained power, frightening and pure.

"What if it gets away from me again?"

"It surely will," Aldren said. "Such things are inevitable. The only thing you can do is focus on what is most important to you—what's worth saving."

"Ruen." She remembered his name as if he had been the dream, and this her only reality. She stood up, and her body was an adult's, though weak and fragile.

The tower melted around her. The black stones faded, as if all the filth was being drained from her memory. She closed her eyes against the swirling, turbulent cleansing.

She smelled the harbor, but when she opened her eyes, the scene had changed. Her mind couldn't process it at first.

Ruen stood thirty feet away, fighting two men at once. A third man floated in the water, his right arm and chest contorted at an odd angle in the water.

She was lying on Ruen's raft. Cerest crouched over her. His crumpled face showed concern, but Icelin noticed he held a dagger slackly in his right hand.

"Are you well?" he asked.

She licked her lips and tried to speak, but she'd been in her mind too long. The words came out as incoherent mumbles.

Cerest leaned closer. "Say it again, Icelin. I didn't hear you."

Icelin didn't repeat what she'd been trying to say. She brought her knee up and crushed it into Cerest's stomach.

He lurched back onto his right elbow, losing his balance when he tried to bring the knife to bear. He pitched over the side of the raft into the water.

Icelin sprang to her feet and immediately saw that Ruen was in trouble. He held off the two men at his right and left flank, but the man on the crow's nest was frantically cranking a crossbow into position. He propped it on the lip of the nest to steady his aim.

Cerest thrashed in the water. He grabbed for the raft. Icelin kicked him in the face. Blood exploded from his nose; her heel had knocked it out of position. The elf cursed and backstroked, putting a safe distance between them.

Lifting her arms, Icelin chanted a spell and brought her hands together, as if she were cupping them around the crow's nest. The basket of rotting wood burst into flames that rose up around the man with the crossbow.

The man shrieked and dropped the weapon. It landed in the water and sank. The man dived from the nest, fistfuls of flame eating at his clothing. He hit the water belly first.

The men fighting Ruen had their backs to the crow's nest. They tried to turn to see their companion's fate, but Ruen wouldn't give them a respite. He clipped the shorter of the two in the jaw, spinning him half toward the water and upsetting his balance on the bones of the leviathan.

It was all about balance. He kept them both at bay because they couldn't keep their feet. If they'd been on level ground, Ruen would have had several of his bones crushed by now.

While the shorter man steadied himself, Ruen dodged a

roundhouse punch from a man wearing a mail vest and thick gauntlets. Built like a brick, this man would be harder to move with simple punches.

Icelin picked her spell carefully, focusing on the chain links pressed tight against the man's body. She could feel the trembling in her fingers as she worked through the complicated gestures.

Two spells, by the gods. Give me two spells without pain, Icelin pleaded. Lady Mystra, I can't pray to your memory. I never knew you. But if any goddess can hear me . . .

She flexed her fingers and released the spell. Her vision blurred. Nausea rose in her gut, and she felt cold, sticky sweat clinging to her forehead. She forced past the sickness and concentrated on the brick man's mail vest.

There was no visible change. Ruen took a glancing punch to his shoulder from the shorter man. He answered with a kick that took the man's right leg out from under him. The short man grabbed an overhanging bone, perhaps a rib of the long-dead creature. The bone snapped off. The man grabbed wildly for his companion and buried his fingers in the mail links.

The brick man roared in pain, and the shorter man cried out as well. Smoke rose from the brick man's clothing where it had pressed against the metal links.

Wide-eyed, the brick man patted his chest, touching hot links wherever his hands rested.

Ruen shot a quick glance at Icelin across the water. He jerked his head in acknowledgment.

"Let me help you with that," he told the brick man. He aimed a kick to the man's midsection. The brick man howled and fell backward into the water. A chorus of snakelike hisses rose from where the hot metal touched the cold water. The brick man sank to his chin, a look of relief crossing his face.

"Get back up 'ere!" cried the short man. He dodged a second kick from Ruen. "Help me!"

The brick man shook his head and swam away. He was obviously done with the fight.

Icelin turned her attention from Ruen to Cerest, who was climbing onto the raft behind her. His knife was gone, but he looked furious enough to kill her with his bare hands. His nose was a red, twisted mass on his face. The blood seeping into his scars made him look like a demon. Icelin remembered the scene outside the tower, when the newly scarred elf had looked up at her young self in agony.

"I remember now," she told him. "The tower. My parents. Elgreth. Did you really think it was safe for us to go in, Cerest? Or was that just what you told yourself? The same way you convinced yourself it wasn't your fault that they died?"

"I had to weigh the risk and reward," Cerest said. There was no remorse in the words. "The knowledge and artifacts we might have found would have enriched all our lives, including yours."

"Oh yes, my life has been enriched indeed," Icelin said.

"I was more than willing to take care of both of you afterwards," Cerest said. "Elgreth could have used his scar to unearth treasures unimaginable. He'd become just like my father, a god of magic—the very aberration I never thought to see again. But he refused to help me. He forced me to look to you."

"And here we are," Icelin said, "in another plague den." She listened to the sounds of fighting behind her, Ruen's muffled cry of pain as he took a blow to some vulnerable part of his body.

"I'm sorry," she told Cerest as she came to a silent decision. "You named me, Cerest, but you were never my family. I thought my family was Waterdeep and a sundries shop. That would have been more than enough for me. But my family is everywhere: Waterdeep, the Dalelands, Aglarond, Luskan—even a burned-out tower. Their footsteps can be heard in the tombs and lost places of Faerûn."

"You can be more than they ever were," Cerest said. "You survived, when Elgreth did not."

"I survived because my gift is different," Icelin said. "Poor Cerest, I share your curse. I don't have Elgreth's sense of magic. I only know memory."

She took a step toward him and lifted her hands, the palms facing each other. Cerest flinched, but only for a breath. His eyes reflected the blue glow illuminating her fingers. He was transfixed, watching the power swirl in the empty air between her hands.

"What are you doing?" he asked.

"Protecting what I have left," Icelin said. She felt the cold touch her palms. She thought it was the first taste of the frost ray forming, but the sensation spread up her arms and lingered around her shoulders.

Icelin looked up and saw the wraiths swirling silently, less than ten feet above their heads. Like Cerest, they seemed transfixed by the radiant glow that was now climbing her arms. Her flesh glowed cerulean, far beyond the scope of the attack spell.

"What's happening?" Cerest demanded. He looked up at the wraiths. Icelin followed his gaze. Beyond the undead, another blue glow was forming on the bones of the leviathan. More of the creatures dived and chased the light around the bones. Like mad fireflies they soaked up the raw spell energy.

"It's the spellplague," Icelin said. Her magic had released the long dormant energy. The wraiths were finally going to have their feast.

"Get off the raft," Cerest cried. He grabbed her arm, trying to tow her toward the *Ferryman*. "If we can make it to some cover—"

Icelin stumbled and fell. On her knees, with one hand on the raft and the other caught in Cerest's grip, she looked up and saw the blue light descending the magnificent bones, a waterfall coming down a mountainside.

"It's too late," she said. "Ruen!" she screamed, and turned to see the monk holding onto one of the rib bones for support. He clutched his chest with his other arm. The short man lay at his feet, a strip of blood leaking from his mouth. His eyes stared vacantly up at the doom working its way down to them.

Ruen jumped into the water. He surfaced five feet from the raft and started to swim to her.

"No!" Icelin waved him off. "Go down," she cried. "Swim down, as far as you can. Get away from the light." She could barely see him now. The light was so bright, she had to squint. "We'll be behind you."

Ruen hesitated. Icelin could almost see him calculating their odds. "I'll try to find an air pocket around the ship," he said. Then he was gone, diving beneath the surface. Icelin crawled to the edge of the raft to follow, when suddenly a heavy weight hit her from behind.

Her breath gone, Icelin fell flat to the raft. She could feel Cerest pressing his body against hers.

"Get off!" she cried, but her scream was lost in the cry of the wraiths. They dived and hovered around the raft, blocking her escape into the water.

"They still smell the magic," Cerest shouted. His strength held her immobile. The blue light fell over them in a curtain.

The glare brightened to a painful intensity, and suddenly everything went black. Icelin thought she'd gone blind.

Blinking reflexively, she felt a warm breeze against her face. She looked up and saw a crescent of sunlight spilling over a pile of stone. It was the remains of a rooftop.

She was back in the tower. The heat continued to build, just as it had in her vision. Her two realities were merging, past and present bridged by the spellplague.

But this time something was different. Icelin rolled onto her side and saw the body lying next to her. Cerest was staring, disoriented, up at the sunbeams and the tower roof.

He doesn't know where he is, Icelin thought. His mind is joined to mine by the plague.

"What happened?" The elf sat up and swung toward her. His face paled visibly. Icelin turned to see the specters of her parents and Elgreth searching the tower. They went about their exploration, smiling and laughing, oblivious to the two figures sitting on the ground.

Cerest's lips formed the name of his old friend, but he couldn't speak. His eyes welled with unshed tears. Icelin couldn't believe the sight.

He's in pain. This pains him. Does he know what's coming? She looked up at the light. It fell in sunbeams and blue threads. Did Cerest know how few breaths stood between his friends and oblivion?

She reached out, against her will, and touched the elf on the shoulder. "Cerest," she said. "Close your eyes."

"What?" He turned to her, gripping her shoulders. "It's them, can't you see them? They're alive!"

Icelin winced at the pressure he exerted. His hands trembled. Half-crazed joy shone in his liquid eyes.

"They aren't real," Icelin said. "This is memory. Everything's going to burn, Cerest." Maybe us too.

"No!" He shook his head. Sweat dripped from his hair. "Not this time. I'll be able to warn them this time. I'll get them out before anything happens."

"They can't hear you," Icelin said. She closed her eyes. She couldn't watch it a second time.

Cerest continued to hold her in a crushing grip as the heat built to a roar in her ears. She heard the screams. Cerest's raw shriek pricked icy needles all over her flesh. She tipped her head forward, resting against his chest while he wept and screamed, over and over.

He was seeing everything as he had never seen it before—from the inside of the inferno. Elgreth had long since carried her young self away, but the memory and Cerest's imagination had taken over. She could hear her mother crying out for her husband and for Cerest. The smell of burning flesh filled the air.

To distract herself, Icelin conjured an image of Ruen, swimming deep in the rotting harbor. She prayed he'd found safe haven from the plague's reach. He'd already drowned in its grip once.

And what about Aldren, Darvont and Bellaril? Would they be safe inside the *Ferryman*, or would the plague consume the ship and crush them all? She held onto the screaming elf and hoped that one of Aldren's deities would take pity on all of them.

CHAPTER 21

Tallmantle heard Tesleena's scream a breath before the explosion. The keel of the *Ferryman* erupted in blue fire. Debris shot thirty feet into the air. The flames spewed toward the sky in an arcane geyser the likes of which he had never seen.

"Halt the boats!" Tallmantle raised a hand, but the men were already bringing their oars up from the water to watch the spectacle. A shower of blue flame and what looked like humanoid forms were raining down over the harbor.

"Gods above," said Deelia, who was behind him in the boat. "Are those people?"

"No," Tesleena said. She was in the boat adjacent to Tallmantle's. Her voice sounded detached from her body. Her eyes stared, unfocused, at some distant point on the horizon. "They're sea wraiths." A crease appeared in her forehead. "I understand. My thanks."

Tallmantle looked at the wizard. "What does the Blackstaff say?"

"He's too far away to know how much damage was done," Tesleena said. Her eyes shifted, centering on Tallmantle. "Which also means he has no way of knowing if it's safe to approach. He can't return to the city now. He leaves it up to you to decide whether to go in."

"What do you think?" he asked her.

"I will go," she said without hesitation. "But it's likely anyone who was in the wreckage was killed instantly when the spellplague pocket erupted."

Icelin awoke staring into darkness. She flexed her fingers—grateful that she still possessed the appendages—and cast a spell using the least possible amount of energy.

A pinprick glow lit her fingertip and spread to her whole hand. By its light, her eyes adjusted to her surroundings.

She stared up at the sky. It took her a long time to realize that the *Ferryman's* masts and rigging had been incinerated by the spellplague blast. Small fires burned at various points along the *Ferryman's* length.

The entire ship had listed far forward, but by some miracle the leviathan's bones held it stable and prevented their being crushed under its weight. The small chamber created by the wreckage had been reduced to half its size, but Ruen's raft was miraculously still intact. Gaps yawned in the planks like missing teeth. Water seeped freely across the ship's surface, but for now it stayed afloat.

As her vision adjusted, Icelin became aware of the bodies. There was one on either side of her and another draped half on the raft and half in the water directly across from her. She could smell the burning, the singed flesh and hair. Her breath quickened.

The body on her right stirred. Icelin swung her spell light toward the movement. Her wrist stopped in midair, caught in an iron grip.

Icelin's heart lifted. "Ruen," she whispered. She removed his sodden hat from where it had fallen over his face. His skin was wet but unmarked by arcane fire. His eyes, when they opened, were the familiar rust red color. "Are you all right?"

He nodded and released her wrist. "Hat, please," he said.

Icelin helped him sit up and put the hat back on his head. "How did you manage not to get that thing incinerated or lost in the harbor?" she asked.

Ruen looked at her, his expression grave. "Magic," he said.

Icelin had the urge to laugh, but it died in her throat when she remembered the other bodies. She moved the light away from Ruen. Her spell illuminated a face she didn't immediately recognize. The man was beautiful, his face smooth-skinned and symmetrical. His long golden hair fell across ears that were pointed like needles.

"Merciful gods," she said. "This is Cerest."

Ruen looked over her shoulder. The elf's face had been perfectly restored. His eyes were open and staring glassily at something invisible in the distance. The expression on his face was both peaceful and sad.

Icelin put her hand against the elf's cheek. It was ice cold. "He's dead," she said.

"So is this one," Ruen said, checking the man draped across the raft. He put his hand against the man's chest to find a heartbeat, but they both saw the burns on the man's face and torso. His skin was blackened, and his hair was gone. His clothes had been burned to brittle strips that turned to ash when Ruen touched them. His chain vest had melted into his skin.

Ruen met her gaze. Icelin knew they were both thinking the same thing.

"Maybe Aldren's magic protected them," Ruen said.

Icelin shone her light around the wreckage. The entrance to Aldren's chamber was now underwater. The channel they'd used to get the raft into the wreckage was filled in with debris.

"We'll have to swim out," Icelin said. Her gaze strayed involuntarily back to Cerest's face, perfect now in its death pose. "Why did it happen?" she asked. "Why were we spared?"

"I don't know," Ruen said. "We're already scarred. Maybe we're immune to the plague now."

"Cerest was scarred," Icelin said, "in body, if not magically. Why would the plague restore him and then kill him?"

Maybe it hadn't been the plague. She remembered Cerest's

anguished screams inside the tower. "He saw my mind," she said. "In that breath we were joined, he saw everything he'd done, for the first time. He was inside the tower with me, watching my parents die."

"A perfect memory," Ruen said. "Maybe Cerest's mind couldn't survive that kind of clarity. To have all the defects of your own psyche laid out for you in a ring of fire—not many people could face it and live."

"So this," Icelin said, touching the elf's smooth face, "this is memory. His last memory." She felt an overwhelming wave of sadness—for her parents, Elgreth, and for Brant. So many lives destroyed.

"We should get out of here," Ruen said. "There's no telling how long the structure will hold."

"The Ferryman's Waltz is over," Icelin said quietly. She turned away, leaving Cerest on the raft, staring peacefully up at the sky.

They swam out of the wreckage together, Icelin's bobbing light leading the way. Gray mist clung to the harbor's surface. In the distance she could smell the Hearth fire burning. The orange glow gave the impression of a false dawn.

Out of the darkness, Icelin saw the line of boats coming toward them. Lantern light swayed at each prow. Icelin could see there were at least two men in each boat.

"Think you can take ten of them?" she asked Ruen, who was treading water next to her. "Leaves eight for me."

"Only ten?" Ruen said. His face twisted with a gallows humor smile. "Bring me a true challenge, lady."

The lead boats drifted to a stop practically on top of them. Icelin squinted up into the face of a woman in robes. She wore a tense frown, but she seemed more interested in the wreckage than in the two figures in the water.

A tall man leaned down to Icelin. This man she recognized immediately, though she'd never expected the Watch Warden to come for her himself.

"Warden Tallmantle," she said. "I understand you've been looking for me."

"Well met, Icelin Tearn," Tallmantle said, inclining his head gravely. "Would you care to come aboard?"

"I would, and if you've a spare blanket or two, I'd be weepingly grateful for those as well. But I've a problem. Three of my friends are trapped in the wreckage. We can't get to them."

" 'Ware!" shouted one of the men at the back of the group. "We need more light over here."

Tesleena spoke a word, and the surrounding harbor lit as if a miniature sun had risen.

A single small boat drifted toward the group. Her oarsman was hunched over, forcing the craft through the water.

The Watch officer nearest raised his crossbow. The oarsman lifted his head, and Icelin shouted, "Stop! He's a friend."

The crossbow stayed aimed at the deformed man. His tentacles undulated across his shoulders. He continued to row toward them, undaunted by the stares.

When Darvont got close enough to Tallmantle's boat, Ruen grabbed an oar and hauled the boat in the rest of the way. There were two figures lying side by side in the bottom of the boat. Icelin recognized Bellaril and Aldren, but she couldn't see if they yet breathed.

The deformed man slumped against the side of the boat, exhausted by whatever toil had brought them out of the wreckage. Tears streaked his face. Icelin could see him stroking Aldren's robes. Her heart lurched painfully.

She swam to the boat, but Tallmantle was closer. He bent over the prone figures. "The old man is dead," he said. "The dwarf lives."

"The Art is around her," Tesleena said. She put a hand on the dwarf's shoulder and rolled her onto her back. Clutched between her two hands was Aldren's staff. It pulsed with pale, crimson radiance, but it was clear at Icelin's touch that the item had been drained. It was nowhere near as powerful as it once had been.

"Is he truly dead?" Icelin asked. She saw Tallmantle nod, but she was looking to the deformed man. He met her gaze and seemed to understand what she was asking. He nodded. The sorrow in his eyes pierced her.

"It was what he wanted," Ruen said.

"He protected Bellaril," Icelin said. The Art requires a focus, Aldren had told her. She lifted the staff from the sleeping Bellaril's arms and cradled it in her own. "Thank you," she murmured. "In Mystra's memory, thank you."

"In Mystra's memory," Tesleena whispered. The words echoed down the line of boats.

EPILOGUE

Icelin sat outside the Watch Warden's private office, awaiting her audience and her fate.

It was strange, to be alone in the small chamber, not to hear the constant flow of the harbor and the people on the twisted walkways. She felt, in some ways, that she'd lived her whole life in Mistshore, and was only now venturing out into the sun-washed world.

She ran her hands over the bodice of her dress, marveling at the softness of a fabric that was not stiff with salt water and grime. All trace of the harbor stink was gone from her body, though her hair had been a struggle. She'd ended up cutting most of the muck out of it. The strands barely brushed her shoulders now, and the shorter locks at her temples were stark white. She ran her fingers through the strands self-consciously.

The forced haircut had yielded another secret of her past. Tesleena had seen it first: a faint, almost indiscernible blue light appeared at the back of her neck when she drew deeply on her memory. Tesleena said the spellscar was a circle broken in two places, the lines so thin she would never have seen them unless she'd known to look.

It was one of many things she was going to have to grow accustomed to in her new life. Another was the staff resting beside her on the bench. The red light had fallen dormant, but she could recall it again with a word of power. She had divined no further secrets from the item, but she was satisfied with her small progress. For now, she used it mainly as a walking stick.

It had been five days since her confrontation with Cerest and her second exposure to the spellplague. Since that night, exhaustion overtook her easily. She found herself leaning on the staff often to maintain her equilibrium.

Her strength was slowly returning. Tesleena had assured her it would, though they both knew she would never again be as spry as a normal twenty-year-old girl.

Tesleena had also told her if she stopped now, she would likely live another twenty years or more. Icelin hadn't asked what the last several days had cost her in longevity. She didn't want to know. She would change very little of what she'd done in defense of herself and her friends. Whatever time she had left was the gods' gift. She didn't intend to waste it on regret.

A door to her left opened, and Kersh came through. Icelin stood to greet him, but he got to her first. The Watchman wrapped his arms around her and lifted her onto her toes.

"Have a care for an aging woman," Icelin said, laughing.

"Not a chance," Kersh said. He pulled back to arm's length and regarded her with mock sternness. "Every time I let you out of my sight you work yourself into more trouble."

"Lucky for you I'm too stubborn to let anyone do away with me," Icelin said.

"Are you well, Icelin?" Kersh looked at her intently, as if he could take her apart piece by piece to find any deficiency. "I don't expect you to ever forgive me, but as long as you're all right, I can be content."

"I'm more than well," Icelin said. "You followed the right course, Kersh. I should have trusted you from the beginning."

"We should have made ourselves more worthy of your trust," said a voice from the open doorway.

Icelin looked beyond Kersh to see Daerovus Tallmantle towering over both of them. He regarded Icelin with an uncertain expression. Icelin had never expected to be on the receiving end of such a look from the imposing Warden.

A memory came to her, with crystal clarity as always, of

another time when she had sat in this chamber. She'd been much younger, and Brant had been with her, holding her hand.

When she looked into the Warden's eyes, she knew he was remembering that same day.

Kersh squeezed her hands and stepped away. She felt suddenly adrift. She looked at him imploringly, but he shook his head and smiled. "I'll leave you two to talk," he said. He gave her hand another squeeze, the Warden a salute, and left the room.

"I am truly sorry," Icelin said, "about Tarvin, and any other men you lost these past nights."

"Tarvin was our sole loss, and that was none of your doing," Tallmantle said. He sat on the bench across from her and gestured that she should resume her seat. "I know you're tired," he said, "so I'll be brief. Cerest is dead. What of his men? Are any of them still hunting you?"

Icelin shook her head. "The only ones that might be are a pair of elf women Cerest had working with him. I don't know who they are or what their fates were."

"They are the Lock sisters," Tallmantle said, "well known dealers in antiquities and magic. We believe they hired a portion of the men who hunted you, but we have no evidence linking them directly to Cerest, other than your testimony." His mouth twisted. "They have already lined up several witnesses who will swear they were giving a party the night you were kidnapped."

"I don't want to go after them," Icelin said. "Cerest was the one bent on hunting me. They should have no interest in me now." She thought of Bellaril, master now of Arowall's Cradle and all its men. The dwarf woman had her own score to settle with the sisters. Icelin had no doubt the women would be made to answer for what they had wrought in Mistshore.

"What will you do now?" the Warden asked, surprising her with the change in topic.

"Do the charges against me still stand?" Icelin asked.

"One," Tallmantle said. "The outstanding charge of evading

a Watch summons waits only for my signature to dismiss it."

"My thanks. You will not be popular for that decision in some circles," Icelin said.

"You overestimate our enmity," the Warden said. "Tarvin was the exception. Any others who privately held you responsible for Therondol's death have changed their opinion, based on the events that have transpired these past days." A faint smile lit his features. "You've shamed them, my lady, by choosing deadly Mistshore as a safer haven than the Watch." His smile faded. "You shamed me, as well."

Icelin shook her head, unable to believe what she was hearing. "You have more reason to hate me than anyone. Therondol was your son." Her voice cracked. "I know what it's like to lose yourself to that kind of grief."

The world had stopped working the night she'd lost Brant. Right and wrong became concepts that belonged to other people. Perhaps she was more at home in Mistshore after all. At least she could understand the place now, what created and sustained it as well as what kept it apart from the rest of the city.

The Warden put a hand on her shoulder. Icelin couldn't meet his eyes. She remembered that day, sitting in his office with Brant. His face had been gray, lifeless as he read the account of the fire and his son's death.

"I would have been glad of someone to punish that day," Tallmantle said, as if reading her thoughts. "But it wasn't you I wanted. I stopped believing in the gods that day. I didn't care whether any of them lived or died, because I thought they had forsaken this world. They'd forsaken my son."

Icelin did look up then, but she couldn't read his expression. "Do you still believe that?" she asked.

"I don't know," the Warden said. "I've learned to put my faith in this city and the men and women who serve to keep it thriving. I look to them for aid and inspiration when I need it. So far, those forces have been enough to sustain me."

Icelin nodded. She knew that kind of strength. Ruen and Sull and Bellaril had been hers. "What will happen to him?" she asked.

She was speaking of Ruen. They both knew it. "He did bring you to the Watch, as I instructed, though it was after considerable delay," the Warden said. "Unfortunately, it's been made clear that he can't be trusted to act under our direction. That leaves two options, as I see it."

"You can't send him back to the dungeons," Icelin said. "I owe him my life."

"I don't enjoy the prospect," the Warden said, "which is part of the reason I inquired after your immediate plans. Will you take up your great-uncle's shop and stay in Waterdeep?"

Icelin shook her head. "I considered it, but no. My family wanted me to see more of the world than Waterdeep."

It was a desire she'd never found in herself before. But she knew the breadth of her life now, and the urgency and wanderlust in her blood had flared. The time to begin her journey was now or never.

The Warden nodded thoughtfully, as if he'd been expecting her answer. "I suppose I could recommend a period of banishment from the city for Morleth. A man of his resources should have no trouble finding a direction in the world. Perhaps that direction will coincide with yours."

Icelin grinned. "You might ask him about this course of action before you undertake it. He may vastly prefer the dungeons to being saddled with me indefinitely."

"I have already asked him," Tallmantle said. "He has agreed to keep an eye on you for me."

Icelin didn't know how to respond. Her throat constricted around emotions she couldn't begin to handle. "My thanks," she said roughly, "for everything."

"Gods and friends go with you, lass," the Warden said, "wherever you choose to walk."

When Icelin stepped outside the barracks, she didn't immediately see the monk. Ruen stood in the shadow of a building several paces down the street.

"Were you waiting for me?" she asked when she reached him.

"I would have waited in Tallmantle's office with you," Ruen said, uncrossing his arms, "but I can only spend so long in the place. I break out in a rash."

Icelin fixed a look of annoyance on her face. "So the Warden thinks I need watching after does he? What makes him think you're the man for this task?"

"I'm still alive," Ruen said, shrugging. "No small accomplishment, where you're concerned."

"Hmmm," Icelin said. "I suppose you're right. Will you be vexing me the entire journey?"

"At least halfway there and back."

"I see. I suppose I'll have no choice but to pay you back in kind." Icelin took a step closer to him and leaned in. When it became clear she was about to kiss his cheek, Ruen stepped back, his hands on her shoulders.

Icelin smiled up at him teasingly, but he didn't return the humor. His eyes were shadowed under the brim of his hat.

"Don't," he said simply.

"Don't what? Don't kiss me now, or don't kiss me ever?" she said. "You already know the outcome. What can it hurt?"

"I don't know anything," Ruen said. "Nothing is carved in stone."

"Finally, he admits it. His gift is not infallible," Icelin said. She brought his gloved hand to her lips and kissed the back. "Congratulations."

"Mock me if you want, but you're not giving up either," he said. "You wouldn't be leaving Waterdeep if you didn't think there was something to find in the world that could help you."

"I admit it freely," Icelin said. "Aldren's burden was lifted. But if such a cure doesn't exist for me, I'll live the remainder of my life as well as I can. And I'll have my taste of adventure besides."

"Lead on, then," Ruen said.

Icelin nodded, but she did not turn in the direction of the city gates. "I have a stop to make first, to Sull's shop."

"It's closed up," Ruen said. "Going there won't change anything."

"I know," Icelin said, "but I need to go anyway."

They walked in silence, and Icelin was surprised, when she turned onto the butcher's street, to see Bellaril standing in front of the shop. She held the signboard with its painted haunch of meat in her hand.

"I didn't expect you'd get roped into helping him," Icelin said when they walked up.

"Didn't think it myself," the dwarf woman said. She made way as Sull's bulk crowded the doorway. The butcher's bright red hair caught the sunlight. His teeth flashed in a wide smile when he saw Icelin. He dropped the hammer and nails he was carrying into his apron pocket and went to her.

He swept her up in a hug that was ten times as crushing as the one Kersh had given her. Icelin had no breath left to protest.

"Almost done here," he said when he released her. "Just need to board the windows for winter, then we can be on our way."

"She came to make you reconsider," Ruen spoke up.

Icelin elbowed the monk in the ribs. She smiled sheepishly under Sull's black glare. "I'll be fine, Sull. Ruen's coming with me, and what about your shop?"

"Got it all with me," Sull said. He trotted around the side of the building and came back with a small cart and pony. "We need provisions, and I'm goin' to see to it you don't starve on hard rations. Besides, I've got recipes for the road," he said proudly. "There are spices and meats out there in the world Waterdeep never sees. How can I pass up the chance to bring some back?

This is research, is what this is, an investment. Got nothin' to do with you," he said, grinning broadly.

Icelin looked at Ruen, who shrugged. "I don't mind eating good food," he said.

She appealed to the dwarf woman next, but Bellaril shook her head. "Nothing to me if he goes or not, but I'm staying. The Cradle's a mess, and I'm still looking forward to dealing with the pretty elves," she said, a wicked light gleaming in her eyes.

Icelin sighed. "Fine. You're all baggage, though, and nothing but."

Ruen bowed. Sull grinned wider.

When they passed beyond the city gates, Icelin silently composed the letter in her head.

Dear Grandfather,

I leave today on a new adventure. Faerûn calls to me, and I'm willing to hear what she has to say. Wish me good fortune, and know that wherever I go, I carry all of you in my heart.

Love always,

Icelin

Forgotten Realms®

A Reader's Guide to

R.A. Salvatore's The Legend of Drizzt™

The Legend

When TSR published *The Crystal Shard* in 1988, a drow ranger first drew his enchanted scimitars, and a legend was born.

The Legacy

Twenty years and twenty books later, readers have brought his story to the world.

Drizzt

Celebrate twenty years of the greatest fantasy hero of a generation.

This fully illustrated, full color, encyclopedic book celebrates the whole world of The Legend of Drizzt, from the dark elf's steadfast companions, to his most dangerous enemies, from the gods and monsters of a world rich in magic, to the exotic lands he's visited.

Mixing classic renditions of characters, locales, and monsters from the last twenty years with cutting edge new art by award-winning illustrators including Todd Lockwood, this is a must-have book every Drizzt fan.

Celebrating 20 Years of Drizzt

Forgotten Realms, The Legend of Drizzt, Wizards of the Coast, and their respective logos are trademarks of Wizards of the Coast, Inc. in the U.S.A. and other countries. ©2008 Wizards.

FORGOTTEN REALMS®

They were built to display might.
They were built to hold secrets.
They will still stand while their builders fall.

THE CITADELS

NEVERSFALL
ED GENTRY

It was supposed to be Estagund's stronghold in monster-ridden Veldorn, an unassailable citadel to protect the southern lands . . . until the regiment holding Neversfall disappeared, leaving no hint of what took them.

OBSIDIAN RIDGE
JESS LEBOW

Looming like a storm cloud, the Obsidian Ridge appears silently and without warning over the kingdom of Erlkazar, prepared to destroy everything in its reach, unless its master gets what he wants.

THE SHIELD OF WEEPING GHOSTS
JAMES P. DAVIS

Frozen Shandaular fell to invaders over two thousand years ago, its ruins protected by the ghosts and undead that haunt the ancient citadel. But to anyone who can evade the weeping dead, the northwest tower holds a deadly secret.

SENTINELSPIRE
MARK SEHESTEDT

The ancient fortress of Sentinelspire draws strength from the portals that feed its fires and pools, as well as the assassins that call it home. Both promise great power to those dangerous enough to seize them.

Stand-alone novels that can be read in any order!

FORGOTTEN REALMS, WIZARDS OF THE COAST, and their respective logos are trademarks of Wizards of the Coast, Inc. in the U.S.A. and other countries. ©2008 Wizards.